Pursuing a Masterpiece

"In this gripping and beautifully complex novel, Sandra Vasoli invites us to travel across both time and space in pursuit of the discovery of a lifetime: a long-lost piece of artwork by Hans Holbein the Younger relating to the seismic and scandalous relationship between King Henry VIII and Queen Anne Boleyn. In doing so, Vasoli has crafted a thrilling, emotional masterpiece; a thick and sublimely descriptive journey which not only leads to the recovery of a lost provenance trail, but which also leads to spiritual enrichment and self-discovery. Vasoli's characters are rich, relatable, and messy, and at its heart, this is an artful account of the triumphs courage, of friendship, and of growth. A sensation."

—DR. OWEN EMMERSON, author of *The Boleyns of Hever Castle*

"*Pursuing a Masterpiece* is a riveting, fast-paced historical adventure story, with a rich and nuanced cast of characters who remain with you long after you've bid them a reluctant farewell. Beautifully written and astoundingly well researched, Vasoli artfully takes the reader on a spellbinding journey through the ages. A delight for any history lover!"

—NATALIE GRUENINGER, author of *The Final Year of Anne Boleyn*

"A joyous and sumptuous read! Sandra Vasoli indubitably crafts a wonderful tale of discovery, intrigue, and determination; blended with a marvelous passion and methodical capacity for archival research. *Pursuing a Masterpiece* transports the reader through the centuries, breathing life once more into some of history's most tumultuous and enigmatic periods. Zara Rossi's pursuit of a painting of the sixteenth century's most infamous and legendary royal couple reflects the dreams and aspirations of every Tudor historian, author, reader, and enthusiast. History doesn't get more alluring than this!"

—DAVID LEE, historian and author of *The Queen's Frog Prince*

"Sandra Vasoli expertly guides us on a gripping, twisty journey through the ages on the hunt for one of history's most remarkable portraits. Readers will cheer for Zara as she uncovers each clue with her stunning knack for solving the most enigmatic of puzzles. True to form, Vasoli has recreated each era with incredibly rich detail. One can't help but feel the tingle of salt spray on their face as they sail across the Atlantic, inhale the sweet island and spicy rum scents of the Caribbean, hear the charged whispers of the demi-monde, and feel a tremor of fear in the presence of sly aristocratic Nazis at the height of their power. *Pursuing a Masterpiece* is a triumph!"

—ADRIENNE DILLARD, author of *Keeper of the Queen's Jewels*

"From the opening scene you are hooked on this gripping historical thriller. Beautifully written, so the reader is drawn in, feeling as though they are with the characters. Sandra Vasoli has fit the story into eras so extraordinary, that one has no choice but to follow the quest for the painting as desperately as does Zara, the heroine."

—JAMES PEACOCK, founder of *The Anne Boleyn Society* on social media

OTHER BOOKS BY SANDRA VASOLI:

Anne Boleyn's Letter from the Tower

Truth Endures: Anne Boleyn's Memoir − A Novel

Pursuing a

MASTERPIECE

A NOVEL

Sandra Vasoli

ISBN (print): 978-1-958725-02-3
ISBN (ebook): 978-1-958725-03-0

Book design and production by Domini Dragoone
Cover image © Yelena Strokin
Author photo © Regina Miller

Published by GreyLondon Press
Gwynedd Valley, PA
www.sandravasoli.com

GREYLONDON
PRESS

For Tom.

And Hank (old and new).

Chapter One

SEPTEMBER 2016

ROME

A thick envelope peeked through the mail slot and dropped to the floor with a soft thud. I glanced over, then placed my cup with its remnants of the morning's third espresso on the counter. One look at the familiar handwriting and my stomach began to churn with an unsettling blend of anxiety and annoyance, peppered with guilt. I picked it up and shoved it deep into the recesses of a textbook sprawled across the kitchen table along with unopened posts, newspapers, and other assorted clutter. Today—especially today—I had no inclination to see what it held.

I was rushing to a critical appointment. An opportunity I'd been longing for since I had moved to Rome.

Grabbing my phone and throwing a battered leather satchel across one shoulder, I paused at the door of the flat to shoot Antonio a quick text.

"Meet you afterward?"

His reply was equally swift; phone right next to him, as usual. "Certo! Message me as you leave, and I will wait for you at Arlú. I'll get a table, and we'll have an aperitivo. Can't wait to hear what you discover."

Pulling the door closed behind me, I ran down the stairs to the street. It was just a short walk on Via Baccina to the bus stop in Rome's Monti neighborhood. The next Number 40 would take me almost directly to my destination, and well in time for my appointment.

The bus was filled with sleekly dressed Roman women on their way to work. I looked down at my outfit with a momentary pang of dismay. Maybe a little more care of my selection for such an important interview would have made sense, but I had a bad habit of being unconcerned about my clothing. I'd never been the girl dying to wear the latest fashions. Self-consciously, I smoothed my skirt, which was a distinct departure from my usual faded jeans and t-shirt. I hoped my beige cashmere sweater would add a touch of refinement; I wondered if the fact that it kind of matched my tan suede boots might help? And at the very last minute before leaving my flat, I'd scraped my thick, dark auburn hair into a loose braid and fastened the watch my parents had given me as a college graduation gift. It was the only jewelry I had on, although I wore it more out of practicality than adornment; it would be useful as I marked the passage of the precious hours I hoped to spend in the restricted sanctuary.

I was to present myself at the Admissions Office, hoping for a coveted entry into the Vatican Archives today.

And I was extremely nervous.

THE BUS SQUEALED TO a halt as we neared Vatican City. I slipped off and made my way across crowded, cobbled St. Peter's Square to Porta Sant' Anna, where a Swiss Guard waved me on to a glass building. There, a dour security official grunted "Papers?" and relieved me of my passport and student visa and handed me a badge which allowed me inside the perimeter of the Vatican property. I stood, awestruck, in the middle of a courtyard next to an ornate marble fountain bubbling away, and gaped at the vastness of it all. The entrance to the Library was tucked away in the corner, so, mouth dry and heart pumping, I walked the remaining length, and pulled at the doors to enter the waiting room. Once inside the marble vestibule, I tried to settle on a hard-backed chair with a few others who waited for the Secretariat to assess our requests for admission. Third in line, my foot jiggled awaiting my turn.

For a grad student like me, a young American woman pursuing a Ph.D. in paleography at La Sapienza Universitá di Roma, it was an immense privilege to be considered for admission to the Papal Archives in order to study ancient texts; I intended to use this opportunity to identify the core premise of my doctoral thesis. It would be an unusual and very special grant, since I'd only published two papers; I had not written or co-authored a book—in fact, I had few substantial credentials with which to support my request. What I did have, however, was the recommendation of Antonio, whom I intended to thank effusively that evening over our cocktail—even more so if indeed I was one of the researchers selected to enter the Ancient Manuscripts room that day. Professore Antonio Moretti was a renowned academic—a brilliant art historian, he taught courses in Visual Arts at Sapienza—and his were always the first to fill at registration. Antonio's lectures were packed with students—most of them young women, enthralled with the acclaimed and charismatic professor. And somehow, he'd become my unofficial advisor—my mentor. In fact, it was his connection that had initiated my dialogue with the Library Prefect, allowing me to present my documents with the aspiration of approval to study alongside the elite scholars of the world.

"Signorina Rossi… Zara Rossi?" The call snapped me to attention. Clutching at my bag, I stepped into a spacious whitewashed office to be greeted by the bald and bespectacled Admissions Secretary. He nodded and gestured for me to sit opposite him at his expansive mahogany desk, upon which he had spread my file. He gave it a cursory glance, then peered at me. Leaning forward on his elbows, he rubbed his hands together. "What brings you here today, Signorina? What do you wish to study?"

"Signore, I request to see documents pertaining to the English withdrawal from the Roman Catholic Church—specifically, the personal letters of Pope Clement VII, written in 1533 or 1534."

Bushy grey eyebrows raised, lips pursed, he shook his head slowly. "That may not prove possible. Personal documents written by the popes are kept in the Archivo Segreto, the Secret Archives, and there is no admission to those collections unless by prior special approval."

At the slump of my shoulders, the secretary's assistant arose from a desk tucked in the far corner and quickly stepped forward to confer with his boss. He caught my eye and nodded just slightly as if to reassure me he had the situation well in hand. They whispered for a moment before the secretary queried, "Signorina Rossi, for what purpose do you wish to study these documents?"

Immediately, the assistant brashly suggested, "Per cinema? She must be writing for the cinema in America." He gave me an appreciative glance.

I ignored him. "Dottor Segretario, I know precisely the collection I need. If only you might be able to obtain it for me today, I would be so very grateful... it is Caponiani 239: The Assorted Letters of Pope Clement VII." I leaned in and gazed hard at the aging official, offering him the most charming smile I could muster. After a slight hesitation, the secretary turned toward the younger man and whispered instructions in Italian. The assistant picked up the phone on the desk, dialed, and his tone was polite but insistent as he spoke with the other party. "Sí, sí... per favore guarda... subito! Sí, grazie." I knew he'd been speaking with someone responsible for the Archives, and as the call came to an end, he winked at me.

The secretary shrugged. "We will see what we can do, Signorina, but unfortunately cannot promise anything. This particular collection has not been pulled from the stacks in almost two hundred years and as a result, it may be difficult to locate. However," he grinned broadly, "we have requested a prompt and thorough search for you. Buona fortuna. The best of luck with your research."

With that, I reached across to shake the secretary's hand, and his large grasp encompassed mine. The warm grip didn't budge, so I pulled away. I was also very aware that the assistant hadn't stopped staring at me. I shot him a withering look and mumbled, "Thank you so very much for all of your help", and turned, with relief, to go.

Passing through the electronic security gates, peering high into the turreted stone staircase, I felt as if I'd be climbing to heaven. So I sucked in a breath, clutched my pass, and marched up and up to the Manuscripts room. As discreetly as possible, I opened the door and peeked inside. Within, I saw a surprisingly simple, whitewashed chamber with a vaulted ceiling. It was notably unadorned, but niches in the wall held busts of personages I assumed to be brilliant contributors to the history of the world—or maybe they were popes; I couldn't tell. Researchers were scattered throughout, seated on hard wooden benches with documents of unimaginable antiquity and value placed before them on equally austere tables. With a little shiver of pleasure, it registered that today, I was to be one of those scholars! At the head of the room, librarians were attentive, carefully observing the quiet activity and occasionally rising to distribute or collect the three volumes permitted to each individual on any given day.

I tiptoed into the chamber so I wouldn't disrupt the silence and was instantly aware of the unspoken code: if invited within, you'd better conduct yourself with the utmost respect. Otherwise, your entry privileges would be revoked, never to be reinstated. I sat gingerly at my assigned table and waited, peeking around with unabashed curiosity and utter astonishment, observing what the experts were studying. Volumes filled with Coptic Greek inscribed on papyrus, illuminated medieval manuscripts still vivid with color deposited by monks hundreds of years ago, and at the front of the room, three women studied what were certainly Michelangelo's drawings of the dome of St. Peter's Basilica.

I knew this sweater was going to itch, and I regretted having worn the hellish thing as I began sweating with tension. I was really thirsty, but what if I was summoned to pick up my volume while out getting a drink of water? Maybe they'd just replace it in the hidden stacks and I would have missed my chance. An hour passed. When I could no longer stand the uncertainty, I crept to the front and quietly asked one of the curators if my book was going to be delivered. She shook her head and mouthed, "I do not know. Not yet." Deflated, I returned to my seat to resume the torturous wait.

At last, a clerk appeared from behind the desk, trundling a cart bearing a large leather-bound book. At a nod from the curator, I jumped to my feet and scurried forward, to be rewarded at last with the volume I'd requested; it looked as if the secretary was right; it must not have been touched in centuries because it was covered by a sheen of dust.

My hands were trembling as I opened it. Ahhh! I was instantly gratified by that peculiarly delicious odor associated with books of great age: animal skins stretched and processed into fine vellum, ink dipped from inkwells so very long ago, oil from the scribes' hands as they scratched letters onto the page, and the accumulated dust of eons.

Somewhere in that tome, I hoped to discover Clement's reaction when King Henry VIII of England split from the Church of Rome in 1534—the beginning of the Reformation. The pope's conduct during that very turbulent time in Church history would form the focus of my Ph.D. thesis.

Just the thought of two mighty and forceful leaders at spiritual combat was fodder for the imagination: the bombastic Henry VIII pitted against a powerful Medici Pope, Clement VII. Rome must have been set on its edge when the Christian world was split in two by the English King, who demanded an annulment from his first wife to marry his adored Anne Boleyn.

Thwarted by Clement's refusal, the enraged King dismantled the Catholic Church in England, withdrawing his financial and spiritual support from Rome. Pope Clement must have been equally livid. Did he rant and rave to members of his Curia? Was he humiliated …? Did he seek revenge? I wanted to see writing in his own hand in the hope that I could find out. As far as I was able to tell, no one had written a paper about how the pope reacted to Henry's defection. The politics of that era, both in England and in the Vatican states, were rife with scandal, intrigue, and manipulation, and I couldn't wait to dig into it all.

The thought of reading letters, or better yet, original reports from spies about Henry's behavior, thrilled me. What a good story it would make! And my transcriptions would form the focus of a fantastic thesis and dissertation. Because I wanted, more than anything in the world, to excel in the pursuit of my Ph.D. and form the foundation of a respected and admired career.

So, doggedly I hunted, lifting the corner of each delicate page to scan its contents. I found folio after folio of beautiful, spidery script, all in Old Italian. Scanning each page, I looked for something to describe the epic battle between Henry VIII and Clement. But there wasn't a word—no mention of the English King at all.

Slowly, the feeble light seeping through the windows started to shift as the afternoon waned, and I felt a crushing sense of disappointment. All too soon, the readers and assistants started to clear the tables for closing. Biting my lip to hold back tears, I gathered my belongings and reluctantly closed the precious volume. I just hated to let it go, so in the few remaining minutes, I opened Cap. 239 once more and turned to the very back of the book.

This time I noticed the last two thin sheets were fused, as parchment will often do. Delicately I pried apart the edges to reveal pages stiffened by centuries. My heart fluttered. Stuck tightly to the inside of the back cover was a small, folded sheet of thin vellum. As others around me packed up and left the room, I slid my nail under the corner and pried it loose, then, holding my breath, unfolded it. Slowly it gave way, and I smoothed it before me. Leaning closer to see faded lines of script, I grabbed my magnifying glass, and peered through it at the enigmatic writing.

I glanced up as the head curator cleared her throat and motioned me to draw my session to a close. I paid no attention to her; instead, I resumed inspecting this strange little gem I had just found. At its top, the paper was dated: *11 Giugno 1534*. 11 June 1534. And its heading was readable as well: *"Mio Stimato Santo Padre"*. My Esteemed Holy Father.

I scanned the length of the small page, and at the bottom, frowned blankly at the signature. It was inscribed with the stamp of a Maltese Cross and the legend:

Grand Master of the Order of St. John
Villiers de L'Isle-Adam

It was a note, consisting of about ten lines scrawled in an unsteady, cryptic hand. I pored over it with my glass.

And there it was. On line four: "King of England Henry Eight."

By line five, the word *ritrattistica*, which I knew represented a portrait. Many of the characters were barely legible, but I saw the word '*Spie*' which meant Spies! And in Italian, "they have reported great danger, the matter is one of the most desperate urgency." Then, written with a quill which had been thrust heavily into an inkwell, a word appeared, gouging the small, fragile page. I blinked:

"Sacrilegio."

One final pronouncement remained:

"King Henry and Anne Boleyn portrayed as false gods."

I exhaled a low whistle and blurted, "Holy *shit*."

The curator, tired and grumpy after a long day behind the desk, stalked over to me. "You will have to leave now."

I looked pointedly at my watch, which said 4:56 pm, then glared back at her, no longer the meek supplicant, and snapped, "I still have four minutes, is that not correct?"

She scowled, turning on her heel to march back to her station while I scribbled, copying every word I could make out. There was no time to try and interpret any of it. My hand flew as I transcribed it all, to study later.

And there, at the very bottom of the page, that seal and the signature of a long-departed man called Villiers de L'Isle-Adam.

Having pushed privilege to the limit, I knew I ran the risk of never being allowed in Ancient Manuscripts again, so I scooped up my pencils, notebook, and magnifier and approached the desk as penitently as possible to return the book, with the note replaced in its hiding spot. There, I offered the still sullen curator an apologetic smile and a slight dip of my head and backed out of the room.

Once outside the boundaries of the Square, I leaned against a wall, panting as if I'd just run up a flight of steps.

What the hell had I just found?

"ZARA! IT'S LOVELY TO see you!" He rose as I approached the table, pulled out my chair and helped me to get settled. And there they were: the butterflies which always made their presence known whenever I was in his company. Thick dark hair sprinkled with grey, a piercing, hazel-eyed gaze, and an aquiline nose countered by a distinct jawline provided him with classic Roman looks. Not only was Antonio handsome, but he had the charming manners of a well-bred European.

"I will say, though, that you look a bit tired. Of course, that does you no injustice. Was it a challenging day?"

"It was overwhelming, Antonio. You didn't tell me how intimidating the place is. But oh, I loved every minute of it!" I recalled my interaction with the librarian and snickered, "All except for the grouchy woman behind the desk, guarding the documents as if they were part of her personal fiefdom."

He chuckled too, and, as usual, I enjoyed watching the outer corners of his eyes crinkle.

"I guess she didn't like it when I whistled and blurted 'holy shit' in her Ancient Manuscripts sanctuary." I gratefully lifted my Campari soda.

"You did what? You're far too irreverent, Zara Rossi! You better hope they don't put a black check next to your name, with the words nessuna ulteriore ammissione: 'no further admission.' But you know... that's one of the things I like about you best. Your impertinence. So, what did you find that caused you to blaspheme? Tell me. I'm dying to know."

I took another sip, and from a little dish of antipasti, speared an olive with a fork. I chewed thoughtfully, and by the time I swallowed, I'd made my decision. I was about to lie to my mentor: by omission.

"Oh, it was a fantastic afternoon, and I got to see lots of letters that Clement's scribes had written for him. There was one written to Alessandro Farnese, promising him a Cardinalship if he completed the assignments arranged for him. Clearly a bribe. Pretty intriguing, right? And tricky to decipher; some of those monks had atrocious handwriting. Good thing they weren't being paid for their efforts and only labored to earn their places in heaven. Oh! And, yes, I found a fascinating letter providing payments for Pope Clement's mistress, Simonetta—the mother of his illegitimate son. Did you know that she was a slave—and a Moor? It was a great scandal. That little find is what caused me to express myself so inappropriately."

I chattered on, hoping I could throw him off track. I bit at the inside of my cheek to avoid saying more despite the slightest of shadows detectable in his expression.

"Nothing else?" Antonio pressed. "Nothing written by Clement about England's belligerence? Nothing at all about his enemy, Henry VIII?"

"Not a single thing. Can you believe it? In that entire volume, not a word."

"What a shame, Zara. I'm so sorry. A bit surprised, though, knowing your aptitude for finding intriguing documents. Well, I guess we'll try to get approval for another session in the Archives—though it won't be easy. And by the way, you haven't forgotten our discussion, have you? When I told you I'd be thrilled if we could collaborate on a project and co-author a paper?"

"Antonio! You know I'd love to have another shot at finding something amazing in Clement's papers—of course, I would be eternally grateful to you if you might possibly arrange it. And..." I shifted in my seat, picking at the napkin in my lap. "... without doubt, I am aware of your very generous offer to work together. However, I... umm... it has to be the right thing, you know? Or I would just feel like your apprentice—which I am, obviously—but I'd never feel worthy of being your co-author."

Antonio lifted one eyebrow, and pursed his lips just a little. He seemed ready to say something, so I quickly motioned to call the waitress over. "Let's order. I'm starving."

BACK IN MY FLAT later that evening, as I retrieved books littering the kitchen, the morning's mail delivery slipped from one of them and fell onto my foot. The envelope seemed to glare at me incriminatingly until I picked it up. I mean, who even *wrote* letters anymore? Answer—my father. Although I had to admit, it was one of his more endearing eccentricities. You might think that a man who had spent years as the Chair of Radiology and Neuroimaging at Massachusetts General Hospital would employ a more tech-savvy method of communicating with his daughter. But regularly, my mail slot would produce an envelope of fine stationery, addressed in his bold hand, containing several sheets regaling me with family news, updates on his work, and always—*always*—his default plea to reconsider the path of my "ill-chosen" education. I ran my finger under the flap and tugged at three sheets, filled with my dad's unmistakeable writing. I scanned it: *"My dearest Zara—I hope you are enjoying some great autumn weather, because it's done nothing but rain back here in Chestnut Hill. We all feel sodden, and rather gloomy. At least I am extremely busy, with two new protocols to evaluate and critique, and more on the way..."* Then he added the news that my cousin was getting married in late spring, so please put it in my calendar to attend, and finally... *"So, how are things going with your classwork and your projects? Are you enjoying them? Because I was just wondering if you'd come into the labs with me next time you are home. You know, just to check out some of the really fascinating stuff we're doing in here? It's pretty interesting. In fact, I think you might like to puzzle a few things out. There are a couple researchers in here who could certainly use your help in putting some complicated datapoints together..."*

I had to admit that his letters always tugged at my heart. But... oh, Dad... really—do you know me?

As I pulled cheese and bread from the fridge and tried to assemble a little late supper, I recalled, with a shot of pride, how, upon my graduation from Harvard, I'd received an invitation to enter the Medical School there. As if it was yesterday, I could hear my parents express their joy. "Zar, do you realize how few—some years, not any!—graduating students are offered an unconditional entry into Harvard Med?" My dad was almost giddy. And then Mom added, "It really is incredible, Zara. Most kids, after graduation, have no idea what comes next. And here you are, with a fabulous opportunity just placed at your feet! We are so proud of you!"

Oh yes, they desperately wanted me to accept. But when I informed them that I intended to study in Rome—and would be pursuing a Ph.D. in paleography (the analysis of ancient documents), Dad, especially, made no effort to conceal his bitter disappointment.

His outrage had been forceful. "Why the hell would you do that? You'll make no money at all! And where on earth will you go to find a job, young lady? You'll end up buried in a dark, musty library as a manuscript geek for your entire life. It's such a waste. You have the brains and ability to be an excellent physician, or pursue scientific research. I simply don't understand." That particular conversation ended abruptly, like so many others, in a face-off. I stalked away into my room, slamming the door behind me.

I didn't—wouldn't—waver, though. So, in the end, Dad gave in. Because he knew me—I was so like him: every bit as headstrong, defiant, and relentless in my pursuits. He realized I wouldn't be dissuaded; in fact, I was precisely what he had described: an intellectual geek.

I buttered bread, laid cheese between the slices, and slid it into a pan to grill it. As I worked, my thoughts ran unabated. An acrid cheesy smell startled me back to the present, and I grabbed the pan just as the sandwich started to burn. I put it on a plate and plopped down at my kitchen table to eat. I should have turned on some music or TV. Instead, my thoughts swam with memories of my teen years: the whispers about me—labeling me as 'peculiar' or 'eccentric.' I knew teachers thought of me as some kind of savant. So, maybe they were justified. As for friends, I'd never been great at reaching out to people, although just like everyone else, I wanted to be admired. Secretly, I envied the popular kids who could easily laugh, tell jokes, throw their arms over their friends' shoulders. That ability had always evaded me. I had a few friends. Mostly they were like me—bright kids who were interested in subjects others thought way too nerdy. I tried to convince myself it didn't matter that girls in my class were busy chatting on the phone or going to parties to which I hadn't been invited. But there were times when it really hurt. To console myself, I hid in libraries where I took comfort in immersing myself in mysteries of the past. Imagining that I inhabited the most exciting places and times throughout history soothed me—I was somehow able to connect with the long-lost scholars and scribes who wrote, leaving us accounts of their lives years ago. They were my friends, and they didn't make fun or sneer at me from their ancient pedestals.

Those sure weren't the most pleasant memories. I took the plate over to the sink to wash up. At least, once I'd entered Harvard and had a chance to burrow in the Library's Archives and Manuscripts, I had found my joy. I discovered a unique talent for untangling ancient writing recorded on archaic sheets of parchment, vellum, or papyrus. It quickly became known to the academic community that I was able to decipher documents no one else could. The challenges always inspired me, since I regard venerable documents with great esteem. Their secrets long to be revealed in whispers from antiquity: discoveries beckon those who spend countless hours in pursuit. And I was undoubtedly one of those treasure seekers, wishing to unearth clues wistfully sought, yet rarely found.

I went into my bedroom to get the backpack I'd dropped on the floor after my visit to the Library and the drink with Antonio. My desire to make an astounding discovery in the world of archives was equal to my intention to earn a Ph.D. Because what if—just what if—I did happen to find something electrifying? Something to rock the global community of famous historians? It would catapult my career into the stratosphere. It would validate my choice—make my mom and dad proud of me, and others would know, once and for all, that they had been wrong about me.

So, I thought with satisfaction, today I had been welcomed into the motherlode of the world's primal writings: the Vatican. I pulled my notebook from the backpack, opened it in front of me, and stared at the scrawl created in those last frantic minutes in the Archives. Scanning the pages, I couldn't make sense of anything, though, because nagging at me was the question of why I'd held back from telling Antonio about the note. He would have been thrilled with my discovery. At our very first meeting, when I'd sat self-consciously in his office, unable to look him in the eye, he said, "Zara. I've been told that your professors at Harvard acknowledge they have rarely—if ever—seen a talent like yours: your almost innate ability to recognize and understand texts too difficult for even the most esteemed scholars to decipher." He studied me. "How did you learn to do that, may I ask? Is your father an archaeologist, by chance?"

"No... no, he's not. He's a physician. Quite a skilled one, actually. Both he and my mom would have liked me to follow a scientific path. But I love untangling old documents. It's my thing." I raised my eyes to peek at him, but nervousness overcame me, and I resumed studying the wooden floorboards.

"Well," he said, "I will be extremely interested to observe your unique abilities. And, who knows, if the right project comes up, maybe we might be able to work on it together. I don't offer that to many students, you know. But let's keep our eye out for just the opportunity. What do you say?"

"I'd be incredibly flattered, Professor Moretti."

"And likewise, Miss Rossi. By the way, we will be working together as mentor and protégée, so why don't you call me Antonio? We are quite relaxed here at Sapienza."

I nodded, thanked him, and slipped out of his office, feeling both pleased and flustered all at the same time.

And now, this hidden letter I found might be just the right subject.

After all, it might amount to nothing, while—if I had unearthed some long-hidden clue—didn't he deserve to know about it? It was Antonio who'd arranged my visit. To make matters worse, I was all too aware that my feelings for him were complicated. When we were together, my palms grew sweaty, and the surroundings seemed to fade away. I tried to ignore the jitters which were prompted by his warm and direct gaze, but was rarely successful. Could he possibly be attracted to me? Probably not—I was sure his interest was focused elsewhere. Probably on my ability to read documents he wished he could but hadn't the skill. That must be it.

I turned to my computer, clicked the mouse, and it blinked to life. I needed a distraction from the dilemma, so instead of the always-distasteful strain of dealing with my feelings, I buried myself in focusing on the notes from the day. First question: why had the note been hidden in that book? I guessed it must have been some-how buried in Clement's collection of letters. Maybe, as the letters and documents were gathered for preservation, this inconsequential scrap of paper had inadvertently been stuck to a larger document, and was never noticed in its hiding place. With the limited info I had, that was as good a guess as any.

Working my way through the early Italian, my translation read:

'11 June 1534
My esteemed Holy Father:.'

The first three lines were so faded as to be illegible. On line four,

"King of England Henry Eight... portrait...."

Some unreadable words followed, but then,

"... and our spies signaled great danger. The King Henry and Anne Boleyn are portrayed as false gods. Holy Father, this is a matter of dire urgency. The king's representation is the greatest sacrilege. As I report this threat to you, my life is in great peril. Yet the portrait must be confiscated. With your permission, I will command the Knights to find it and bring it to you.

I seek your blessing and your immediate instruction.
Grandmaster of the Order of St. John
Villiers de L'Isle-Adam"

It was extraordinary! What was the Order of St. John? And an unholy portrait in which Henry VIII and his queen were represented as gods?

My keyboard clicked furiously as I searched for insight. Who was the enigmatic Villiers de L'Isle-Adam? A simple query opened a world of information about a medieval religious order: originally the Knights Hospitaller, then the Order of St. John of Jerusalem, a staunchly Roman Catholic, zealous society, which thrives in the present day as The Order of Malta. Fascinated, I read article after article about the mysterious Order. With a huge presence in Rome, it is one of the oldest institutions in Western civilization. It was founded in 1113 (which seemed absolutely crazy!) and was a crusading force for God in the Middle Ages. Today, it branded itself as a diplomatic, humanitarian ministry. But still, the Order was fraught with speculation and secrecy.

L'Isle-Adam was its revered Grand Master from 1521 until his suspiciously sudden death on the Island of Malta in August of 1534. So it seems as if the private message I'd chanced upon, written to the pope, had been despatched just before L'Isle Adam died, being dated the 11th of June 1534. And apparently, he had been a great personal friend of Pope Clement VII; in fact, the rules of the order proscribed that the Grand Master was answerable only to one earthly individual: the pope.

My attention shifted to the painting, described in such ominous terms by the Grand Master. Hunting for a dual portrait of Henry VIII and Anne Boleyn, I was bewildered. There was not a single record of such a painting. I combed the websites of every one of the national portrait galleries, the British National Archives, the U.S. Library of Congress, searched back copies of The British Art Journal, and read all I could about the portraiture of Henry VIII. Stiff after several hours, I stretched and went to the kitchen for some tea. Leaning against the counter with my cup and thinking about the dearth of any reference to the painting at all, it became clear there was no known depiction of the King and his second wife—certainly none which conveyed the level of alarm signaled by L'Isle-Adam.

BY 3:00 A.M., MY EYES were scratchy and my back ached. My computer wasn't going to reveal anything which would shed light on the portrait described by L'Isle-Adam. Still, I sat for a long time, pondering. What if the note I accidentally discovered was real evidence that a dangerous icon of the King and Queen *had* existed? But why would it not have been recorded somewhere? And why was there no indication that anyone had searched for it? It made no sense. The word "sacrilege", in particular, haunted me. The definition I found was unsettling: *the crime of stealing what is consecrated to God.* What could possibly have happened in 1534 that seemingly challenged Divine authority? And, if this painting had been destroyed, or perhaps hidden, did something terrible occur as a result? After all, the note was a communication between two of the most powerful people in the world at that time. For sure, the notion that such an artwork might have been invisible for centuries seemed absurd. But I knew my early documents. It was authentic, and it was almost 500 years old. Of that, I was certain.

At last, I switched off lights and shut down my laptop, heading for my bedroom. I hoped I could sleep, but my head throbbed with riddles. However, I was certain of one thing: I would not tell Antonio about this discovery. It was mine.

If, due to a bizarre wrinkle in time and circumstance, that little clandestine note was the key to a painting which would be coveted by the entire art world, and a momentous discovery to master historians and leading theologians around the world, I intended to find it.

By myself.

Chapter Two

LATE AUTUMN 1533

PALACE OF WHITEHALL
LONDON

The library doors thudded to a close. Cromwell engaged the ornate brass lock with a sharp snap. No intruder would be granted entry to this most secret of meetings.

The massive, polished oak table reflected stacks of leatherbound books, all the property of Henry VIII. At its head sat the Sovereign and arrayed along both sides were his wife and second Queen, Anne Boleyn; Thomas Cranmer, Archbishop of Canterbury; and Thomas Cromwell, Secretary to the King. Hans Holbein, an unusual addition to this noble company, looked confused and somewhat uncomfortable. But the King, Henry VIII, had summoned the prominent court painter to travel immediately from his home and family in Basel, Switzerland to attend the meeting, and a command from Henry was a command to be obeyed.

"Gentlemen. My Lady." The King's sharp scrutiny sought to read each face. "I, along with your gracious Queen, have called you here today to discuss an exceptional—a most unconventional—undertaking."

The men around him settled themselves accordingly. One did not interrupt Henry Rex. While age had thickened his formerly lithe frame, it had also deepened his voice, affording a personal gravitas which he deployed to strike just the exact tone of command. At 42 years, enhanced by his mighty height and breadth, Henry VIII was a monarch to behold. Brows knitted, lips pursed in concentration, eyes that challenged others with steely superiority—he knew he was imposing. His raiment, as always, was calculated to underscore the magnificence that was Henry. Suspended from his neck by thick shining ropes of gold swayed two spectacular jewels which glinted with his slightest movement, reflecting the dancing beams of late autumn sun still flooding the room: one, a weighty golden ship flying before the wind, the helmsman at its stern steering the craft, the other an extravagant silver-gilt cross studded with diamonds.

"First, Sirs: be aware," the King growled warningly. "The information I am about to share with you is to be kept confidential. I will tolerate no leak, not even an allusion to the subject, outside this closed gathering unless expressly agreed upon and approved by me. Is this understood?"

"With certitude, Majesty," the three men responded in dutiful unison.

As he spoke, the Queen simply inclined her head, betraying no hint of what she already knew was to come.

"Good. Then the matter before us is this: I intend to commission a painting from you, Master Holbein." Henry fixed the bearded painter with a stare that would intimidate the bravest of men. "It is to be an extraordinary work—the composition of which will test the limit of your extensive talents—but, if correctly executed, it will mark your place in perpetuity. You will forevermore be renowned as the artist who documented a pivotal event in world history."

All eyes shifted to the German-born artist. After a short pause, Holbein nervously cleared his throat.

"Your Majesty, I know not yet what you expect of me, but I do immediately assure you I will use every scrap of ability God has given me to complete whatever you have in mind—I pray, complete it to your greatest satisfaction—and of course, to that of Her Royal Highness," he tacked on hastily, deferring to Anne.

At this, her lips betrayed the slightest suspicion of a smile. She knew—how well she knew—the objective of this painting. She understood just how much it meant to Henry. And indeed, if accomplished according to the vision she and her husband shared, it would be one of the most powerful portrayals ever created.

The royal pair exchanged a glance: she composed, her bearing dignified; Henry, as always, splendid in appearance and manner. But the Queen equaled his brilliance. With the confidence gained by recently having easily birthed a healthy and hearty infant—albeit a girl child—Anne wore her position of wealth and power with complete self-assurance. And why should she not? Her striking, though unconventional, beauty was indisputable. A highly colored complexion, smooth and unlined, belying her age of 32 years; dark, expressive eyes thickly fringed with lashes, shining with vitality and intelligence; glossy chestnut hair tucked into a French headdress matching her gown of deep blue velvet liberally strewn with sapphires, pearls, and diamonds. Taken altogether, it was apparent why the King remained devoted to the new wife he had worked so hard and waited so long to win, even if she had not, as yet, given him that which he demanded above all: a son.

The partnership they shared as they sat shoulder to shoulder, inclining toward one another in solidarity, was evident.

"The specification of your brief will come in due course, Master Holbein, after I first describe the intent driving it."

Anne placed her hand lightly on the King's sleeve, slender fingers drawing attention to a single ring on each hand: the dazzling emerald flanked by diamonds which Henry had given her upon their marriage, and a luminous pearl set in gold—presented to her by her husband at the birth of their daughter Elizabeth. "I implore you, gentlemen, do pay heed to what the King has to say, for you will find it to be the foundation of a monumental shift in our way of thinking." She spoke confidently. "I know I was greatly moved by his revelation."

The King shifted in his seat, assuming his maximum height and blocking much of the light pooling on the table. "Esteemed Councillors, you are each well aware of my beliefs concerning the Church of Rome and the Holy See, of its long line of Bishops and their flagrant transgressions against the faith, those which defy God's glory. You two above all, Archbishop Cranmer and Secretary Cromwell, know how deeply this dilemma has, for many years now, rent an open wound in my soul."

"Our frustrations have been as nothing compared to your own tribulation, Majesty," Cranmer commiserated somberly.

"Yet this pope—Clement!" Henry positively spat the name of the man whom he had come to regard as his nemesis. "This papal pretender, has consistently—insolently—denied the truth of God's Word by refusing to dissolve what any fool could have recognized as my unlawful marriage to Katherine of Aragon. His arrogant disregard has been, of course, reinforced by his Curia—all of them falsely believing that such a decision lies exclusively within the pope's jurisdiction, which it most definitively does not! If he grasped even the fundamental principles of theology, he would know that it remains within the purlieu of God's command, and God's alone."

He calmed a little then, not without some effort. After all, according to the mandate of Rome and Clement, he was a man who currently carried two wives, the second illegally wed. No amount of rationalizing, debating, or cajoling had been able to convince Clement to dissolve Henry's marriage to Katherine of Aragon, and bless his union with Anne.

Henry did not like to lose.

"Gentlemen, I am here to tell you that I have been illuminated with God's Truth. And as a result, I am prepared to dedicate my entire life to its advancement and His glory: the True Knowledge of His Word."

Anne was glowing with pride. She cast a glance around, and her eyes narrowed as she assessed the reactions of the three. Both Cromwell and Cranmer, of course, were familiar with the monarch's near-obsessive intention to release his association with the Church of Rome, but they had never heard him speak with such passion, such conviction. To a man, they leaned forward in fascinated anticipation—or apprehension—of what was to come.

"You are already aware that, even as we speak, Parliament is drafting articles describing England's separation from the pope and the Roman Church. But they will not reveal the Truth in its entirety—the world is not yet ready for such a message. But, my good advisors, you are ready. I will now disclose it for you."

The Archbishop, lips pressed together, stroked his chin, while Cromwell attentively cocked his head to one side. Holbein, meanwhile, remained frozen in place, the only demeanor he imagined appropriate for a humble man in such august company.

Henry paused, his authoritative look betraying a hint of awe. "God Almighty has bestowed upon me a great blessing. You see, He has disclosed His plan for my life. At first, I resisted, perhaps due to a lack of faith, but after a time, I have come to accept what He has ordained. For the Lord God has commanded that I—Henry Tudor, King of England—will henceforth be regarded as Constantine, Emperor of the Church: in fact, as the new David, King of Israel! That I am now as one with Josiah, the Almighty King of Judah!"

Each man's brow knitted fiercely to grasp the breadth, the import, of what their Sovereign was attempting to describe with such fervor. Henry's gaze met each face, and his intensity caused tremors. He took note of, even relished, their bewildered astonishment.

"Yes, gentlemen, you may indeed stand in wonderment, but it is indisputable," he continued. "God has spoken to me directly and granted a divine proclamation. I am Peter, the rock upon which a whole new Church shall be built! The Lord Himself has said to me, 'Henricus Rex, I give thee the Keys to the Kingdom of Heaven, and command that whatever thou bind on earth will be bound in Heaven: whatever thou loose on earth will be loosed in Heaven. And thus do I decree that thou, Henricus, Sovereign Ruler of England, are chosen by Me to build a New Church—the One True Church—and that in thou alone I place my trust!'"

The King scanned the room and added, "My loyal and beloved subjects, I tell you that my mission is this: to destroy the papacy of Rome. Once and forever."

It was then that it began to dawn on his listeners. The full extent of their ruler's ecclesiastically seismic claim.

The very air seemed to thin throughout that vast chamber. Only from a corner of one window came movement as a fly buzzed and battered frantically against a high pane as if desperate to distance itself from such a cataclysm. It was only long after, when the fly had dropped, spent, and still no one ventured to speak, that Henry smiled unexpectedly, mercurially, almost as if passing the time of day.

"It is this very instruction from Our Lord, Master Holbein, that I wish for you to proclaim, by incorporating the most subtle codings within a magnificent portrait, to be viewed and understood at first to a select few of my faithful subjects. Only when I determine that the time is right will I expose its message to all common men. It will be your portrayal which we will use, with guidance from God, to prevail on the hearts and minds of the faithful, turning them away from the unlawfulness of the Roman Church, opening their eyes to their new leadership: their true passage to heaven."

His shining eyes locked on the artist, boring into his very soul.

"So, tell me, Holbein. Are you up to the task?"

Chapter Three

EARLY OCTOBER 2016

LA SAPIENZA CAMPUS

I paced restlessly, waiting for my friend to appear for our lunch date. Uncomfortable from the dampness of my T-shirt clinging to my back, I wondered how it could ever be this hot and humid. It was October, and I longed for the sugar maples of New England putting on their spectacle, turning brilliant shades of red and ochre. Oh, for just a breath of crisp autumn edge to freshen the air! I'd lived in Rome for two years, and I'd grown to love it. How could I not? Around every corner, the astonishing sight of a 2000-year-old ruin parked next to a modern-day pharmacy or shoe store, the museums chock full of art and antiquities, and the food! The tiny restaurants casually serving the world's best, freshest pasta, cheeses, steamed or fried artichokes. But, in my estimation, the heat could definitely take a break, so I did miss my New England fall.

I found an arching stone pine and took advantage of the little patch of shade just outside the paleography building on campus. Checking my phone for the time, I squinted against the bright sun to scan the quadrangle in the hope of seeing Carolina headed in my direction. I heaved a sigh. It was more than a little annoying since there was no sign of her; she was late today, as often. I should have canceled; I was far too busy to nibble lunch and make small talk, even though I had to admit that Lina's company was always enjoyable, especially when we got to laughing raucously at her dry, biting wit.

During the two weeks since my visit to the Vatican Library and the revelation of the tiny, unassuming scrap I found in the volume of papal letters, I'd thought of little else, determined to find further information—no matter how trivial—which might shed light on the note's arcane message. I probed the Sapienza library system databases: no easy feat since it was an immense network covering fifty-nine libraries, over three million books, thousands of journals and periodicals, as well as a treasury of rare books, historical archives, and the archives of premier museums. After multiple all-nighters—countless hours of work—nothing. Not a single entry referring to the mysterious portrait that had caused Grand Master L'Isle-Adam such angst over 480 years ago. But the fact that I had yet to unearth any corroborating evidence had done nothing to deflate my resolve. The note existed, that was indisputable. Certain of its authenticity, I would not be swayed from the opinion that somewhere there had to be confirmation that such an image existed. Or at least, that it had at one time.

All-nighters had become the norm. I wasn't a great sleeper anyway, not that it mattered much, because in bed all I did was toss and turn, running the loop in my mind about why a warning from the Grand Master of the Knights of Jerusalem to the pope remained, yet there was no sign of its subject. Equally gripping was my need to understand the "sacrilege" that had driven L'Isle-Adam to write to the pope offering his army of knights to locate the portrait before it wreaked catastrophic damage on Holy Mother Church. This, followed closely by the Grand Master's death just two months later? I was absolutely driven to find even a single shred of a clue.

After scrolling through hundreds of possible links and scouting dozens of articles and book excerpts, yet coming up empty-handed, a thought so obvious occurred to me that I clapped a hand to my forehead, muttering "you dumbass" to myself—which drew a bemused glance from the bleary-eyed student sharing the library table. It took mere seconds, then, to discover that the Magistral Library—the principal library of the Sovereign Order of Malta, the modern-day representation of the Knights Hospitaller, Knights of the Order of St. John of Jerusalem, then Rhodes, and finally today, the Knights of Malta—houses the world's most complete collection of the Order's history.

Furthermore, the world headquarters of the Sovereign Order, along with its Library, was located just across town. On Rome's chic Via Condotti.

Twenty minutes late, Carolina Orsini sauntered across the grass and plumped herself down next to me. Lina possessed that unique quality that allowed her always to seem poised and composed. She was never flustered, and I had never seen her perspire gently—much less sweat—even on the dog days of a Roman August. Smoothing her lustrous dark hair, she tucked a wayward strand behind her ear and gave me a double-cheeked kiss in greeting, adding, "Ciao cara mia, I hope you haven't been waiting long?"

I fumbled in my backpack, locating an old rubber band which I used to pull my own thick mane off my face. I hoped a ponytail would ebb the trickles running down the nape of my neck. "It's okay. I've got a lot to think about, so the time passed quickly." I was distracted and barely offered her a greeting in return. "It's nice to see you," I tacked on, almost as an afterthought.

Lina turned to face me on the bench and her sweeping glance was one of appraisal. "Mamma mia! Guardati! Look at you, Zara. What's going on? I mean... this..." and she made a circular motion which encompassed my face and hair, then swept wider to include my whole person. She sat back, surveying my appearance with an undisguised look of surprised disapproval. "Tesoro, I know you are not one to fuss over yourself… and may I say how lucky, how blessed, you are to possess a gorgeous face and a body men swoon over without any additional adornment, but we, as women, can't always leave our appearances merely up to God's gifts, now, can we? I do think He expects us to help Him along, just a little. D'accordo? So, what is it that causes you to be so, shall we say, disheveled?"

Suddenly I was aware of how I must appear, since I hadn't showered that morning, nor had I even given a second glance at what I'd dragged from my closet to throw on before I left the flat. Feeling a little embarrassed, I shrugged. "I guess you're right, Lina. But in all honesty, I couldn't care less right now. I'm so entirely focused on something big—so big—much bigger than anything I could ever have imagined. Who gives a hoot how I look?!"

"*Hoot?* What is hoot? Well anyway, we should put your last comment aside for a moment, and can you tell me what you're doing? What's so big that you can't shower? And… oh my… those eyebrows! They are screaming for some wax… but allora, what is this monumental crisis?"

If it had been anyone other than Lina delivering such a message, I'd have packed up my bag, ended that conversation abruptly, and never initiated another one. But we'd formed a friendship in the very first months of my move to Rome. We were in the same class, and one afternoon we went for coffee and had found that, although we may have outwardly seemed quite different, in reality we were not. We shared an Italian heritage and as a result, understood each other's facial expressions and gestures. Maybe most importantly, I respected Lina. She was highly intelligent, studying toward her Ph.D. in linguistics, and it just so happened that we both came from educated, wealthy families. Even though she may have appeared soft, she was anything but—a fiercely independent nature made her, in every aspect, a worthy competitor. I quickly came to admire Lina and feel that, perhaps, I might trust her—and these were sentiments I didn't bestow readily.

Maybe the second or third time we'd hung out together, she had said, "Zara, I bet most of the girls you grew up with didn't understand you, d'accordo?" She watched me closely as I looked away, unable to reply. "Well, mi amica, my new friend, I think you are fascinating. You're unusual—in a good, beautiful way, you see? You're so smart, you are curious, and you have... how shall I say... una molto bella disordinata. You are messy but enchanting, all at the same time. I guess I'm able to see what they missed."

I'd felt tears prick at the back of my lids, but sniffed and willed them away. "Thank you, Lina. That means a whole lot coming from someone like you." I remember regarding her enviously. "You seem to have it all figured out. I mean, who you are, what you want to do... All that." She was shocked, then laughed uproariously. "All figured out? Zara, don't you know that no one has it all figured out? But let's promise to share with each other any secrets to the key of life that we discover. Okay?" And in that moment, our friendship was bonded.

She repeated, "So? Well? What's the big finding?"

I did feel that Lina had my best interests at heart, but I wasn't prepared to share too much of my discovery. "Well, remember when I went to the Vatican Library a couple weeks ago? Let's just say that I discovered something. An item small in size, but with the potential to be one of the biggest discoveries the art world—or even more broadly, the composite worlds of art and history—has seen in decades. Maybe more—maybe in hundreds of years!"

Lina's eyes grew wide. "What? Are you kidding? What is it? Does Antonio know? And what are you doing about it?"

"No! I haven't informed Antonio! And please do not mention it if you happen to see him." I paused. "Don't ask me why I haven't told him, because I don't know... I don't know... I just don't want to. Something, a gut feeling, is telling me not to reveal anything to him. This is my discovery, and I want it to remain that way. In fact, you're the only person I've mentioned it to, Lina, and I'm pleading with you to keep it private. It's very important to me that no information is leaked until I know more about what I may or may not have found."

With a sigh and a little shake of her head, she responded, "I can do that, cara mia, but will you share nothing with me? You are asking a lot for very little in return, you know."

"Okay. Here's what I can disclose. I found, in a volume of letters which had belonged to Pope Clement VII, a small note which looks like it was accidently left there many, many years ago. It referred to a portrait which may have been painted in the 1500s that held some kind of mystery, some long-ago threat to the Church—if the painting exists, or ever existed at all. And, the kicker... there's no historical record of it anywhere."

"Well, what makes you think it was actually painted? What if this note, as you call it, was just a fraud?"

I shook my head emphatically. "I know my documents. That note was real. It was definitely written when it was dated. And furthermore, I was able to verify the handwriting, so the signee wrote it. But from there the trail dies. That is, until I had a revelation last night at the library. The headquarters of the ancient organization whose leader wrote about this painting, along with their huge archival collection, is located right here! In the city!"

"What organization? And where is this headquarters?" Lina endeavored to keep pace with my rapid delivery.

"The group is known as the Sovereign Order of Malta. And their headquarters, the Magistral Palace—which I plan to visit as soon as possible—is on the Via Condotti. I am betting I can find something there, even the smallest detail, which will provide a lead."

Lina leaned back against the tree and regarded me carefully. "I will keep your secret. I don't understand why you can't tell your advisor—a man who clearly holds you in high esteem both, ah... personally and professionally. But I respect your decision. And I certainly don't know enough about your field of specialty to try and guess at what you've found and why it may shake the world of art history. But there is one thing I know for sure: if you think you are trotting yourself down to this 'Magistral Palace' on one of the most fashionable streets in the world looking like that, my friend, you are sadly mistaken. Non é permesso! I am making an appointment at the Nardi Day Spa for you. You are getting a head-to-toe makeover."

"No way, Lina. I've no time—"

"Silenzio! È fatta! It's done! Now let's get lunch.

Chapter Four

NOVEMBER 1533

WINDSOR ROYAL PARK

T he imposing circular castle tower of Windsor cast its long shadow over the hills which gently sloped to the Royal Forest. They rode companionably. Stretching ahead of them was a path blanketed with pine needles and the crisp leaves fallen from a dense copse of trees bordering the forest. Even as the Palace faded into the distance, pleasant whiffs of woodsmoke and roasting meat drifted from the kitchens. The aroma blended agreeably with the smell of well-oiled tack and impeccably groomed horses. As King Henry shifted in his saddle, his powerful courser—the horse he favored for hunting—shook its head with a jangle of bit and bridle. Archbishop Thomas Cranmer's sleek bay palfrey pricked its ears at the sound. As the two men approached the wood's depths, bells from Windsor's Curfew Tower pealed, signaling the noon hour.

They chose a path through the woodland which accommodated them both, riding side by side. The Archbishop had requested an audience with the King; he had serious matters to discuss— concerns which had kept him sleepless since the King's revelation. Henry offered to talk while they rode out on that brisk November day, a suggestion readily accepted by Cranmer, an avid horseman who relished the opportunity to ride the expensive gelding Henry had gifted to him, especially in the royal hunting grounds adjoining Windsor Palace. He had rehearsed in his mind how he would initiate this conversation; still, he hesitated. The subject was of such magnitude that he was apprehensive about engaging the King—but discuss it he must. He withdrew a kerchief from a pocket in his jerkin and scrubbed at his forehead, drying the glaze of sweat that had appeared despite the fresh breeze.

"Your Majesty, I hardly know how to express the veneration I hold for you and your... ah, most eminent stature in the eyes of God. Yet I will readily admit that your words took my breath away. It seems to me, Your Grace, that what you envision will have an enormous impact on the realm. And beyond our borders. For the consequences, you must concede, will certainly be far-reaching. Of course, you will be aware of this. How, Sire, do you intend to counter this reaction?"

Henry rode on, unperturbed. It was as if his vicar had asked what he wished to have for supper. "Thomas, your concern is what I would expect of you, nothing less. Indeed, there will be great turmoil. But change is already upon us, and it must happen. It is God's will. You well know the present situation to be intolerable. Disgraceful! Souls are waiting, crying out for salvation. Only by eradicating the corrupt Church of Rome and the codification of a new religion will they be helped. The Almighty Father will have it no other way. He depends on me to carry out His mission here on earth."

The horses' hooves thudded softly on the pine floor. Cranmer felt the blood drain from his face. "Your Grace, what mean you when you say eradicating the Roman Church?"

Calmly, eyes forward, Henry replied. "I mean that I have a divinely ordained calling to purify the Church by seizing power from Rome—by destroying the papacy—the figurehead of all that has become noxious and evil in its midst."

Cranmer drew a sharp breath. "By raising an army, you mean? By marching on Rome and the Vatican? Is this your plan, Majesty?"

"Not immediately, no. As I said, a revelation of this new order will take time, Thomas. After all, Rome ne s'est pas faite en un jour! That city wasn't built in a day; nor will we see its immediate undoing." Henry's bellowing laughter at his pun echoed in the hallowed stillness of the forest.

Cranmer chuckled in unity but felt little mirth. "Your Grace, I apologize for my ignorance. Tell me please—in detail—what you intend."

Henry pulled his horse up and, dropping the reins, allowed him to graze. Cranmer likewise halted, facing the King. The palfrey contentedly lowered his head to nibble blades of grass that poked through the matted forest floor.

"Thomas, my Archbishop, allow me to be clear, for this is how it will be: I am Christ's divine disciple. Not the pope, or any other mortal. And I have been called to extinguish the corruption, the errors, the customs and abuses by which the children of God have been bound to the Roman Church and its clergy for centuries. Écoutez-moi! Hear me well! I can and will use any offensive necessary to attack Clement's pomp, avarice, and tyranny—his prideful ambition."

Cranmer tried to swallow, but his mouth felt as if was lined with wool. He watched as Henry stroked his horse's flank, idly scanning the forest glen for a hapless red deer which might wander nearby. The cleric ventured softly, "But what about the heads of Europe, Majesty? Charles of Spain? What of your ally, François? Do you really believe that France will bow to your command? You and François have been, at times, friends, at others, enemies—but you have always united against the encroachment of Suleiman, the Turk. If, or rather when, François becomes outraged over your pronouncement, how will you unify the forces of Christ to battle the Turk, should he invade?"

"I fear that prospect not, Thomas. God will show me the way. And He will provide the resources necessary to arm ourselves for the holy battle ahead. To that end, we will begin at once garnering funds. The riches hoarded by the Church—the incalculable wealth stored within its monasteries and cathedrals. They are not to remain the property of the Holy See. I will abolish them and claim their fortunes to underwrite this, the most righteous of pursuits."

Cranmer struggled to grasp the enormity of what he heard. He, too, stroked his horse's neck anxiously. "But what of resistors, Your Grace? For you know there will be those."

Henry's pensive gaze vanished. "Watch me, Thomas! I will do everything necessary to the preferment of God's Word. And I will defend to the death my right and title. Refusal to believe and act accordingly will be met with punishment: corporal punishment of the most merciless kind. We will begin here at home, but let this warning be heard across all Christian lands. On behalf of our Lord God Almighty, I will not be denied! Let Rome quake in fear. Unless they succumb, the sack of 1527 will look like a celebration. This is my shining moment— God has entrusted me to act on his behalf, and act I will."

Archbishop Cranmer looked away. He straightened his cap and resigned himself to the strategy Henry had presented. Which was, after all, his only choice.

The King gathered his horse's reins and moved off, Archbishop Cranmer in tow, to follow a beam of light that pierced the forest's gloom at the trail's end.

AUSTIN FRIARS

RESPONDING TO THEIR MASTER'S subtle signal, the house staff at Thomas Cromwell's palatial London residence moved quickly, parading steaming, silver-domed dishes into the hall. Candelabra and a warming hearth blaze cast flickering light, picking out the somber features of Thomas Cranmer and, across the table, those of Cromwell, his host. Once they had placed the platters bearing the evening's repast on the sideboards and had poured full measures of claret in each goblet, they silently departed. The heavy studded doors were securely closed, and a careful check of the surroundings assured that no one lurked within range of hearing. Only then was their first word uttered.

"Well, Thomas. You know why we dine together this evening, aside from the fact that I need no excuse to enjoy your company, sir," Cromwell opened. "The King's pronouncement. It took us all aback, did it not? As you know, I pride myself on anticipating his requests, his needs, and when possible, his thoughts. It is a hard-earned skill that has enabled me to deal with Henry—usually with great success. But this? This I did not foresee. Oh, the man is devout. For all his intimidating swagger, he spends time on his knees. I have oft wished I could be privy to the conversations he conducts with God, as I wonder if he uses the royal 'We'."

Cranmer's lips twitched at Cromwell's drollery. "I cannot lie and say I expected what we were told, either. In truth, it nigh knocked the wind from me. Nonetheless…" He sighed and sank lower in his plush chair. "…nonetheless, the situation has been laid squarely at our feet, Tom. What does that mean for us? It means there is little time to waste. We must act. 'Tis delicate and dangerous indeed, this matter, and delicate is how I picture our necks if we are not well able to move forward in accordance with our Sovereign's expectations."

With a chortle, Cromwell stood, reached across the table for the decanter and poured another glass of wine for himself, raising a questioning eyebrow in Cranmer's direction, who placed a hand over the top of his goblet.

Cranmer brooded over the untouched plate before him. "So, what then do you make of this, Tom? His Majesty's revelation is confounding, saying the very least. Oh, I concede that our collective thinking has clearly shifted away from Rome's stifling jurisprudence and that we've had to place oversight of all matters of faith into the King's hands, but now to be informed that he's had visions? That he's been appointed directly by God as His designate on earth, akin to Simon Peter himself? It borders on the profane; you do realize that?"

Cromwell gave a slight shake to his head. Thomas Cranmer was his friend, and in actuality, there were few whom the King's Secretary trusted. He was a lawyer, after all, and knew how easily a man might turn on his closest ally were it a case of gaining riches, even quicker if it meant saving his own neck. But Cranmer was different. They'd forged a bond of shared clerical and constitutional strategy during the madness litigating the King's Great Matter. So, he felt confident to speak openly, as he would not have dared had it been anyone else at that table.

"There is not one amongst the King's closest council who believes a move to separate from Rome is the wrong course for England. God Himself knows we've spent countless hours in debate and study, and it is the only logical conclusion. But..." Cromwell considered his words very carefully. "...although we are well aware that he does consider himself—in his definition—divine... I'd had no previous indication that His Majesty sees himself as a King of Jerusalem, the Rock of a completely reborn Church, intending to challenge the institution of Rome to achieve his end."

The Archbishop leaned forward, elbows akimbo, fingers pressed together, steeple-like. "Well, there's no doubt he believes it to be true, Tom. With every fiber of his being. I heard His Majesty's confession only this morning, and afterward, we talked. Without revealing more than I am able, I can tell you that, while he is committed to the path Our Lord has laid before him... well... he has moments of self-doubt. He wishes, of course, for no one—maybe above all, the Queen—to have even an inkling of his apprehension. I did my best to provide reassurance that God will steer him appropriately. I guess it worked, because he seemed, at the self-same time, humbled, yet exalted—and I did wonder, then, at his inner peace."

Both men sat in uncomfortable reflection until Cromwell shrugged. "But how are we to know the real truth, Thomas? Come to that, why should we assume that what he asserts is not, after all, God's command? What proof would we conjure to discount his claim?"

Cranmer gestured and refilled the cleric's chalice with the blood-red wine. "We have none. Yet, it is nigh impossible not to imagine that he will ask—demand!—his subjects acknowledge him unconditionally as equal to Simon Peter, the Apostle most loved by Jesus Christ. And that can only invite one outcome."

"Theological chaos. And war," Cromwell retorted flatly.

Reluctantly the Archbishop nodded agreement. "Yes. He will be secretly regarded by many as having gone mad. As demented as the Holy Maid of Kent, who is captive and raving like a lunatic in the Tower even as we speak. Of course, Henry can rightfully counter his naysayers, those desperate to exploit his flaws, by arguing that Peter was notably human too, and fallible."

"Yet Jesus forgave him. Of course."

"Not only forgave him his betrayals, Tom, but founded His Church on the shoulders of an imperfect, albeit devoted, follower. Therefore, why might Henry not be a second Peter? His commitment to God and Faith is without question, his sweep and influence far-reaching. And so far as his will to achieve goes? Well, you and I have both stood witness to how single-minded, how damnably obdurate, he can be. So, why might it not be a tenable thesis? We are taught that man is made in God's image and that each of us carries the spark of divinity. So, is it unimaginable that Henry's spark is ignited and that he now stands in divine service to God?"

Cranmer paused, searching Cromwell's carefully composed expression for agreement, before hazarding, "Which is why I, for one, have decided to accept the King's revelation fully." A mere flicker betrayed a near-imperceptible breach in the Secretary's practiced reserve. But thus committed, the Archbishop took a deep breath and pressed on. "If the King swears that he has been so ordained, Tom, then, in my mind, he has. And I shall honor him thus."

Cromwell nodded thoughtfully. "I have to agree with you. You are a practical theologian, Thomas, which is why we work well together. You speak rationally. I value that, so I shall follow suit—the course which I, too, had decided before this evening would present my only option. I state here before you, Your Grace, that I consider Henricus Rex not only Sovereign of the Realm but Christ's directly ordained vicar. What it may mean for us, for England, and the rest of the world, I shudder to think. The message will not go down easily, that is certain. I will do my utmost to dissuade him from reckless and violent action, but it will be as it will be. I could say more, but I choose to leave it at that." He removed his cap and raked one hand through his hair. "May God help us."

From the open grate, the last log spit a shower of sparks. Cromwell stood, stretched his legs, and selected a hefty chunk of oak from the basket near the fireplace. Placing it carefully on top of the glowing embers, he stood in thought for a few moments, leaning against the elegantly carved mantel.

Cranmer nodded in agreement, and sat staring as the flames burst into an orange pyre. Silence hung heavy in the chamber, save for the crackle and hiss of the hearth. Finally, the Archbishop looked up, and regarding his still untouched plate laden with cold, congealed food, wrinkled his nose. "So, for now, to less weighty matters, my friend. With your permission as host, let us serve ourselves some more palatable fresh roast that still steams on the sideboard, eat well, and then play cards. Tomorrow I shall meet with Master Holbein to ascertain his predilection toward this matter. If he does not believe, he will not be able to execute."

"And if he does—and let us hope that he does—we must quickly discuss this painting in depth: what message it must convey. The King and his Queen will be anxious to meet with Hans to begin planning. They hope for the entire project to be completed by year-end. What imagery Our Royal Highnesses have in mind, I know not. But suffice to say our esteemed Hans will have many sleepless nights ahead, so he better rest up while he can. This little task is going to consume him until it meets the demanding satisfaction of both Henry and Anne."

ON THE FOLLOWING DAY, immediately after morning mass, the Archbishop sat with Hans Holbein in a small, private closet adjoining the library in Windsor Castle. Archbishop Cranmer opened the discussion, reiterating the expectation they had heard directly from the King just days before. Appeal made, he leaned back and observed the painter from across the table's expanse. Even though Holbein had pledged his dedication to the King while in the meeting, Cranmer needed to know if, in fact, he possessed the commitment to see it through. And thus, he placed the question before Holbein once again. He waited.

Holbein had listened without interruption. A man of few words at the best of times, his reply was careful. "Your Grace, I am but a simple painter. What do I know of these things? On the other hand, I need no persuasion to be convinced that the pope has misled the people of the Faith. Even to a humble man like me, it is apparent that the mighty Bishops of Rome have not provided the moral compass needed by the faithful. Change is required."

"Meaning, Master Holbein?"

"What I mean, Your Grace, is my offer: I pledge my conviction to Henry, King of England."

Cranmer studied Holbein, but in the artist's mien he detected no artifice. "If you take this on, Holbein, it will be a great service to His Majesty, for I can scarce describe how profoundly important this is to him and thus to us all. The King's plan to reveal his ordination is a gradual one. As you can understand, a depiction of our royal couple, incorporating the proper allegories befitting such an astounding truth, must be designed and executed with the most exquisite skill. Have you thought about it? Have you an idea about how you would proceed?"

Holbein rubbed a grizzled chin, calluses on his dye-stained hand rasping against the short beard. "To be truthful, Your Grace, in order to successfully carry out the King's wishes, I must have assistance. I am well aware of the project's secrecy, Archbishop. Acutely so. But I would like to consult my friend and colleague, Nickolaus Kratzer, to help with the design and imagery. There is no other man who compares in this regard. Indeed, it was his guidance upon which I depended to compose my painting of the French ambassadors, which Your Grace has previously been so kind as to compliment."

Cranmer rose from his chair and went to the window. He pushed wide the mullioned glass. A cold, steady rain was falling, and gusts of wind caused the flailing branches from a nearby sycamore to relinquish their few remaining, soggy leaves.

Hans spoke to Cranmer's back. "Your Grace, you can be well assured that Nikolaus, as Royal Astronomer, is a dedicated servant of His Majesty. Might you, therefore, consider discussing the possibility with the King and advise whether or not he would be agreeable to allowing Kratzer knowledge of the subject matter?"

With a shiver, Cranmer pulled the window closed and fastened the latch. He turned and faced Holbein. "Henry well knows Kratzer as a true man of science and trusts him. He's relied on him for many years and, as far as I know, he's always found Nickolaus's knowledge of the heavens and mathematical formulae to be without equal. Nor, I believe, does the King find him to be in any way biased or excitable. So yes, I would assume His Majesty will permit him to collaborate with you on the painting's theme and schematics as long as he can assure us that he'll betray no word of it."

"I feel sure that will not present an obstacle, Your Grace."

"I shall arrange a meeting to make our request of the King with some urgency, Hans. In the meantime, though, ponder this: the King was deeply moved by your double portrait of the French ambassadors De Selve and Dinteville. And as you know well, the Queen was exuberant about it and well pleased to contribute to your stipend, having declared it to be one of the most stunningly beautiful, realistic, and enigmatic paintings she has ever seen. Indeed, she could not stop talking to Henry about it." He pulled a chair from beneath the table and scraped it across the floor until he was seated eye to eye with Hans. Cranmer looked at him, unblinking. "But, Holbein, that painting, it sets a high bar, you know. You must be aware that a large portrait of the King and Queen together—one intended to convey such a powerful message—will need to be much more brilliant." He shook his head. "You have proven yourself to possess great talent, Hans, but I do not envy you this ambitious task."

Holbein sucked in his breath and looked away. Slowly, he exhaled between tight lips, rubbing at his forehead. Cranmer remained still, silent. If the man could not assimilate what this task would require, and if he was reluctant to take it on, it would be better to know right away. Cranmer wondered what he would do if the answer was negative, or even doubtful. This he knew: Henry would not be pleased. And Holbein's burgeoning career in the Tudor court would almost certainly come to a grinding halt.

The painter raised his head. Slowly, he nodded and grunted his assent. "I will do it, Your Grace. I will take on the task, and do my utmost to convey the King's holy message using sticks of charcoal and pots of paint. May God be with me to do it honor." He extended his hand to shake Cranmer's. The Archbishop momentarily wondered how such a paw could possibly create incomparable beauty with great delicacy, realism with subtle brushstrokes. But after all, that was Holbein's magic, and God knows it was about to be put to the test. The painter now had no choice but to create a masterpiece.

For better or for worse, an agreement had been forged.

PALACE OF GREENWICH

THE KING WAS GENIAL, noisily demolishing an ample dinner washed down by a vintage he favored, the latest having been sent to him by François I as yet another peace offering following one of the *contretemps* which regularly arose between the French and English kings. The Queen, tucked in close to her husband, gown gracefully arranged, giggled at his witticisms, affording him her full attention and generally charming him as she was so able to do. Anne, Henry's love for seven years and his Queen for one, had mastered the art of beguiling her husband while asserting her opinions in the politics of his court whenever she was able.

Cromwell took in the scene as he, Holbein, and the Archbishop waited in the doorway to be announced, drawing a silent breath of relief to know that their planned meeting would, at the least, get off to a good start.

"Your Majesties," Cromwell greeted while all three men bowed low.

"Thomas! Come forth! My Lord Archbishop, Master Holbein, all three of you, please join us." Henry motioned for the usher to set additional places. "Wine! Gentlemen, are you hungry? There is sustenance aplenty. Pray help yourselves."

The instant they were seated, at their elbows appeared servants with platters heaped with roast venison, thick slices of boar, and steamed vegetables. Cromwell feigned appreciation; food was the last thing on his and his companions' minds. "Your Grace, you and the Queen are too generous. But we thank you and are delighted to be

invited to dine with you both. Although, of course, we have important business to attend to this afternoon, which, as you commanded,
is why we are here."

Anne spoke up. "Equally are we eager to discuss the matter with
you, gentlemen. But let us finish our meal and drink to the project at
hand before we begin." She raised her goblet. "À notre grand succès:
to our great achievement!"

Each, including the King, drank to an auspicious initiation of the
project intended to take shape that day.

Once the ushers had cleared the table, only a platter of sweet-
meats and a bowl of apples remained on the white napery. A fresh
round of wine was poured before all servants were dismissed from
the King's presence chamber, whereupon Henry pushed his chair
back to stretch his long legs before him. He was ready.

"Come tell me then, Master Hans," he rumbled. "What say you
about this venture? What ideas do you have?"

Hans stood before his Sovereign, shifting his weight from one foot
to the other. He seemed ready to speak, but then hesitated. Henry
cocked an eyebrow, prompting an answer.

"Your Highness, my mind has been awhirl with images these past
days since you shared with us—and I am humbled to be included,
Sire—the knowledge of your ordinance as the Lord God's appointed
founder of a new theology. But I contained my thoughts because I
must first understand what message you have in mind before I get
carried away with presumption. So, with the greatest respect, I ask to
hear from you and the Queen what you envision." He turned diplo-
matically to Cranmer and Cromwell and supplemented, "Gentlemen,
your contributions will be most gratefully received, as well."

Henry hesitated but a fleeting moment. "I have envisioned this
for some time now, Hans. I see in my mind's eye a large composition; not quite life-size, but it must be very impressive in length
and width. It will achieve two aims: first, to provide the message of

my appointment by the Spirit of the Lord as the divine founder of His new church. And second, but of equal importance, guidance to a heavenly reward for all who see it and understand. Of course, it must affirm the pivotal role Her Royal Highness has played in our enlightenment. She has opened my eyes and ears to the message God delivered; for, were it not for Queen Anne, we in this kingdom might be ensnared throughout eternity by the tyranny of the Holy See."

"Indeed so, Your Grace," the Archbishop murmured, not intending to be left out of the conversation.

Henry lifted Boleyn's fingertips to his mouth and kissed them delicately, causing her to beam with delight. "So, Holbein, hear me well! Your work must illustrate the Queen at her finest: detailing her as no portrait to date has been able. It will display her unequaled beauty, fine intelligence, boundless courage, and abiding faith. It is to be a portrait of My Lady Anne as much as one of myself. I want all who view it to be awestruck by our harmony as England's royal couple. In essence, it must emphasize her importance to me while celebrating my steadfast love and respect for her."

"And indeed, your appraisal is more than amply justified, Your Majesty." Holbein nodded awkwardly. "I only pray I can fulfill that expectation, but I have never been one to shirk from a challenge and am impatient to begin."

"Although I understand you first have a request to make of the King," Cranmer prompted gently, sensing Holbein's nervousness.

The painter knew he ventured into dangerous territory. The monarch had earlier made the implied penalty for breaching absolute secrecy all too clear.

"I must ask, Majesty. May I include your Court Astronomer in the planning of the schematic drawings? No one matches Nikolaus Kratzer in subtle messaging—in conceiving the icons to be used and laying out the geometry and perspective of such a work. His consultation was invaluable in creation of the Ambassadors' portrait and the imagery it incorporates. At the same time, I can assure you he will be as close-lipped as a corpse."

"I give my assent, Master Hans," the King answered solemnly and without hesitation, then winked at Cranmer. The artist's discomfiture was their little joke. The Archbishop had already broached the subject with him.

"For which I am greatly indebted, Your Grace." Holbein looked relieved. "Now, can you tell me more regarding the symbols which are most important as we begin to create the concept? What does your imagination hold?"

"There must be a rock as the painting's foundation," Anne interjected firmly before Henry could respond. "The rock upon which the new Church will stand, proud and strong. And accompanying that—keys. The holy Keys to the Kingdom of Heaven."

Henry lifted the heavy chain hanging about his neck and dropped it with a thud on the table in front of them. Attached was the golden ship, flying through seas of a storm, its helmsman strong and erect. "As well as this, my symbol, Sires. The Barque of St. Peter, which I, Henricus Rex, will now guide through all coming turbulence to its safe harbor. I am, and always will be, Fidei Defensor, the Defender of the True Faith entrusted by God Almighty to steer a righteous course. Thus, must this Barque be represented also, Holbein."

Archbishop Cranmer, pacing back and forth in front of the warming fire, occasionally rubbing his hands, halted: the discussion had veered squarely into his territory now. "It is said in John, Chapter 21, that Christ asked Peter if he loved Him. Peter committed that he did, just as our King has, without remonstrance. Our Sovereign has demonstrated his unfailing love of the Lord over and over throughout his life. Thus now, as Christ then asked of Peter, it will be the King of England's duty to feed God's lambs—his sheep. Can you embody that truth too, Holbein?"

The painter took notes as they spoke. He looked up only when the silence became noticeable.

The King, raw emotion causing his voice to waver uncharacteristically, said quietly, "Hans, it will be your privileged mission to paint validation of my intimate relationship with Jesus Christ: I am entrusted with the protection of two of the most cherished relics known to humanity—remnants of Christ's suffering and death. There are many who have claimed, in the past centuries, to know where remnants of Christ's cross are hidden. But it is I, through the blessing of Jesus, who own the single remaining piece of the cross that Christ carried and upon which he died." Mighty Henry stumbled as he uttered the words, and had to gather himself before continuing. "And even more wondrous: I am the only living person who knows the location of the Sangreal—the wooden dish in which Joseph of Arimathea caught the remaining drops of Jesus' divine blood after his death."

At the revelation of these two secrets, the present company became reverentially quiet.

After a time, Henry spoke. "I will have you render, Holbein, concealed within the painting, code for the whereabouts of these treasures. In that way, and in the event something should happen to me, there will remain worldly evidence of their existence."

Holbein appeared overwhelmed at what he'd just heard. "I am humbled, Majesty, by your confidence in me—that I might aptly depict such profound miracles. I can only pray that my hand and heart will be divinely guided as I work."

Everyone in the room, including the King, were suddenly intensely aware of the significance of what had been proposed. No one was quite sure what to say.

So Master Cromwell, bowing his head, murmured, "Confirming Vicarius Christi. That Henricus Rex is now Christ's Vicar."

HOLBEIN, CRANMER, AND CROMWELL stepped through the palace's sturdy outer door to meet the blast of a whipping wind. Brown, sere leaves, the sad remnants of a glorious autumn, whirled in crazy vortexes at the center of the courtyard. Holbein seemed impervious to the bite of the raw draughts. Cranmer tried stoically to withstand their sting as if it was his penance for the day. While Cromwell tugged his cloak tight about his neck and shouted to be heard above the rising gale blowing down-Channel from the North Sea.

"Gentlemen, we are now bound to see this crusade through. Whatever we might believe in the depths of our souls must henceforth remain private."

"Indeed." Cranmer gave in and wrapped his woolen coat as close to his body as he could manage. "We move in one direction only. Master Holbein, you have the authority to meet with Kratzer and draw up a carta. With all haste, create a concept of how to depict the King's message. Remember! It must represent our King and Queen with the distinction they rightfully expect—as a loving, unified couple. Cromwell and I will review your initial plans before we show it to Their Majesties. And Hans—don't tarry! His Majesty is not a patient man, and this project looms large on his agenda."

"I'll do so, my lord," Holbein yelled as he hunched to ward off a blast. "I intend to go now and take shelter in Kratzer's chamber, and we will work on our draft."

Cromwell clapped both men on the shoulder, at which point each headed purposefully in a different direction. It occurred to him that their divergence seemed similar to the violent parting of the ways imminent for Henry VIII, King of England and Wales, and Pope Clement VII, Bishop of Rome. He turned to shout to each his wish of good luck, but at that very moment the wind snatched the tail of his cloak and lashed it across his face, obliterating his vision.

HANS RAPPED ON THE door of Kratzer's room and was bidden "Enter." The dwelling was found only by following a maze of narrow and meandering hallways to the wing of Greenwich apartments reserved for the resident intellectuals and scholars of Henry's court. Inside, it was small and cramped, but clusters of beeswax candles burning brightly fortified the afternoon's waning light. Although his living quarters were spare, Kratzer's stature as Henry's Astronomer Royal was distinctive by his unusually generous allowance of fine wax candles—an extravagance the King approved so the astrologer and mathematician could effectively work at night, his preferred hour of productivity. The crowded space was cluttered with rolled and flattened parchments, books open to pages displaying enigmatic drawings, sketches of extraordinary instruments tacked to the walls, and several prototypes of cosmological devices tucked into corners. On the desk, before the single window, stood an impressive astrolabe. Nikolaus's most prized possession and extremely valuable; it had been made specifically for him by the master instrument-maker Gemma Frisius in Louvain, Belgium, and had been carefully and expensively shipped to Greenwich. The object fascinated the King, and he and Klaus spent many hours conferring with it, inspecting the heavens.

Klaus Kratzer greeted his younger friend warmly, sweeping papers from a chair to the floor and motioning for Hans to sit. With a grunt, Kratzer lowered himself onto the stool near his desk. "Of late, Hans, my hip has been bothering me. If only my devices could prognosticate whether my mobility will return, or if I will forevermore be destined to limp, propped by that dratted cane." He grimaced as he settled himself on a pillow, and reaching for a flagon of ale, he poured a tankard and passed it to Hans. Filling one for himself, he took a hearty quaff. He raised his left leg to prop it on a small shelf with some effort, then looked directly into Holbein's eyes. "So... tell me. Why your insistence on this meeting, without even passage of another day?"

Hans swallowed a mouthful and placed his tankard down carefully, thoughtfully, as if it were made of fine, thin glass. "What I have to tell you, Klaus, you may find difficult to believe. In fact, you may hear and never believe. That will be your choice. But I ask you, as my friend, to help me—to guide me and offer your inspiration and wisdom. For, surely, I need it."

Kratzer leaned forward, intrigued not only by Holbein's words but by the strangely vulnerable look on his face—a face which was usually rugged and impenetrable.

Holbein began. "Not quite a week ago, I was summoned to meet with the King and Queen, Secretary Cromwell, and Archbishop Cranmer, a strange enough occurrence in itself. But even more extraordinary was the King's purpose: to inform us of a powerful manifestation he has experienced and to ask if I would commemorate it in a painting. He demanded complete and total secrecy, but I have asked him if he would permit me to include you in the small circle of those who know so that I may seek your instruction as I create the composition. He agreed but only on the condition you will not share the information with anyone. Can you give me your word, Klaus?"

"I will. Yes. What, pray, is it?"

"The King makes ready to separate from the Church of Rome and his domination by the pope. Through his course of prayer and devotions, he has been called by God to assume the mantle of leadership of a new Church. But not merely leadership, you see. Instead, he says God requires Henry to become the new St. Peter. The King will stand upon the rock supporting an entirely new Church, one which will abolish the hypocrisy of the past and emerge victorious and righteous. Klaus, His Majesty is fully convinced he is tantamount to the Kings of the Old Testament and that he is as important to God and the Holy Trinity as was Simon Peter. Perhaps more so! He absolutely believes this—as does the Queen. And he wishes me to depict this new image in a painting, replete with symbolism—magnificent—a full-length portrait of him as the foundation of the Church, alongside his Queen."

Kratzer blinked and rubbed his forehead, staring through the window into the darkened, stormy evening. In truth, he was an atheist—strictly a man of science. And to that end, he had learned to discreetly detach himself from the profoundly religious overtones which directed almost every aspect of life. He'd determined how to carefully converse with individuals at Court—both clerical and secular. It was his passion to learn how the workings of the world and the heavens beyond directed human behavior. However, he remained closely allied with Sir Thomas More, Henry's Lord High Chancellor, who was a devout follower of the Roman Church. If More were to learn of the King's stunning declaration, he would actively rebel—of this there should be no doubt. And More would not be the only one in Henry's court to abhor such a claim. The clergymen who had resolutely objected to the divorce between the King and Katharine of Aragon: the forbidding and unpleasant John Fisher; clever, devious Stephen Gardiner; and that unctuous enemy of Queen Anne, the Spanish ambassador Chapuys, to name but a very few. He imagined their reactions would be considered treasonous. And for that matter, what of the pope himself, along with the rest of the Roman Catholic world? By a cock's testicles, what was Henry thinking?

This pronouncement would surely set the cosmos on its edge. Brutal, bloody wars had raged throughout time for less—much less. What would a claim such as this incite? No wonder it had to be kept a secret. But for how long?

"Hans, do you believe what the King has told you and his advisors? If you do, I respect your opinion. You must know, though, it runs counterpoint to all I believe, all my training has instilled in me."

Holbein's face was impassive. "My personal views are irrelevant. Suffice to say, I must paint him as such, Klaus," came the simple answer.

"Then, my friend… I shall help you."

By the time the evening had drifted into the early hours of the following day, and the candles had burned low, Holbein and Kratzer had devised their plan.

Chapter Five

EARLY NOVEMBER 2016

ROME

Squeals of feminine laughter could be heard coming from behind the closed office door. There were always girls, students both undergrad and doctoral, clamoring for his attention. Antonio's classes were fascinating, without doubt, and it wasn't easy to sign up for his lectures since they were some of the first to fill to capacity. But it was pretty clear that many of his students had no genuine interest in pursuing a career involving the history of language. In fact, I was certain there were more than a few who were intent on exploring the language of love with Professore Moretti.

So I waited, leaning against the wall in the hallway just outside his office. My patience rewarded, the door opened at last, and two very attractive young women lingered at the threshold, chatting and giggling as long as they could. Finally, I heard a chair grate against the floor, and Antonio's head appeared as he politely ushered the girls out. As they passed, they gave me a dismissive glance. Then he caught sight of me, and his relief was evident.

"Signorina Rossi!" He pointedly looked at his watch. "Thank you for being so prompt for our meeting... do please come in..." He waved the two girls on, motioned me inside and firmly shut the door.

"Grazie a Dio!" He sank into his leather chair after pushing one over for me. "I've had student appointments all afternoon. Lord, but they're tiring! And those last two… I'm not sure how they qualified for Sapienza, but neither shows the slightest interest in the course content. I'd hazard a guess that they have a bet to see who gets invited to my apartment first. Bad news, ladies: neither of you."

I afforded him a half-smile. I'd heard Antonio protest before, like when his classes were booked up with female students and a talented young man couldn't register, or when the dean asked him to add one more lecture and it was immediately filled to standing room with women.

"I'm delighted to see you, Zara! I wanted to talk with you about a few ideas for a project. One of them might be useful for your dissertation, or could even be something we might work on together. And anyway, it's nice just to be able to relax with you." His smile was so warm and engaging, and as usual, I felt both flattered and uncomfortable, all at the same time.

We chatted about books and papers, and Antonio told me about a unique archival document he heard had been acquired by the Biblioteca Nazionale Centrale in Florence. "It's an interesting piece, and apparently, it was part of the collection which belonged to Lorenzo de Medici. Which, speaking of the Medici, brings me to another point, Zara: I still can't credit that you weren't able to locate anything on the feud between the Medici pope, Clement VII, and Henry VIII." He paused and shook his head quizzically. "It just seems strange that throughout an entire volume of his letters, there was no mention of it. Are you certain you looked carefully enough?"

I stiffened in defense. "You know how thorough I am! And even though my time was limited, I'm utterly certain there was not a word in that book. Maybe he kept a private journal? But if so, that would be in the Secret Archives, and I would have no access to it." I met his direct gaze. "Oh well… there are so many other interesting subjects to explore. Small loss." I pulled my notebook, which had been perched on his desk, just a bit closer to me.

"Well, okay then. Of course I believe you. Let me make a note so I can contact the prefect tomorrow and see if we can get you back into the Archives. Would you want me to come with you this time? Two pairs of eyes?"

I didn't know what to say. His referral was critical to my entry, but I wasn't thrilled with the idea that he just might find the note I had tucked back and away in its resting place. So I said, "Oh, how kind of you to offer, Antonio! I'd love to go back. But I actually have a few leads I'm working on in our library, so… maybe later. Maybe we can do that next semester. Let me see how I get on with what I have." The thought of passing up another visit to the Archives made me feel almost physically ill. But what else could I do?

He glanced at his watch. "Well, let's go get a drink, shall we? I could use a glass of wine or two after such a long afternoon. Will you join me?"

"Okay. Let me just visit the ladies' room for a minute, and then we can go." I collected my books, placing the notebook carefully on the bottom of the pile, shifting them to the chair as I rose. "I'll be right back." While in the washroom, it occurred to me that I'd have to do a better job of steering the conversation away from the topic of Clement's letters if I intended to keep the mystery of the painting to myself. I'd need to decide on another focus for my thesis, and I'd better get it done, soon. I dried my hands and crossed the hall to return to the office. Antonio's back was blocking the doorway. Maybe he was on the phone? He heard me approach and stepped aside to allow me to enter. With a start, I noticed that my books were rearranged, and he was mopping up spilled coffee. My notebook—the one in which I'd transcribed the sixteenth-century message—was on the desk, open. My heart started racing, and I quickly closed the notebook with a snap and scooped up the remaining pile. "What happened?"

Coolly, Antonio answered, "I'm so clumsy! I spilled my coffee and wanted to be sure I blotted up the mess before it dripped onto your papers for you... there! It's all taken care of. I need a drink. Andiamo. Let's go."

Chapter Six

NOVEMBER 2016

ROME

The several days following that meeting with Antonio were unsettling. Headed into town, I was so deep in thought that when I stepped out into Piazza Ungheria, a not-so-SmartCar, careening around the corner, narrowly avoided sideswiping me. I leaped aside while its driver, shaking his fist out the window, yelled, *"Hey! Attenta! Stupida!"*

"An' fuck you too!" I screamed back, wishing I'd been fluent enough to have retorted in Italian.

Trying to calm my racing heart, I arrived at a classical four-story Italianate townhouse on the square. The Nardi DaySpa was on the first level. I pushed the door open to be greeted by a composed young lady whose fresh, understated look perfectly reflected the serenity of the cool grey reception area. I drew a deep breath, determined to use the afternoon to relax, maybe even forget briefly about lost paintings and inquisitive university professors. Probably Lina had been on to something. Maybe indulging in some beautification would do me good.

Although the day's appointment hadn't been my idea, I wasn't a complete stranger to the interior of an upscale salon. There were a number scattered in and around Chestnut Hill, Massachusetts, where my parents lived, and I'd be packed off, muttering under my breath, to one of those when home from college and invariably needing a radical sprucing up. My father still lived there, in that same large brick English Colonial house. My mother had become a well-known, highly desired client of the top salons in the village. She was a lavish tipper, and not that much effort was required to make Christina Rossi emerge looking beautiful. She always had been a ravishing woman. And not only that, but she carried herself with an air of confidence, something I was aware of and wished I could emulate.

The attendant led me to the treatment area, where I changed into a thick, fluffy robe, then stretched out on a comfortable chaise waiting to be called for my massage. Following that, I was to have a facial, haircut, and styling, and finally, a makeup application. Not at all certain I'd be able to dedicate the required hours to such indolence without the urge to escape to the nearest library, I willed myself to unwind and obediently followed the masseuse into the warm, deliciously scented chamber.

The setting, meditative music, and sheer indulgence of the experience caused my thoughts to drift, and they came to rest on my mother. I was practiced at shifting my attention away from her, but blocking something so insistent requires skill, and this time, I lost. The images ran through my mind, undeterred.

What I remembered—at least the stand-out memories from my teen years and early adulthood—was my determination not to emulate the life my mother had created for herself. Back then, I thought I knew what was most important. And she was a housewife—in the most traditional sense, there was no question that she ran an impeccable household. But that was it! That was all! And for the life of me, I couldn't understand her not wanting something more. What made her path stranger still—at least in my eyes—was the fact that the former Christina Castellani had been known as an intellectually gifted free spirit, planning a great future practicing law—a profession I imagined she would have excelled in, had she pursued it. After all, no one could out-argue my mom when it came to free-wheeling discussions about almost any topic. And she read prodigiously and widely. But apparently, the best-laid plans... In her senior year at Wellesley, she and her friends attended a party at Harvard, and there she'd met the man who was to become my dad. He'd been a first-year med student in those days, tall, self-assured, and, according to Mom, incredibly handsome. He became her first genuinely steady boyfriend, and soon she was spending more time on the Harvard campus than on her own. By the time Christina graduated *magna cum laude* with a degree in sociology, she and Daniel Rossi were talking marriage. Sure enough, in July of 1977, they became engaged despite Dad still having two years of medical school to complete. So, while Dad finished school, he and his bride moved into a small apartment where Christina nobly abandoned her own career path to work as a secretary, simply to earn enough to cover rent and groceries.

Happily, soon after Dad completed his initial medical training, the by-then Doctor Rossi was accepted into a neurosurgery residency at the University of California in Los Angeles. There he excelled, so much so that he was invited to do additional study in the renowned neuroscience program at King's College, London. So he and Mom packed up and settled in London for a few years. As the story had been told, many a time, she loved living in the London neighborhood of Mayfair, and had lots of friends who wanted to socialize with the young and vibrant American wife of a rising medical star. They had a box full of dog-eared photos from those years, and as a kid I pored over them: Mom and Dad dressed to go out; snapshots of them at glamorous parties with Mom somehow always outshining the wealthy, polished British women. But the stories included the downside: underneath the elegant appearances lurked heartache. Several miscarriages had left my parents child-less into their thirties.

It was only after their final move to Boston, where my dad was appointed to a staff position at Mass General, they discovered—much to their delight—that my mother-to-be was weeks into a pregnancy. To their great joy, I was born early in February of 1990. I think for my mom, it must have been a longed-for turning point. She dedicated herself, with all of her typical zeal, into being the best mother she could be. And as I grew, I came to realize that, for her, mother-hood meant fashioning me in her own image.

I suspect, from those very earliest days, I never showed promise of matching that ambition.

Massage completed, I returned to the relaxation area to await my next service. Teacup in hand, I glanced in the mirror before being seated. One look at my wild and outrageously unkempt hair and overgrown brows triggered a vivid memory mixed with a grudging concession that maybe Mom had been on to something all along.

It was hard to forget the many scenes from the past…

"Zara, darling, we're almost ready to walk out the door. Can't you please, please, run a brush through your hair? And where are your stockings? You know you can't go to an awards dinner for your father with bare legs under your dress," Mother called as we rushed to leave for a banquet at which my dad would be honored. I was a junior in high school, already beginning to look at universities, and the plea from Mom was a constant refrain. Even after we'd climbed into the car for the ride into central Boston, her favorite theme continued relentlessly.

"Zara, you are almost seventeen. You simply must take more care with your appearance. Okay, I know it's not your first concern, but regardless, it is important. When you go to college interviews, what will the admissions officers think? And how I would love for you to speak up—offer a brief smile, even—to people when they're address-ing you. Surely that's not too much to ask?"

"I suppose not, Mom," followed my default sullen retort.

"I know you aren't interested in dating as yet, but it would be nice if you could make at least some effort to reciprocate the interest shown by some of the well-mannered boys in town. One day it will be important to you, you know. Very much so."

I'd been glad to be in the back seat, free to roll my eyes heavenward. The last thing I'd cared about was the driveling attention of teenage boys. Such a waste of time! It may have been what my mother wished for me, but I'd then reflected smugly, I was deeper, so much more mature, than that. Instead, I thought about the trip we had planned for the summer: a family vacation in London and Rome, where I intended to indulge myself in as much archaeology and library hunting as time—and Mother—would allow.

Oh, admittedly, I knew she'd been proud of me when I was accepted into Harvard as an undergrad. When she found out that I'd opted to read ancient history and archaeology—probably not her first choice for me—she remained upbeat. "I'm so excited for you, Zara," she'd said as we were selecting the essentials I'd need to move into my freshman dorm. "What a great start to your career. But please, honey, don't dismiss the benefits of socializing during your free time. And, of course, it's okay to wear jeans, but make sure you have a cute top on, and your hair is shiny and brushed out. And a little natural-looking makeup would be great. There'll be so many wonderful friends and young men to meet."

"Mom! I'm not going to college on a husband hunt!" I'd snapped, "There's so much I want to do—and chasing every guy who says 'Hi' doesn't factor in."

"You may say that now, honey, but we only want the best for you. I don't think you are the kind of individual who will want your Dad and me to bankroll you forever. Right? Let's be honest: you'll never be a big earner. Not from the academic path you've chosen. There's nothing wrong with considering the benefits that an affluent and well-connected husband could bring you. Can you understand my point?"

I remember just staring coldly at the back of her immaculately coiffured hair and thinking how it was it that my mother, the woman who had birthed me, didn't understand me at all?

And so, I went to Harvard—and loved it! Loved every minute of my studies and the people I met who shared my major, studying the past by deciphering fossils, relics, and other clues. It was there that my fascination with paleography was born, particularly after I'd first been exposed to some of the priceless documents held in the University Archives.

But I'd never been able to shake off the drawbacks. Every visit home consisted of the comfortable pleasures of being with family and old friends in surroundings so familiar, only to be countered by the frustration of having Mom harp on me about my appearance and inexplicable lack of a boyfriend. Dad didn't exactly help either. He, for his part, wanted me to reconsider my educational direction altogether. Oh, I loved my parents, but we never conceded those excruciating arguments. During those teen years when everyone seemed to be searching for themselves, when girls try to sort out what kind of women they want to be, I had to admit that I was probably more confused than most. Who, exactly, was I? A feminist? An intellectual?

Certainly, I never felt like a traditional homemaker kind of woman. I tried so hard to figure it out, and the idealized versions of myself veered madly from archetype to archetype. I had parents who'd been high achievers in school, and that imprint was left indelibly on my psyche. So, that much, at least, was clear. But when it came to relationships, I failed, often miserably. And the pain involved shoved me further and further into my shell. And on both sides, any familial peace we achieved seemed to be conditional.

The aesthetician layered a mask over my cheeks as I lay on the table, eyes closed. She had been working on my skin for just a little while when she said, "Cara, you are a truly lovely woman. Such exquisite bone structure and your skin is beautiful even though I can tell you do very little to keep it that way. Why don't you take better care of it?"

Sounds familiar, I thought resignedly. Her words uncannily echoed my mother's.

Achingly, I relived the family dinner that had taken place just before I returned to school in the spring of my senior year. All I had left was to finish finals and then prep for graduation. Even though my GPA was just shy of a perfect 4.0, and I had a plan mapped out for graduate studies, Mom hadn't even tried to conceal her disappointment that I hadn't developed a wider group of friends and that none of those was a romantically oriented male. Still determined to shape me in her own perfect image, she'd taken me shopping just the day before and had bought me reams of clothes, few of which I intended to wear. That afternoon, she'd come to my room, holding a small square box enrobed in soft grey velvet. Sitting on my bed, she said softly, "Zara, I know we've not seen eye to eye. But I never want you to doubt my love for you. I will always be there for you, no matter what you decide to do."

I eyed her uncertainly as she held out the box. "I want you to have this. It's the bracelet your father gave to me before we were married—the first substantial gift I received from him before he had much money." She smiled wistfully. "That's why it means so much to me. Anyway, I want you to have it, and maybe you will wear it one day—maybe when you go out with a man you love, or maybe even on your wedding day."

I hardly even tried to hide my disdain. She added, "Look, darling—whether or not you wear it really doesn't matter to me, although you may not believe that right now. I want you to have it to remember me by and to know I will always love and support you while always being proud of my wonderful girl."

She opened the box, and on its bed of velvet was a beautiful, gold circle bracelet, studded all around with ten diamonds. "Isn't it lovely?"

I remember waiting quite a while before responding. "Thanks, Mom. It's a wonderful gift, and I appreciate it: truly, I do. Whether I will ever wear it with a boyfriend—or even more far-fetched, on my wedding day—I can't say. But I am grateful. Let's just leave it here, though, Okay? I can't risk anything that valuable in my dorm room. Look, I'll put it in this drawer for safekeeping."

Apart from that somewhat unexpected interlude, it hadn't proved to be one of the most congenial visits. I longed for the moment when I would leave the U.S. for Rome: my intended destination for graduate school. At least there, a much greater distance would separate us, and I wouldn't have to listen to her lectures as frequently. I'd packed up my bags to leave for the remaining three weeks of my college life— and it became a silent, resentful few hours. Finally, I said, "See you later," and pulled out of the driveway to head back to school. I don't even remember waving goodbye—I was that disillusioned.

The very next day, as Mom backed out of that same driveway to go to an auxiliary meeting, a trash truck, driving way too fast for a residential street, with a screech of tires, slammed into her BMW. The full impact had been on the driver's side, and she was killed instantly.

Under the sheet, my hands clenched into fists, nails digging into my palms. Despite my effort, tears slipped down the sides of my cheeks as I lay on the treatment table, creating rivulets in the clay mask the aesthetician had applied, as I desperately fought to overcome my bitter remorse and grief.

Chapter Seven

DECEMBER 1533

WHITEHALL PALACE

Henry's excitement was palpable. His eyes sparkled, cheeks ruddy. When he was in top spirits, he laughed easily and paced restlessly, sharing his warmest camaraderie with those present. He and Anne were to sit for their portrait for the first time that day.

An appropriate studio had been carefully selected in the newly renovated portion of Whitehall. Whitehall (formerly York Place) was just one of the magnificent residences owned by the late Cardinal, Thomas Wolsey. Upon his demise, it became a Crown property, intended as Henry's grand city palace. Anne loved it, too, since she had worked alongside Henry and the architects to redesign and decorate it. Whitehall was her special residence; Katherine never had, and would never, if Anne had anything to do about it, cross its threshold.

Holbein found the studio's location eminently suitable, with ample windows affording an eastern exposure and a most favorable morning light. Early in the day would be the designated appointment time for sittings with the King and Queen. Immediately after they attended matins in the Chapel Royal, they'd agreed to come directly to the studio for a short period during which Hans could record what he needed while they posed, silent and motionless.

They were less likely to be missed early forenoon—Henry could offer excuses to his ministers and reappear to conduct business by mid-morning. By the time dinner had been completed, and as the day wore on, Hans knew, Henry became distracted and was not always in the pleasantest of humors.

The King was satisfied with the preliminary plans shown to him. In fact, he was delighted. Hans had first reviewed the ideas with Cromwell and Cranmer as instructed and received a substantial endorsement. It then remained to sketch the initial design concepts for the King and Queen, hoping they would agree.

When Hans and Kratzer had done their initial thinking, an idea occurred to them which they both hoped would inspire the king, as it had them. The German artist and his compatriot had tapped into their combined personal connections in Flanders and managed to borrow a copy of an unusual, beautiful work by the illustrious Bruges artist Jan van Eyck. Margaret of Austria had long owned the original painting. While Holbein had only glimpsed it once when visiting the Hof von Savoye, the Habsburg royal palace in Mechelen, it had affected him deeply: so much so that he'd never forgotten it. Only through extraordinary effort was he able to locate a copy which a Ghent merchant had commissioned. The wealthy burgher had agreed—for a hefty fee, of course—to loan it to them for a short time.

The borrowed painting leaned against a wall in the studio, where the pale golden sunrise provided just the suitable illumination by which to admire it. Gathered round were Henry and Anne, Holbein, and Cromwell. Kratzer and the Archbishop sat apart at a low table near the hearth. Despite being a copy, the work had been executed with enormous skill. A full-length double portrait, the people featured were known to have been Giovanni Arnolfini and his wife, Costanza Trenta, wealthy Italian residents of Bruges. Clothing of great elegance and refinement worn by the couple indicated their affluence: each article superbly tailored with fabric that was luxurious.

The position of the man and woman was unusual. They were both angled such that the viewer could see them clearly, but they faced each other. The technique of posing sitters in a three-quarter perspective was one masterfully perfected by Van Eyck and one that Holbein had long admired and emulated. It made the viewer feel as if he or she shared the room with the couple. At first glance, the chamber seemed simple, but that perception was quickly dispelled as the eye traveled the composition's quadrants. Known immediately to the likes of Hans and Nikolaus, but virtually invisible to the eye of the viewer, was the precise orthogonal orientation of the painting's geometry. The couple and the perspective of space surrounding them caused the eye to focus on a vanishing point: a meticulously rendered convex mirror in the very center of the chamber and of the painting itself. Presumably, Van Eyck wanted the viewer to reflect on worldly aspirations, but perhaps then to be drawn inward—as if the central mirror reflected the state of one's soul. Henry's court painter and royal astronomer had already devised the geometric pattern they would recommend for the double portrait of the King and Queen, and Van Eyck's work, though completed almost exactly one hundred years prior, was an expert example of such a plan.

Henry and Anne peered closely at the wooden panel, exclaiming over each newly discovered icon beautifully placed within the composition. The mirror was especially fascinating, featuring medallions around its frame, which showed scenes from Christ's Passion when studied with a magnifying glass. Anne squealed with surprise when her inspection revealed that the mirror reflected two tiny figures just inside the door facing the couple.

"Who are these two, Hans?" Anne was thoroughly engrossed in scrutinizing every detail with her glass.

"It is believed, Madame, that one is Van Eyck himself. He often added his identity to his work. I do not know who the other man is, though. But you will see that the painter signed his name just above the mirror and below the chandelier."

"What does it say? I can't quite make it out."

Hans used a narrow brush to point out the words as he read them to the Queen. 'Johannes de eyck fuit hic 1434', or 'Jan van Eyck was here 1434'.

"Oh, how clever of him, and bold! I think you should also sign the painting you are about to execute, Hans. Do you not agree, Henry?" She turned to the King inquiringly.

"I do. This will be the work of our Master Holbein's life. There is no reason why he should not claim it for the centuries to come."

But what most appealed to Henry and Anne as they studied Van Eyck's portrait of the Arnolfini's was the posture the man and woman had adopted for their likenesses. Giovanni Arnolfini (the husband) stood to the left near an open window, indicating to the viewer that he held an important position in the greater world beyond the chamber. From there, he gazed steadily and confidently at his observers. His wife was placed near the bed, remindful of her calling to beget children, and to care for the interior life she and her husband shared. The man's hand was raised in an oath, while his left hand was joined with his wife's right: the consent which symbolized the unity of their pledge of faith.

"Thomas!" Henry called over his shoulder to Cranmer. "Do come see this! Is it not the perfect ploy to represent my spiritual appointment from Our Lord and, at the same time, emphasize Queen Anne's importance to me—and the new faith?"

He turned to Hans. "The painting is wonderful! It allows me to imagine so much more vividly just how I want our portrait to appear. Of course, ours will be far more glorious, grander, but there is much about this image I admire greatly. I am pleased that you were able to acquire it, Hans and Nikolaus, so we may learn from it."

Anne slipped her hand into Henry's. "Gentlemen, do you see that the lady appears to be with child?"

Nikolaus replied, "I have been told, Madame, that it is merely the folds of her garment in a representation of the fashion of the day because we believe that Costanza Arnolfini died a year before the completion of the painting."

Anne looked more closely. Slowly and quietly, she shook her head. "No. No, I do not for a moment think it was simply the drape of her gown. Her face—see that distant look of contentment and knowing? Her hand is gently placed upon her belly just so, and her other hand confidently held in her husband's. It is spiritual, surely. But in this likeness, she expects a child. Yes... I am certain." She fell silent, then, but the wistful expression she wore said that she longed for their portrait to render her in the very same way: pregnant with her second child, this time a prince.

Using Van Eyck's Arnolfini portrait as his reference, Hans arranged Henry and Anne in the room, the King's right shoulder aglow from the light streaming in from the open window above and behind, with Anne standing to Henry's left.

"Hans, with His Grace's approval, I wish to be depicted like this." And she placed her hand upon Henry's forearm. "This will be the symbol of our connection, our caring and support for one another, and my ability to gently guide my husband if called upon to do so." She sought their approval. "Gentlemen, do you agree?"

The all-powerful, mighty King Henry glanced at his wife and Queen, and laid his other hand on top of hers in silent acknowledgment of her wish.

Positioned thus, the painter stepped back, head tilted, eyes narrowed, assessing the overall effect of the royal couple in the chamber. Next, he opened the shutters to the window a bit—then closed them ever so slightly, each time examining the effect on the painting subjects. When he felt it was right, he had Kratzer measure the shutters' precise aperture, and notate the exact hour using his clock, so he could best replicate the lighting each time the King and Queen sat for him.

Once preparations had been completed, Hans commenced his drawings. From a bulging, worn leather bag, he selected a stylus made of an alloy of silver with a bit of copper. He faced a tall frame of oak panels upon which had been affixed paper covering the entire mount. Holbein had commissioned special paper from a renowned mill in Hertford, the very first of its kind in England. The ready-primed white sheet had been brush-treated with a textured finish to afford it the abrasiveness necessary for the technique of silver-point drawing. When the paper was inscribed using a wire of silver inserted into a wooden rod, there remained a glittering metallic line. Hans used this technique following the influence of masters of the craft like Albrecht Dürer, Van Eyck, and Leonardo Da Vinci. As he adeptly piloted the stylus, he would often select a crayon of either red ochre or black chalk to add shading and form to the figures. To sketch angles of the chamber in the background, he used a black charcoal pencil. It was not long before the forms of Henry and Anne began to take shape on the paper.

After a time, while the King and Queen sat gratefully at the table to take some rest and refreshment, Hans stepped to one side, after which Nikolaus limped over to assume a stance in front of the panel. Peering through a special eyeglass and employing an unusual device he called a caliper, he measured each quadrant of the page, the distances between the figures, the window, the sketched chamber angles, as well as the overall dimensions. He wrote and calculated in a small leather-bound journal, eventually using the pencil to lightly write notations on the drawing itself.

Henry watched, fascinated, as he chewed an apple. "What are you figuring, Klaus?"

Kratzer half turned, calipers in hand. "Your Majesties, every dimension of this drawing—which of course will be translated into the final painting—is based upon the geometry of three, representing the Trinity. You, Sire," he said, with a nod of his head, "will be poised on the page in such a way that you will represent the centrum of the triad, eternally united with the Father, the Son, and the Holy Spirit."

Henry looked pleased while squinting to regard the borrowed painting again. "Hans—see the window? In the Van Eyck, there is little, if any, view to the outside. But in your rendering, I want the observer to look through the open casement to a most specific view. In this way, we will provide a powerful message to the faithful."

"As you wish, Majesty. What have you in mind?"

Dreamily, he mused, "I think a pastoral scene with rolling hills. And scattered across the landscape, sheep… this must be, as the Lord our God has asked me the same question He posed to Simon Peter: 'Henry, King of England, lovest thou me?' And I answered, 'Yea, Lord; thou knowest that I love thee.' And the Lord said, 'Henricus Rex, Tend my sheep.' This I intend to do."

Anne smiled at her husband, eyes shining with admiration, while the Archbishop nodded ponderously. "Indeed, there is so much tending to be done, Your Majesty. A great deal of good you can accomplish for a flock in search of the care of a righteous shepherd."

Nikolaus wrote rapidly in his notebook while Henry continued. "In the distance, beyond the hills, Hans—and note my words, for this is important!—I wish for you to paint the Mount and the Temple of Zion. Create it as if it were a beautiful castle, perched high on a far cliff, illuminated by heaven's glow. It is God's home, and thus it will be mine when I fulfill my destiny."

Henry looked about and found that each pair of eyes in the small chamber were focused, unblinking, upon him. So, he disclosed: "Zion is the palace of David—the temple of Our Lord. But it will be mine, too, on the day the Lord tells me He is pleased with me when I bring His wishes to fruition. Then will I dwell in Zion as the Lord God's great and obedient King."

The King's Secretary, his chief cleric, the Astronomer Royal and even the painter wondered exactly what those wishes were and whether England would have to raise a mighty army, and endure much bloodshed, to deliver them.

NOVEMBER TRANSMUTED INTO A bitingly cold December, and though he worked almost incessantly on the project, Hans began to feel dismay at how tediously long each step took to completion. Although the King was anxious to see progress, he, like Hans and Nikolaus, was not prepared to sacrifice excellence for speed, so he remained tolerant, instead expressing pleasure at each accomplishment.

Every morning Hans arrived at the studio in the pre-dawn gloom to haul in the considerable supply of wood and candles which had been left the night before by porters who had no idea what lay beyond the stout door with the sizable iron lock. Once inside, he stoked the waning embers in the brazier, feeding it hefty chunks of oak so the chamber would be sufficiently warm if and when the royal couple came for a sitting. *When* was always at the same time: just after morning mass, once the sun had fully risen. *If* depended upon whether Hans could design the segment he was working on by himself on a particular day or if he required a live sitting. By mid-December, Hans had finished the preliminary sketches. He planned to review them with the royal couple before Christmastide and hoped their response would be favorable.

One evening, sharing a simple supper with Nikolaus, his brooding was so apparent that Kratzer thumped his tankard on the rough wooden planks of the table, spilling half and startling Hans from his private ruminations. "What's the problem, Holbein? You are anything but a pleasant dining companion this night. There is an issue which concerns you?"

Hans stuck his knife in the knob of bread on his plate and sat back. "I worry, Klaus. I worry more than I've ever done. The drawings are complete, but they are nothing compared to what I must create as a finished work. We both know this undertaking is the culmination of my livelihood as an artist. It does not matter what other commissions I might be offered or who else I am asked to paint. What could be more demanding than this? And what will become of me if I fail, miserably? I tell you, the King asked if I was up to the task. As I sit before you tonight, I know not if I am."

"Hans! You are too hard on yourself, man! Why the self-pity? Your gift is beyond measure. The portraits you render make it seem as if the subject sits right there, in the room. No one else paints like you."

"Thank you, my friend. But your praise is far too generous. In truth, every time I begin a project, I battle self-doubt. Usually, the efforts end reasonably well; my patrons are pleased their money has not been simply tossed into the river. But this endeavor has me sleeping little and eating less, just drinking too much in an attempt to bury my anxieties. It's not the structure of the painting, you see—the room, the symbols—none of that gives me concern. Klaus, what causes me to toss and turn in the wee hours is how I am to present the King's message yet capture his humanity and divinity? He is a complex man—and we well know he can be ruthless. But with my artist's eyes, I do see it: the sensitivity and lightness. He has both strength and tender grace… Ergo, how do I lay raw color on a hard surface so it will shine a beacon into his very soul? This I must do, or it may as well have been any artist—any young apprentice of a reasonably decent school of painting—selected to create this masterpiece of a lifetime. And the Queen? Beauteous Anne. She deserves to be painted so in the years to come all will know her as she is: radiant, exceptional. She is such an extraordinary woman, one whose looks never fail to inspire, especially when her moods shift and change like the sky in an approaching storm." He spread his broad hands before him, seeking his friend's understanding. "Here, you see, is my plight."

Kratzer had rarely, if ever, heard Holbein speak so plaintively or with such raw emotion. "Hans, if it is of any help at all, I tell you true: I have confidence you will excel. I know you have the talent. Your soul will guide your hands if you allow it. The image you create with brushes and pigment is going to deliver an astounding message to the world. Of this, I have no doubt. The painting will be renowned, esteemed for as long as it may exist."

"I am grateful for your encouragement. And I hope you are right. For if I fail, and the King is bitterly disappointed, my position in court—and my reputation—will be finished. At least in England. I'll be required to return to Basel permanently and there to the wrath of my wife Elsbeth, who writes to me constantly with warnings that she is none too happy about having been left with two children to raise on her own." With a rueful shake of his head, he noted, "In weighing the two options, Henry's temper might just be the lesser of two evils."

Chapter Eight

MID-NOVEMBER, 2016

LA SAPIENZA, ROME

It was the week before Thanksgiving. Of course, that holiday meant nothing in Rome; Italians don't celebrate the day which is so beloved by Americans. I was grouchy, because I'd always enjoyed being at home, anticipating a big Thanksgiving feast, loving the autumn colors, watching football on Sunday afternoons with my dad. And this year, just like last, I would remain in Rome, studying and eating pizza. Or, should I say more accurately, being consumed by the enigma which had grabbed me and wouldn't let go.

I'd met Lina for lunch between classes, and we sat in the student café.

"How did you enjoy your day at the Spa, Zara? I must say, they did work some magic on you. You look *bellisima*! You see? It's not so hard, now, is it? To keep ourselves, shall we say, well-maintained?"

I looked at her, and snorted a little laugh. "Lina, you are the best. Honestly, somehow you make everything sound so simple, so easy! Okay, I guess you are right. But not everyone can look effortlessly polished like you do, day in and day out, you know."

She shrugged. "I don't see why not... a few products here and there, and ecco qua! There you have it! Facile!"

Just then, one of Lina's friends stopped at our table. After Lina gave her a double-kiss greeting, the girl nodded at me, then pulled up a chair to visit. As they chattered away in rapid Italian, I was bored, so I pulled my MacBook out of my backpack, flipped it open, and was instantly absorbed in searching the Vatican Library catalogue, typing in terms to expand the complicated indexes. It was a time-consuming process, but I just had to persevere, in case I might be able to find something, anything at all, about the obscure portrait.

I guess my mad clicking of the keys caused Lina and her friend to stop their chat and look at me curiously. I didn't notice, not for several minutes. Not until Lina cleared her throat. I glanced up, and her friend said, "What are you doing? Working on a paper? Why so intense that you can't have lunch and a conversation?"

I wanted to snap at her. But she was Lina's friend, so I stopped myself, and replied, "Oh! Mi dispiace; so sorry. Ahh, actually, yes, I am working on a project which is due soon. In fact, I have to run. Have a good afternoon, ladies." I closed my computer, shoved it back into my bag, and with a quick wave, stood to go.

"I'll see you soon, right, Zara?" Lina gave a little shake of her head, but then offered one of her smiles, so I returned it.

"Yep, right. Of course, Lina. See you later." I was happy to go, having neither time or tolerance for her friend's judgemental attitude. I headed for the library: my respite. All I wanted to do was to spend hours digging, searching, excavating for information which just had to be there. Somewhere, somehow, I was going to surface evidence that my painting not only existed but would be found. I didn't care how long it took, or how many hours—if my doctoral studies were put on the back burner, well... so be it.

I realized, with a start, that nothing mattered to me as much as hunting for this painting. Nothing.

Chapter Nine

JANUARY 1534

THE GREAT CARRACK SANT ANNA
GRAND HARBOUR, MALTA

T he Grand Master was in a foul humor.

Having been tersely summoned to the main cabin, Weston already anticipated that he would be the recipient of a vitriolic rant. He rapped on the door of the spacious lodging in the ship's hold.

"Enter, Captain Weston!" came a growl from within.

Weston ducked, stepped across the threshold, and was confronted by the venerable, 66-year-old Philippe Villiers de l'Isle-Adam, Grand Master of the Order of St. John. Having survived Suleiman's grueling six-month siege of the Order's former headquarters on Rhodes, an ordeal which had ended in their humiliating defeat and forced exile, he'd led the search—crisscrossing the Mediterranean, for a new base for his beloved Order—a frustrating quest which had lasted seven long years. Still, the man wore his nobility well and looked remarkably resilient. Enough so that William Weston steeled himself for the confrontation which was, apparently, to come.

"Sit, Captain."

Obediently, the ship's commander lowered himself into a chair. The Grand Master, tall and stately even at his age, proceeded to stalk before him.

"Are you ready to set sail?"

"Yes, sir. Thank you for coming on board to meet with me before I depart. My first mate is completing the final inventory: we hope to embark by evening if the weather holds."

His comment was met with a glowering stare. "Have I sufficiently emphasized how crucial this mission is, Captain? My expectations are high and they will be met. Any hope of our continued survival on this God-forsaken island rests with you, and you are well aware that our needs are extreme. You will return, not only with the supplies we require but with a firm commitment of funds from the wealthy Catholic heads of Europe, who, by the way, are never hesitant to ask for our protection and aid. It's past time for them to step forward and provide us with the finances we desperately need to restore this ancient pile of rubble into an edifice worthy of our Knights." He paced unabated.

Weston tried to soothe. "Highness, the existing walls of Castrum Maris are stout and its infrastructure has proved formidable. It's been a military citadel for many centuries. We can transform it to suit our purposes and give glory to God."

"Ah, yes. More backbreaking labor. Of course we can, Weston. And we will. Because that is what our Knights have sworn themselves to so do." He scowled at the ship's captain: an English nobleman whose family was deeply committed in allegiance to Henry VIII. His voice dripped with bitterness. "And forget not, sir, that one of your main objectives is to secure material support from your illustrious king. Oh, his promises are bounteous, but his follow-through? It's non-existent. That is unless it suits purposes of his own."

"Highness, I feel confident that His Grace the king will provide you with the sponsorship he has pledged. He is a man of his word; I know this to be true."

L'Isle-Adam shot Weston a cynical look. "Really? Then let us examine the facts, Captain. Three years ago, Henry and his accomplice, the exorbitantly prosperous Cardinal Wolsey, promised me monetary aid toward the recovery of Rhodes. Since then, Wolsey has succumbed, the victim of his avarice. Henry has appalled the Christian world with his demand that the pope grant him a divorce from a woman who has done him no wrong, and he has asked anyone and everyone who would listen to align with his desires. But as for my needs—and the promises he made? It's as if they evaporated in the exhalation of his very own hot air. To date, have I seen a shilling, Sire? Not a one."

The ship pitched and yawed before the stiff winter wind, even though it was anchored within the Grand Harbour's shelter. L'Isle-Adam grabbed at the corner of the desk and braced himself to avoid falling.

Weston collected his thoughts, venturing, "Most Eminent Highness, the bronze cannon sent by my Sovereign, and the quantity of armory, longbows, crossbows, and halberds? All were intended to back your quest. I feel certain funds will follow."

"No... no, they were not, Captain Weston. They were tokens! He tossed me a few crumbs, smiling broadly all the while, to hurry me on my way and rid himself of the annoyance of dealing with me—this, even though so many of his noble subjects are members of our Order. And I tell you this: I shall not forget that when the Order was in need of a new home, he did nothing. Thus, if he should ever require our protection, I will be sure to return favors in the measure with which they were given. Henry, King of England, is no ally of mine."

Weston thought it prudent to allow the Grand Master to have the final word, knowing he would not win this particular debate. So, with a bow and a sharp salute, he backed out of the cabin. No sooner had the door closed behind him than he rubbed the back of his neck and sighed heavily, grumbling, "God's blood! I am too damned old for this," and set off to go above deck to ready his crew to set sail.

Sir William Weston had enjoyed great privilege in his career as a high-ranking member of the Order of St. John. The Weston family had long been associated with the Order; three of his uncles had served well and bravely in religious military campaigns. Now William, at sixty years of age, was not only the Order's current Lord Prior of England, with headquarters based in the fine Priory of Clerkenwell, London, but also served as captain and commander of the Order's magnificent carrack Sant Anna. The Sant Anna was an ironclad wonder, probably the largest ship sailing the Mediterranean. This three-masted marvel was fully armor-plated, and its six decks housed fifty big guns and reinforced cannons, small calibre guns on its mast tops, and an array of bombards, falcons and falconets making up its significant armory. Onboard, Weston commanded over three hundred men.

Although Sir William's career had been distinguished by his service to the Order of the Knights of St. John and his dedication to the faith and the pope in Rome, he also held the prominent position of a high-ranking noble in the court of King Henry VIII of England. The Westons were a very prominent family committed to the service and good graces of their Sovereign. The art of how to finesse a temperamental and unpredictable king, taught by father to son and uncle to nephew, had been imprinted on young William. It had served him well, and both Henry VII and his son, Henry VIII, had rewarded the family with wealth and lands. Now, notably, Sir William's nephew had also achieved a high position in the king's court. Young Sir Francis Weston was a gentleman in the King's Privy Chamber; knighted the previous June.

As a result of these allegiances, Weston found himself in the intractable position of being wedged between two dominant and commanding men, each with a demand to fulfil his own singular aspiration. He dreaded the journey and his commission. Convincing Henry to act against his will would surely be an impossible feat. He wondered if perhaps his nephew Francis might be of some help.

His sense of duty overriding his misgivings, he made rounds, issuing commands. Atop the main mast, the red banner bisected with the sharp white cross snapped in a fresh breeze; seamen strained to unfurl the sails. As soon as the anchor was weighed, the vessel, driven by a following wind, began to power through the Grand Harbour's entrance, and Weston's onerous quest was underway.

Chapter Ten

LATE NOVEMBER 2016

ROME

S cudding clouds, resembling puffs of grey smoke from a man's pipe, lent an ever more melancholy cast to an autumn afternoon already bleak and depressing. Like almost every other day during the past two weeks, I felt labored—as if my arms and legs were weighted—trying unsuccessfully to maintain focus on the tasks at hand. The joy I usually felt from the pursuit of my daily endeavors had dissipated. The visit to the salon had somehow released in me a tide of emotion I'd long been striving to control. Reluctantly, I trudged east on Via Condotti; even though the purpose of my journey to this handsome part of the city should have filled me with excitement, my insides felt hollow and I didn't know why.

Crossing Via del Corso, on my right, loomed the immense façade of Santissima Trinità degli Spagnoli—one among the intricate web of Catholic churches spanning the city. On a whim, I climbed the steps, pulled open the heavy wooden doors, and slipped into the cool interior. Inside such massive structures, composed almost entirely of marble and stone, the temperature never really varied. Like an excellent Roman wine cellar, winter or summer, one could expect conditions that were consistent, hence allowing the visitor to concentrate on the purpose at hand: either consumption of wine, or prayer, depending on the situation.

How I hated dealing with raw sentiment. Usually, I was successful in suppressing it, finding a way to distract myself, pushing the unpleasantness firmly beneath the surface, and denying it permission to seek confrontation. But since that day, when thoughts of my mother had forced their way into my consciousness, I couldn't rid myself of them. Not only did I painfully regret how I'd behaved as an irritable teen, especially during the last precious months I'd shared with her—but what remained was an anguish of confusion. Round and round in my head swam a fundamental question—why had she given up a life of intellect and advocacy, choosing instead to be a housewife? She'd seemed content, though—at least in my peripheral view as her daughter. And while she'd professed to be proud of my academic accomplishments, was she, really? Or did she want me to default on my intellectual abilities to pursue a more traditional life, one that she may have believed would bring me greater happiness and contentment in the long run?

I found a pew halfway along the nave and gratefully sank into it, dropping my backpack next to me. There was no denying it was a stunning church, its thick walls a swirling pattern of moss green and brick red marble, side chapels well lit, each offering elaborate paintings of saints absorbed in the rapture of their devotional lives. The altar was particularly beautiful, tranquil, and my gaze rested upon it, even while my thoughts swirled in an eddy of confusion.

Whatever the truth about Mom, she had left me struggling to know what a woman should be. I'd certainly never had a confident sense of myself, and now all my many perceived inadequacies congealed and stuck in my craw like a rotten meal. What was my place in this world, this universe? Was my mom somehow successful in censoring her true nature, or had she genuinely been happy and fulfilled? If so, I wondered what her secret might have been, and now, of course, it was too late to ask.

What, then, had she expected of me? And I guessed the bigger question was: what did I expect of myself? I knew I longed to achieve something special, and I didn't think I would ever be happy by subordinating my life and a career to a husband—even a wealthy and smart one. My instincts told me that it would take much more for me to justify my existence. And along with that, I somehow felt the bewildering need to bring distinction to all that she might have been. I could not waste the intelligence I had inherited from her.

I glanced about the church, hoping that just maybe one of the saints (or angels—I'd have happily settled for a garden-variety angel right then) would float down from his roost high above, sit beside me and help sort through my maze of conflict. Perhaps I was completely misguided, and my way of thinking was horribly arrogant. What right did I have to project my assumptions on others, including my mother—now gone? The pain was almost unbearable as I dwelt on the loss. My mom was robbed of the opportunity to see her child grow into adulthood. We had, I reflected bitterly, an unfinished relationship. If only I'd grasped the opportunity while I might have, instead of remaining obnoxious and self-righteous.

Groaning at the utter impossibility of it all, I glanced at my watch. It was getting late, and I needed to complete this self-imposed mission today, as it might be weeks before I'd have time to return. Finals and several papers were due all too soon. Sniffing and dabbing at my eyes with a tissue, I gathered my bag and emerged from that blissful solitude onto the busy street and resolutely headed for the Magistral Library, the archives of the Sovereign Military Order of Malta.

Chapter Eleven

FEBRUARY 1534

ANTWERP

Holbein and Kratzer huddled gratefully before a warming fire in the rough but hospitable Gulick tavern. They had sailed into the port of Antwerp earlier in the day, concluding a bitterly cold, uncomfortable voyage from England after crossing the winter-rough North Sea. Hans hungrily dug into his Flemish stew, and Klaus shifted his chair to aim his left side directly toward the crackling wood fire. His hip felt no better, and the bone-numbing cold aggravated it even more. He sipped at his dark ale and mused on the fact that this taxing journey might be his last. He couldn't have refused Hans's request to accompany him, though. He was committed to helping him complete the daunting project which was well underway. And Hans certainly needed a collaborator on this particular undertaking!

Holbein, for his part, welcomed the slow return of feeling to his frozen hands and feet, the rich, aromatic stew renewing his sense of well-being. It was also pleasant, he admitted to himself, to hear the sound of the Brabantish dialect—it was close enough to his native Swiss German that he understood well and could speak passably. Being in Antwerpen, a prosperous and cosmopolitan city, promised a welcome respite from the constant strain he had been enduring in

England—even if the trip would be short and the February climate best endured under a thick coverlet.

The king's painter wiped his beard with a towel and gave a satisfied grunt. "Tomorrow, then, Klaus, we will arrive as early as possible at the Guildhouse of St. Luke. That is, if you are able to drag yourself from a warm bed blessedly set on a firm floor instead of a tiny cot in a ship's hold, pitching and swaying all the night long."

"I will do my best, but without making any promises." Kratzer smiled with relief as he noticed that the sturdy ale was slowly relieving the pain in his side. He motioned for the tavern maid to bring them both refills, then tasted the roast rabbit and found it much to his liking. "So, how do we go about meeting someone who can fulfill your needs, Hans?"

"I have the names of several individuals who are reputed to be premier *vendicolori*—color merchants. Predominantly they are Venetians doing business in this city. But first, I want to speak to the guild master. We must be certain we are only dealing with purveyors of unquestionable integrity. There is far too much at stake to take risks."

"That, indeed, goes without saying." Klaus thought warily of the exorbitant quantity of guilders he and Hans had carefully hidden amongst their belongings. It was unnerving to be carrying that much currency. Neither Hans, nor certainly he, would be able to defend themselves against an attack by thieves and would have to depend solely upon a careful air of discretion and unassuming behavior to protect them.

Henry had supplied them with enough of the new Carolus golden guilders to enable them to seek out and purchase the most lavish—and most expensive—pigments available anywhere in the world. And Antwerp, as the leading European commercial market in luxury trade, which included tapestry weaving, diamond cutting, silks, and glass blowing as well as painting, was the best place to locate and acquire such prized materials. Almost all of the precious raw material for pigments used in manuscript illumination, majolica, and glass decorating and painting was imported from Venice, the European hub of fine trade, for those who could afford such substances. That canal-resplendent city had been for some time the center of trade from the Middle East, and the specialists who dealt in brilliant colors were able to not only provide the powdered pigments but also offer information on the latest techniques to mix and apply paint so its luminosity would leap from the board and strike the eye of the viewer, eliciting gasps of admiration. The trick would be to ably seek out the correct merchant, assess the quality of his materials, and transact a notably sizable purchase without encouraging discussion about the patron or the subject of the extravagant project. After all, the community of such painters and patrons was limited and well known. And in the art world of the day, gossip provided the very stuff of life.

ERICH ALBRECHT WAS MASTER of the Guild of St. Luke, that of painters and artists. Holbein and Kratzer had secured an interview with him and arrived promptly at the well-appointed guild house, positioned in a most prominent spot on Antwerp's lively Grote Markt. The guild master led them into his office, where dark and richly paneled walls were liberally hung with paintings, all executed by guild members. Once pleasantries had been completed and all settled comfortably, the slight man with a hooked nose asked in German, "What can I do for you, gentlemen?"

Holbein withdrew a rolled paper from his pack. Smoothing it, he said, "Herr Albrecht, I am a humble painter who has been given a unique opportunity. I will be working with a senior artist in his growing school. We were asked to supply London and the surrounding area with some of the finer materials being used today: brilliant pigments, a few of the excellent oak panels available here in Antwerp, and a handful of badger brushes which practitioners of the trade so covet. The school is funded by a consortium of well-to-do landowners who wish to promote the art of classical painting in the countryside around London. Can you help us?"

Albrecht peered over his wire spectacles. "Ah, my dear Holbein, and Herr Kratzer, you are both Germanic, no? What then accounts for your residence in England?"

Kratzer reacted quickly. "For my part, I sought work as a mathematics tutor, sir, and have gained employment with a wealthy farmer—to live at his estate and teach his seven children. My friend here, whom I have known for many years, was commissioned to paint a family portrait. Once that had been completed, he chose—actually, we both decided—to stay in England."

"It is most unusual that a modest painter and a mathematics tutor would seek art materials from the world center of such trade." His eyes narrowed dubiously. "But then… where else would aspiring artists in the backcountry of England find the substances to improve their work? So perhaps it's not all that peculiar. What is it, then, that you would like to purchase? Not all merchants coming into Antwerp deal in the same materials, you understand."

Hans cleared his throat. "We have been asked to acquire a considerable quantity of ultramarine. You know, so as not to have to send a representative back to Antwerp again any time soon—just to conserve money, as you might imagine. And we would also like to purchase a supply of the beautiful vermilion made here. Some malachite and… a handsome parcel of fine gold leaf."

Eyebrows raised, the master sat back in his chair, his gaze scanning their rough, humble garments with barely concealed disdain. "You do realize that what you ask will cost you a large sum, a great deal of money? Are you certain you can pay what will be required?"

"Yes, sir. At any rate, we will purchase as much as our allotment will afford. Can you, therefore, recommend to us an honest, and hopefully, considerate, merchant?"

Albrecht hesitated briefly, then pulled a scrap of parchment from his desk drawer. With his quill, he scratched out a name and address. "Go and see Signore Giulio Pisani. He is a renowned exporter of fine colore. You may tell him that I sent you."

"Vielen dank, Herr Albrecht. Thank you so very much." Hans and Kratzer stood, bowed in acknowledgment, and made their way toward the door.

Once outside, Klaus turned to Hans. "Do you think he's principled? I wonder if he will share information about the two rural oafs who just happen to want to buy a ransom's worth of gold leaf and the most expensive blue pigment known. It makes me nervous, Holbein."

"Well, we won't have any way of knowing, will we? Not unless we're set upon and robbed. So all we can do is visit this Venetian trader, see if his materials are as superb as we hope, make the transaction discreetly, then slip quickly out of Antwerp and head back to London. If I don't have enough of the dazzling ultramarine to satisfy Henry—or for that matter, the gold—I may just as well dump the whole mess into the Thames."

DURING HIS FREQUENT BUSINESS trips to Antwerp, Signore Pisani lived in a lavish, rented townhouse filled with visible signs of wealth: tapestries, glassware, fine majolica plate, and paintings all displayed in abundance. He was also as polite and refined a gentleman as Holbein and Kratzer had ever met; not at all, it seemed, discomfited by their rough and ready attire. After serving wine in beautiful silver chalices, he took them into a studio room and, from a cabinet, opened a drawer and withdrew a sample of the most vivid, intensely blue powder Hans had come across in his years as a painter.

As they examined it in awe, Pisani explained how he had a particular contact in Persia, someone who had an ownership in the mine from which this lapis lazuli was extracted. He described how lazurite—the blue crystals of the stone lapis—are pulverized and processed according to a closely guarded technique, which is difficult and time-consuming and only known to certain master colorists. Pausing in his explanation, he stroked a finely groomed beard with sparkling, ring-laden fingers.

"Precisely how much blue do you require, signori?" Pisani asked nonchalantly.

"As much as we can afford, sir. We are also commissioned, as you may have been told by Master Albrecht, to purchase the excellent gold leaf available through your dealers."

"I see... Well, then. Let's discuss numbers, shall we? And if we reach an agreement, I will show you the technique you must employ to work the blue pastello—it is the ball of powdered pigment, beeswax and resin. That is how it is transported, you see—to extract its precious dye. I will add the gold to the price, as well as vermilion and malachite powder. The bill will be substantial; I hope you understand."

After he factored the complex calculations on vellum with a quill of peacock feather, he slid the page across the table to be assessed by his visitors. Holbein studied the figures and nodded in assent. "Thank you, sir. That is acceptable. Please prepare our package, and I will count the money to provide your payment in gold."

If Signore Pisani was surprised, to say nothing of gratified—for he had asked a far greater price than he would have been happy to settle for—then he was too shrewd a gentleman to show it.

Transaction completed, Holbein and Kratzer emerged onto the square to be greeted by an icy sleet that pelted their faces and coated the cobbled street. The rush of cold air felt refreshing, though, after the strain of making such a huge purchase. His cloak laden with precious blue pastelli, Hans also carefully guarded the sack he carried, hiding their gold sheets. They began the treacherous walk to the shelter of their inn on the Zirkstraat.

The sleet intensified as they crossed the square and soon had turned into blinding, swirling snow. Hans motioned to Klaus to duck into an alley which he knew was a shortcut to their tavern. As they made the turn, through the thick veil of white, Hans spotted a figure following close behind. The back of his neck prickled in apprehension. The figure was hunched but insistent in narrowing the distance between them. Hans and Klaus tucked closer to the houses lining the alleyway, hoping that the overhang would keep the snow from obscuring their vision and deter the pursuer. Klaus kept slipping, unable to move quickly enough, and the figure lurked ever closer. Hans attempted to shift his pack in preparation to defend himself if needed, but in the split second that his attention was diverted, he was viciously clubbed from behind by a blow that knocked him to the ground. His head bashed against the stone wall, and a searing pain caused him to gasp while he struggled to remain conscious. He heard Klaus cry out. Hans called to his friend but couldn't see him: blinded by snow and a warm flow of blood, he frantically felt for the strap of his leather sack, but, alas, it was savagely yanked from his grip. There was a scrabble of boots on the cobblestones, a churn of white, and then he heard receding footfalls as the thief took off, quickly lost to sight in the curved alley.

Desperately, Hans crawled to where Klaus lay motionless. He knelt beside him, lifting his head and calling to him. Klaus moaned before his eyes fluttered open.

"Thank God, Klaus! I thought you were gone." Hans cradled his friend's head and shoulders until he was fully alert. "Can you stand, man? We have to get out of here."

With help, Kratzer slowly got to his feet. Although he was limping severely, he was able, just barely, to walk. Hans snatched the cloak from the ground where it had been pulled from his neck and, to his relief, felt the package still safe in its inner pocket. He blotted the blood from his forehead and scanned the area for his knapsack in the certain knowledge that he was wasting his effort.

And he was right. It had vanished.

Slowly, painfully, the two men hobbled through the drifts and deepening shadows to finally arrive at the inn. The barmaid looked questioningly at them as they pushed open the door, letting the wind blow a blanket of snow into the room.

"What's happened to you? And here I be thinking you two was respectable gentlemen," she observed. "An' shut the door! You're lettin' in the ice!"

"Even respectable sods can suffer a bad turn, girl. Too much drink and a fight. We'll be fine. Just hold your tongue and put up a couple of tankards to take to our room."

Stony-faced, she grudgingly filled two steins to the brim before handing them a loaf of bread and some cheese. They stumbled to their room, threw off their cloaks, and fell into chairs. Hans pulled the leather parcel containing the loaves of raw ultramarine from the inner hiding place in his cloak. His great relief was blunted, though, by the loss of the sack, which had held the gold leaf and the purse containing the remainder of their guilders.

"Well... we're alive. That's good. But we have no money to get us back to England. And we lost all that gold—half of the reason we made this accursed trip."

Hans sat up and drained his tankard in a single swig while Klaus inched tentatively onto the bed. "These wretched old bones of mine. I believe you owe me mightily for going on this adventure with you, my friend."

It didn't help. Hans felt miserable enough already. "You're right. Never should I have put you in this position. And it's been for naught."

"Not entirely, Holbein. Look." Moving slowly, wincing, Kratzer opened his jerkin, still wet with bloodied snow, to reveal an inner pocket. From this he withdrew the parcel containing the sheaves of gold leaf. He dug deeper and magically produced the small leather purse with a jingle of remaining guilders.

"How the devil did you have those? I placed them in my sack!"

A long draught of ale was required to wet his throat before Klaus replied, "I transferred them from your sack while you were receiving instruction on how to extract the dye from the blue loaves. What a stupid place to have concealed gold! It's the first target anyone would spot if they were to loot us, which is exactly what happened. It is a very good thing someone in this couplet has any wit at all. And may I say with all due respect, Master Painter, that's not you."

Hans refrained from a most unmanly inclination to physically embrace his friend. "I can't agree with you more and thank you from the bottom of my heart, Klaus Kratzer. Allow me to stumble back downstairs to bring us a further flagon of the strongest ale that wretched serving girl has. We need it. And tomorrow—if we can walk—we will book ourselves a return passage home."

Chapter Twelve

APRIL AND MAY 1534

PALACE OF WHITEHALL
LONDON

The cool stillness of that early spring morning was disrupted only by the soft rustling of a family of mice which had taken up residence in the room's far corner and the rhythmic clicking of a palette knife against marble as Holbein meticulously mixed the coming day's batch of pigments.

Far enough along towards the project's completion, Hans worked alone in his studio. He was now known around court as the King's Painter, and his status had risen significantly. Welcome indeed, as an accompaniment to the title, was regular payment from the King's Privy Purse—which was quietly supplemented by bonuses directly from the King's hand upon completion of progressive stages of the task. But for all Holbein's increased prosperity, it had done little to calm the uneasiness which nagged him constantly as the work neared its conclusion.

By mid-January, the preliminary drawings had been completed; meticulously reviewed with the King, Queen Anne, and Kratzer. The four conferred, discussing timing for the progressive stages of work. Henry, always keenly interested in evolving styles of architecture, music, and art emanating from the Continent, announced, "Hans, recently I've partaken in conversations with some of my ambassadors to Italy, more precisely, those sent to Venice, and I hear there is a new technique in painting, used for portraits and human figures. Some of the finest Venetian artists work directly on stretched and prepared cloth to replace heavy oak panels. What do you know of this?"

"I am aware that a strong linen fabric called canvas is being employed in Italy, Sire. The painter Raphael occasionally worked on canvas, along with the renowned Tiziano Vecellio, when they did portraits of wealthy patrons in and around Padua and Ferrara. Even 'il divino,' Buonarotti—called Michelangelo—has experimented with canvas, though he claims he is not much of a painter. I've corresponded with some artists I know who've observed this method, and I certainly find it worthy of consideration. It's said that when the surface of the material is properly prepared, paint flows on it like softened butter. And there is no doubt it makes a work far more portable than one completed on wooden boards. As for its permanence, of that I know little—nor do those using it, as yet. But certainly, any painting done on a completely malleable surface can be rolled up and protected if needed... Although, having said that, I've not yet tried the method myself."

Henry pursed his lips in thought. "Then do so now, Holbein. I want you to learn as much about the mode as you can. It is my wish to have the painting executed on this new canvas. If the master Italians are using it for their most prosperous patrons, then the King of England will have his portrait rendered in the same way."

Hardly surprising, therefore, on that very afternoon, a worried Hans wrote several urgent letters of inquiry to colleagues in Italy. As an avid learner of new techniques being developed by his peers, he made it his practice to regularly correspond with painting schools he admired. He rummaged through an overstuffed chest to locate two recent letters he'd received from the Florentine School and scanned the text. 'Sir, our illuminators have recently used both gold leaf and hammered silver to coat parchment and the newly refined textile surface called canvas...'

Of course, almost every master painter Hans knew wanted to emulate the methods developed by the genius Van Eyck. The painter from Bruges had changed a longstanding approach to mixing pigments by using unique combinations of oils, solvents, and particular kinds of varnish where needed, and mostly by applying layers of oil paint wet on wet, thereby replacing the previous, static method of employing quick-drying egg tempera. Hans had experimented with some of the techniques invented and perfected by Van Eyck. The master painter's influence on the Flemish artists was a prime reason they were so in demand; their formulas glided onto the surface so thinly that they created incredible depth and luminosity. And this effect is what Hans hoped to achieve with his project.

Meanwhile, Holbein knew his contemporaries in the Netherlands were using different oils to mix with their pigments, depending on the tone and color desired. The formerly common use of linseed was now only applied to dark colors because it had a darker cast and appeared to yellow even further over time. For bright, sharp colors, which is what he hoped to achieve, poppy oil or nut oils were now being successfully used. But his choices must depend upon the unforgiving English climate. Hans would have to determine which oil would be best, along with the mixing ratio of fat to pigment to solvent. Colder, damp weather required one approach, while heat and dry conditions, another. Layering the paint—thin and glossy or thicker and textural—would help achieve the effect he sought. He also knew that some of the Italians added crushed glass to their pigments to give their work an astonishing brilliance, and he considered trying that to lend a celestial effect. Although Hans was familiar with these means, he was all too aware of Henry's demand to bring the latest, most advanced approaches to bear in this, his masterwork.

After impatiently waiting for what seemed an eternity, Holbein received several responses to his letters, along with a large package sent from Florence containing several lengths of canvas. He tore open a folded and sealed document from the prestigious Bellini studio to find, with great relief, detailed instructions on preparing the canvas for the application of oil-based paint. Almost immediately, he cut a piece of the cloth to experiment.

With Klaus overseeing the process—his inquisitive nature demanded a part in the research—Hans carefully prepared a mixture of glove glue and a finely sifted ash, which he applied to the stretched and supported canvas in thin layers. After each application, he polished the surface to even it and then used a prime layer of very pale grey paint. This procedure he repeated several times, allowing each application to thoroughly dry before adding the next. The process took some time, but in the end, Holbein had achieved a surface that was as smooth as honed marble, betraying no trace of the base canvas's warp and weft. After stroking on his mixture of oil and pigment, he grunted in satisfaction when the brush glided across the prepared canvas with an ease he had not before experienced. He then experimented with applying a Venetian Amber varnish over portions of his test painting and found the effect remarkably to his liking.

The next challenge was to practice prepping the pigments so he might obtain the most brilliant, the most vivid colors possible. And this must be done using as little of the precious raw materials as he could manage. They spent days in his studio; Klaus reading aloud the manuscripts which offered recipes for the making of various colors; measuring, mixing, heating, and stirring. Together, they decided upon the best possible formula for reconstituting the unique vermilion red purchased in Antwerp. The unholy stink it created required them to stuff the cracks in the door with rags and open wide the windows of the small studio so as not to pass out from the fumes. But the result was worth the effort, for the pigment produced a stunning, glowing red unlike any he had used to date. Next, he concocted a beautiful pink extracted from wood exported from the exotic land of Brazil. Green, deep and alluring, came from Verdigris out of the south of France. And a rich, creamy hue like that of the golden sun was called Naples yellow and originated in Italy's southernmost region.

But the color most highly prized, and the one he and Klaus had almost lost their lives acquiring, was the blue extracted from ultramarine. Carefully, almost reverentially, Hans unwrapped the parcel they had brought back from Antwerp. In it rested ten solid balls of a hardened dough-like substance, a blue so deep it appeared purple. Now Hans and Klaus had to meticulously follow the instructions given to extract the usable pigment from the hardened sticks.

Klaus stoked the fire and placed a bucket of water over it to warm. Once it was heated, Hans added two of the lumps just long enough to soften them, then lifted them out and began kneading. Together, the men pulled and stretched the dough until it was pliable again. Using a clean vessel with fresh water, they immersed one ball at a time, and Hans kneaded and massaged it in the water, folding, pushing and pressing the dough as more and more of the pigment came out and fell to the bottom. For hours, they took turns kneading the ball until the material itself became like a sponge which held only the impurities while, at the bottom of the deep bowl, lay a thick coating of blue—a heavenly blue like that worn by the Madonna in her sublime images. Hans was transfixed. He gave thanks the parcel hadn't been stolen and decided then and there that such a final product was worth every ache, pain, and cut endured on that back alleyway in Antwerp.

On that April morning, the colors he intended to use were mixed, and a small amount of each dabbed on the palette he held in his right hand, thumb protruding through a hole in the board. Brush poised in his left hand, Hans faced the canvas already stretched tautly and firmly tacked to an oak frame, the whole supported by a wooden easel built specifically to support it. The canvas itself was quite large—its width almost spanned the length of his arms when held outstretched, height close to Hans's stature but then, the king had specified a near life-sized depiction of he and his beloved—and the sheer bulk of the mighty King Henry alone would require a lot of room.

Before laying down the first brushstroke each morning, Hans would stand back and narrow his eyes to appraise the work's progress. It had always been his practice to critically observe what he'd accomplished on the previous day. And each appraisal invariably concerned him. It seemed, although he'd often concluded his last day's work with a sense of satisfaction, somehow the next morning's review filled him with despair. Nothing about it pleased him, and he was starting to believe the portrait would never come together as it appeared in his mind's eye. Reluctantly he asked himself, What choice do I have, at this point?

None, came the brutal answer. None but to forge on, doing the best you can, and be well prepared to accept the consequence.

As he pondered, a sharp rap at the locked door made him start nervously. He scuttled across the room to peer through the peephole, fearing it was the King, who would undoubtedly be impatient to observe progress now that Hans was applying color to the underdrawing. Like many artists, Hans was reluctant to show patrons his renderings until the coloring was almost finished, with only the very final touches yet to be added. He had discovered that premature viewings almost always ended in disappointment and dreaded the possibility that Henry, although well pleased with the conceptual drawings, would be thoroughly dissatisfied with the result.

Opening the door a crack, he was relieved to see Klaus, whom he hadn't encountered in several weeks since the King had been keeping his Court Astronomer busy, calculating astrological predictions for the coming year.

"Quickly!" Hans waved his friend inside so he could close and bolt the door behind him. "Glad to see you, man. How've you been?"

"Well occupied, Hans. The King has me burning a supply of candles which must cost a small fortune, working at all hours to provide him prognostications for the future."

Although they were alone, Klaus then lowered his voice. "Between you and me, my friend, that assured, gleaming exterior he takes such pride in is full of cracks which may run deep. He is always unnerved about the possibility he will contract some awful illness and has me analyzing every astrological chart possible to assure him he will remain healthy. But not only that: in truth, he is often uneasy about the course he has chosen. But he'll never admit such uncertainty to anyone—I think not even to his wife. He desperately wants the cosmography to bolster his position."

"And does it?"

"To a certain degree, yes. Nothing runs counter to the decisions he's made so far. But precisely what his longer-term strategy is…? That I do not know since he tends to keep much to himself. I think he's well aware of what must be done to realize this professed divinely ordained role and position himself as the leader of the Christian world, but outwardly he's cavalier about it. Of course, that is Henry's way. But he is anxious, believe me. He fears the possibility of abject failure and, to Henry, nothing is as grievous as rejection or, worse, scorn. So, in addition to my astrological reassurances, he is greatly dependent on this painting to represent him in the light he envisions. He badly needs it to reinforce his strength of purpose."

"And thank you, Sire, for thus helping reinforce mine," Holbein retorted. It was precisely that message which filled him with foreboding. Resignedly, he stepped around the easel's legs to resume his position in front of the canvas and picked up his palette. For the first time in almost a month, Klaus followed him and saw what Hans had created. It was then that the astronomer became strangely still and uttered no sound. Becoming aware of his friend's unusual reticence, Hans glanced over his shoulder to find Kratzer wide-eyed, mouth agape.

"What, man? It's terrible, isn't it? God help me, I knew it."

Attempting to regain his composure, Klaus spluttered, "Holbein! Look at it! Have angels visited you while you toil alone in this tiny cell? How... how have you produced this—this... jewel?"

"Jewel? Do you not see what I see, Klaus? It's common! It doesn't shine with the light I had hoped for. I am mightily discouraged." Shoulders hunched, he covered his face with his paint-stained hands.

"Oh, my friend. You are mistaken. So terribly, terribly wrong. Of course, the work isn't yet finished, but what do I view? I am standing before a masterpiece the likes of which I have never before encountered. Have you completed Henry's and Anne's faces?"

"Almost," the master painter retorted gloomily. "I just have some final strokes of the brush to add light and a tad more dimension. But they are as near to complete as my overestimated talent will allow."

"Henry's expression! As I gaze upon it, I am awed! It perfectly captures our monarch's strength, humanity, and, incredibly, his pledged sanctity. It is beautiful beyond description! While Anne...? Hans, this representation will live beyond her years and portray her exquisite features and extraordinary spirit forever. What you have done—what you are doing..." He shook his head in awe. "It is, quite simply, remarkable."

Hans, who well knew that his trusted comrade was a man of science and pragmatism, not given to affectations of any kind, was suffused with immense relief.

Voice choking with gratitude, he murmured, "Thank you, Klaus Kratzer. I think you may have just saved my life and sanity. Yet again!"

ALONE IN WHITEHALL'S MAGNIFICENT library, Hans paced; his footfalls echoing on the polished floor; mouth so dry that no amount of ale could quench it. At moments he felt as if he might vomit, so he sat to pour himself a sizable beaker of wine and swallowed it in two gulps, hoping it would settle his lurching stomach and bolster his courage. Then, unable to remain seated, he jumped to his feet and stalked the chamber's perimeter again, sweating profusely. A heavy brass key rattled at the door's lock eliciting a rising wave of panic, which Hans struggled to contain. Hinges creaking, the door began to swing open. The moment he most dreaded was at hand.

Hans was to unveil the finished painting to Henry, King of England, and Anne, the Queen. This was his day of reckoning.

He studied, one final time, what he was about to deliver and realized that, in truth, he was pleased. He knew he could not possibly have done any better. That didn't mean, however, that Henry would share the sentiment. His thoughts returned to the previous year and the many months he had spent working on a portrait of the two French ambassadors, Dinteville and de Selve, and the lavish praise he'd garnered when that painting was viewed. Indeed, as he contemplated the portrait of the King and Queen, Hans knew it far surpassed all of his other work. He was not even sure how he had done it. He murmured a prayer of indebtedness, knowing his hand had been divinely guided. His prayer quickly included the humble but urgent request that the painting would please his Sovereign King. And that his career would be saved.

The pale, yellow morning light streamed through the leaded windows and cast a perfect illumination on the portrait. Its frame was magnificent, carved, and gilded by the premier woodcarver in London, and the frame's subtle golden tones accentuated the liberal use of gold leaf throughout the painting. Placed on a library table, leaning against the oaken stacks, it was positioned exactly at eye level for optimal viewing. Hans drew a deep, slow breath, and for the first time in many months, his anxiety left him as he exhaled. He felt light. His painting glowed; as he'd dared to hope, it emanated an exquisite radiance, and Hans was proud. With a relieved sense of hope, he let the velvet drape fall back into place.

He turned to greet the King and Queen who had just entered the room, bowing low and respectfully to them. His voice was even, steady. "Good day, Your Highnesses. How pleased I am to see you this morning."

"And we you, Master Holbein." Anne gracefully moved across the floor with a rustle of dove grey silk. Considering the privacy of the meeting, there were no serving staff present, so she poured a goblet of wine for her husband and inquired if Holbein would like one. He demurred, "Thank you, but no, Your Highness."

The Court Painter then turned to the King. "Majesty, please excuse me if I seem nervous, but I am all too aware that your expectations are high indeed. I can only pray that I have fulfilled a fraction of your wishes."

"I feel sure you have done a remarkable job, Holbein. But let us not delay further. I am anxious to see it! Show us your work!"

Hans led Anne and the King to the table upon which the painting reclined. They moved to stand directly before it and lifted their eyes only when Holbein pulled aside the cloth.

Anne raised her hand to her throat and uttered a soft cry.

Henry merely stood silent—so much so that Holbein's newfound calm began to crumble, and he felt a fresh sweat break out under his tight collar while, within the room itself, all that could be heard was the pop and hiss of logs burning in the hearth.

Finally, the King turned to Hans, and his eyes were wet with … were those royal tears?

With a voice quiet and deep with emotion, he said, "I hoped but did not dare to dream of this, Holbein. It exceeds anything I could have imagined. It is marvelous. Sacred! You have accomplished what

I'd longed for—indeed, somehow you have achieved the work of a lifetime in this singular painting." The King grew quiet and once again studied the portrait. Finally, he turned to face Hans, and said softly, "I offer you my deepest gratitude, my admiration and respect, and that, sir, is something I do not give freely."

Hans flushed red and awkwardly lowered his gaze. "Your Grace, I am honored to the point of speechlessness. I am but a rough and humble man and know not how to express my thankfulness to you and our gracious Queen. Therefore, to compensate for my lack of poise, may we examine the work in detail? I am much more comfortable discussing paint."

Henry bellowed laughter which relieved the moment, and chairs were pulled so they might sit and analyze the creation.

Not unlike the double portrait of the Arnolfinis', Henry and Anne were represented standing in the mid-ground of the painting, each at a three-quarter turn, facing the viewer but aligned toward each other. The overall effect was an explosion of rich color, the extravagant pigments used to their greatest advantage, and the technique of thin layers of oils applied to the prepared canvas resulted in a look that gleamed as if lit from within. Henry's image, majestic and imposing, yet engaging, was adorned in deep royal purple, his long, elegant swing coat liberally threaded with gold leaf. The jerkin and doublet worn under the coat were of white velvet, traced in silver and gold. The fabrics looked alive, natural, as if one could reach out and touch them, actually feel the silky softness beneath one's fingers. Anne's gown and train were of the luminous, heavenly blue seen in depictions of Mary, the Mother of God; its cut designed to noticeably reveal the blessed news in which she delighted—as she had so fervently wished, she was expecting her second child with the King. Both the King's and the Queen's faces were extraordinary likenesses, the flesh tones delicately rendered, expressions alive with perception, eyes focused on the viewer, inviting knowledge of the secrets to be revealed. The King's left hand was extended, and his wife's right lay lightly atop his forearm in a symbol of solidarity. Henry's right hand was raised, the first two fingers and thumb extended, third and fourth fingers closed in a recognizable sign of benediction. Atop each head was a holy diadem, brilliantly executed in gold leaf.

Anne had brought her magnifying glass and inspected every element of the complex work. Her beautiful image was positioned before a pair of ornate doors, and with the aid of her glass, she read aloud the words which appeared to be carved into them: "Ps XXIV VII Lift up your heads O you gates And be lifted up you everlasting doors And the King of glory shall come in." In front of the King and Queen was a table covered by a carpet of the Orient, and on it were numerous objects. Although he had seen outlines of them in the drawings, Henry exclaimed over each as if it were the first time. His voice rang out, jubilant. "Hans! The Keys of Heaven! They look as if they are real, lying there, crossed. As if Jesus had just placed them in front of me."

Next to the keys, gleaming gold and heavy with solid symbolism, lay a ship seemingly carved from precious metal—the barque of St. Peter, now to be helmed by Henry the King. And in the very middle of the table, washed by the light of a pure white taper—the Divine flame—was an innocuous-looking dish. Only the most learned would know it to be the mysterious and hallowed sang real, the bowl into which the dying Christ's blood had been spilled. Next to the dish was a papyrus, lettered with hieroglyphs, evidence of its existence, and clues to its secret location. Henry professed to be the solitary living man who knew of its whereabouts.

While the royal couple was engrossed in their examination, Hans snatched a moment to savor his relief and joy at his achievement. He was immensely glad the task was over and that by all appearances, both King and Queen were well pleased with the result. Anne remarked, "Hans, just as we discussed, you have the King standing upon a rock embedded in the floor. He is the rock upon which the New Church will be founded. Oh! I just adore the parables you have created here! I feel as if I could view this beautiful painting and the story it tells for days on end and never grow weary of it. I know that anyone who looks upon it, for however long it may survive, will feel the very same sense of wonder and awe."

"And your representation of the landscape seen through the window at my right is superb, Holbein." Henry rubbed his red-gold beard with pleasure. "The hills are rolling, dotted with sheep and lambs—my lambs—the ones I am to tend. And just there, in the distance, is the castle: The House of Zion." Taking the eyeglass from Anne, he inspected closely and found carved into the windowsill the characters 'II Sml V vii'. He strode across the room to lift a heavy volume, and placing the Bible on a nearby table, opened it, paging through until he found the particular passage he sought. 2 Samuel 5:7. He read aloud, "Nevertheless David took stronghold over Zion which is now the City of David..."

At that, the king sat back in reflection, a beatific smile erasing all uncertainty from his face.

"Look, Henry!" Anne pointed to a shadowed corner in the painting. There, leaning against the wall, was a curved shepherd's staff. The very staff Peter used to lead his flock, which would now be Henry's symbol of guidance.

As the viewer's eye roamed over the image, it came to rest on the center—the focus—the vanishing point. There, fantastically rendered and mounted against a wall of dramatic vermilion red, hung a golden cross featuring a dome of glass at its center. With a magnifier, one could see, within the dome, a splinter of ancient olive wood. The King and Queen were respectfully mute as they marveled over this depiction of the one remaining piece of Christ's True Cross.

As the observers endeavored to absorb all they beheld, each took note of something which might easily have been missed. As the eye luxuriated in the visual display of extravagant, rippling velvet worn by the King, it could be seen that his bent knee was partially hidden by the folds of his coat. His foot was triumphantly planted upon an object which lay on the rock floor. The light played upon its surface; the shining metal had been crushed under the heel of the King's boot. It was, very obviously, a spoil of war. Only then did it come clear: the mangled plunder was nothing less than the hallowed papal tiara which popes have worn through the ages. Its smattering of gems winked helplessly. The golden Triregnum, which had represented popes as the fathers of kings, governors of the world, and vicars of Christ—now decimated by the force of Henry's victorious stance.

And at the bottom of the spectacular painting, Hans had etched a single word: *Obedientiam.*

SO ELATED WAS THE King with his dazzling portrait that he immediately arranged for an elegant supper to be served that very evening in the library, and sent forth a summons to Archbishop Cranmer, Master Secretary Cromwell, Astronomer Kratzer, and Master Painter Holbein to attend. He couldn't wait to unveil the finished artwork to Cromwell and Cranmer, who had seen little of it as it progressed. His Grace the Archbishop and Secretary Cromwell sent their grateful acceptance, while Kratzer, utterly exhausted from the long hours at work on his astrological charts and feeling ill from a chest cold, respectfully declined. Holbein thanked the King and Queen effusively and also made his excuses, saying he felt that same cold coming on and wished not to be in the company of the pregnant Queen while coughing. Privately, he wished nothing more than to have a simple supper and collapse to sleep, finally unencumbered by worry for the first time in over six months.

All that day, Henry remained ebullient. Finally, after several tedious afternoon hours reviewing and signing documents, he collected one of his favorite noblemen and a member of his Privy Council, Sir Francis Weston, and proposed a game of tennis. Weston was an athletic and entertaining young man of 23 years who idolized his King. They enjoyed great times together, and Francis well knew how to compete with an energetic Henry who was, in fact, two decades older, skillfully allowing him to win when prudent and according to His Royal Highness's mood, yet always giving him good sport.

Together they crossed the green lawns to the recreation center on the palace grounds. It was a favorite element of Henry's masterful redesign of Whitehall, and he'd created courts for tennis, jousting, bowling, cockfighting—all pursuits he reveled in and thoroughly enjoyed as antidotes to his often-trying daily existence. Throwing an arm across Weston's shoulders, his boisterous laughter rang out, signaling staff who scurried to ready the tennis plays.

"It's been some time since we had a match, eh, Fran?"

"Indeed, Your Grace. I can only hope you have wisely used that time to practice. Then just perhaps, you might have a slightly better chance of beating me. But I doubt it!" Weston winked at Henry and chucked him with an elbow.

The King snorted in mock derision. "I have not a concern. You may be younger, but look at you! You are puny, man. I told you that you need to bulk up. Add some muscle to that wiry frame. You think women admire long and lean? They like a man with strength! And they really like to watch a winner. Which, without any doubt, will be me."

They assumed their places on the court, each on one side of the net, grasped their racquets, and Henry called out, "Good luck, for you shall need it, Sir Francis!" before powering the first blistering serve his way.

An hour and a half later, sweating and breathing hard, Henry continued his day of delight, having soundly beaten his good friend. They were toweling off, making ready to return to the Palace's apartments, when Henry, suffused with bonhomie and unable to contain his joy, leaned across to Francis. "My friend, I have something I would like to show you. Only a very few know if its existence as yet, but you are one of my closest councilors, and I see no reason to withhold it from you. Come to the Library this evening at six of the clock for supper. Join me, the Queen, and two others, and I will reveal to you something spectacular."

Weston stopped scrubbing himself with his towel at Henry's eagerly conspiratorial tone whence, resuming his subordinate position of councilor to his King, he bowed.

"Your Grace! I am honored by your gracious invitation to be included in whatever revelation might take place. I will most certainly be there at the appointed time, and thank you, Majesty."

THE LONG LIBRARY TABLE had been laid with white napery, silver plate gleamed hearthside, and stewards began to set dishes of fragrant roast meats and stewed fish on the sideboard, readying them for serving the guests. Across the room, surrounded by fine beeswax candles and washed in amber light, stood the easel, upon which was a draped frame. The Archbishop arrived first, followed by Thomas Cromwell. Seated near the fire, sipping wine, they quietly conferred, both anxious to see what had come from the monumental meetings held the previous November. Moments later, they looked up, startled, to see Sir Francis enter the room.

"Good evening, Weston." Cromwell's brows knitted in confusion. "But with respect—why are you here? I don't mean to sound rude, but I believe this to be a private meeting."

"I can't say, exactly, Sir Thomas. I played tennis with the King this afternoon, and he invited me. Actually, he insisted I come. He was in exceedingly high spirits. And as we well know, one doesn't disregard the King. If he asks me to come, I come."

Cromwell and Cranmer exchanged furtive glances. What was Henry doing? The revelation of his plan, to be accompanied by the painting, had not yet been mapped out. However, there was no time to consider further, for into the library on a rush of perfumed air swept the King accompanied by Anne.

"Gentlemen! Good evening!"

Not since the announcement of the Queen's pregnancy had they seen Henry in such excellent humor. His smile was broad, and his stance tall and self-assured. In a deep and resonant tone, he announced, "What a special delight we have in store for you this eve. I am glad we are here, together." He motioned for the servers to fill glasses with the royal cellars' finest vintage. "Let us toast this, an exceptionally successful fulfilment of the agreement made six months ago. The achievement of which will herald a change so far-reaching, so significant, that it will mark a turn of the page upon which history will be written." He raised his glass. "To a dazzling triumph!"

They all drank, calling out, "Hear-hear!"

Weston did so, too, although he still had no idea to what he toasted.

The Queen whispered in her husband's ear, and he announced, "We shall view the masterpiece first, then we may continue to discuss it while we sup. So, let us arrange ourselves to afford each person an excellent view."

As soon as they were settled, Henry stood before them and announced, "Today I witnessed this in its completed form, and I will tell you I was astonished. When the painting was commissioned, I held hope it would represent my message in a spiritual, impactful way. Never, though, did I imagine it would move me as it has. My Queen and I are convinced it is one of the most magnificent works of art ever created. Perhaps I am biased, but I think not. Therefore, I leave it for you to judge for yourself." And with a flourish, he removed the drape.

Neither Cranmer nor Cromwell expected to see anything like what was carefully positioned before them on the library table that night. Upon the revelation of the canvas, each individual uttered a gasp. Dominated by gold leaf, ethereal blues, purples, and augmented by intense reds, the painting had its astounding effect on all present. It was moments before anyone spoke.

Cromwell was the first to find voice. "Your Majesty. Never have I seen an artwork quite so beautiful, so masterful. Your painter Holbein has somehow done justice to the subject—a remarkable feat due to the momentous directive it conveys. I am elated, Sire, that it has turned out so very well. You must be gratified."

Beaming, Henry nodded. "Indeed, I am, Thomas."

Archbishop Cranmer quickly spoke up. "Your Highness, truly, I did not know what to expect. I have thought of little else over the past months except for fulfilling my role in advocating the message you wish to convey. When I see this work, so obviously divinely inspired, it reassures me. God's hand is marked in this accomplishment. He is with us."

Sir Francis Weston was overwhelmed and did not voice a single sound. The sheer beauty of Holbein's painting, his masterful execution of the many mysterious symbols, Henry's and Anne's radiant likenesses, Cranmer's and Cromwell's words, all had a stupefying effect. Henry, noticing that his much-loved young courtier was pale and moved to stillness, encouraged the small party to sit at table and dine. "As we eat, we will view the painting, and I can tell you about each and every icon which the Master has included in this, his work of a lifetime. And, Francis, I will explain to you how we have come to this miraculous point."

And so they gathered at the table and ate, drank, and celebrated late into the night.

Chapter Thirteen

EARLY DECEMBER 2016

ROME

The sharp, insistent trill of my phone startled me as I turned the corner from Via Bocca di Leone onto Condotti. My nerves were raw anyway, and I just wanted to let the damn thing ring. It ceased for a minute but started sounding again so I pulled it from my bag to see that it was Antonio calling. Maybe it was urgent since he'd dialled twice, so reluctantly, I answered.

"Hey Antonio. Che c'é? What's up?"

"Oh, am I interrupting, Zara? Were you studying or something? You sound a little irritated."

"I'm sorry. Didn't mean to come across so brusque. I'm actually headed to the library to do some res—I mean, to finish a paper." I realized, as distracted as I was after leaving the church and the soul-searching I'd subjected myself to, that I needed to remain guarded. It was getting more and more difficult to hide this quest I was on from Antonio, who was both intuitive and very inquisitive.

"It's just that I haven't seen you on campus for a while, so I was wondering if everything is okay? And I thought maybe we could have a drink and antipasti, or something. How are you coming along with your Ph.D. thesis?"

I didn't say anything, so he quickly added, "You know, I can help. That is, if you'd only ask. So... do you want to grab a bite?"

I was silent long enough that I heard him say, "Zara? Are you still there? Can you hear me?"

"Thanks, Antonio. Sure, yes, I can hear you. I'm sorry, but I have a bunch of work planned for late this afternoon and evening. But— I'll take a rain check, if that's good with you?"

"Rain check? Oh! You mean, we can do it another time, right?" He sounded disappointed.

"Again, I'm sorry. And thanks so much for asking me. But I'm sure I will see you on campus in the next couple days. And I promise—I will go over with you what thesis proposal I've come up with. After all, your opinion is super important to me. Okay? Thanks for calling. I have to run now. Buonasera. Ciao."

I hung up before he could say anything else.

For a moment I felt bad. I'd been rude to him. And if things were different, I might enjoy lingering with him over wine and a delicious antipasto. But how did I know if he was going to probe once again about what I'd seen in the Vatican Archives? And what if I lost my cool and let something slip? I could imagine him saying, 'Let's go back there together. Let's take a look at that note again! I'll help you hunt for the source!' Then the search would be his, not mine. And all the credit would go to him. I could just see his name listed first on the published paper: 'Dottore Antonio Moretti.' Not Dr. Zara Rossi. Maybe I'd end up with a brief mention in the acknowledgements section, but I'd certainly not be the author. I'd have to return to my basic studies in the scant hope I'd be able to validate myself in some other way. My stomach clenched at the thought. No! This search had become way too important to me. Although, I had to admit, at the moment I wasn't doing a great job of finding anything at all. Maybe I should just acquiesce. His sources might be much more effective than mine.

I looked up as I walked and there it was. The Magistral Palace. With that singular glance, my resolve was renewed. Who knows? In that building just might be the key I'd been searching for.

I squared my shoulders and crossed the street.

Chapter Fourteen

MAY 1534

THE GRAND PRIORY OF THE ORDER OF ST. JOHN CLERKENWELL, LONDON

Francis Weston arrived precisely on time at St. Johns Gate, Clerkenwell Priory, and reported his name to the guard stationed there. The creaky portcullis was raised without delay, allowing him to enter, and a uniformed soldier escorted him to his destination—his uncle William Weston's luxurious apartment.

Sir William was not often in England, as he had for years traveled the world commanding the Order's ships and fighting for its causes. But now, he had been instructed by the Grand Master to spend time in London, doing business with the King and checking on operations at the Priory. Hardly surprising, then, that during his stay, he would want to see his nephew, who had done so well for himself achieving the rank of Knight of the Bath, Privy Councilor, and close confidante to Henry VIII. Moreover, since Sir William was under strict orders from his Grand Master, Philippe de l'Isle-Adam, to meet with Henry and wheedle funds from him, William thought that perhaps his nephew's relationship with the King might be put to good use.

First admiring the Lord Prior's spacious, grandly furnished suite of rooms, Francis then turned his attention to the older man, who, although very grey and a little stooped at sixty years old, was still possessed of a firm grip and a sharp, flinty glance.

"Uncle William! How very good to see you again after so much time!" Francis's warm nature was evident in his greeting, as he was truly glad to see his father's brother, whom he hadn't encountered for many years.

"And likewise, my dear Francis. Look at you! It's hard for me to realize you are the same boy I knew when we last met. I think at that time, you were a skinny young buck who took pleasure in slipping salamanders and frogs into the ladies' purses at a family banquet. Do you recall?"

Reddening slightly, Francis admitted he did. "Sadly, Uncle, I haven't entirely rid myself of that mischievous streak. I do indeed like a good practical joke."

"Then watch your step, young sir. I imagine the King has little patience for that kind of irreverence. But you must have learned the rules well, or you would not be in such close contact with His Grace."

"Oh, quite to the contrary! You'd be surprised, Uncle. Henry has a great sense of humor and enjoys a jape as much as the next fellow. But, of course, he does have to be in the right humor for the joke to be on him."

"I can only imagine how true that must be, so whilst you retain your head, nephew,' Sir William retorted dryly, "let's dine, and we can converse as we do."

As they sat to their meal, Francis provided his august relative with news of the family, political happenings in and around court, and general gossip amongst the nobility until, as very ample pours of wine were consumed and sweets were served, their talk flowed ever more freely. His sensibilities well lubricated by the ever-full goblets, he leaned toward his uncle and quietly confided, "The most unusual thing happened last night, Uncle. The King invited me to dine with him and the Queen, in company with Archbishop Cranmer and Thomas Cromwell, in the library at Whitehall. I knew not what the meeting concerned, but when I arrived, it became clear we were to discuss some highly significant matter."

William's eyes narrowed as he straightened in his chair. Such privileged intelligence, particularly royal espionage, was meat and drink to any Knight of the Order. "You intrigue me, Francis. Tell me, pray?"

"Well, it turned out that the King had called us together to unveil a painting he had commissioned."

"A painting, you say?"

"A portrait, Uncle. Executed by Master Hans Holbein, who, as you may know, is one of the Court's premier artists. But unlike just any portrait, this one is, it seems, so meaningful that His Grace the King stated it would change the course of history."

William motioned for a servant to refill Francis's glass and sat back, encouraging the young man to continue.

"On its face, one immediately notices that the portrait is a double one, quite large indeed, of our King and Queen together which is, unto itself, unusual. And it is magnificent, Uncle. I can truly claim never to have seen any artist's work to approach its equal. Executed with the latest techniques in oil, on a new surface called canvas, and using the most expensive pigments money can buy, one would expect it to be remarkable—and it is, just breathtaking." Francis came closer to his uncle's ear and lowered his voice, although there were no servants within earshot. "But, Uncle, even more amazing is its subject matter. You see, it depicts something extraordinary the King feels he has been called upon to do."

"Called upon by whom, nephew?"

"By God Almighty, sir."

The Lord Prior of the Order of Saint John of Jerusalem blinked. "To do what, precisely?"

Francis's eyes were shining. "Oh, Uncle William, in all my life I've never witnessed such a revelation. I tell you true: I was struck dumb by it all. It's nothing less than that our own monarch has been called to revolutionize the Papal Empire, root and branch," Francis revealed triumphantly. "That he, Henricus Rex, has been ordained by God to establish a brand new church on the ashes of the old, corrupt one. And as amazing as it sounds, the Lord has surely christened our King as the new St. Peter: the new David, King of Zion." Francis sat back to appraise how his words were affecting his uncle. He was gratified to see that the Prior was staring at him, mouth slightly agape. The young courtier took another quaff of wine before continuing. "And this portrait will cast the message abroad employing exquisite, coded iconography most artfully woven within. Indeed, sir, did you know that King Henry holds the only splinter of the True Cross? And that he alone protects the hidden resting place of the Holy Grail? Can you imagine? All this is represented in the profound work of art. And soon, the King will reveal his divine eminence to the world using this portrait as an omen. I'm—actually we, I mean me and the illustrious company I am clearly now a part of—we are certain that those who see it will be overwhelmed accordingly, and be moved to follow Henry, abandoning their lifelong devotion to the pope. When that happens… oh, can you just picture the repercussions such a shift in faith will cause, Uncle? The world will see a new day, unlike anything it has witnessed since the founding of Christianity."

The Prior was stunned into silence—but just for a moment. Then, wanting his nephew to continue, he nodded in implicit agreement. "That is, as you say, monumental, Francis! So, this incredible experience only took place last evening? I assume, then, that the Pope as yet knows nothing of this—of the King's divine elevation? And the painting—what will happen to it now? Will it be publicly displayed?"

"I think not yet, Uncle. The King will decide where and when he will reveal it. Until that moment, it will remain hidden in an undisclosed loca—" Francis halted abruptly. The wine Uncle had so liberally plied him with was very strong. "Ah… oh no… perhaps I have revealed too much. Of course, this information is being held privately for now, sire. But, after all, you are my family, and a man of God, so I know you can be trusted."

"Well, of course, beloved nephew. That you command my absolute discretion goes without saying."

Young Sir Francis Weston thought for a flash about the King's stern admonishment for absolute privacy regarding the portrait, but the heady wine had thoroughly numbed his good judgment. However, he cast a questioning look at his uncle, thus being reassured to see his esteemed elder composed and seemingly unperturbed. So he smiled, pleased that his eminent relation should know just how far he, young Francis, had risen, and continued to peel his orange.

LATE THAT EVENING, LONG after Francis had stumbled back to his own lodging at the royal palace, Lord Prior Weston gathered tapers, grouping them on his desk to create a pool of light on the blank parchment he'd unfurled. He assembled quills and ink. Every so often, he paused in his preparations to lean against the desk and swill weak ale, trying to offset the sour stomach which plagued him after listening to Francis's astonishing news. Weston suffered a temperamental digestion at the best of times; when circumstances grew unpleasant, he could count on his stomach to bubble and ferment like a cauldron, and tonight his discomfort was intense. His trusting nephew, with childlike *naiveté*, had unknowingly discharged a veritable eruption of information the likes of which the Prior had not in his life encountered. Henry, King of England, considered himself divine and intended to destroy the papacy to found a new *creed*?

The sheer audacity! The concept was appalling! And to think he believed—has actually stated to others—that God ordained him to take such action? The claim that he, Henry, was now God's instrument on earth, replacing St. Peter, proved his lunacy. Henry Tudor—a King of Israel? It was ludicrous in the extreme and a monstrous defiance of all that was sacred. Francis had made it clear the King planned to annihilate the pope and the Roman Church as it has been known and revered for centuries and to stand victorious on its ruin. The mere thought caused bile to backswell into Weston's gullet. At that very moment, Henry might be raising a mighty army to march into Rome, invade and plunder the Vatican, murder Pope Clement, and take over all that was hallowed to the Christian world.

Trying to ignore his dyspeptic gut, Weston dipped a quill into the inkpot and poised to write an urgent, dangerous, and most secretive letter to the Grand Master. This would not be an easy missive to compose. L'Isle-Adam was expecting to hear of Weston's success in gaining a commitment of gold from Henry, yet now the Prior must, instead, reveal shattering news which, since he was a subject of the English King, could well be considered traitorous. He had no alternative, however. He was one of the highest-ranking officials of the Order. Each Knight was sworn to protect the faith with his very being.

Leaning heavily on his elbows, Weston propped his forehead on his hands, then ran trembling fingers through thinning white hair, reflecting on his many fulfilling years with the Order and his long and distinguished career. He'd been a resolute soldier, never fearful, unwilling to back down in defense of a noble cause. The risk of this particular duty was very high, though. If discovered, the message would undoubtedly cost Weston his life—and that of his young nephew. Nonetheless, heaving a deep sigh, he raised his head and surrendered his fate to God.

The ink from the quill flowed dark, like drying blood, as his fears took shape on the page.

Chapter Fifteen

EARLY DECEMBER 2016

THE MAGISTRAL PALACE OF THE ORDER OF MALTA ROME

V ia dei Condotti 68 is a building spanning two city blocks, although one wouldn't know it, hidden as it is behind gates. Above flew the brilliant flags of St. John and The Hospitallers. I showed the guard my approval to study in the Library, and the gates silently opened to allow me access. I walked across the courtyard, much smaller than the Cortile di Belvedere at the Vatican, stepped across the entry threshold and into a richly appointed reception space. Central to the marble lobby was an emblem—the Maltese Cross—which overlooked all who entered. A pleasant receptionist checked my documentation, handed me a badge, and directed me to the Library.

I'd previously completed all necessary forms, and in the sections which required me to state the object of my research visit, I decided to say I was interested in the tenure of Grand Master L'Isle-Adam and the Lord Prior of England under Henry VIII, William Weston. Of course, I made no mention of the note or the portrait, but I hoped that the study of these two men might reveal some tip worth chasing. At least, it would be a start.

I got settled in a study carrel in short order and had before me several volumes of letters and papers from Weston's tenure. The melancholy I'd carried with me, and my experience in the church, still weighed heavily. But I was always comfortable in a library surrounded by books, and I began to relax.

Paging through the volumes, an amassed collection of general ledgers, inventories, military orders, reports from Knights stationed at locations across the Christian world, I soon found myself yawning. My lack of sleep and heavy mood was taking its toll as the afternoon wore on. It seemed there was nothing in this litter of ancient bureaucratic trivia worth spending more of my time on. With a sigh of resignation, I decided to pack up and head home, maybe grab an early dinner, hit the books, then go to bed.

But then, just as I was closing my notebook, a young man with wire-rimmed glasses and an unruly shock of dark hair—likely an intern—peeked over the edge of the carrel.

"Signorina?"

"Sí?" My reply was terse. I was ready to close up shop and didn't look forward to any delay.

His face was eager, though, so I softened my tone. "Sorry. What can I do for you?"

In good English, he explained. "I understand you are researching Lord Prior William Weston, and I happened to come across this little volume, mistakenly tucked away in the wrong section. I thought perhaps, Signorina, you may find it of interest."

On tiptoe, he reached over the lip of the carrel to hand me a small, leather-bound book. "I think it may be Weston's personal giornale; at least that what it appears to be, to me."

"Well. Grazie mille, then. I will be glad to look it over." The student intern seemed pleased with himself as he left the book with me, departing with a quick backward glance and a smile.

Stifling another yawn, I opened the tightly bound book and

began to page through. Within minutes I could tell that it was a diary of sorts, apparently written by Weston himself. He must have kept notes and added editorial comments, some in the margins, others as full-page narratives, recording his reactions following battles, sailing missions, and commanding ships. His writing style was descriptive and colorful, so I began to perk up a bit as I read his entries. Mostly, they followed a chronological order and, although some seemed undated and out of context, there was a page dated July 1527 which recorded remarks on his pleasure at being appointed England's Lord Prior by the then Grand Master, L'Isle-Adam. That name, splayed on the parchment, started my heart racing, and I began to skim each page. Weston's records seemed to grow briefer as his level of responsibility increased, and some events warranted only a few lines.

But with just three pages remaining, I delicately turned to a new leaf. Dated 30 May 1534, Sir William Weston had begun his entry:

> *"My distress knows no boundary. On the day previ-*
> *ous I gained urgent knowledge of a disaster so imminent*
> *and painful that I scarce know how to confront it..."*

Sitting upright, spine like a ramrod, breath shallow, my eyes rapidly traveled the page taking in every neatly inked syllable.

> *"I have been told by someone whose name I shall protect that the King*
> *Henry is to assume the mantle of Faith, as commanded by God, to revoke*
> *the Church of Rome and to lead the Christian flock anew. From whence*
> *he truly believes this I know not: just that he is soon to take control by*
> *force of the Pope's authority and avow his place as St. Peter of this time. I*
> *know too that there be an icon, done by the master Holbein which interprets*
> *the King's intent. This painting which I have not seen is said to repre-*
> *sent Henry as King of Israel and his wife the Queen as his consort..."*

My God! My head pounded. So, it must be true! It was true—a painting did exist—and somehow Weston had gained knowledge of it.

"... *I know not if he hopes to conquer the Church in Rome by force but I fear the worst. The icon will be used to propagate his word and to win subjects. It is believed to be hid somewhere in White Hall palace, yet few have seen it. I know this from a witness who has called it a wondrous and miraculous likeness, painted to inspire anyone who lays eyes upon it. Hereby, I have done my duty and informed Grand Master L'Isle-Adam. It is our sworn vow to protect and defend the Faith, Mother Church, and our Holy Father the Pope. What he shall choose to do about such treacherous news I cannot say but on this page I confess my betrayal of my Sovereign King. If anyone shall read this and report me as traitor then so be it. I shall accept my punishment as a last act of conviction to God, in whose mercy I trust.*"

I could hardly breathe. To think I'd almost left these archives, probably with no intent to return. And here it was, right in front of me. Proof! To Weston, it represented a sacrilege and an ominous menace to the pope and his domain, and his obligation to the Order he loved and served had won out over loyalty to his King. It was so unbelievably dramatic! Then it must have been he who'd reported on the portrait's existence to the Grand Master, and to make it even more incredible, with that act he summarily committed treason. I was shaken. The revelation was more profound than any I might have possibly imagined or hoped for.

Oh, how I longed to snatch that small, seemingly insignificant book, hide it in my backpack, and escape! For a wild moment, I actually thought I would try. I was manic with elation and disbelief at what the intern had handed me. I felt like running up to him and kissing him.

Finally, I was able to calm myself enough to begin to think clearly. Carefully, I transcribed each word, every mark on the page. I took note of the page location and the small marking on the binding. Discovering nothing else in the remaining two pages of the journal, I looked again in the ledger to see if there were any additional validating markings. I found none.

The afternoon was drawing to a close. My previously listless heart was racing.

Cured of my lethargy, I packed my things, made sure to bid the head archivist and the intern a very warm goodbye, and expressed my thanks—for I now knew I'd return, probably quite soon—and left the Magistral Palace, my thoughts swimming with 16th century intrigue.

I'd barely got into my flat when I ripped my coat off, threw my pack onto the table and dug out my notes. I studied every word I'd transcribed. It seemed that the portrait was by Holbein. Hans Holbein—who, my research revealed—was the official portraitist of the Tudor Court under Henry VIII. I read about him, and saw that he had done a remarkable double portrait called The Ambassadors. It was unusual for the time because double portraits were not the norm. But it seemed that the painting L'Isle-Adam described to the pope was indeed a double portrait—of the King and Queen. I pored over Holbein's paintings online. Their realism was absolutely stunning. Some of the individuals he painted looked like they might, at any moment, open their mouths and speak. It must have been some arresting work of art, that was certain. Oh, I was dying to see what it looked like! And it had icons! Those mysterious, unique symbols scattered across masterful paintings of the day which told their own story, if they could be interpreted. But, Henry as the King of Israel? That depiction must have set heads spinning—that is, for anyone who might have seen the image. And it seemed like not many people had been privy to it.

I kept evaluating Weston's entry, line by line. I landed upon the phrase "take control by force the Pope's authority..." No wonder the Grand Master—whose role it was to avow and defend the pope and the Holy Roman Church—must have been in a full-blown panic!

This was far more gripping than I'd ever imagined. Weston mentioned he'd been told the painting was, at one point, in the Palace of Whitehall, London. I couldn't help but wonder if by some strange occurance, it might still be there, hidden away?

I had to go. To London. To Whitehall.

Chapter Sixteen

JUNE 1534

PALACE OF WHITEHALL
LONDON

The buckets were heavy; Gabrielle's back ached, and inevitably she stumbled, sloshing water all over the thick Turkish carpet. With a furtive glance to see if anyone had witnessed her carelessness, she was relieved to find herself completely alone. That was typical for midday, deep within the secret lodgings the King had built for himself in his beautifully refurbished Palace of Whitehall. Quickly, she blotted the water with towels, hoping the color wouldn't run and leave an incriminating stain on the oak parquet floor.

Gathering her supplies and again hoisting the heavy bucket, she continued through to the King's bedchamber, hobbling into the privy gallery then onwards to its two antechambers, which she had been instructed to clean thoroughly. Once a fortnight, it was her job to dust, wash, and sweep every corner of these rooms; she was the only chambermaid permitted to do so, and the task must be completed quickly, thoroughly, and without displacing a single item even by a hairsbreadth. Nor was she allowed to tell any of the other servants what she observed in the private lodgings. She knew that to do so would incur instant dismissal. Perhaps an even more severe punishment.

Gabrielle placed her water bucket and the pail containing her cleaning supplies in the corner of the room and assessed the task. This particular chamber appeared to be one in which the King did some personal reading and writing. There were two desks, a carved wooden casket filled with writing implements, and several inkwells. Candlesticks of silver-gilt topped with beeswax candles were liberally scattered about the room, and a shelf was tightly stacked with books. Several comfortable-looking chairs could be moved to either write or read. However, Gabrielle took careful note of their locations to leave them exactly as she found them. This floor, too, was carpeted, the soft pile extravagantly luxurious. The room looked almost as it had when she'd cleaned it two weeks prior—apart from one notable exception. Now, in an embrasure near the paned window stood a sturdy wooden structure, an easel, providing support for what appeared to be a painting—a large one in an ornate frame. However, its subject was obscured, draped as it was with a swath of purple velvet.

Her curiosity was piqued. But it wasn't her place to look, so she resisted temptation and began her work.

Gabrielle LeVasseur was a Frenchwoman. More than that, she was a well-born Frenchwoman. She guessed that was why the associate steward had hired her in the Whitehall kitchens. Her graceful manners and elegant speech soon impressed the head steward. As a result, she was promoted to chambermaid working under Lord Sandys, the Lord Chamberlain for the King's personal residences. Still, it was a hard job—after all, someone needed to clean those inner chambers. The noble members of the King's Privy Council were certainly not going to perform such menial tasks for themselves. So, Gabrielle became one of a few trusted servants permitted behind closed doors of the innermost, secret lodgings of the King and Queen in their new palace. She was grateful for the work, and the job was a source of pride—although her current position was still a far cry from her origins, from what she had been used to as a girl growing up just outside the city of Rouen in France.

There, Gabrielle's family were respected members of the upper bourgeoisie. Her father was a successful merchant, as was his father before him, and as far back as family lore allowed, the Vasseurs had been privileged to live in comfortable wealth. She and her two brothers were well educated; Gabrielle's father, Louis, although a grim and implacably rigid man, believed that his daughter should receive the same advantages as his sons. Her cultural refinement could only help attain a lucrative marriage, after all, which would be suitable for Gabrielle and very good for the family. So, the middle child of Louis and Marie LeVasseur sat with tutors alongside her brothers, learning to read and thus master the concepts of theology and philosophy. She was pretty, with long and luxurious blond hair; she rode well, executed fine needlework, and knew how to organize a prominent and well-to-do household. Their spacious Château de Rouen governed a property of many hectares, and Gabrielle was used to being served by a large household staff, a bevy of gardeners, stable boys, and groomsmen to care for their many excellent horses.

Wiping her forehead with the back of her hand to catch a trickle of sweat as she polished and dusted, Gabrielle daydreamed about how pleasant life had been: her family home warmed by fires in every hearth, paintings hung on the walls—even the giant tapestry her father had commissioned in Bruges which took pride of place in their great hall. Unlike many families, even wealthy ones, they had books piled in the library and delicious food on the table. Of course, her father's things were not nearly as fine as those owned by the King, but her present life certainly provided a harsh contrast to what she had known—and what she thought she would have known—for the remainder of her days.

With chapped fingers, she pushed some escaped hair back under her coif and straightened briefly to ease her sore back. To avoid becoming immersed in the melancholy which at times threatened to engulf her, Gabrielle reached into the pocket of her woolen smock where her fingers closed around the smooth stones of her rosary. Just touching it brought her comfort. As she continued her tasks, her lips moved, silently reciting the Ave Marias and the Pater Nosters, the ritual at which Gabrielle was so practiced that she scarce needed to feel the beads to know her place in the Rosary's chain. The fact that she was still able to observe her very devout Catholic faith was a blessing. It bolstered her spirits on the hardest of days.

Her faith was, without question, the most essential aspect of her life. Her family was fervently Catholic, actively repudiating the opinions of some who were intrigued by the rising swell of religious reform in France. Her father did business only with other sworn Catholics, and friends of her father and mother shared the Vasseurs' ideology, or they were quickly and permanently shunned. She saw it as a saving grace that there were many dedicated Catholics in the community of the Court of King Henry VIII.

A smile played about her features when her thoughts came to rest on the other joyful good fortune in her life: her husband, Mathieu Dauvet. She looked forward to seeing his handsome face, even though it would be many long hours into the evening before they could be together. She still had a number of chores to complete, and Mathieu, a stable hand, would also be occupied into the night, caring for the King's horses. The King's Master of the Horse, Sir Nicholas Carew, was a challenging taskmaster. He expected perfection; and between the heavy stable work, keeping the horses perfectly groomed, tack oiled, and a myriad of other jobs, it was a rare occasion when she and Mathieu could be together when they were both not completely exhausted.

While the court was in residence at Whitehall, the husband and wife had a little corner they called their own in the great kitchen complex. There, they kept the few things they possessed; nearby, a small supply closet sometimes allowed them to sneak away when they might want some privacy. Living in an alcove was hardly what she had been accustomed to, that was certain, but it was warm and, after the day's consumption of fare by the massive court was completed, there was often extra food available so, all in all, it was not too bad.

Gabrielle was devoted to Mathieu. Her loyalty never wavered, even though it was that very devotion that had caused her profound loss. He was her husband, and she'd taken vows to commit to him in both good times and bad. When she was a girl in the company of women who'd gathered socially at her family's estate, she'd been privy to the chatter and gossip which provided fodder for the shallow society in which well-dressed, affluent ladies eagerly recounted stories of illicit love between wealthy members of the aristocracy and their servants. Those tales, always titillating, were whispered from behind delicately gloved hands. Although relished, such drama was looked down upon with self-righteous disdain. Gabrielle eavesdropped and heard the stories but never, in any lifetime, imagined that she would one day be the subject of such tawdry scandal.

But she'd been wrong and thereby learned the harsh lesson that one can never really predict the course of one's own life.

At her parent's estate, Mathieu had been the groomsman responsible for caring for Gabrielle's horse. When she was to ride out for the day, she could be sure that upon her arrival at the stable, her mare would be saddled—groomed beautifully—tack freshly cleaned, her saddlebag neatly packed with any supply she might need, and best of all—a handsome, well-built, smiling stable boy ready to assist her in mounting her horse. Upon her return, there he would be, his sweet face welcoming and helpful. Gabrielle soon found that she used any excuse she could conjure to spend time at the stable, professing to a love of horses when actually, it was a growing infatuation with Mathieu which drew her. She'd been delighted to learn he was from a very pious family, even if they were desperately poor, and that his father had been greatly pleased when his son's abilities with horses had landed him the position of stable hand at the Château de Rouen. He, like his family, was an ardent Catholic. Gabrielle knew her Mathieu made time to attend Mass each day. His commitment to God gave Gabrielle an especially warm feeling about the object of her growing affection and drew her to him even more.

They were both 17 years of age, idealistic and romantic. It wasn't long before mutual attraction turned to love. Gabrielle was captivated, yet she agonized over what was fast becoming a dilemma. It was an impossible situation. Her father was actively seeking prospective husbands for her, all from well-to-do landowners in northern France, even from as far as Paris—and little wonder. As one among many of his commercial assets, she was beautiful, well-educated, and charming—a fine prize with which to barter. Gabrielle was introduced to several men, and meeting each of them created dread, which added to her turmoil.

She leaned into her work, scrubbing the marble hearthstone fiercely as memories flooded her. In vivid detail, she recalled one particular afternoon when her father, Louis, had hosted a visit from a prosperous vicomte from Alençon and his son. They were there to evaluate the lands owned by the Vasseurs and, more importantly, assess Gabrielle's suitability as a potential bride. Obediently, but fighting a sick feeling in her stomach, she'd entered the hall to encounter a gross, ridiculously overdressed man and a young boy. Perhaps 12 years old, the boy was tearing at a chicken leg, jaw grinding noisily, lips smacking the air. He never once looked up from his plate but kept shoveling food into his pimple-strewn face.

Once she was seated, her father said to the boy, "Monsieur Guillaume, I would like to introduce you to my daughter, Gabrielle."

Only briefly did the awful child glance in her direction, showing not a flicker of interest, before quickly resuming the activity more important to him: grabbing handfuls from a platter of sweets just placed on the table. His parent, also busy consuming whatever had been placed within his reach, studied Gabrielle for a moment barely longer than had his son and casually extended a grease-laden hand across the table to her father.

"She will be acceptable."

Father had beamed. A successful transaction accomplished.

Gabrielle remembered feeling about to vomit, whispering, "Excuse me", then running blindly from the room, up the stone stairs, and into her bedchamber. Once inside, she'd closed the door behind her and twisted the key in the lock. She spent the rest of the afternoon, face buried in her pillow, sobbing until her eyes were like raw embers. Only eventually did she calm, having reached a decision. No matter her father's wishes, she was not going to be condemned to a life spent with such grotesques! More than that—she resolved never, ever to marry any man only by her father's choosing. As the light from her bedchamber window began to fade, she rose, splashed her face with cold water, and defiantly slipped from the manor house, heading for the stable. It was quite late in the day, and to her great joy, she found Mathieu finishing his tasks. Gabrielle told him to retrieve her mare from the fields and saddle her. As soon as the horse was ready, she clambered astride and pulled Mathieu's hand. He jumped astride, riding behind her. She felt free, and her relief was like a balm as they set out in the deepening twilight across fragrant July fields and meadows. After riding for some time, they came to rest near a stream that ran through a thicket of woods Gabrielle had always loved. There they dismounted and spread a blanket on the banks of the bubbling creek.

Even as she meticulously washed the windows in the King's writing chamber, Gabrielle's face flushed remembering that night. On the blanket, as stars pricked the sky above, she and Mathieu had made love. It was wonderful, magical, and, while she hoped God would forgive her sin, still, she had not an instant of regret. She committed to Mathieu, and he to her. They knew not how, but they would be together. She would not marry a man her father bartered for her, and she would tell him so when the time was right. After that, he would simply have to accept the idea.

How innocent she had been, how optimistic… how foolish!

When, in the following months during preparations for her wedding to the oafish son of the Vicomte d'Alençon, it became apparent that Gabrielle was with child, a screaming confrontation with her father revealed the truth about her and Mathieu. She informed her father that she would marry the stable hand, and there was nothing to be done about it. Her father promptly forbade her from seeing him again, informing her that Mathieu would be banished. When she retorted that no one, not even he, would command her, she was expelled from her home, ordered never to return.

That very night, she and Mathieu gathered two small bags of belongings and left the manor. Neither parent was present to wish her well.

Oh, how she had cried! She'd loved her family and her home. She especially missed her mother, who had been distraught that fateful night, but who had been ordered to keep her tongue and not ever to contact Gabrielle as long as her daughter insisted upon marrying a stable boy. So, Gabrielle and Mathieu clung to each other and, using some of the meager amount of gold she had been able to secrete away, booked ship's passage from Calais into England, where they had already determined to start life anew, together.

It had been an awful crossing—stormy, with the tiny vessel rocking violently in the deep swells of the Channel—and Gabrielle sick as a gutter dog. It had been a difficult early pregnancy, and now this dreadful voyage. In the middle of the night, she awoke in their cramped and stinking quarters with a pain that felt as if it would tear her in two. Mathieu, frightened for her very life, comforted her as best he could until that appalling moment came when a gush of blood told the truth about what she had most feared: she had lost their child.

Gabrielle found that every time she relived the horrible night in the hold of the ship, she cried. Cried for the baby she had lost and would have loved, and for the fact that she and Mathieu had been unable to conceive again, even in the five years since she had left France. Dusting almost complete, she stopped work to mop her tears with a clean rag. She willed herself to stop sniffling and squared her shoulders. There was nothing to do but live—each day like the last. It was hard to envision any life other than what they'd been able to carve out for themselves. At least, she thought, they did have each other. And God. She'd always felt the nearness of God and tried very hard to do what she believed He asked of her. She had long come to accept that her infertility was a rebuke for having conceived a child out of wedlock. Happily, she and Mathieu had been married by a local priest as soon as they'd arrived in England, so no need to worry about that any longer. With hope and prayer, perhaps one day they would yet become parents.

She reloaded her buckets with the used cloths, brushes and brooms, and prepared to leave. Glancing around the chamber to ensure all was in place, her attention was captured by a singular beam of late afternoon sunlight which pierced the window and illuminated the velvet-swathed frame. Although the rest of the chamber was in shadow, the stream of light was bright, beckoning. Unconsciously, she reached for her rosary beads and fingered them for just a minute before, hesitantly, approaching the easel. So insistent was the shaft of brilliant light that she wondered if it was a sign being conveyed to her. The beacon never faltered but seemed to point out precisely what she should do; whereupon she stood before the shrouded work and whispered a prayer.

Cautiously she cast around, even peering apprehensively into the next chamber to ensure she was alone before reaching out to feel the silky velvet. Then chambermaid LeVasseur lifted the drape.

She had only intended to steal a peep to satisfy the urge that, mysteriously, seemed to be driving her, but what confronted her as she exposed that great painting under its protective cloth nearly knocked the wind from her body. Fearful or no, she could not stop staring at the image which had been hidden deep within the King's most private spaces with great deliberation.

Her eye traveled the entire range of the work, and the longer she stared, the more horrified she became. Gabrielle's education and reading in theology allowed her to clearly interpret what was depicted in this most astonishing work of art. It had been executed, quite deliberately and with much aforethought, to convey a message—an epistle which would cause any God-fearing Catholic man or woman's blood to run cold.

It was sheer profanity... more than mere impiety... it was a sacrilege... in fact, it was blasphemy!

Heart hammering in her chest, she let the drape fall back into place before hastily gathering her cleaning materials and scuttling white-faced from the chamber. Curiously, the beam of light that had first beckoned to her had faded from view.

LATE THAT NIGHT, WHEN other exhausted servants who slept nearby in corners of the kitchen were grunting and whistling, Gabrielle shifted fitfully on her straw mat. She kept her whisper low and her mouth close to Mathieu's ear as they huddled together beneath their rough blanket. She dared not risk anyone else hearing.

"Mathieu, are you awake? I can't sleep. All I can think of is that painting and the images I saw. You have no idea what a terrible jolt it was."

"But you only saw it for a few minutes, Gabbie. How can you possibly know what it meant?"

"Hush! Keep your voice down. If we are heard, I will be let go. Or worse!"

"Alright," he croaked. "Tell me what you think it was about. Why not just a portrait of the King and Queen? He flaunts them everywhere. The man loves to look at his own image, that be certain..."

"Mathieu! Shhhhhh..." Gabrielle hissed. "Any courtier, if he were to hear you speak such, would have you arrested! Anyway, it is more than just their portrait. So much more! It's horrifying, yet it's beautiful. It's the most breathtaking yet corrupt work of art I've ever seen."

"Well, I haven't seen as many paintings as have you in your privileged life, so I concede you know better than I. Why is it horrifying?"

"He thinks he is divine, Mathieu! It must be clear to anyone who knows about the symbols of St. Peter. It shows the King in all his magnificence, and he wears the signs. Every badge of Jesus' apostle Peter, the Rock of the Church—these are now worn by Henry the King... His hand is extended in a blessing! He points to the lambs of God! In the distance is the House of Zion, his palace—and he has close by the staff of St. Peter. And... he stands resolutely on the Rock. The ark of Peter, the True Cross, they are all there. And over them all towers Henry and Queen Anne. Mathieu, there are carvings in the painting which refer to Scripture, passages which tell of the King's place as God's patriarch on earth! How can he present himself in that way?"

Mathieu struggled to comprehend. "So, what do you believe it means? Oh, why did you have to look? Gabbie! Now we are at risk!"

"I know, I know. But there was a sign! God told me to look. He directed me with a beam of light. And now I must do something about it."

"What do you mean, Gabbie—do something? What can you do? Nothing! You must forget you ever saw the accursed thing. You can never speak of it again. Else you endanger yourself—both of us. This is the King you are talking about, you realize that? He'd have us thrown into the river with a millstone around each of our necks without another thought! No—it's impossible. Maybe we should leave? Find another noble house to work in, get away from what you know sits upstairs, haunting you."

"Mathieu, you're wrong! I have to act! Why do you think God asked me to look? It is plain from this portrait that Henry thinks he's the head of the Church. Soon enough, he's going to display it for everyone—he's had it painted for a reason, and he's not going to keep it hidden forever. And it will cause chaos within the Catholic Church and for the pope. It will be far, far worse than the rumblings going on now. Then what will happen to our beloved faith, Mathieu? What will we have left to us?" She choked back a sob. "I tell you, I must rescue our Church from this desecration, even though it seems unimaginable: me, a little chambermaid, a nobody. But God's command was clear. And if you can't help me, Mathieu, I promise you I will understand. But you have to know this, my love: I will do it on my own." Tears welled up and spilling over, ran freely. She struggled to keep her trembling voice from waking anyone nearby.

Mathieu took a deep breath and ever so slowly exhaled. He placed his lips close to her ear. "Gabbie, you know I'd never let you take this on yourself. What you suggest runs counter to every instinct I have, but I will be with you. I am with you. So… what shall we do?"

Long into that night they whispered, only stopping momentarily when a random cough or shifting body nearby caused them to fear being overheard. By the time the first glimmers of dawn softened the kitchen's darkness, and the scullions rose in their misery to stoke the hearth fires for the day's cooking, they had hatched a scheme. While also, on that night, Mathieu came to know just how much he loved his Gabbie because to console her, he'd agreed to commit an act that was utter madness.

The two weeks which followed were draining, each day filled with the laborious demands on the servants who enabled the palace's enterprises. When the King, Queen, and full court were in residence, accommodating their needs was a massive effort and kept Mathieu and Gabrielle occupied from dawn to dark. At night the couple would, despite their fatigue, lie awake till the other servants were safely asleep to formulate and fine-hone their plan. The idea would take courage and a great deal of fortitude, but it also would require money, of which they had none. So, Gabrielle unwrapped, from her scant and treasured possessions kept in an old, tattered muslin bag, a small brooch. She had been wearing the jewel the night she and Mathieu had been banished from her home in exile and had successfully kept it hidden from prying eyes and avaricious fingers ever since. Made of gold, with three small pearls and a central ruby, it was the only reminder of her refined past life that she still possessed. Through inquiry, Gabbie learned of a pawnbroker in the city, and one afternoon when she was able to escape for a short time, visited him to exchange the brooch for several crowns, knowing full well she would never again see the jewel she had loved.

With that crucial gold in hand, they gathered a few necessary tools and supplies by filching them when no one was looking. The stresses they endured were immense and took their toll as, with the passage of each day and night, both husband and wife became increasingly agitated and fearful.

But Gabrielle was unwavering. She prayed relentlessly about it. In her prayers she knew she heard the voices of Jesus Christ, and sometimes His Mother, Mary. They murmured to her, "Gabrielle, we count on you. God will strengthen you. Have no fear and you will be protected in this calling. Keep us close." Thus her conclusion was always the same. This is what God has asked of her. And she could not—she would not let Him down.

It came her day to clean His Majesty's innermost chambers. After the conclusion of dinner, the King and some of his courtiers went hunting for the afternoon, whereupon the head steward instructed Gabrielle to gather her supplies and make haste to complete the task before the Royal's return. She believed, though, that the King and his cronies would be out late since the weather was fine, and Mathieu knew their Sovereign never rushed to return if the hunting was good and the horses were fresh. So, she assembled her buckets, rags, water, and brooms. She'd found a long, cylindrical, two-handled basket which was a great help in carrying everything, while, into her apron's pockets, she secreted a sizable length of twine and a stout, exceedingly sharp knife.

Heart thumping, she nodded to the King's guard who sleepily stood at his post, and she entered the privy suite. Quickly, she went about her business of scrubbing and sweeping, dusting and burnishing. At one point, she was startled by the appearance of a steward, who delivered a fresh supply of beeswax candles. He'd looked about at her work appreciatively as he left, saying, "His Grace must be glad of you; looks like you do a goodly job. You are a lucky one to have this duty, all on your own in here."

Not another soul came into view for the entire afternoon while she worked.

The chambers were sparkling—her job done as the day waned. By then, Gabrielle felt as if she might faint with fear, but her fingers found her rosary, and from it she drew strength. Stealthily she moved to the easel, on which was braced the portrait, just as it had been two weeks prior. Holding her breath, she folded back the velvet drapery and encountered the images of King and Queen peering down at her. She retrieved the knife from her apron and with a flick of her wrist, sliced through the canvas as close as she could to the frame. With a muted rustle, it fell away and settled on the carpeted floor.

There could be no going back now. Knowing full well that if anyone entered the room at that moment, her life would be over, Gabrielle stooped and hastily rolled the canvas into a tube and tied it with the twine she had brought. It wasn't easy; the painted surface didn't bend well. But she was able to slide it into the broom basket, tucking a few brushes in along with it, handles exposed, to convince anyone she might encounter to assume her burden unremarkable. Finally, pale and panting, she carefully coaxed the drape back into place until it was impossible to tell that beneath that Judas-shroud, nothing remained but a gaping hole. Desperately, she hoped it would be some hours before the theft was discovered.

A rough pinch of both cheeks returned some semblance of life into her face; a slow and deliberate breath allowed her heart to calm a bit. Then, assuming a false air of confidence, she shouldered her supplies and made her way back to the scullery. She would stow the basket with the brushes, and the painting, in a small closet. Night was falling and no one would look in there—no one would have need to look inside Gabrielle's cleaning basket.

She anxiously waited for Mathieu to finish his duties and join her. She couldn't possibly eat a thing but instead stuffed some dark brown bread, cheese, and a joint of mutton into a parcel and hid it near their alcove.

At long last, he appeared. Gabbie felt terrible because he looked so haggard. Had it been up to him, they would never be risking their lives in this way. But he'd agreed, and she knew that in his heart, he felt they were doing the right thing—that which God had inspired them to attempt. They exchanged knowing glances but kept silent, waiting for the people who inhabited the kitchen space at night to settle into their much-needed slumber. As soon as the area was quiet, Mathieu produced a gunny sack he had salvaged from the horses' feed. Creeping into the closet, Gabrielle retrieved the painting and slipped it into the sack then, with shaking hands, tied the mouth closed with twine. They each pulled on their rough cloaks, freezing nervously in place when someone nearby grunted. Snatching the few bundles they'd prepared, they quickly made their way to the door leading to the open courtyard. It was fortunate that the King's guards were rarely stationed there, so they slipped through the yard and used the path Mathieu frequented as a short-cut to the stables.

The night was moonless, but the sky was littered with stars, and the temperature mild. Gabrielle silently mouthed a grateful prayer, interpreting it as a sign that God guided her mission. Just behind the stables, they entered the woods. The paths were well known to Mathieu, and they needed to go by foot to the nearest village, where a small but ample payment had bought them the use of an older, dependable horse, along with the sworn silence of its owner. God's blessings would surely be needed from that point on, for they would have to hide by day and travel by night until they reached Dover. There, they would use even more of their precious gold reserve to buy passage aboard a cargo ship headed for Calais.

To France.

To home and freedom.

Mathieu and Gabrielle LeVasseur-Dauvet prayed that they would be long and irretrievably gone by the time the revered painting's loss was discovered. And indeed, they were, well on their way to Dover, cowering in barns during daylight and traveling rutted roads in the waxing light of the late spring moon.

Chapter Seventeen

EARLY DECEMBER 2016

WESTMINSTER, LONDON

The magnificent, looming towers of Westminster Abbey fell into the distance as I strode with great purpose, headed north on the road of Whitehall. My map told me I would pass the Banqueting House just before arrival at the Ministry of Defense building.

Once there, I hoped I could talk my way in for a little tour. I turned back to peek at the venerable Abbey again. I was yearning to go in there. I'd never been. Surprising, since my mom and dad had lived in London. But somehow, our overseas family trips had most often been to the Continent: Rome, Florence, Milan, and Paris. Oh, how my mother loved Paris.

But Westminster Abbey! Such history! And I so wished I could dive into it. I knew there was a brilliant collection of illuminated manuscripts housed within; and just to tour the gravesites of so many people who drastically changed the course of history… Maybe later I would be able to squeeze in a quick visit. But I was only here in London for a day and a half. In fact, I had to get back because no one knew I'd left Rome. Maybe that wasn't the smartest move; I realized that I should have told someone where I was—but all I could think about was trying to gain entry into any remaining structure of Henry

VIII's immense palace, Whitehall. Even a sniff of the painting's past was worth pursuing. My confidence had been restored after finding the jaw-dropping entry by William Weston and I was eager to see what I could find out, so I hurried along.

Once I'd determined to come to London, I thought briefly about asking Lina to join me, but decided against it. I knew I could trust her for secrecy, but I hadn't yet shared all of the information about my search. And she was busy working on a massive paper. I had no time to lose, I wanted to see what I could dig up. I booked my flight, and spent the rest of the afternoon reading about the palatial estate once renovated and occupied by Henry VIII—along with his wife and queen, Anne Boleyn.

York Place had been the city property of the fabulously wealthy Cardinal Wolsey, Lord High Chancellor to the King. But when he was unable to achieve the annulment Henry demanded, Wolsey was banished from court. Upon Wolsey's demise, Henry and Anne were thrilled to assume ownership, and immediately employed top architects, builders, and craftsmen of the day to completely refurbish the residence. Henry loved it because not only was it centrally located within London, but he delighted in fashioning it as a pleasure palace, featuring every recreational sport available. Anne loved it equally. It was her palace; not her predecessor's, Katharine of Aragon's. Anne and Henry were married there, in one of the towers, and years later, Henry died at Whitehall. In other words, in my estimation, there were lots of reasons why a painting so critical to the king's mission should have been at that very palace on display, perhaps even hidden there for future generations to see.

There was one huge problem: almost all of the palace had burned down in a great fire in 1698. Most of the buildings which comprised the estate were destroyed. The rest, damaged, were taken down. Reading this, I became distraught. It seemed highly probable that if the painting had remained in Whitehall it was lost in that very fire.

But a slim hope remained. Somehow, the extensive wine cellars which had been built by Wolsey, and then used by Henry VIII, had escaped fire. It was in these cellars that both Wolsey and the king had stored their most expensive, coveted vintages—including, I read, the first shipments of champagne to be exported to England.

I reasoned, if there had been a fire, and there were irreplaceable items which needed a rush to safety, why not in a cellar? After all, it did escape the all-consuming flames. With that knowledge, I wanted to have a look around. Not an easy feat, because tours are rare; almost non-existent. I'd placed a call in to the switchboard as soon as I arrived in the Heathrow Airport, and spoke with a nice lady who told me she wasn't sure if a tour could be arranged, but I jumped in and said, "Oh, you have no idea how I would appreciate your help. I'm working on my Ph.D. and just a glimpse of the former building from the Tudor era would be enormously important."

"Well, come over this afternoon, Miss. Bring all of your ID with you. It's a long shot but maybe you will have some luck."

"Thank you!" I almost shouted. I was pretty excited, and grabbed my bag and ran out to clamber into a cab to take me to the Westminster area of the city.

I walked up to the gates of the ministry building and told the guards I had a previously arranged appointment. A phone call and a check of my ID allowed me to enter the white marble lobby. I reported to the receptionist, telling her that I hoped to have a quick tour of the wine cellars, to complete some research for my Ph.D. She looked doubtful, so I pulled out my Sapienza student ID card to try and convince her, sliding it under the glass so she could take a look. When she began to shake her head, I jumped in: "Truly, Ma'am, I would not need to be there for long. Is there anyone at all here who might allow me to have a peek?"

A deep voice behind me said, "Did I hear you want to see the Tudor wine cellar? For research?"

I whirled about to be greeted by a pleasant-looking officer. "Yes, that's right, sir, and I've come in from Rome just hoping to see them."

"I'm Major Sam Cooper." He extended his hand.

I shook it, looking hopefully at him. "How nice to meet you. I'm Zara Rossi, a student at La Sapienza university in Rome. I'm working on my Ph.D. in history, and a glimpse at the cellars, since they are what remains of the old Palace, would be so helpful."

"I see. Well, I'll be honest with you. I've never seen them, and I'd like to. So, I will escort you."

I was almost overcome with joy but pulled myself together as we stepped into a nearby office and Major Cooper processed a temporary security badge for me.

And then, we were off.

We passed through an airlock, and as we made our way through back corridors and a staircase or two, all descending, the Major told me about how the entire cellar had to be moved intact by encasing it in a vault. "Can you believe this thing remained all those years and no one knew about it until the new ministry building was renovated in the 1930s?"

"It's just incredible," I said as we came to the exterior of the vault. "Five hundred years old. I wonder if there are any bottles of wine still hidden in the walls?"

Major Cooper chuckled, and opened the door, switching on the lights. I stood in awe as the room revealed itself: whitewashed brick with a gorgeous vaulted ceiling, gothic style ribs of stone holding up the interior. Around the circumference was a stone track: a watercourse which would have kept the air sufficiently humid and the temperature cool. It was a sophisticated cellar, and in its day it protected a valuable commodity. We both wandered about, enjoying the aura of a Tudor king who well knew how to live.

But I didn't see any place where other treasures might have been stored. "Major, are you aware, if when this room was moved, were there any access points attached to it? Any hallways, or ante-rooms perhaps?"

"I can't say that I know for certain. It was back in the thirties. But there is a tale that when it was encased to stabilize it, there was a storage room which had mostly crumbled, and a bunch of artefacts were found in there. Some of them quite collectible, so the story goes. But what happened to them, I have no idea."

"Would you know if there was any artwork? Paintings, perhaps?"

"Gosh, I have no idea. But I did hear there were some very interesting things."

I could feel my hope dissipate. How would we ever know if one of those interesting artefacts was a painting of the king and queen? "So, where do you think those items went, Major?"

He chortled, "Hah! They probably ended up in the stately homes of members of the House of Lords, if I were to guess. But there's nothing remaining." He took a last look around and muttered, "I have to get myself invited to one of the parties they have down here..." And he allowed me to step out first, closing and locking the door behind us.

Back in reception, I thanked Major Cooper gratefully, returned my badge and went back onto the bustling street. Wandering along till I found a pub, I popped in, sat in a tiny corner booth and ordered a pint. It was disappointing, sure. But I didn't really think I would find the painting there, anyway. I had at the least hoped for a hint, and that much I did gain, even though it wasn't a promising one. Maybe the portrait was, in fact, in the attic of one of the massive stately old homes somewhere in England. That, I reflected, would make things really difficult.

But not impossible. There wasn't a riddle or a puzzle I couldn't solve.

I can do this, I thought.

I'm a Rossi.

Chapter Eighteen

JUNE 1534

THE KING'S PRIVY CHAMBER
WHITEHALL PALACE

"Beloved God *ALMIGHTY*!"

A howl pierced the discreet hush of the King's private chambers late in the morning. Sir Henry Norris leaped to his feet, all but strangling on the piece of buttered bread he'd just popped into his mouth and bolted frantically for the royal closet where he feared his monarch had been taken with some kind of fit.

At first glance, Henry VIII of England on his knees, broad back to the doorway, appeared to Norris as if the King was at prayer—perhaps overcome with religious fervor. Then he noticed the shoulders trembling, and a clenched hand laden with bejeweled rings thudded heavily to the floor for support. Norris tore his stare from the disturbing scene and scanned the room for the source of Henry Tudor's distress. There! In a window embrasure, a blue velvet drape which just the previous evening had completely concealed the King's pride and joy had been ripped aside. While, behind it, stood... nothing. Naught but thin air. Witnessing the gaping space felt obscene somehow, like peering at someone unclothed without their permission. With effort, the chief groom dragged ashen-faced Henry to his feet.

"Your Grace, sit here." He guided him to a chair and quickly poured a measure of ale. "Drink. It will fortify you."

Obediently, the king gulped the brew, gripped Norris's arm like a vise, and choked, "What's happened? How?! How could it be missing?"

Young Lord Norris's jaw clenched and unclenched as he worked to control rising panic over what they'd just discovered. "God's eyes… I tell you I know not, Your Grace. In my wildest imagining I could never have foreseen this!"

"Call for Cromwell. Now! We must see Cromwell. Immediately!" His bark was sharp, hoarse.

Norris left the King alone for a few anxious moments, ran to find a page to beckon Cromwell to the inner chamber with the greatest urgency, and returned swiftly to sit with His Majesty while Henry slowly regained some color.

Secretary Cromwell had fortuitously been meeting other councilors nearby. His face a grimace of dismay at the desperate summons, he hastened into the room to see the King hunched over a table. The statesman's eye quickly traveled to the void at which point even he, a steadfastly unflappable lawyer, could barely stifle a gasp. "Your Majesty, how dreadful! God knows my distress must be nothing in comparison to yours…" Cromwell's voice trailed off as the King lowered his head to his hands and morosely began to knead his temples.

Only after some minutes did Henry look up, eyes bloodshot with barely controlled rage. "Thomas! How did this vile theft occur? Only a few knew of it! Who betrayed me like this?!" His menacing glare slid from Cromwell to Norris. Both courtiers chose to remain silent, gazes averted.

The King's mood shifted to anguish. "If only I hadn't stubbornly insisted it remain here. My treasure! If I'd stored it in the Jewel House as I knew I should, it might still be in my possession."

His groan was pitiable: a rare self-recrimination. "I am heartsick. It was so very beautiful. And it meant so much. Its message. Its meaning and purpose..."

Norris jumped as Henry's mighty fist slammed to the table. "I should have attended to my instincts! Its time was not yet at hand, but I had to have it near to me. And now it's too late for this—this miracle—which can never be replicated. I swear by God's holy blood, I will avenge this affront!"

The Secretary allowed his King to lament a few minutes more, then urged, "Sire, we must act quickly. Establish the identity of those who may have committed the heinous crime and make plans—if there is any chance at all it might be restored. Time is of the essence."

"Yes, yes—of course, Thomas, you are correct. I last saw it early yesterday morning, before I went to Mass. Afterward, I held meetings and dined, then went out hunting until almost dark. When I returned, I did not enter this room—I played cards with Heneage and Weston in my bedchamber, then retired early. Only this morning, seeking documents for the day, did I enter. I had to have another look, so I pulled back the drape. Never would I have expected what confronted me! Someone—a vicious criminal, a traitor, crept in here between the mornings last and today. But who, though? Surely it cannot be one from my closest circle, my most loyal and beloved friends. A spy, then! A Moor! A papist dog?! But among those contemptible blackguards, who could have gained access to these secured rooms?"

Cromwell measured his response carefully. "You haven't revealed your plan to anyone other than a few from your Privy Council, Majesty. Therefore, only they know of its significance—so, somehow, news must have been leaked. It appears likely that the traitor is a zealot. Perhaps a conspirator paid someone to sneak in here yesterday whilst you and your attendants were otherwise engaged..."

Henry's growl was menacing. "I'll have every godforsaken cart leaving London ripped to pieces. We will interrogate every individual—man, woman, or child—until the felon is discovered and exposed. And then…woe to whomever that may be! He—or she—will plead for death, but it won't come until I've wrested my entire revenge."

Cromwell waited until the King had finished his tirade. Then he ventured, "With great respect, Sire, I advise you to do nothing of the sort. It will but fuel the fire of rebellion against your mission. We must first lull the villain into complacency while meticulously investigating those who have had access to your quarters. They will be easy to enumerate, so we can surely determine who committed this atrocity. I will call for an immediate inventory of visitors permitted beyond the Watching Chamber over the last several weeks. We shall establish a list of names and discreetly probe. I'm confident we will find the man who was brazen enough—and senseless enough—to defy the King, as well as the command of God Himself."

Henry was silent for a moment before heaving a wretched sigh. "As you suggest, Cromwell. You tender, as ever, wise counsel. Commence your investigation with all speed. As for my holy mission, without doubt, this has dealt a heavy blow. I will pray ceaselessly, though, and know that my prayer will be answered. God's sacred purpose will be achieved. He is sure to show me a way forward so long as I place all my trust in Him."

"Indeed, Your Majesty, His light will guide you. That is certain."

Momentarily calmed by such reassurance from his closest and most trusted advisor, Henry strove to gather himself and recalibrate his thinking. Ever confident of his own invincible power, he left it to others with the command to search for the painting and the perpetrator.

Discovery of the painting's theft surely caused great tumult within Henry's innermost circle. The King was beside himself with despair over the loss of something which could never be replicated. The Queen, too, was bereft, knowing what a blow this had dealt her husband and the strategy to achieve his great and holy purpose. She sorrowed over the loss of such a resplendent depiction of her, *enceinte*, carrying what was most certainly the male heir to the Tudor dynasty.

And, as they had promised to the distraught King, Thomas Cromwell and the Palace's Lord Chamberlain Sandys amassed a roster of the names of every individual who might have crossed the threshold from the King's Watching Chamber into his private apartments. The list was not long; it included the King's closest councillors, the Archbishop of Canterbury, Sir William Weston, the Lord Chamberlain and the two trusted ushers who delivered supplies and served meals in the apartments. Each individual was brought before Cromwell and thoroughly interrogated. In the end, though, the internal probe didn't produce any likely suspects. Instead, the King dispatched a small, trusted army of knights to search far and wide, across every conceivable land, with the instruction to recover the painting and wreak a painful death upon the criminal responsible for its theft.

Before they finalized their search of the people who had been in residence at the time of the burglary, Cromwell and William Sandys did one last run-through. With lists and reports spread before them on the desk, they conferred and checked off name by name. As the last inked signature was ticked, the Lord Secretary sat back, exhausted. "Well, it looks like this ends it, William. For the life of me, I cannot think of a soul who might have had the lunacy to break in here and steal something so cherished by His Majesty. Whomever it was must be crazy. By God, they had better pray they are never found, because he will cast the hounds of hell on them." Both men sat in thought, then Sandys piped up. "Do you think it could possibly be one of the people who cleans the rooms? Who is that, anyway? Who does these apartments?"

Cromwell scowled, shook his head and said, "What? That's preposterous. I actually have no idea who does the cleaning. There's one girl I've seen and she is so timid and so tiny that she can hardly lug her scullery basket to and fro. Never her. I think it was a spy... one of the slithery serpents who manage to sneak in on occasion. And for that matter, we'd best be more careful about hindering those trespassers. Otherwise, we could ultimately be blamed. And wouldn't that just be the height of irony."

"Indeed," said Sandys.

They gathered their papers and records and left the chamber, headed to dinner.

Chapter Nineteen

DECEMBER 2016

ROME

The insistent knocking turned to a hammering of the heavy brass knocker on the estate's oak door. It wouldn't cease, and from my nook in an upstairs chamber, I waited for one of the house staff to respond and answer it. The knocking became ever more forceful. I was thoroughly annoyed, because I had just reached the most beautiful passage in the book I was reading, *Le Roman de la Rose*. I'd been inspecting the gorgeous illuminations, especially the one of the two lovers in the book's dream sequence, standing next to one another, holding hands. I placed a ribbon to mark my page and reluctantly closed the book. The knocking hadn't ceased so I would have to answer it myself. Holding my skirts aloft, I descended the stone staircase, crossing the great hall to the door. Without a servant in sight, I opened the door to greet an unfamiliar young woman in maid's attire. What on earth could she want, and why was she knocking at our chateau door?

"Bonjour Madame," she said as she curtsied to me. "J'ai un message urgent pour vous."

An urgent message? For me? I was startled by her fervent expression. But before I could reply…

...MY EYES BLINKED OPEN. The previously bright afternoon light which usually flooded my bedroom had faded to the point of near-darkness. I was confused. The knocking continued. I jumped up in complete disorientation, and went to my apartment door to open it a crack. There was Lina, face full of concern.

"Zara! What are you doing? We are supposed to meet Antonio and my friend Giancarlo. Like twenty minutes ago! Do you remember?"

I still felt like I was in the dream I'd just had. I guessed I'd laid on my bed for a quick rest in the afternoon and had fallen into a deep sleep.

"Oh, Lina! I'm so sorry!" I shook my head trying to clear it of the images which were still vivid. "Come in. Just have a seat and let me get myself together. Can you call to tell them we'll be late but will still meet them?"

"Sure, I can do that. What happened? It's dark in here! You look like you had some kind of nightmare! Were you sleeping?"

I switched on a few lights and stepped into the bathroom to splash cold water on my face and run a brush through my hair. "I fell asleep, yes. And I had the weirdest dream. I still feel like I am there."

"Where? You are where?"

"In an estate. In France. A very old estate. Reading a medieval manuscript, a poem about a dream... the poem's dream was about romantic love. I was the mistress of the chateau... And someone—it must have been your knocking—was at the door. None of the servants answered it, so I had to stop reading the book and when I opened the door, a young maid was there to tell me she had an urgent message. But, before she could tell me, I woke up. It was incredibly strange!"

"Wow, Zar. That's a crazy one! But sometimes those afternoon sleeps make weird dreams."

"Yeah, they do. But somehow, it seemed more than that. I'm not sure. I gotta say, it's left me with a creepy feeling. Like...I don't know...Do you think it could have been some kind of sign?"

"Sign? Like a prophecy?" Lina grimaced. "I hope not. I find those things scary. I like the real world. The here and now, you know? Come on, let's go before they get tired of waiting for us and leave the bar." She hustled me out the door, and we went down into the street.

But I couldn't get the maid's face out of my mind. And I couldn't help but wonder what urgent message she'd had for me.

Chapter Twenty

OCTOBER 1534

CHÂTEAU DE ROUEN
ROUEN, FRANCE

On a gorgeous autumn morning, Gabrielle contentedly lingered before an open window in the estate office of the Vasseur château, smiling to herself as she looked out across the hills rolling down and away from the house. She had always loved this time of year—the beautiful russets and golds of the beech trees as they prepared for winter, the waving pale yellow feathers of tall grasses, the freshness to the air, and warming fires: it felt like home. And home it was.

Although there'd been days and especially nights when fear had all but consumed her, she and Mathieu had somehow managed to reach Dover undetected. There, using their wits and some of the precious gold to barter, they'd slipped aboard a ship which was to sail the spice route ultimately destined for India. They crossed the Channel, and landing in Calais, resumed travel on foot, hugging the coast traveling through the westernmost region of Flanders into France. All the while, they never let the sack which held the secret out of their sight. When they slept, it lay next to Mathieu, his knife always within reach. At the port of Honfleur, they picked up a barge which glided southeast on the Seine following its curves and bends, until finally into view came the beloved spires of Rouen Cathedral. Gabrielle wept tears of joy while Mathieu roughly brushed his arm across his face to hide his own emotion, and the rugged bargeman who had allowed them to ride with him wondered about the young woman with the tattered, poor gown and cloak, yet spoke like a lady, and her commoner husband.

The couple had spent many anxious hours discussing their plan for a return home. Gabrielle was ready to throw herself at the mercy of her father, beg him to allow them to stay, and offer to do menial work in exchange for shelter and board. She had no intentions of asking her father to allow her to resume the life of privilege she had once known.

Their destination was at hand. Gabrielle could do little about improving her appearance: her clothing torn and dirty, Mathieu's not one rag better. But she stopped at a stream along their final walk before passing through the gatehouse of the manor to wash her face and arrange her hair as best she could. Heart in her mouth, she glanced tremulously at her equally tense husband as she raised the heavy knocker of the door and let it fall with a thud. The big, familiar portal swung open and after a moment of confusion, Etienne, who had been the household's head steward since Gabrielle had been a child, cried out in recognition.

"Madame! Oh, Madame, entres vous, s'il vous plait! What a shock it is to see you, but how wonderful! Come—be seated. Please, please wait but a moment and I will beckon your brother."

Hesitantly, Gabrielle and Mathieu entered the main salon where she lowered herself into an ornate, upholstered chair, thinking how bizarre it was to feel uncomfortable in a room she'd known so well, her ragged gown an ironic contradiction to its tasteful appointments. As a former, lowly-ranked servant, Mathieu could not bring himself to sit. Instead, he paced anxiously, wishing only that he could blend into the surrounding woodwork.

Footfalls on the polished floor preceded the arrival of her brother, Jean-Jacques, a year and a half older than Gabrielle and the sibling whom she had loved most and with whom she'd shared so many adventures as a child. She had missed him terribly on that night when she and Mathieu had been banished from her home; he had not even been summoned so they could say their goodbyes. She'd left the house never to see him again—not until the present moment, as they stood face to face. It took him but a flash before he'd gathered her in his arms and held her.

Voice thick with emotion, he cried, "Gabbie? My Gabbie—I never thought I would see you again! Truly, I thought you might be dead! Where have you been these years… and what has happened to you … and Mathieu—always my favorite stable hand?"

"My husband now, Jean," Gabrielle corrected firmly.

"Your husband?" The look of bewilderment on her brother's hand-some, bearded face told Gabrielle all she needed to know. That her parents never conveyed to her brother what had happened that night. And the realization made her even sadder, thinking he'd believed she had wilfully abandoned her family.

"It's a long story, sweet brother. I would hope to tell you all of it, every bit—but first I must ask: may we stay here? I am prepared to tell Father that Mathieu and I are very willing to perform any service needed—we can clean, take care of the horses, help in the kitchen… anything. But, of course, I do not expect him to accept me back as his daughter, a lady of the manor, and understand his unwillingness to do so. But we need a place to stay—to live, and we will be ever grateful if he would permit us to remain, albeit as simple servants of the household."

"Oh, Gabbie… our father died three years ago. He came down with a fever and was gone in a matter of days. And then Mother…" Jean's voice cracked. "… our dear mother left us a mere six months later. So now only I reside here along with my wife Marie and our son, Jacques—we are the owners and caretakers of Château de Rouen."

Gabby's breath caught in her throat. Both her parents gone? "And Julien?" Gabrielle asked, dreading the answer.

"Our younger brother Julien entered the clergy and lives at the monastery of Saint-Denis. He is very happy there, he tells us. So, beloved sister—" He turned to Mathieu. "—and my brother by marriage, you are both most welcome here and, of course, you must stay. This is your home, Gabbie, and it will remain your home for as long as you live, or for as long as you wish to stay."

He rubbed his hands briskly then. "I will be interested to hear your tales, and we will do that when we have supper this evening. You must be starving so we will sup early. But now, first things first: we must have you both clean and dressed. We shall do our best to restore you to at least a semblance of prosperity before the evening's meal—although I must say it seems we'll have our work cut out for us, eh?"

And with a wink, he summoned a maid for Gabrielle and a valet for Mathieu—who felt exceedingly uncomfortable at the prospect but who obediently followed the young man to the private chambers to be dressed, pampered, and preened as a gentleman for the first time in his life.

That night, before a crackling fire, fresh from a scented bath and wearing a lovely damask gown loaned by her new sister-in-law, Marie, Gabrielle sorrowed for the loss of her mother and her father. As she looked around her, though, she was almost overcome with gratitude and joy. Her good fortune in being able to return home and take up her rightful place was not lost on her as she fondly gazed at her husband, seated next to her. He'd never looked so handsome, in an embroidered shirt and soft lambskin jerkin, beard trimmed and groomed, velvet hat in place. It amused Gabrielle that Mathieu appeared as if he'd been born to wear such luxuriant fashions despite his resistance to the initial idea. Barely able to contain their hunger, they eagerly consumed a supper of roast veal, boiled carrots with a sweet glaze, stewed leeks and mashed turnips. It had been years since Gabrielle had tasted wine of the quality her brother's cellars contained—Mathieu had never been so indulged.

Once the meal was complete, and a compote of fruit in sugar and cream served, Gabrielle began to narrate, with Mathieu's occasional interjections, their time working for the court of Henry VIII, a drudgery never eased by their having had to move from palace to palace depending on the King's whim and the season.

"I can see that the work must have been hard, sister," Marie empathized, her eyes fixed on Gabrielle's hands, still red and rough as any scullery girl's.

"It was that. But at least we had a roof over our heads, food in our bellies, and a warm place to sleep at night. And the best part— we were able to attend Mass almost every day. There were a goodly number of deeply devout Catholics in our midst, which gave us comfort, although, particularly in the last year, there's been increasingly strident talk about reforming the Church. There are those who insist that change must happen and happen soon. I do not agree; both Mathieu and I feel that the Holy Church has served the faithful well for over a thousand years, therefore, why should it require change, Marie? It is God's Church; it is in place to give Him glory and to challenge that would be a sacrilege. Do you not agree, Jean?"

"I do. Of course, the reformers have been busily at work here for some time as well. But as yet they haven't gained sufficient hold to upset the balance of Catholics who will stay true and loyal to the pope and to the Church in Rome. And I—we—are among those."

Gabrielle described how the Chamberlain had eventually selected her to clean the new apartments King Henry had renovated for himself and his Queen, Anne Boleyn.

"That must have been a daunting responsibility, Gabbie! To have access to the English King's most personal space and to be entrusted with the care of his belongings. I have heard that he is a man of leonine proportions and character, and that his new wife and Queen, the Lady Boleyn, was in our Queen Claude's court for some years—not too long ago. Curiously, Henry has always been either a great friend or just as often a bitter enemy of our own King, François." Jean's voice lowered as if fearful of being overheard, even by his closest staff. "Pray tell, what did you see in those, his most secret spaces?"

Gabrielle hesitated. She placed her hand gently atop Mathieu's arm, looking at him with love and the closeness built from their mutual commitment and endurance. In the flickering candlelight, she saw him nod assent.

"Mon frère, we have something of grave import to tell you…"

Chapter Twenty-one

MID-DECEMBER 2016

ROME

I should have been working on my thesis proposal. But instead, there I was, curled up on the couch in my flat, MacBook on my lap, scanning websites and reading about the drama of Henry VIII, his doomed queen Anne Boleyn, and their Lord Prior of the Order of St. John, William Weston. Oh, and the pope. The bishops of Rome of that day lived anything but boringly pious lives, it seemed.

From his journal, it had been revealed that Weston had informed Grand Master Philippe Villiers de l'Isle-Adam of news about the sinister painting, which threatened the wellbeing of Pope Clement VII, and the Roman Church.

And I also knew, with evidence I'd uncovered in the Vatican Archives, that L'Isle-Adam had conveyed the danger to the pope. At least, he had written a note. Whether or not the pope saw it, I could not be sure. Spies and secret operatives were the order of the day, and it may have well been purloined and had somehow made its way into the back of the volume I studied.

Biographical data relayed that a previously healthy Grand Master L'Isle-Adam died in Malta on August 21, 1534, mere weeks after the date of the note he wrote to the pope. Was it a suspicious death? Might someone have seen his communiqué and poisoned him? It was possible, certainly.

Then, in what seemed like an unusual confluence of events, Pope Clement VII died precisely 36 days after his devoted servant, L'Isle-Adam. What theater! This was the stuff movies were made of!

And to add an even more tragic element to the saga, Queen Anne suffered her first miscarriage just months after someone told Weston about the painting. A year and a half later, she had a second, heart-breaking failed pregnancy. By that time, her queenship was virtually over, because Henry imprisoned her after she was falsely accused of infidelity. Somehow, the wife he had desperately sought—the one he'd insisted be included in the painting which would reveal his mission—was brutally put to death at his command.

I stared at the portraits of her (none of them painted from life, but beautiful and moving, all the same) and felt a heaviness in my heart. She must have been so strong, so brave. And I very much believed she had loved her husband, the King. Might her death have been punishment for overstepping her bounds? I'd read how she spoke out vehemently for the causes she believed in: certainly not the accepted role of a woman, even a queen, in that day and time. I became quite emotional at the thought, and couldn't help but wonder if things had substantially changed for women, five hundred years on.

I continued to read. After Anne's death, Henry and Cromwell plundered and dissolved the Catholic monasteries in England, using the bounty to bolster the coffers of the Crown. It seemed that the Order of St. John was no exception. On the 7th of May in 1540, the royal mandate arrived: terminate England's Priory and its Order, with immediate effect. Upon hearing the command, Weston collapsed.

He perished that very day.

I closed the lid of my computer and sat there for a while, feeling strangely linked, somehow, to these people who had been so devoted to their causes, their beliefs. But unlike me, they all seemed to know who they were. It sure seemed as if they all understood their precise mission in life. I, on the other hand, struggled every single day with that dilemma. One thing, though, I did have in common with these extraordinary characters of the past.

Yes. At the core of it all: the painting. It held an exceptional lure.

Chapter Twenty-two

DECEMBER 1558

FORT SANT ANGELO
ISLAND OF MALTA

C rimson wax dripped soundlessly onto a leaf of vellum. Quickly, an assistant pressed a gold stamp engraved with the eight-pointed cross into the wax: the symbol of the Order of Malta. The scarlet seal was positioned at the top of a sizable document. Emanating from the cross were rays, gorgeously leafed in gold. Beneath the entire device were inscribed the words: *Ordre Souverain de Malte.* To the bottom of the page, the Grand Master added his signature with a flourish: *Fra' Jean Parisot de Valette.*

Before allowing his secretaries to carry forth the proclamation, Valette scanned it once again. The decree was to be issued to the Grand Prior of each of the seven langues of the order: Provence, Auvergne, France, Italy, Aragon, England, and Germany. They, in turn, were commanded to disseminate the information contained therein to every Knight through ranks high and low.

Valette, a man of lifelong devotion to God and the Church, tall and handsome, even at 63 years of age, fluent in numerous languages, had committed himself to the pursuits of the Order. Having joined at twenty years old, he'd served under—and greatly admired—the legendary Philippe Villiers de l'Isle-Adam.

As if it were yesterday, Valette recalled an incident that had occurred over twenty years prior, one that shaped his life and career within the Order. On a blistering August afternoon of 1534, L'Isle-Adam, suffering the cruel pain induced by what his doctors were convinced was poisoning, and recognizing that his final hours were upon him, had summoned Valette. In a private audience, the dying Grand Master told the younger Knight he was certain Valette would one day be called upon to serve as leader of the noble Order.

"Jean Parisot," he rasped, "you will endure many trials. I foresee them as tests any lesser man would find impossible to face. But you, my son, have been gifted by God to rise and triumph. Therefore, I need to tell you something you must know. A watch you must keep, a task you must fulfill! It is of the utmost importance—" The old man choked, striving for breath. Valette grabbed a cloth, wrung it in cool water, and mopped the sickly pale brow, moving the strands of white hair away from his neck. Sweat bathed them both; the heat was stifling. Placing a chalice to the elder's lips, Vallette prayed the wine would revive L'Isle-Adam. He feared the man's final breath was imminent before he could know of the challenge he was to face.

With effort, Grand Master L'Isle-Adam gathered himself. "Jean, I have been informed of an immense threat which faces the Church— one which confronts the pope. It has the potential to make the peril posed by Suleiman minor by comparison." He paused to catch his breath, which came in shallow gasps. Valette helped him to sit up further, bolstering his back with pillows. This seemed to help, and the Grand Master continued.

"The King of England—Henry—has been at war with Clement for some time. He sought a divorce from his wife, Katherine, the Queen."

"Yes, Your Eminence. This I know. Henry is a man of my age. I am aware of his theological battles, waged across the academies of Europe, to win dominance over the pope. He has, as is right and just, been unsuccessful. Our pope has remained steadfast."

"Indeed, he has. But not without resulting detriment. Henry is not a man to be trifled with. He is mighty—and determined. There are spies dedicated to the Church and faith who have been told that the English King intends to strike at the Church of Rome—to overthrow the pope—and to assume a place he believes has been ordained for him and him alone: the founder of a new Church, rising on the ashes of the old. Our beloved Church, which St. Peter established follow-ing the word of Jesus Christ! Henry represents himself as the new St. Peter for the ages to come."

Blood had rushed to Valette's face. Raw anger swelled within him, and he strained to remain in control. "My dear Eminence, how do you know of this? It's incomprehensible. A travesty!" He waited while L'Isle-Adam drew enough strength to continue.

"I am told of a painting which the King had commissioned. Its rendering tells the entire story, depicting Henry as the new King of Israel, St. Peter of the coming day. He stands triumphant upon the papal tiara, crushed beneath his feet. The painting is rife with sym-bolism, all pointing to his intention to vanquish the papacy and take over the Church, establishing his own Church. This painting exists, and he will use it to recruit his army and attack."

Vallette's head swam with the enormity of the report. It seemed incomprehensible—yet he knew Henry to be a man of incredible arrogance and resolve. The information must not be doubted.

In a feeble voice, L'Isle-Adam struggled to continue. "Jean, I have informed Pope Clement of the threat, though I hesitated to pro-vide too much information in a letter. I am uncertain whether it ever reached His Holiness. If it was intercepted it surely may have been the cause of my life's end. I'm soon to leave this world and know not who will succeed me. There are but few candidates I trust. Therefore, I leave this instruction with you—you, who will see it through, no matter the price you may have to pay. I believe in you, Jean Parisot de Valette." He raised his bony hand and shook his finger toward the sky. "Seek and find this blasphemy! Deliver it to the Vatican so the pope and his curia can conquer the usurper and restore the people's hearts to the One True Faith. Do not let Henry succeed! Find this symbol and show him it is a desecration of God's divine presence on earth! Do not fail me, my son."

His arm dropped weakly, as his time grew short with the rattle of death evident in every gasp, so Jean made the esteemed warrior as comfortable as he was able, called the aides who were caring for him, and turned to depart. With tears stinging his eyes, he gently placed his palm on the old man's forehead, saying, "I promise you, Eminence, that you have left your news in good hands. Pray for me, and I will do the same for you. Good-bye and God speed."

IN 1557, AFTER A long and dedicated career to the mission of the Order of St. John, Jean Parisot de Valette was elevated to Grand Master. As one of his very first acts, he diligently engaged contacts he knew who might be able to trace the whereabouts of the mysterious, threatening painting. He paid for spies to infiltrate the King's court, listening for talk that might imply an army was being raised to march on Rome. Stealthily, he observed the movements of Henry VIII of England: the religious monasteries he ruthlessly tore apart plundering gold, statuary, monies, and lands owned by the Church for his use. Nothing his spies uncovered, though, led him to believe that Henry was amassing an army to wage war with Rome. However, Valette was well aware of the theologian Martin Luther and the potent sweep of religious reform gaining hold in England and Europe. And although the Roman Church remained strong, Valette never lost sight of the possibility that someday, Henry might resume his aim to conquer the pope and the Holy See. When the King died in 1547 and the battle between the Reformed religion and the Catholic faction reached a fever pitch, Jean Parisot renewed his efforts to locate the painting.

A few years after he had assumed the role of Grand Master, a paid informer appeared before him to report that it had long ago been stolen, and no one knew of its location, or for that matter, anything about the identity of the thief. The informer added, though, a rumor from an anonymous source which alleged that it had been smuggled into France. Always conscious of the promise he made to L'Isle -Adam, Jean refocused his efforts within his home country, fanning out spies far and wide. All of those inquiries proved fruitless.

The written proclamation Vallette issued to each of his Grand Priors, then, promised any Knight who might discover the painting and return it to him would receive the most coveted of plenary indulgences, absolution of all sins: a direct path to heaven to sit in glory with God and Jesus Christ.

Thus was the message broadcast to the world of the Order of the Knights of St. John of Jerusalem. It spread like a blistering fire. A mission to find the lost painting ignited a passion within the Knights' idealistic souls, and the portrait's legend was born, one which persisted through the ages.

Chapter Twenty-three

APRIL 1575

CHÂTEAU DE ROUEN

G abrielle knew she was dying. But her pain was not severe, and in truth, she was content.

With a flourish of the feathered quill, she signed the document and shook a measure of ponce on the vellum to blot the ink. Satisfied, she reviewed the final product.

It was her last will and testament.

At 58 years of age, she had outlived her brother Jean-Jacques, his son Jacques, her monastic younger brother, Julien, and most sorrowfully, her beloved husband, Mathieu. Only Jean's wife Marie survived to keep her company on this earth—and bounteous God be praised—Gabrielle and Mathieu's son, Alixandre.

Stiffly and with visible discomfort, Gabrielle hobbled from the desk to a padded chair by the library window. How good it was to have lived these forty-some years in her family's ancestral home, which remained as comfortable today as it always had been. Having been ably managed by Jean-Jacques until his passing, the estate was now the responsibility of Alixandre. He'd become the owner of Château de Rouen upon the early death of his cousin, Jacques the younger, who, but for a most dreadful riding accident, would have inherited all by virtue of primogeniture.

Oh, how proud Gabrielle was of Alixandre and how blessed she and Mathieu had been to have such a son! He had been born on her thirtieth birthday, past the time when she or her husband thought she would ever conceive again. And to add to their joy, he had proved an intelligent and respectful young man in every way. It was reassuring to know that as she prepared to depart this world, she and Mathieu would leave their mark in the person of Alixandre LeVasseur. Mathieu had generously endorsed his son's taking of his wife's family name, knowing it would allow Alixandre and his heirs great benefit. As indeed it had, for not only was Alixandre an exceedingly wealthy landowner but he had been elected a member of an esteemed Order: one which was held in high regard by not only the nobility of France but its King, Henri III.

Nothing was to bring Gabrielle greater happiness as her days dwindled. At just twenty years of age, her son had been appointed a Knight of St. John of Jerusalem, an order reserved for only the most devout, courageous, and well-born among men. His dedicated service to the Order would allow him, in turn, to secure a place for his sons and their sons. In this way, the family Vasseur would take their long-term position in the standing of an ancient, highly respected assembly dedicated to serving the pope and the Church.

The will would be witnessed, stamped, and sealed, then placed in the family vault where other essential papers were kept. To accompany it, she had completed a critical codicil. This document repeated those precise instructions which she had already imparted to Alixandre. It described Gabrielle's wish to hide and protect something which she had carefully safeguarded for many year: a painting, the work of the late master Holbein, commissioned and owned by the former King of England, Henry VIII.

Once she and Mathieu had revealed the story of its discovery to Jean-Jacques, the canvas had been carefully wrapped in layers of cloth and leather to preserve it. Immediately thereafter, they had it installed into a corner chamber excavated in the family crypt beneath the chapel of the château. Finally, the vault was blocked off by a wall of stone and mortar, never to be opened again.

Gabrielle LeVasseur died peacefully on a lovely day early in May. It was a contented death, as much as death could be. She'd shared her life with a man she had loved from girlhood, and together they had weathered rough times. But their dedication to one another and to the faith they shared had seen them through. And, in the end, they were rewarded with a life of comfort and the joy of a son. Gabrielle wouldn't have had things any other way.

She went to her God confident that not only had she lived a good life, but that she had followed His instruction and forever suppressed the emblem of heresy she had found.

Chapter Twenty-four

DECEMBER 2016

ROME

The sculpted faces scowled, tracking us with their unseeing eyes. We wandered through the Portrait Gallery of the Palazzo Massimo Museum, marble heads populating the room they now inhabited, quite a departure from their lavish homes of origin.

Lina and her new friend Giancarlo, Antonio, and I had visited the splendid museum that afternoon. We'd enjoyed ourselves poring over the antiquities, especially studying in amazement the mosaic art crafted by early Romans. Now we were headed to the café for a coffee before returning home for an evening of work and studies.

"I am always fascinated thinking about how those wealthy early Romans lived, aren't you?" Lina asked. "What I would give to have been able to wander through one of those immense villas, draped in a toga with a laurel wreath around my head! Especially the Villa di Livia... the garden frescoes were just bellisima!"

"It was surely an impressive place," Antonio added. "Livia Drusilla was quite a woman, it seems. She had two marriages to powerful and brutal men and became Empress Julia Augusta during a time of corruption, jealousy, and plenty of bloodshed. But she lived in one of the most beautiful houses in the countryside near

Rome. Apparently, the entire villa was frescoed and mosaicked, all by the top artisans of that era."

"Wow, I do wonder what it would have been like to be a woman with that much power. And money!" Lina sipped her coffee thoughtfully.

"Well—" Giancarlo looked at his new girlfriend with amused admiration. "—somehow I feel you would have slipped quite easily into the role of empress, Lina."

She gave him a nudge in the ribs with her elbow, then nestled a little closer.

"Zara, so… did you enjoy it? The museum?" Antonio prompted me. Momentarily startled, I realized I had no idea what they'd been talking about.

"Oh! Oh yes, of course! Sure, I did. Why?"

"No reason other than I'd hoped you had a good time. I love visiting museums in the winter. Too chilly to be out and about. Would any of you be interested in seeing the inside of Castel Sant'Angelo someday soon? It's connected to the Vatican, you know, by secret tunnels. I might be able to get us access to see the passageways."

"Sure, I've never been in there. How about you, Lina. Want to go?" Giancarlo was eager to cement this new relationship.

"Sí, sí. Absolutely! And Zara? How about you?" I looked up in time to see Lina giving me a slightly disapproving stare. She raised her groomed brows in question.

"Um, yes. Sure. I'd love to." I was pretty certain they'd asked me to go to another museum, but honestly, I was deeply entangled in thought, trying to figure out what my next step should be, searching for the portrait. And I was getting nowhere.

"Okay, then, let me see what I can arrange, and I'll let you know." Antonio stood to put on his coat and scarf. "I've got to run; I have a faculty meeting in an hour. Grazie á tutti for a great afternoon. Ciao Lina, Giancarlo." Then he turned his attention to me, giving me a hopeful, but uncertain smile. "Zara… I'll look forward to seeing you back at campus."

"Yes, of course, Antonio. I'll stop in to see you soon. And thank you—thanks again for this afternoon." I hoped I sounded warm and gracious, but I wasn't sure. I'd just been too preoccupied.

Once he'd departed, and Giancarlo had also slipped away to go to work, first giving Lina a charming kiss on the hand, she sat there shaking her head and contemplating me.

"What?" I said. "What's wrong?"

"Oh, cara mia. How can I even begin to tell you? You are so distracted! Your head is in—where do they say? Head in the sky! What, oh what, are you thinking about? What is so perplexing?"

I slumped lower into the booth. "Lina, I know. I know I was probably rude. Right? Was I? But I'm telling you, this mystery I am involved in… I just can't think of anything else! I am fixated on it. I'm sorry."

"No need to apologize to me, Zara. But, Antonio. He plainly tries hard to gain your attention. Not just your attention, but your admiration. Your *affetta*: affection. Don't you feel that for him? At all?"

"I think I do, Lina. At least, I might. I'm not sure, really."

"Oh boy! That's some confusion you've got there. Well, I hope you are able to figure it out. Because it's clear to me that he has feelings for you. And let me tell you, he is an exceptional man. I'm not sure he will remain interested forever if he doesn't get any tenderness in return." She gazed at me earnestly, her chin propped by a fist.

"Ohhh," I sighed heavily. "I don't know what to do about it. Before I can solve that riddle, I have to make headway with this other problem. Really, at the moment, there's room for nothing else."

"Well, Zara. I'll help you. You just need to share it with me. I'll help if I possibly can."

"Thanks, Lina. You are honestly the best. I'll, well, I'll let you know."

We pulled on our coats and went to catch a cab.

Chapter Twenty-five

LATE JULY 1715

THE PIRATE SLOOP *POSTILLON* OFF THE EASTERN COAST OF ISLE OF SANTA CRUZ CARIBBEAN SEA

Latitude 17°45' 11 / Longitude of Paris 67° 00' 15

At three bells in the middle watch, a mighty force hurled him from his berth. His head slammed into the bulkhead, and the crash of books, crockery, wine bottles, and guns hitting the deck was deafening. A keening wind sliced through the tiny porthole, and cold seawater rushed over his feet while he struggled to stand.

Over the wind's howl, La Buse could hear his crew shouting, "Mates! All hands to the sails!" Cursing, he hauled himself upright, grabbed a scrap of cloth to blot blood flowing from the gash in his forehead, and crawled toward the main deck. "Fils de putes!" How did those sons of whores not smell this storm coming? And why was he allowed to sleep until he was thrown from his bed? He should have been summoned at the earliest sign of it. His first mate and the bosun were going to pay for this mistake. Coming above, he was shocked to find they were struggling to stay afloat in a vicious sea, the sloop pitching savagely, rain driving in blinding sheets so dense that he could barely make out his crew.

Monstrous waves rocked *Postillon* so violently that the impact of another following sea would surely cause it to broach, and then they'd all be no more than ballast, capsized, and tossed overboard. Men crawled across the deck, desperately trying to stabilize the ship by hauling on the rigging to reduce the mainsail in the face of hurricane-fuelled winds. Stinging salt spray blinded La Buse, his commands blown away long before they could be heard. Buse grabbed a deckhand by the neck and bellowed into his face to find first mate Vane. The terrified boy squealed, "Oui, Capitaine!" and disappeared, slipping into the black of night.

Even the buccaneer ferocious enough to be infamously known as La Buse—The Buzzard—was suddenly overcome with fear as a wave arose and towered over the deck of the hundred-ton sloop, hovering as would a cutlass before the downward strike to smite a head from its shoulders. A second later, the sea cliff collapsed onto the foredeck with a deafening roar, instantly sweeping six men of her seventy crew into the roiling sea.

As *Postillon* yawed to recover from the wave's blow, out of the darkness loomed a specter—the new mate he'd just taken on.

"Vane!" he screamed. "Who can steer this slop pail? Put him at the helm NOW unless you want us all to dive to the devil!"

An ashen-faced First Mate Charles Vane scuttled off, hanging on to the railing for dear life. The captain shook his drenched head, muttering that he should never have taken the useless cur off the hands of the pirate Hornigold after that drunken bet in Nassau. The new mate had best do his job and rally his sailors or—if they didn't all perish first by swallowing seawater—he'd be neatly disposed of. Aye, any crewman lucky enough to remain alive after this forsaken night would watch as Vane danced the hempen jig over the water until the sharks circled before being dropped into the drink.

Buse clambered along the deck, shouting above the din to the deckhands who fought to regain control of the heaving vessel. "Strike the mains, Mister Boucher: we'll run before the wind on the storm gib! Haul it IN, man!"

Good God Almighty, had none of these imbeciles ever sailed through a storm before? Yet most of them had been at sea for years—and they looked it. Scarred, skin leathered and brown, but few teeth left in their heads. When it came to the moment, though, when seamanship was in dire need, there they were, scrabbling about like hens whose necks had been chopped in two.

The tempest raged on. Lines snapped, canvas whipped, sounding as if it would rip apart. The hull moaned and creaked under the strain. Explosions of thunder immediately overhead accompanied by slashes of lightning piercing the black sky were enough to stop a heart in mid-beat.

The following hours were brutal. The sloop climbed wave after immense wave. Men labored to keep the ship afloat even as the boom took charge and swung violently, exploding the skull of a young boy who had just joined the crew and catapulting two other sailors into the demonic night. The Buzzard had lived through many a savage storm, and this one was nothing to toy with. But with any luck, Postillon would withstand the storm and they—at least some of her crew—would see the dawn.

The captain left his men to battle the typhoon and lurched below deck to his quarters. Waves had breached the lower galley, and water sloshed across the deck. He ripped a leather cord from his neck, and with the brass key which hung from it, unlocked a deep, broad trunk lashed to the bulkhead near his bed. Lifting the lid, he heaved in relief that no damp had yet seeped into the chest. Anyway, some of what was locked inside could withstand a little seawater. Even in the dimness of a single lantern, the contents glimmered and winked at him. Spanish gold and plenty of it, round, perfect coins minted for

Philip V, thick chains, bars, gemstones gamely reflecting what little light there was, and a collection of dowry jewels which had been intended for the new Spanish queen, Elisabeth of Parma.

The Buzzard had fared well when he attacked the *Santa Cristo de San Ramon*, reputedly one of Spain's richest galleons, in the shallow waters near Eleuthera. Unsuspecting and ill-prepared, encouraged by pistols pointed at their heads and Toledo steel at their throats, its crew had readily surrendered chests full of gold, jewels, and well-crafted armaments to the smaller but far more agile sloop commanded by La Buse.

He was a buccaneer—a gentleman of fortune, as they're known—and he excelled in the black art of piracy. Not that he, as a young man (nor his wealthy family, for that matter) would have ever thought he'd end up plying the seas, attacking ships under Spanish and English banners, and relieving them of their cargoes as his plunder. Quite to the contrary. Olivier LeVasseur's childhood and youth had been spent at his family's ancestral estates in Rouen, France, where he received the education of a privileged heir. His father, a landowner like the generations before him, was a man who loved the sea and wanted above all to become a skilled sailor. It was only natural, then, that the father would wish to pass his love and knowledge of the seafaring life to his two sons. So, he arranged for his boys to be taught by the best navigators in the world: the Knights of St. John. Men of the LeVasseur family had long been members of the Order of St. John of Jerusalem—and so, too, became Olivier and his brother, Louis. Young Olivier learned well, and at the age of 22, was able to procure a letter of marque from his king, Louis the Great. He was elated at the prospect of leaving France behind and living his life aboard ship, so, letter in hand, he set out as a corsaire, patrolling the seas, defending the French against Spain during the War of Spanish Succession. It was a bold life, filled with adventure, and he soon became known as an exceptional seaman, one with a fearless streak. Rough and tenacious, he'd quickly developed a reputation for swift and brutal action to overcome an enemy, gaining the fear and respect of his crew. When the war ended, he, along with the other French corsaires, was recalled to Paris. Upon reflection, LeVasseur defied the imperial order. Instead, he commandeered a small sloop, crimped a few black-hearted rogues to come aboard, and began hunting the western Atlantic near the Caribbean Sea on the lookout for poorly-armed English or Spanish merchantmen. As his notoriety grew, so did his fortune.

One hot day, drinking in the shade of a Nassau tavern, he met the Englishman Benjamin Hornigold and Hornigold's first mate, Edward Teach. Hornigold was a crusty salt, commander of a sloop called *Happy Return*, of all sarcastic monikers, and had spent the past months harassing vessels in and around the south Atlantic, seizing many and taking over whatever cargo they carried before setting them afire, using the spoils to finance his next expedition. Teach—a man with a baleful, dark glance and sharp wit—and Hornigold boasted about their exploits, and by the time an entire jug of rum had been consumed, the three had formed an unholy alliance. They would traverse the seas across trade routes from Europe to the islands of the Caribe, each in his own vessel, pooling their resources. And so they did, working mainly as a unit to surround and overcome their prey. Only occasionally did the three fight like mongrels amongst them, but ultimately, they split the loot, making them very rich. And, in that corner of the world, very much feared.

LA BUSE DUG DEEP into the trunk, scraping through coinage, yanking golden collars and chains aside, as his fingers sought and finally found what was of most concern to him. They closed around a long, cylindrical, hard leather case. He pulled it out to inspect it for water damage, and to his great relief, saw none on its heavily waxed surface. Just for a moment, he considered opening it and withdrawing the glorious prize it concealed. Every time he touched the case he was consumed with the same desire. But knowing he couldn't possibly manage it while the ship gyrated so erratically, he shoved it back into the chest and locked it. Carefully, he replaced the key in its permanent home around his neck and returned to the after deck to command his crew and try to keep the ship afloat in the howling storm.

It was well after dawn when the winds had settled somewhat and the sea, while still rolling, became navigable. The skies were grey and rain spit intermittently, but the worst of the hurricane had roared northwest to ravage the Bahamas and wreak havoc on Florida's coast. *Postillon* had survived, although severely damaged. A goodly number of her complement of pirates had not.

Grateful to find himself still alive, the captain rounded up his rag-tag foc'sle rats—those who remained. He wasn't one to indulge a crew, but after such a night, they looked like phantoms.

"Messieurs, you've done your duty this night. There's many of us lost forever, may their souls lie in repose in Davey's locker." Turning to the cook, a man by the name of Defay who hailed from Saint-Domingue, he called, "Defay, supply everyone with plenty of grog and salt-pork. Let us eat and drink to our good luck and continuing health. We will have a sea-cheer for the survivors and for *Postillon*, who saw us through the horror of last night."

A jubilant swell rose from the ragged crew. "And Vane! You and Bosun Prinston set our course. We will run up the trades to catch the winds of Santa Cruz. I want us raising the south shore harbor by noon tomorrow. We have repairs to make, and we need fresh crew to replace those lost."

"Aye, aye, Captain." The silver ring in the mate's nose bobbed as he nodded vigorously. He and Prinston leaped to their feet and made their way to the fo'cs'le to follow orders.

Captain LeVasseur descended into the hold to review his charts. In the galley, he passed a cabin boy and stopped him. The youth quavered before the ship's fierce commander.

"Young sir. Go aft to my quarters and clean up the mess on the deck. Clear all the trash away and find me when you're finished. I'll give you a cup of wine." Hardened to suffering as he was, he still felt for the crew, especially the young ones, who had seen their lives pass by more than once in the small hours of the previous night.

Waiting for his quarters to be cleared, he climbed to the after deck and stood at the rail, appreciating the growing patches of blue sky above, drinking in the fresher winds as the storm blew away to the west. *Postillon* was tacking south by southwest toward Santa Cruz. There was a steady breeze abeam, and the ship slipped along, her bowsprit dipping into peaceful waves. A light spray dampened his face as he gazed out, using his glass to catch the first sight of land. While he was glad for having come through the night alive, Buzzard was not a man who feared death either. Pursuing the life he'd chosen, one couldn't be constantly vigilant for one's safety. To sail the Atlantic, to ply the waters of the Caribe, to command a ship manned by renegades, slaves, and men hungry to build on their own fortunes through spilling the blood of others—all required a ruthless abandon. And while he was callous—had no moral qualms about slitting a throat or hanging a man when necessary—such lack of empathy didn't take the place of keen thought. The successful privateers were men whose wits were sharp as a razor's edge. The Buzzard intended to become one of the richest men captaining a ship from the Caribbean to Europe, and maybe even beyond. Yes, there was much to see—even more to possess—and he was not at all ready to reach the end of the line, especially in a storm. So, quietly, he gave thanks in his way.

Running a rough hand across his face to wipe off the spray, he reflected that he needed a shave, and probably a haircut, too. Buse was a man of two distinct characters: a wealthy Frenchman born, educated, a Knight of St. John, his visible manner belying his true temperament. He was handsome—at least that is what he was told by women in the ports where and when they made landfall. He was sought out by the most beautiful of the island girls and slave women alike. They loved to run their hands through his thick black hair—which he kept cropped short to avoid it becoming home to fleas or other vermin. They all admired his heavy gold earrings, set off by a strong, clean-shaven face. A powerful physique was a great advantage, and even if he were to remain in port for an extended stay, would never allow himself to run to fat, nor imbibe too much rum. He'd often seen the results of over-indulgence: watery, red-rimmed eyes, teeth that grew loose then were spat out one by one, a paunch and a stooping posture, the sure sign of a slow reaction when challenged. He kept his skills sharply honed and spoke in a soft voice—which somehow was all the more ominous since it was known he would readily send a man to his death by the most gruesome means, if warranted. His crew paid attention and stayed in line.

He called for Vane, and the bosun, Josue Prinston, and the three sat at a table with the captain's charts before them.

"Men, barely did we survive the night, that be certain. But it's God's truth I should string you both up for not summoning me as that storm took hold. I'd think you both are aware your neglect could easily be seen as a threat of mutiny." He glared at them from under thick black eyebrows. "But only because I am in good spirit and feel grateful for my life this day will I overlook your grievous error. Mark me, though! If there is just one more blunder, even the smallest mistake, be assured you'll pay the price. Especially you, Vane. I gave you a chance when others would not, only because I heard a tale or two of your seamanship. It didn't show itself last night. Be warned, your life hangs in the balance."

"Captain, you have my word such as it is. I offer amends for my mistake. You'll see only the best of me from now on. It's just that I knew you'd had some drink, and the gale blew up much faster than I anticipated. I was wrong. It won't happen again." The already unnerved Vane did his best to appease the captain. He was well acquainted with the title "The Buzzard". And its meaning.

Prinston, who'd sailed with this captain before, was equally remorseful. He knew La Buse was reputed to be one of the most ambitious buccaneers in the southern seas, and Prinston wanted to remain part of his crew, with his head firmly attached to his body, in order to earn a dole of the riches they plundered.

"Pardon, mon Capitaine." He nodded deferentially.

With a final scowl, LeVasseur spread open the charts. "Let us look at our current position, and how we intend to approach harbor in Santa Cruz. We sail due south past the Buck Eyland, then tack southeast around Oost Point and Oost Ende Bay. We shall then set a course sailing west, hugging the southern shore to pass through Manchenil Bay, around Vaythius Point and come in at Bay of Cane Garden where we should be able to drop anchor, the soundings being about two and a half fathoms. Does your gut feeling tell you the winds will send us to our destination by sundown, Bosun?"

"Aye, sir, I do believe they will. I already have lookout posted for'ard and at the masthead on land watch. Once we sight it, then it shouldn't be long before we round the island and sail into anchorage."

"So be it, then. Vane, let me remind you that, once anchored, we remain as discreet as possible. I want no attention from anyone ashore. We have the men pack the goods which'll be rowed to the beach, and once on land, we descend into the tunnels carrying provisions and booty. From there we follow them north, to surface again just below MonCoeur. I will check every parcel of stores and examine each chest of treasure before the goods are stowed. As for the treasure—its whereabouts will be known only to me. Once our business is complete, I will make payments as due. I intend to reside in the fort while repairs are being made to the ship until I've had time to scout the island for crew. That is, if there be any island men I consider suitable. I'm not about to take anyone else on as the result of a bet—" At this he cast a derisory sneer at Vane. "—but only capable seamen. With big balls."

"Aye, Captain. We understand. Your orders will be followed to the letter." Vane took the opportunity to remove himself from La Buse's scrutiny, so he yanked at the bosun's arm and they set off to relay the Buzzard's instructions.

Late in the afternoon came the cry "LAND-HO!" Immediately there was much glee, accompanied by toothless grins as the piratical rough humor and bawdy jokes were shared all around. Still, the men had a bit more work ahead before they could enjoy a run ashore, plant their feet on land for a stretch, eat better food, and seek some female companionship.

That evening, safely anchored in the sheltered south shore harbour, and after a satisfying salt pork stew made by the cook to celebrate their safe arrival, LeVasseur stood on deck in the soft, balmy tropical air smoking a cigarro, one of the supply he'd acquired in Hispaniola. Tendrils of smoke curled about his head before being whisked away by the light easterly wind. He felt at peace and was looking forward to a stay at MonCoeur. Although the fortress was not fully inhabited as it had been some years ago, it was still a stronghold for the Knights of St. John. He knew of it, and although he'd never before been on the island, he was in possession of beautifully detailed charts of the waters surrounding the land mass, and the geography, estates and hamlets which made up the island. But they were not the only assets that caused the Buzzard such satisfaction.

Most crucially, he knew of the legendary complex of narrow tunnels which had been excavated and used by the knights to carry supplies and arms to and from ships docked in the southern harbor without attracting notice. They would be perfect for his purposes.

He ducked below into his cabin, which had been cleared of rubble, swept, and impeccably cleaned by the cabin boy, whose respect neared reverential when his captain offered him a pannikin of wine for his work.

After dismissing the young recruit, Buse peeked through the aftermost porthole to see the risen moon, silvering the tops of gentle, lapping waves. He went to his cabin door and locked it. Using the key about his neck, he unlatched the treasure chest, threw open the lid and dug among the gold and silver until he'd reached the hard cylinder. It took effort to drag it out of the trunk and lay it upon the table. A long canister it was—fully half as tall as a man, with a diameter the width of his own head, its weight made greater by a thick waxen coating. At one end was a lid, attached by a buckle, and bearing a lock (he'd had the container made by a saddler he knew in Rouen) and he unlocked and released the clasp, tugging at the cap till it popped off. Holding his breath, he peered inside. He simply had to see it, had to gaze upon it once more before he found a hiding place on the island where it would remain, at least for a good long while, secure from the elements, location unknown to any pilferer seeking to steal his loot. Of course, this was far more than mere treasure trove. *Certainement*, he knew it to be a prize of priceless worth—a value he couldn't imagine—and what was more, it had been actively sought by many for some 180 years. And to think! It was in his possession due to his remarkable little grandmother four times over, a valiant woman known in life as Gabrielle LeVasseur.

Slowly, ever so carefully, he withdrew the rolled canvas from its protective shell. It being a sizable painting, he cleared everything from his table before delicately pressing it open, weighting each corner with handfuls of gold so he could stand back and regard it in totality. It was remarkable, *absolument magnifique*, and once again he was surprised, as he'd been each time he'd seen it, at how beautifully preserved it was. Indeed, his dear great-grand-mére had taken extreme care when she'd hidden it. It had been gently rolled, only possible because it had been painted on canvas—in itself a surprising innovation considering its age—following which, she'd had it encased in multiple layers of liberally waxed cloth and leather, and finally secured in a stone box which had, in turn, been placed in a tomb-like cavern within the walls of the crypt of Chateau Rouen. The stone-masons had covered it up, then whitewashed the entire crypt so it was almost impossible to tell where it had been buried. And there, deep in the wall, it had lain, its location unsuspected as the genera-tions passed—even though the LeVasseur sons were aware that the family had, at least at one time, been in possession of the remarkable portrait, now seemingly lost.

Olivier's gaze lingered on every nuance of the composition. He'd been lucky enough to have known beautiful art in his young life. His family owned a collection which was displayed within their Chateau. Never, though, had he seen any artefact remotely comparable to this. In the lantern light, its color shimmered and pulsed with an intensity that was irresistible. Richly and plentifully adorned with gold leaf, the canvas appeared to glow on its own. LeVasseur knew that the abundance and quality of ultramarine and gold used in the paint-ing's palette could only have been afforded by a king of mythical status—the very one depicted as the painting's subject, Henry VIII of England.

Only a religiously educated man or woman would have been able to interpret the symbolic representations the painter had wrought within the portrait. But Olivier LeVasseur, having been brought up in a devout Catholic family, and as a member of the Order of St. John, was well able to read them. It was indisputable that the paint-ing had intended to present Henry as figurehead of the Church—in fact, it appeared that he had at one time desired to be recognized as St. Peter; he audaciously displayed himself as triumphant over the papacy. It was no wonder that the legend lived even though its location was unknown. The ambition of Grand Masters of the Order since the tenure of Jean Parisot de la Vallette was to find it to present it to the pope, whomever that might be at the time.

Sacrilegious as it might seem to some, LeVasseur could only admire its magnificent pretentiousness. The artist, though Olivier wasn't familiar with his work, had surely been a master of the highest order—that was evident. He grinned, congratulating himself as he recalled his decision to search the grounds and within the walls of Chateau Rouen for the hidden and forbidden treasure.

Whispers of the chateau's legend had been a part of his family's lore for many a year. And once, at a reception, he'd been drinking and sharing stories with a cousin. The young man, son of an uncle who lived on the neighboring estate, asked if Olivier knew of the prize which had been hidden at Rouen many years before. Instantly alert and very interested, he tolerated a longer conversation with the otherwise boring relative, pumping him for as much information as he could. Unfortunately, there wasn't much known—just that something owned by a Tudor king was hidden on the grounds, with the intent that it never be found. That was all Olivier needed to hear. He determined to uncover it.

The project had taken some months, but after meticulously eliminating many places he thought likely, he'd stopped his relentlessly frustrating quest and had simply allowed himself to imagine just what he, himself, would have done had he been hiding something of great value. And suddenly the answer had come to him... where else? The crypt! Rarely visited by any living soul, the family crypt, lying deep below ground, offered a quiet and undisturbed site. Within its confines there would only be two options for concealment: either within a tomb, or behind a wall. Hence, armed with hammer and chisel, a sturdy lever and a lantern, he'd spent weeks descending the narrow, dark stone stairs, and section by section, he'd tapped on the walls to listen for a difference in sound. Just before he gave up, and dreading the thought of having to pry open the tombs of his decomposing ancestors... voilá! A ring of a distinctly different pitch rewarded his ears from one particular corner as the hammer rapped on the stone-and-mortar wall.

His excitement had intensified while, working in the dead of night to avoid detection, he'd chiseled and picked away at the wall where the sound had rung hollow. Sure enough, it took but little labor to recognize that he had indeed uncovered a vault within a vault. Bit by bit, he removed the façade and came quickly upon a long box of limestone. He extracted it from its own grave, tentatively prized open the lid, and was greeted by a scroll covered in layers of cloth and leather. With shaking fingers, he removed the shroud-like wrappings from around a carefully stored length of canvas. By the wavering light of the single lantern, he unrolled the final turn of cloth and gasped at what he'd revealed. In his most fantastic dreams, never could he have imagined the sight that greeted him in that dark, dank, and macabre setting. Olivier knew he had found something spectacular. In the dim light it worked its magic, and he was spellbound.

Now it was his. And he would kill to preserve his ownership of it.

A POUNDING ON HIS door caused him to start. "Who goes there?"

"'Tis Vane, Cap'n. We was wonderin' if you might like to join me, Cook, and Prinston and a few other hands in a game or two of noddy? The sea's calm, there's a bit o' rum in the barrel, and we be betting on each hand—only a little, though."

Buse went to the door and squinted through the peephole. The mate's silhouette blocked all light from the tiny cuddy beyond the cabin. "Indeed not, Vane," he retorted sharply, damning the man's familiarity. "I intend to finish reviewing our charts, then claw back some rest, as you should too. Tomorrow, we have work ahead. You best tell the crew to expect to hoist heavy loads and carry them a distance. The tunnels are narrow and long. All hands to the task, mister. No one is excused."

"Aye, sir. The men will be ready." Vane's shadow disappeared, then, from the hole in the door.

What was it about his second in command, thought Buse, that seemed cagey? He was beginning to understand all too well why Hornigold and Teach had been so ready to rid themselves of the dog. Although not so much a seadog as a sea-pup, methinks, the pirate captain mused, judging by the man's show of nerves during the storm.

THE MORNING FOG DISSOLVED as the sun climbed, revealing a sea blue as a bird's egg with frothy waves breaking on the steep, sandy beach. Stony pines and scrub brush dotted the land beyond the shoreline, the sea birds were wheeling and crying, and *Postillon* was tucked into the narrow anchorage well out of sight of any ships which might skim the southern coast headed west. The crew was busy packing goods which would be rowed and carried ashore. La Buse wandered among the men.

"Mister Boucher, stop yer packing and haul down our colors. We want no passing ships, or islanders for that matter, to see our flag flying and be alerted to our visit. At least, not yet—not until we've had a chance to hide what we own." Boucher immediately headed for the halyard to lower the white flag inscribed with a black human skeleton, Buse's personal emblem, and the very last sight many a merchant sailor carried with him to his watery grave. He carefully folded it and handed it to the captain.

"Prinston, have you got the jolly-boat readied?"

"Aye, Captain. We'll commence transportin' the first load soon as you is rowed ashore."

La Buse was sculled to the beach first and positioned himself in the shade of a tall pine. Adjusting the pitch of his cocked hat to keep the rays of the rising sun from blinding him, he watched as the men, young to old, waded back and forth, the small boat laden with parcels of rations, such barrels of drink which remained, and wooden chests packed with spices, cloth, tobacco, and very profitable sugar—all plunder which had been neatly removed from Spanish and English ships over the past months.

As the men unloaded after each trip, Buse tracked their progress. "Vane, keep up the pace! The men get no grub until all goods are removed from the ship and safely stowed in the tunnel." After each haul, Buse checked off the delivery in his ledger, and often went to tally the stores accumulating on the beach to ensure that what was supposed to be there, was, in fact, accounted for.

The blistering tropical sun beat upon the pale sand while the men grunted and swore, rowing and lugging the heavy wares through the surf onto land. A tattered lot they surely were, headscarves frayed and bug-eaten, the few clothes they owned patched till they could be repaired no longer. Some of the spoils, when finally divided and doled out by the captain, would go toward clothing, at least enough to see them through the next voyage.

Buse trusted most of his crew—those who had survived the storm—but he was never one to lower his guard. Refined he might seem, but it was a certainty that not all the grisly legends about The Buzzard were untrue. Thus, he stood fully armed against a possible ambush from inhabitants of the island, or of a foolhardy decision by one of the crew to try and filch some treasure and make a run for it. Two silver pistols hung across his chest, gleaming in the bright sunlight. His cutlass—a most fearsome blade—was attached loosely at his waist and swung menacingly as he walked. A double-edged dirk, sharp enough to slice with ease through a man's ribcage, was visible in its belt at his hip.

The relentless afternoon heat made the job all the more difficult, but finally, the transfer from boat to shore was complete. The ragtag bunch sprawled in the shade and shared a leather bucket of drink, some bacon, and apples. Somewhat revived, they began the task of hauling everything into the mouth of the tunnel which, it was said, was a direct route to the fortress. Its entrance had been found by several sailors clearing wide swaths in the jungle underbrush with machetes, until with a cry they announced the discovery of the underground passage. The entire crew, though, including Buse, was dismayed to find that the tunnel was not only dank with stale water but exceeding narrow. Only with great exertion could a man pass through carrying two or more sacks or boxes of goods. It mattered not, though. It must, and would, be done. So, well into the night they labored, and to a man, felt as if they would drop dead of exhaustion when, finally, the last shipment was delivered into a stone stockroom within the fortress of MonCoeur. The captain himself transported the heavy trunk filled with his most prized booty while, slung across his shoulders on a thick strap, was that curious leather cylinder retrieved from his cabin. He kept a protective arm around it at all times. As he passed a small knot of men who were lugging a large box, he heard one mutter, "Blimey! What th' divil is in that tube?" And his toothless mate answered, "Well, ya stupid seadog, wha' d'ya think it is? It'd be treasure maps, that's what!"

Buse knew he needed to hide the cylinder, and quick.

By the turn of the middle watch the crew had been driven to a state of collapse and spent the remainder of the night in a tumble-down cattle shed just outside the walls of the fortress. La Buse, on the other hand, was more than pleased to find his own accommodations within the fort to be comfortable. Even though there were just a handful of inhabitants remaining, the former home of Phillippe de Poincy—during his lifetime a respected Knight and founder of the Knights' colonies in these islands—remained adequately furnished and had a kitchen which was stocked with provisions for the residents.

The following morning, LeVasseur rose early, left the fort and pushed open the door of the lean-to where his men snored, still near dead with exhaustion. He kicked them awake, and as they came to, announced, "Swabs, you can thank God you are on dry land for a time. You're free to roam the island. The hamlet of Christianswaern on the north end has some taverns and a few traders. I'll have your shares of loot ready for you in two days' time. Be back here by eight bells in the forenoon watch to collect your dues. By then I'll have decided whether you will join me on my next voyage."

There was muttering, and three men piped up, "We be willing, if you'll 'ave us, Captain!"

"Glad I am to hear of it, lads. Just you be sure you're ready to bleed for profit as I'll take only the most fearless and the most willing to work hearty from among you. Until you come back to collect your divisions, then, all of you have some good times on this island."

The captain left and returned to his quarters, ducking through a stone doorway and under the pink keystone with the Cross of Malta carved into it, flanked by the date 1657. It must have been ordered by De Poincy, who'd been Bailiff Grand Cross when the Knights flourished here in the Caribe. LeVasseur might be a marauder of the seas, but he was still a Knight, and as such, he was a welcomed guest at the fort.

That evening in his chamber, he wrote a letter to his brother. Louis, the younger of the two, had—in stark contrast to his older, but much-loved brother Olivier—fallen in thrall to the life of a dedicated defender of the Faith: a Knight of St. John in the truest sense of the word, who now lived in Rome as part of the Order community, caring for the sick and poor of the city. Olivier and Louis had always been close, and even though Louis had learned the basics of seamanship alongside his brother, he'd shown no appetite for life at sea. So, Olivier had earned his letter of marque on his own and departed for adventure, only returning to France once for a visit home. He'd stayed at the chateau long enough to see to its disposition after the death of their father—and to search for and take the painting, telling no one of his discovery.

It was time, though—especially due to the perilous life he had chosen—to let his brother know of the family's treasure, and how he might recover it in case Olivier was to die at sea, or at the hands of enemies. With quill poised, he hesitated. If Louis was to acquire the portrait—a blatant symbol of defiance and offense against the pope and the Catholic faith—he would lose no time in returning it to the Vatican as his obligation, where it would surely be destroyed. As beautiful and mesmerizing as it was, he was sure he could sell or barter the painting for a treasure more immense than any he might pilfer on the open seas. He had no intention, though, of doing that in the foreseeable future. For as long as he was able, he would keep it. Guard it. Hide it from the world, known only to him.

Without further reflection, he dipped his pen in the well and began his letter: a page replete with the odd symbols and characters he and his brother had devised when they were boys being tutored together in Rouen. There, they had dreamed up a method of ciphers, and delighted in writing notes and letters to each other using the language they'd invented. The hieroglyphs, known only to them, danced across the page under the flicker of the flame, and Olivier mused how perfectly suited they were to conveying the message he now needed to send. He could feel confident that, should the letter be intercepted, no one else would be able to interpret the marks they used, and gain knowledge of the painting's location. After first inquiring about Louis's health and wellbeing, he recorded the tale of the portrait's history, how he'd found it, and that he intended to hide it somewhere on the Isle of Santa Cruz, where it would remain until such time that he removed it to accompany him across the oceans, to destinations as yet unknown.

Once finished, he folded the letter, sealed it with wax, and addressed it to:

Knight Commander Louis LeVasseur
Villa del Priorato di Malta
Roma, Italia

He'd been informed that a ship with a French crew was ready to set sail from the island's north harbor, with the objective of transporting sugar, rum, spices, and tobacco to the European Continent. His letter would be posted aboard, and he'd pay well to have it delivered personally once the ship docked. He hoped it would reach Louis, and that its delivery wouldn't take too many months—or be intercepted by some other dastardly pirate sloop, he reflected wryly, for there was little honor between those sharks who were his colleagues. In the meantime, he'd need to scout the island to find the right place in which to hide his treasure. With a quick glance he reassured himself. For the time being, his trunk, packed full of gold along with the painting, remained secure in his chamber while its key remained safely around his neck.

THE THREE SAT IN the dim light of a small, rustic tavern on the north shore. The landlord had just served them stewed goat, and placed a tankard each, filled with rum and sugar, on the table. The only sound, besides waves breaking on the beach, was that of chewing and an occasional swallow of drink as La Buse assessed the men sitting opposite him. One of the two was Vane, who'd requested the meeting. The other was a most intriguing character, indeed. And it was he who spoke first.

"Bonjour, Capitaine. It's a fine thing to make your acquaintance. I've heard much about you, sir."

"Is that so? It's Monsieur Toussaint. Am I correct?"

"Oui, ça l'est. I am Adolphe Toussaint. And you are the famous Olivier LeVasseur—La Buse, I am told. So, we are countrymen, of sorts. Yes, my father is French. His family is Parisian. But he came to Sant Domingue some twenty years ago to run the sugar plantation he inherited, here in the islands."

"Inferring you were born into some wealth, then. And your mother?" LeVasseur imagined that his mother must be either a slave, or of some island descent. It was obvious, from the look of the man.

"My mother, may her soul rest, was West African." He said no more about her.

"I see. So, you are of mixed race. Are you to inherit your father's wealth when he is gone?"

"I am French Creole, Captain. And glad I am for it." He fell silent, but his scrutiny of La Buse was penetrating. "To answer your pointed question about my personal legacy, you are correct. I will inherit the family's estates. But I prefer to make my own fortune. And I know no better, or quicker, way to do that than to relieve the Spaniards, and the English as well, of the overabundance of riches they carry. I do believe that forcing them to share such abundance will fortify their souls. Therefore, I know it to be a favor I do them. I can then provide some of that prosperity to the islanders, who work so hard and have so little."

"I'm impressed. That is exceedingly noble of you, Monsieur Toussaint." La Buse's tone mocked.

Charles Vane interrupted. "Captain, I asked to meet you today to discuss your plans. I, for one, would like to join your crew, traveling on your next quest. And I wanted you to meet Toussaint here, who has spent many years a seaman and is a friend of mine. God's witness, he's one of the most able quartermasters you'd ever have the privilege to know or to sail with."

"Is that right, now, Vane?" LeVasseur sat back, took a swig of rum, and regarded Toussaint with narrowed eyes. The man was striking. In fact, he was one of the most strikingly handsome men the captain had ever encountered.

Unlike Vane, who obviously found the presence of La Buse daunting for all his spurned attempts at familiarity with his better, Adolphe Toussaint was relaxed, at ease, his gaze firmly fixed on the pirate captain's face. And what eyes they were! An unusual, pale blue—the color of the Caribe Sea, to be accurate—and offset by skin the amber color of an aged whiskey. Not brown skin, but not the color of a white man, either. And his eyes tilted up at the outer corners, bestowing him an exotic look not one often encountered. A square face, generous mouth, a full set of pearl-white teeth and a cleanly shaved head covered by a patterned scarf of fine silk completed his look. As the islander quartermaster waited for LeVasseur to respond, his fingers idly stroked a small leather pouch he wore about his neck.

"What is that you wear, Monsieur Toussaint, if I may ask? I note you fondle it with some tenderness." The ship's captain regarded the medallion-like item with curiosity.

"It is my gris-gris, Captain. My amulet. It was given me by my mother. There are things I keep in it from her people in Africa. Do you know of them? I am *vodouisant*. I follow Bondye, the Creator. And you? Do you call yourself a Christian, Monsieur LeVasseur?"

LeVasseur bristled at Toussaint's arrogant comment. "Why would I not? I was born well, lived well, and God has been good to me."

"I do wonder, sir, because there are many legends which precede you. I will say that not all of them are flattering." Toussaint spoke in a honey-smooth tone.

"That may be. I take no pleasure in inflicting unnecessary punishment, so as long as I can conduct my pursuits in my own way, I am happy to live and let live. It's only when I have the need to persuade—well, then, there's no guarantee about what I might do to achieve my aim."

"Ahhh, an interesting view, Captain, and one I would not disagree with."

"If that's so, Toussaint, let us decide if we are suited to sail side by side. If you choose, meet me aboard *Postillon* tomorrow late in the afternoon. I shall be there to gauge progress on her repairs. You can look her over and we'll see if you are a quartermaster up to sailing under my colors."

"I will be there. And you, Vane?"

"'Deed I will, gentlemen." Vane nodded vigorously. The three drained their tankards, and parted ways.

THE FOLLOWING DAY, VANE, Toussaint, and LeVasseur were forced to seek shelter within the captain's quarters on *Postillon*. Tropical rain lashed the deck, and even though the wind had picked up and thunder boomed overhead, the workmen who'd been hired to rebuild the sloop's masts and repair her hull never slowed their hammering and sawing.

The three walked the length and breadth of the vessel, and as they talked, it became apparent to LeVasseur that the arresting-looking Toussaint indeed knew ships and had steered many. From stem to stern, he'd demonstrated his knowledge of all things nautical. Furthermore, he and Vane seemed to communicate well. Buse was thinking that the two might be just the team he needed to travel with him on his next quest: westward, then skimming the coast of Florida headed north to the rich sailing lanes along the eastern coast of British America.

A flagon of wine was produced, and generous measures poured.

"I should be honored to sail under your command, Captain, if you'll have me." Toussaint raised his glass. His unsettling blue eyes glinted, and the thick gold hoops he wore in both ears mirrored the porthole's light. To be sure, the man had an elegance about him—a quality rarely encountered in the debased company now kept by LeVasseur, who thought to himself that Toussaint's mother must have been a beauty and that women must find the landowner pirate alluring. He also noticed, as the discussion progressed, that Toussaint kept his hand on his vodou amulet, massaging it and feeling the mysterious contents within.

Vane echoed, "I, too Captain, am keen to rejoin your crew. You'll not be disappointed in me this time."

"So be it, men. Then you sail under my flag. We commence as soon as Postillon has been thoroughly refitted and is shipshape."

After a clink of glasses, Toussaint spoke up. "Captain, your first mate here tells me you are in possession of maps and charts which lead to unimaginable treasure. Is that true?"

La Buse stiffened. "What in God's name do you mean, Toussaint?"

Vane be damned! That loose-lipped cur!

With a quick glance in Vane's direction, Toussaint leaned forward and spread his ringed hands on the table. "I'm told, sir, that you have exclusive possession of a, well… shall we refer to it as a certain vessel? Long in size, made from leather, with a lid kept under a sturdy lock and key? It bears concluding that, as you keep it so well protected, it is likely filled with maps of places where tremendous loot lies buried. Might this not be correct? If so, I hereby propose we use those very maps to chart our course well before we sail."

A vein on La Buse's head began to throb ominously. Before anyone had blinked, his dirk was silently unsheathed, and with a blinding stroke he drove it deep into the table between Toussaint's outspread fingers. Toussaint never moved, although his color grew pale, and his eyes narrowed to slits.

In a sinister, quiet voice, Buzzard warned, "Permit me to inform you, Monsieur Toussaint—and you, Vane—what is my business remains strictly my business. You don't inquire, you don't even observe. You will never take it upon yourselves to suggest what I do with my property. As for the 'vessel' you believe you saw? Let us simply say that your eyes were playing tricks. There is no such artefact. Do you understand? You, Toussaint, are fortunate for my good nature, since, as it is, we have just met and forged an agreement. Otherwise, you would now be in possession of a hand with but three fingers. Let me be clear: should anything like this happen again, should you decide to make observations about business which is none of your concern, well, then, let us say I shall feel obliged to see death visited upon you. Both of you."

The Buzzard yanked the deadly point of his dagger free, sheathed it, and followed his new officers as they left *Postillon* and went ashore in the deepening dusk.

Unnerved by their conversation, LeVasseur returned to his fortress chamber. Tomorrow, at daybreak and not a moment later, he must remove the chest with the painting and situate it in its hiding place. It wasn't safe, not even within the seemingly impregnable walls of MonCoeur. After a light meal of bread and cheese, and a goodly draught of whiskey, he readied for sleep. Next to him on his berth was his dagger, his pistol within arm's reach. He blew out the candle and fell into a deep slumber.

He dreamt that he was aboard a schooner slipping across a waveless sea. In his imagining, he lay abed with a beautiful woman, and they were entwined. He heard her soft breathing, and it was pleasurable. She removed a silk scarf which had been tied about her waist and slid it behind his shoulders, then produced a soft white cord and wrapped it about his wrists. In his dream he welcomed her actions. She lifted the corners of the scarf and in one swift motion slipped it from his shoulders to around his neck—and he felt it tighten!

La Buse was jolted from his fantasy by the heavy breathing of the man who knelt over him on his cot. Before he was awake enough to react, he felt the noose about his neck constricting. He thought to grab for his dirk, but he found that his wrists were bound. In the pitch of the night, he was aware that the man had moved to his ankles and quickly bound them as well, so tightly that it cut off the blood flow to his feet. A thick wad of cotton wool was shoved deep into his mouth, along with two plugs into his nostrils. He struggled to breathe, nor could he yell. The leather cord with the key to his trunk was ripped from his neck while La Buse thrashed about the bed before tumbling to the floor.

As his eyes became accustomed to the darkness he watched helplessly as the man unlocked the trunk, dug out its contents and shoved fistfuls of gold into a sack he carried. His heart nearly beat from his chest as he saw the long cylinder emerge. The lid slammed closed, and with the portrait's case tucked under his arm, the man stood over La Buse.

"I thank you, esteemed Captain, for sharing your secrets with me. I know you were reluctant this afternoon, but I was in earnest, so I felt that a bit of encouragement might change your mind. I choose not to inflict upon you the indignity of death, so I will spare you that shame. And now I must hurry, because I've booked passage on the ship leaving port within the hour, headed for my homeland. Although I'm sure the tales of your ferociousness are true, after all, you are just a man. So, before I depart, if you don't mind, I shall leave my mark of dominance upon you, the great Buzzard. This way, everyone will know that you can be defeated. Kindly allow me to provide you with my monogram: A.T."

And thus it was, that, wielding the blade of the captain's own stiletto, Adolphe Toussaint carved his initials deep into La Buse's chest.

As LeVasseur's blood flowed freely and he faded from consciousness, he heard Toussaint, "Merci, mon capitaine. Et Adieu!"

Chapter Twenty-six

MID-DECEMBER 2016

ROME

W e sat across from one another at a small round table in the cozy trattoria, knees occasionally brushing as I shifted in my seat. The pizzas arrived, steaming and fragrant with basil and tomato. We were very hungry and dug in with forks and knives the second the waitress had departed.

"Do you come here often, Luca?" I asked between scrumptious bites.

"Sì, certamente. It's my favorite—they have by far the best pizza in this part of the city. That is, at least, in my humble opinion." He offered a shy smile.

"Sure useful to know about. With all of the fabulous food there is to be had in Rome, there's nothing better, in my mind, than a great pizza. So, tell me, how did you come to intern at the Magistral Library?"

He put his fork down before replying. "I'm working on my Ph.D. dissertation from Università di Roma. My area of study is history involving the Order of St. John of Jerusalem, now known as the Order of Malta, and I'm focusing on the Knights—who they were and are, especially some of the more unusual individuals who've been members of the Order over the centuries. I was spending so much time hanging around the Library that they offered me a part-time job! It seemed like a good idea, and it's turned out to be fun. Well, I guess it appeals to my nerdy side." He chuckled. I liked that he didn't take himself too seriously. His blue eyes were warm and when he smiled at me, the thought occurred that he was cute. "All the members of staff are so nice—so kind, and helpful. I'm glad I accepted their offer. By the way, I was happy I was working when you came back into the Library the other day. I had been hoping you would."

I returned his smile, and was suddenly surprised to realize I was having an enjoyable time.

Just a few days ago, I'd eagerly visited the Library for a second time to comb through their bibliographies in the hope that I might find anything else, even the smallest reference, to the painting. Somehow, somewhere, there must lurk a brief comment in a letter, or even a single entry in an inventory. The tiniest clue would suffice. After all, how could it have simply disappeared? I felt certain there must be some trace, and my instincts told me a lead would be found in the archives of the Order of St. John. I was determined to examine all possibilities. No sooner had I set up my study space than a familiar, tousled head had appeared over the top of the carrel. He'd whispered "Buon giorno" and asked me if I'd join him for a coffee when I needed a break. My immediate reaction was 'absolutely not—I've got too much to do to socialize.' But then, for some reason, I regretted my all-too typical backlash. So instead, I replied, "Okay, sure. Let's go to the café."

He was delighted, and we sat in a corner booth with an espresso each, and a couple of biscotti.

"Mi chiamo Luca Crivelli; é como si chiama?" I took note of the fact that he was very polite, which seemed appealing.

"Zara. I'm Zara Rossi—it's very nice to meet you, Luca." And I reached across to shake his hand.

"Really, Zara, the pleasure is all mine. Are you a student?"

"Yep. Just like you, I'm working on my Ph.D. At Sapienza, in paleography."

His eyebrows had raised in admiration. "Wow! That's quite a difficult specialty, no? You must be very, very smart—as well as pretty."

My knee-jerk tendency to deliver a snarky comeback almost won out, but before I could open my mouth, I bit my lip. In that moment I found that, actually, I appreciated the compliment. "Thank you, Luca. It's challenging, but I do love it."

Long after our espressos had been drained and the biscotti reduced to a few stray crumbs, we'd chatted. Finally, I said, "I absolutely have to get back upstairs and do some work. I need to look through the bibliographies to see if there's anything else of interest I can use."

"I'm happy to help, you know, Zara. And..." he'd hesitated. The long pause was beginning to make me uncomfortable. "...would you possibly consider going out with me some evening for an aperitivo and maybe a pizza?"

He looked so wistful that I didn't delay too long before saying, "Okay, Luca. I'd like to." His obvious pleasure at my response was hard to miss, and I was glad I'd said yes. "But now, honestly, I've got to get back to the reading room. I have lots of searching to do."

Although I pored over the files for quite a while to see if anything else referred, even indirectly, to the lost artwork, nothing did. So, emptyhanded, I packed up, said my goodbyes and returned to my flat, where I promptly dialled Carolina to tell her the news: believe it or not, I had a date! Lina's excitement at the revelation had far exceeded my own. She'd insisted on helping me select an outfit which she considered suitable—and surprisingly, I'd only needed to tone it down a little, ensuring I was comfortable in it. She emphasized that I absolutely must call her when I got home, so we could debrief the evening over the phone.

So, here I was. In an out-of-body flash I saw myself: on a legiti-
mate date with an attractive Italian guy. He was funny and charming,
and kept the conversation flowing. Surprisingly, I didn't have time to
feel nervous or awkward, as usual. We demolished our pizzas and
Luca insisted on paying the check despite my protestations, and then,
wrapped in jackets and scarves, we left the trattoria, strolling out
into the street. He took my elbow and steered me into a little wine
bar on the corner. Sipping a nice Nebbiolo, we chattered for a while,
and I felt relaxed with him. It didn't hurt that we both really enjoyed
talking about our studies.

"Tell me about your visit to the Biblioteca Apostolica, Zara. I am
so jealous! How I would love to spend some time in there, among
those researchers, although I doubt that I will ever get in—at least
not anytime in the near future. I hear you really need to know someone important, someone who can refer you to get an approval."

"I guess that may be true. One of my professors, Antonio Moretti,
is very well acquainted with the prefect, and it was largely because of
his reference that I gained access. It was a daunting experience, yet
magical at the same time. I wish I could go back, but I'm not sure I'd
be granted a second shot."

I savored my wine and watched him closely. He was so very different from Antonio. A youthful-looking face—kind of cherubic, actually.
Unusual blue eyes framed by wire-rimmed glasses, a head of very
dark wavy hair. He had a gentleness about him which I felt drawn to.

"Well, what were you looking for there? Did you discover anything amazing? It must be fantastic for you, since you've said you can
read almost anything, no matter how old it is." He shook his head in
wonder. "I find it so difficult to decipher writing that is in any way
unclear. And so much of it is like a giant puzzle!"

"To answer your question, no, I didn't find what I was hoping for.
And as for my ability, it's just a weird gift I have. I've always, since
I was a kid, found that I have to solve a riddle, or finish a puzzle.

For some inexplicable reason, I apparently see things in a way that I guess others can't. The more convoluted, the better. I just cannot leave something undeciphered. Especially codes. Ancient writing is, in its own way, encoded. With enough time, I can always figure it out. So, how's that for a quirky talent? I guess it will never make me a million dollars, or famous, will it?"

He laughed while paying the check. "Hey, you never know, and anyway, money isn't everything—at least, so they say!" Out we went, into the chilly Roman winter evening and Luca walked me to my stop. As the bus rolled into view, he grabbed my hand and gave it a squeeze. "Will you be back in the Library soon? Do you think we can get together again? I know I'd like to."

"Me too. I think I'd like to see you again, Luca. And by the way, if you need any help reading the early documents of the knights you're researching, I'm willing to offer some assistance."

"Really? Would you do that? You'd sit with me and help unscramble some of those letters and journals? I can't tell you how grateful I would be."

As I climbed onto the bus, I nodded my assent. With a final wave, I ducked into the back, and he was out of sight before I sank low into the seat, overcome with unusual feelings: a blend of warm excitement, happiness, and a curious sense of accomplishment.

Back in my flat, I kicked off my boots, shrugged my coat and scarf to the floor, and curled up on the couch to call Lina.

"Darling Zara!" Her voice was just as fresh and sparkling at 11 p.m. as it was in the morning. "Com'è andata? How did it go?"

"Actually, it was fun, Lina. I enjoyed myself. There were a few times when I felt my resistance rising, but I checked it and kind of willed myself to relax. And you know what? It worked."

"What did you talk about? Where did you go?"

One of the things I loved most about Lina was her ability to enjoy events vicariously.

"Toto's, on Via delle Carozze? Great atmosphere! A small place, but the food was yummy. Pizzas to die for. Then we took a walk and ended up in a little bar for a drink."

"Ohhhh, how fantastic! You planning to see him again, then? Did he ask you?" Lina's voice revealed her relief. I guessed she was glad her friend wasn't a total loss at dating.

"Yes, he did ask, and, before you jump in, nosey—I agreed! Aren't you proud of me?" And we both squealed with laughter. "Mind you, I did fix it to meet with him in a way I'm comfortable with—so, maybe it's not the most romantic setting, but I'm going to help him transcribe some old documents to help with his dissertation."

"Okay, my little hermit. Whatever it takes to make the ship float."

"Lina. That's boat. 'Whatever it takes to float your boat.'"

"Oh, who cares! It's an espressione stupida, anyway."

With a final giggle, we said, "Ciao, see you tomorrow", and called it a night.

THE DAYS BEFORE CHRISTMAS were a mad scramble: every student and professor stressed to the max, papers due, finals underway, everyone needing a break for the holidays. I was looking forward to heading home for a few weeks. I hadn't been home for many months. I found that I was missing my dad, and home. It felt good to know that I couldn't wait to see him and slip into the comfort of the house I'd grown up in. I'd be seeing other family members as well, and I had cousins I loved. We always had a great time together sharing laughs and reminiscing about childhood. We planned to visit my aunt, my mother's sister, on Christmas Eve, and spend Christmas Day with my father's sister and her family. It would be reassuring to be surrounded by the extended Rossi clan—it'd help ease the hollow sting of my mom's absence.

With just two days left before I was to catch my flight to Boston,

I was on my way to the Magistral Library. I'd planned to meet Luca there, and help him review a few journals and letters for his dissertation research. Even though I was busy, I didn't mind spending the afternoon with him poring over old documents. In fact, I was looking forward to it.

"Zara!" His relief and pleasure at seeing me was obvious as he jumped from the seat where he'd been waiting in the entrance hall to the Library. "Oh, I'm so glad you're here! Grazie! Grazie mille. I'm so anxious. I've got to submit my outline and first two chapters right after we are back in session in January, and I need much more substance to have them approved. There's no way I can do it unless I'm able to analyze these documents."

He kept chattering as we climbed the stairs to the Archives Reading Room. "... and I've tried and tried; I get some words, but then there are critical gaps, and it's all so damn frustrating! I'm so thankful you can help!"

I pressed my lips together to hide my amusement. But truly, he seemed to be a nice person, and I was honestly happy to help. Plus, there wasn't much I liked doing better on a wintry afternoon than digging into a good paleographic puzzle.

We were seated together on a bench, notebooks and pencils ready, and several early leather-bound journals propped on the study lecterns in front of us. Of course, we had to whisper, there were other researchers at work nearby, and we were close to one another. I noticed Luca's scent, and I liked it: the faint aroma of citrus; that special lemony fragrance Italians do so well. It occurred to me that I didn't remember the last time I'd been in close enough proximity to a man to notice his scent.

He lifted the cover of the first volume. "I'm scrutinizing the Grand Masters who either had difficult histories, or those who were at odds with the pope of their time. My study is to trace the awkward relationship between the heads of the Order and the Catholic

Church. So, anything I can find about early Grand Masters who were contentious is of help."

"Okay, Luca, let's dig in." And we started skimming pages from the era of Jean de Lastic, the 35th Grand Master. The book we reviewed was a collection of notes and letters from 1448. There were a surprising number of documents in the bound book, and they were in pretty good shape. It didn't take long for my eyes to become accustomed to the mid-fifteenth century handwriting used by the cluster of scribes whose work was in the book. I found a letter addressed to Pope Nicholas V, in which it was confirmed that Lastic would attend the meetings of the Concordat of Vienna. The letter stated that the Order insisted upon conferring with the pope over his selection of bishops, providing references when they deemed it appropriate. At this discovery, Luca was ecstatic.

"Zara, do you realize we've found the very document which might have started the argument between the Order and the Church over selection of bishops and the sovereign council? This is just perfetto!"

"Awesome. Let's keep looking."

The hours crept by as we pored over countless volumes. As I worked, I noticed Luca's frequent glances in my direction; presumably, he was astonished at my ability to untangle letter after letter, page after page. Finally, he said, "We should take a break. Personally, my brain is swimming, and I need a coffee. Let's go to the café, okay?"

Over coffee and sandwiches, he just couldn't stop marvelling at my skill. "You know, I've worked here for a while now, and even among the senior staff and the archivists, there's no one who can read what you are able to, Zara. What are you planning to do with your talent?"

"I don't exactly know. I'm sort of searching for something really unique to provide the basis for my dissertation. And I just haven't found the right hook as yet."

I wrapped my fingers around the hot cup and my thoughts shifted, as usual, to the lost painting. Wouldn't it be fantastic, if I did find it, to use it as the basis of my study? It was impossible, though—it would cause too great a furore. I just wished there was someone—the right someone—I could confide in. I wondered… if Luca was researching the more extraordinary knights, maybe he'd stumble on a lead which would help? But I didn't trust anyone; even though Luca was nice, and I felt pretty certain he was an ethical person, I couldn't possibly share it with him. But, hey, I could fish a little?

"Luca, as you've been doing your digging, have you found anything really unusual? Letters, or maybe a diary or something that seemed out of the ordinary—a little bizarre?"

He frowned and shook his head slowly, but then suddenly brightened.

"Hey, you know what? I just thought of something. This is crazy. It might not be of any value, but who knows? There's a strange little packet of letters stuffed into one of the back shelves in the archives. They've been gathering dust there for a long time. There are a few people on staff who are aware of them, but no one pays any attention. Know why? Because they are in code. I mean, they are really in code. We think they date from the early 1700s. They're bound with twine and kept together, and when you look at them you see that they were written in some sort of invented language—like a cipher. They're all addressed in French, and it looks like they were sent to an obscure Knight, but I forget his name. Anyway, not a single soul would notice if the box went missing. Would you want to take a look at them? I could send them home with you, and I know you wouldn't mention it. You could study them, see if there's anything which might spark your curiosity. I guess you never know."

I was so busy, and I needed to finish up work, pack, and get ready to head back to the U.S., but of course my inquisitiveness got right in the way of common sense, so I said, "Hmmm… yeah, sure. I'd like to examine them. Are you certain you won't get in trouble? You can count on me to not let anyone know. I'll look them over and return them before I leave for Stateside—and thanks. Thanks for thinking of me."

"You don't need to thank me, Zara. I think of you all the time."

I felt my face flush. "Let's go get our things, and head out. It's getting late."

Luca slid from the booth and grabbed his notebook. "Look, I'll just pop into the back and slip the letters in my bag, being sure no one is in there. I'll meet you outside."

"Okay, I'll wait for you. I hope they don't set off any alarms."

"Don't worry, they won't. They aren't even included in the items which are controlled. Like I said, no one cares about them. Wait for me; I'll see you in a few minutes."

I collected my belongings, went through the entrance hall and out into the sharp air. The coolness felt good. I was starting to wonder where this friendship with Luca might be headed, and I got that familiar, nervous knot in my stomach. It was great timing that I'd be away for a while. I could try and figure it out. And as for the letters he mentioned, most likely they would be a whole lot of nothing; but, it was true, you could never be sure, and I didn't have much of anything else going as a lead anyway. It was really curious that Luca said they were written in a cipher. Anyone who took the time to write in cipher must have been hiding something. If the writer could invent the code, I would break it. Just then Luca stepped around the corner and guided me into a coffee shop. There, he told me to open my backpack, and when I did, he shoved the packet of letters in it.

"Thanks again, so much, for today, Zara. It's proved more helpful than I can tell you. Can we meet for a drink before you go home to America?"

"Well, I'm super busy, but we can try. I'll take a look at these and give you a call so I can return them to you, and maybe we can grab a glass of wine when we connect. And... thanks so much,

Luca. I'll see you soon, then." Suddenly I felt self-conscious. With a quick glance at my watch, I said, "Gotta make the next bus. Ciao!" And dashed out the door.

THAT EVENING, AFTER SCROUNGING around in the empty fridge and finally rescuing a few lonely eggs which I scrambled, I made a cup of coffee, and pushed aside the mess of papers and books spread across my desk. Glancing distastefully around my flat and the mess an entire semester had wrought, I thought, *Damn! I better get up really early tomorrow morning to print off my paper, drop it at school, and then pack.* I hated to think about cleaning my apartment before I left for home, but I guessed I needed to do that as well or it wouldn't present a very welcoming sight upon my return.

Eagerly, I reached into the satchel and my hand closed around the packet of letters Luca had stuffed in there. The paper was dry and crisp, the narrow twine rough. I placed the yellowing bundle on my desk right under the lamp and saw that there looked to be five separate envelopes. Each one was addressed to 'Knight Commander Louis LeVasseur' in exquisite calligraphy. From the first envelope, I withdrew the note enclosed. Opening it, I was startled at the sight. Two full pages of closely spaced glyphs greeted me. They were strong and clear—very square with sharp right angles, and some looked like letters of the Roman alphabet inverted or upside down. Each missive began with a greeting and ended with a symbol that apparently represented a name. I quickly slid the other letters from their coverings, examined them and instantly realized that the glyphs were comparable. In fact, I was able to recognize several patterns with just a glance. Maybe this would be a lot easier than I'd expected. I opened my notebook, sharpened a few pencils, and began my analysis.

Entangled in my little world of cryptography, I didn't budge from my seat until I had to get up to go into the bathroom. When I looked at the clock, I was shocked as it was just after 2 a.m. The project wasn't turning out to be nearly as simple as I had naïvely assumed; I wasn't close to being finished, and I'd promised Luca I'd return the letters before I went home. I stretched, gave my bedroom a cursory glance, and decided I'd stay up all night if I had to. I would decipher the writer's code, and know the content of the letters, by morning.

Relatively quickly, I was able to figure out that the code was a version of a shift cipher. Symbols were used with a certain frequency and in a prescribed pattern to make words. The challenge was figuring out what symbols represented which letters of the alphabet. I plugged the patterns into a software program I had—a pretty rudimentary one—but nevertheless it helped me recognize the configuration of letters into words. Slowly but surely, words and phrases emerged. Diligently, I worked until most of the letters had been painstakingly decoded. But they weren't yet coherent—I still had to translate them. Not only had they been written in archaic French, but some included words that had clearly been made up. My ability to read French was spotty, but I used a translation program, and where an invented word was inserted, I guessed at its meaning.

Page after page of scribbles, scratched out words, algorithms and symbols filled my notebook. But eventually the pencilled annotations started to take shape into readable messages.

And I could not believe what I was transcribing.

Each letter described sea voyages the writer had completed. It became apparent that the writer and recipient were siblings because every heading was '*À mon cher frère Louis*': 'To my dear brother Louis'. I read with utter fascination how the writer had sailed across the North Atlantic from the Continent, and round about the Caribbean Sea. At first, his description of sea attacks and battles had me thinking he was a naval mercenary recruited to serve French interests. But into the second letter, he described some barbarous killings, and suddenly it occurred to me. My God, the man had been a pirate! Wow! I ran my hands through my hair, re-sharpened my pencils, and kept working.

He graphically described raiding other ships and always followed the account with what seemed to be an apology, telling his brother the attacks were necessary and would "relieve corrupt and avaricious followers of the King's crown of their burdens of wealth, enabling them to share more equitably with people whose need was greater."

By interpreting his questions, I gathered that the letters' recipient, Knight Commander LeVasseur, was a virtuous and dedicated member of the Order, who spent his time caring for others less fortunate. There were comments about their shared childhood, apparently spent on an estate in Rouen, France. Certainly, different paths in life for brothers who had once been close enough to develop their own private language.

I struggled on. At 8 a.m. a shower and coffee helped revive me somewhat. There were just two letters left. I so wanted to collapse into bed, but although I'd started decoding, I still needed to translate their actual text. I couldn't stop now, so I refilled my cup and kept going. The second to last letter was addressed, as were the others, to 'Dear brother Louis.' In the upper right-hand corner, the symbols indicated it had been written in July of 1715 and its location was MonCoeur, Island of Santa Cruz. The letter began: "My brother, I have a tale I must tell you for you are to be the only living soul, beside me, who will know of it. It will reveal a secret kept by our family for generations..."

My breath caught in my throat. I was now wide awake as I read.

Line by line, the writer revealed the story for his brother: that of their great-grandmother many times over who, while in the employ of the King of England, Henry VIII, had discovered and stolen a portrait of the king and his queen. She had risked her life and that of her husband by the brazen theft but had done so to hide it from the world because its message was, in her belief, blasphemous. It pictured the king as God's representative on earth, replacing St. Peter, and it clearly portended his cruel takeover of the pope and the Church of Rome. That most pious grandmother, named Gabrielle LeVasseur, had interred the portrait in the estate's chateau, intending for it never to be found.

The pencil fell from my fingers, landing hollowly on the wooden floor. Suddenly, my head flushed with heat and my palms were drenched in a clammy sweat. I clasped my stomach as it churned in an unexpected wave of nausea. I felt like I might retch but had to know what messages were contained in the remainder of the note.

The letter continued, relaying the news that once he had been told of the legend of the painting, he could not rest until he'd found it—which indeed he had. He'd taken it with him aboard ship and had henceforth protected it with his life. It was worth a fortune, he said, and his intent was to hide it somewhere on the island of Santa Cruz, near to the Fort of MonCoeur, which had been built and inhabited by the Knights of Malta. The letter closed with an admonishment to never share what had been revealed but to keep the secret as it had been kept for so many years. The letter had been signed, as were the others, by the word 'Olivier' and the rough drawing of a bird of prey.

I was faint—compelling me to clutch the edge of my desk and sit immobile until the dizziness passed. Suddenly, emotion overwhelmed me, and contrary to my character, my eyes grew hot with tears, and soon I was wracked with sobs. Stumbling to my bed, I threw myself on it, crying until I was drained. What in the name of God had just happened? What was this unimaginable secret—this weird revelation—which I alone was now privy to? And why me? For that matter, how did a young woman who worked for the king have the audacity to steal it—based upon her values and beliefs, no less? The courage it must have taken! It seemed almost inconceivable. The portrait had clearly chosen her... and now it had chosen me. I was engulfed by an alarming notion that, somehow, I had been sought out, directed to follow the painting's path. But where? To its discovery? I considered how I'd desperately wanted to find a sign pointing to its existence, its location. Yet now that I had, I was entirely freaked out.

Disoriented and utterly depleted, I fell into a restless sleep.

I don't know how long I'd drifted, but I was jolted awake, certain that I heard my mother calling to me. I sat up, dazed. It was still morning, just before noon, and I felt wretched. Rubbing my eyes, I groaned thinking about how much I had to do that day—I couldn't possibly go back to sleep, which is what I longed for. Slumped on the edge of the bed, I took a bleak look across the room at my work table piled high with papers, notebooks, and trash. Filled with a sense of apprehension yet needing to know what awaited on that final sheet of ancient paper, I forced myself to sit down at the desk with the letter in front of me and scowled at the beginnings of the last decoded message. Fortunately, it was a short missive and, judging by its scratchings and smears, obviously written in haste. I picked up my pencil, and word by tortuous word, dissected its content.

"My dear brother Louis. I write to tell you that I was attacked. My injuries held me nigh unto death, but the Lord somehow saw fit to preserve my life. The intent of the attack was to rob me of much gold, but the deepest agony—greater than that of any bodily wound—was the theft of the painting which has been the property of our family for so long. I ask you, Brother—I implore you—to recover and keep it. It is right now on its way across the ocean: its destination, France—I believe Paris. If you find the wretch who stole it and left me for dead, I will pay you handsomely to have him strung limb from limb, his innards splayed out before him. Please find him, Louis. He is French Creole, his name is Adolphe Toussaint. Find the man. Find the painting. Restore it to our family!
Your brother, Olivier."

Chapter Twenty-seven

CHRISTMAS 2016

CHESTNUT HILL
MASSACHUSETTS

"Your turn. Try and make it snappy, will you?" I challenged.

Dad looked at me with his wry, slightly crooked grin. "You can adopt that smartass attitude all you like, my dear. But it doesn't change the fact that I'm beating you 410 to 325."

"That's because you take forever." I rearranged my Scrabble tiles once again, secretly despairing that I had the worst consonants possible, and not a single vowel. Plus, the board was packed full, with no likely spaces to use. "I think I'll get a Diet Coke while you ponder. Want anything?"

Dad debated a minute, then said "Yeah—two fingers of Macallan 18. Help soften your insults."

I brought the single malt and a Coke back into the study. I looked around with a deep sense of contentment. I'd always loved that room: a classic man's study, with paneled walls, shelves loaded with books—some of Dad's many medical texts, but also lots of our family's massive book collection, overseeing a thick and cozy Oriental carpet, overstuffed chairs and a wood fire blazing merrily away in the big hearth. I had to admit—it felt really great to be home. I didn't realize how much I missed it, and how deeply I'd missed my dad until I saw him, and we'd hugged each other for what seemed like forever, but it was just what I needed.

Christmas had been good. We'd surrounded ourselves with family, and when Dad suggested we have a holiday house party, at first, I objected. I'd always hated parties. The standing around, the whole ordeal of making small talk. But when he asked me if I wanted to host a gathering with him, and I saw how eager he seemed, I couldn't help but agree. We indulgently had it catered by one of the very best catering services in Chestnut Hill, and together, he and I unearthed and unboxed some of our favorite Christmas decorations. That had its moments, since many were poignant reminders of Mom. But we got our fresh Christmas tree, strung lights and placed ornaments, and as always, I loved the sharp, citrusy smell any time we entered the living room.

On the evening of the party, the guests arrived, and remarkably, I felt relaxed and happy. I knew my mom would have been proud of me as I circulated, chatting with people I hadn't seen for some time. I'd dressed for the occasion, too. I had my hair blown out, and makeup applied by a skilled girl who came to the house. When I was assembling my outfit, I'd dug around in a drawer in my room, and found the silver-grey box containing the bracelet Mom had given me, it seemed like years before. I held the box, wanted to open it, but found I couldn't. The memory was still too raw, too painful. So carefully, I replaced it in my dresser, not knowing if I'd ever touch it again.

I did wish Lina had been there, as her vivacious Italian charm would have been a welcome addition to the evening. Nonetheless, I knew she would have thoroughly approved of my sleek silk pants and black velvet top, and my overall much more polished look. So, all in all, we'd had a great time and my visit home had been wonderful thus far.

However, even though I'd filled Dad in on my coursework progress, I'd harbored a secret. My extraordinary discovery was never out
of mind, and I knew needed help. Or reassurance. Or just someone
to whom I could tell about the wild circumstance I'd experienced just
before leaving Rome.

Dad sipped at his scotch and, ridiculously over-pleased with himself, carefully laid his tiles in place on the board. "There! 'Equivocal'.
A 75-point word. How's that?" he crowed.

"It's great, Dad. No doubt, you're the champion…" My voice
trailed off.

He looked up, frowning. "What's up, Zar?"

"Dad. I've got to tell you something. You might call me crazy, and
maybe I am. It wouldn't be the first time you'd have thought that of
me." I gave a rueful laugh. "But I have to tell someone, and you are
really the only one I can trust."

His eyes reflected concern. "What is it, love? You know I'm
always here for you, no matter what."

"I'm sorry; I didn't mean to alarm you. It's nothing dire. But it is
kind of earth-shattering." I chewed my lip and guessed it had to be
time, even though I'd promised myself I would solve the riddle on my
own. So I settled back, snatched a sip of my Coke, took a deep breath,
and began.

"Remember when I went to the Papal Library—the Manuscripts
room—in the fall? Well, while I was there, I discovered something.
Something incredibly strange, and so compelling it's consumed me
since the moment I found it…"

There was nothing left of the fire but glowing embers by the time
I'd finished my tale, having told my father every detail about what I
had uncovered, and what I knew. He sat silently, eyes narrowed in concentration, while I recounted my chance finding of the tiny note, its link
to the Knights of Malta, my visits to the Magistral Library, the Weston
chronicle, and the astonishing coded letters Luca had given to me.

"So, I've come this far, Dad. And I can't just let it go: surely you see that? I have to keep searching. But I truly don't know how. I can't do it on my own, and as I told you, I'm reluctant to let Antonio know about it."

"Why, though, Zara? Isn't he a friend? And your mentor? I thought he was very supportive of you. Why couldn't he be of help?"

"He is supportive. And we are friends." My thoughts flitted to Antonio—my "friend". Was it a friendship, though? Or was it more and I just didn't want to think about it? So instead, I continued. "Maybe he could help. But…" I faltered. It was time to say it out loud, what had been gnawing at me when it came to Antonio. "I guess this is my concern: what if he decides to pursue the painting on his own, and then what if he finds it and claims it as his? It would mean that… well… that I'd failed at something I wanted so much to do, believed I could do. And he would have robbed me of that validation. I know I would be devastated. I'm not sure I would trust anyone again. You know, Dad, that kind of stuff happens all the time—the lowly student discovers something, or invents something, then the senior researcher, or the professor, claims sole authorship. I would totally lose it if that happened to me."

"Oh, Zar, honey. Look, I am not saying it's an impossibility, but truthfully, it seems farfetched. At least to me." He got up, came around to my chair and gave me a warm and reassuring hug. "I can see how much this means to you. And I get it. I really do. But great achievements don't happen very often by a single person. You know that, right? Collaboration is the key. Think on that, okay?" Then he chuckled. "Anyway, us academics, we're generally an ethical crowd of old farts."

"He's not old, Dad! I mean, Antonio—he's not old at all. At least I don't consider forty old."

The denial had escaped me before I had time to think. I surprised myself by needing to jump to Antonio's defense. Why did I care what my dad thought of him? It seemed weird.

So, to close the uncomfortable subject, I heaved myself from the armchair and went to the bar in the corner of the room to pour refills for us both. "I just don't want to risk telling anyone. I feel like… like somehow, I've been called, in an odd way… to search for it. Does that sound insane? 'Cause at times to me, I feel like I am. Yet at others, it's all completely logical. You know, I've thought about confiding in my new friend Luca—but he's just not in any position to help. He's struggling to pull his own thesis together and having a hard enough time with that, and anyway, I don't know him well enough. This is way too important to me."

Dad slowly swirled the golden whiskey in his snifter and studied it. "So, what do you think should come next, Zara? Do you have any strategy in mind on how to continue your search?"

"Well, I've thought about it a lot. In fact, it seems that's all I think about these days. I know what I need to do, but I'm not sure I can pull it off myself."

"What is it, hon? I hear you, and I believe every single thing you've told me. And whether or not you know it, I want you to follow this dream—to succeed. So, what's next, then?"

"I want to go to Paris, Dad, which is where I believe the painting was at one time. Perhaps still in the possession of Toussaint's heirs— you know, the Creole pirate who stole it? Maybe he never moved it on. Maybe it's still there, still in the city somewhere."

He was silent; we both were, for a time. Then he glanced up, smiling quizzically. "So how would you feel if I came with you?"

It took me a minute to register what my father had just offered. But then I looked at him with relief and gratitude, and jumped up this time to give him the biggest hug I could.

"Really? Really, Dad—you would do that? I'd be thrilled if you would come!"

"Ok then, my treasure seeker. Because I believe in you—actually, I always have. Let's book a trip to Paris, and together we'll search for your lost masterpiece."

Chapter Twenty-eight

EARLY JANUARY 2017

PARIS

T he Air France Boeing 777 touched down smoothly on de Gaulle's runway. Although barely able to contain my excitement thinking about the adventure ahead, I had to admit I was just the tiniest bit reluctant to leave the jet's luxurious *La Première* cabin. Dad, equally eager to begin our investigation in Paris, had insisted that, this being a special trip for the two of us, we travel first class all the way. As a budget-conscious student, I didn't feel such self-indulgence necessary, but I knew it was important to him. He'd barely been anywhere since Mom died—only to a few medical conventions—and it wasn't as if the cost was going to be a burden.

I was surprised, and thrilled, that the story of the portrait, and the obscure but definitive clues I'd uncovered, had sparked an unmistakable enthusiasm in him. He'd spent countless hours in the days before our departure reading everything he could find about Henry VIII and his queens, particularly about Anne Boleyn and the advent of the Reformation in England. He'd also researched the Order of Malta, and by the time we took off from JFK to Paris, already carried a sizable folder full of information. I'd paged through it. The mysterious link with the Order of Malta was so intriguing. Scanning the material Dad had gathered, I read the beginning of a paper; it described the Order as The Sovereign Military Hospitaller Order of St. John of Jerusalem of Rhodes and of Malta. The name alone was convoluted. The ancient group tended to pilgrims on Crusades and in the Holy Land. Interesting that the mighty Templars, also a Christian military order, was now defunct, but the Order of Malta continued to thrive. And to think that they were at the source of the painting's disappearance.

I stole a last sip of my delicious mimosa (made with fresh squeezed orange juice and Veuve Cliquot Grande Dame, no less) and sneaked a final lingering look around my snug personal cabin. I sincerely hoped this experience hadn't permanently ruined me for flying economy in the future, but, after all, a trans-Atlantic flight on first was enough to spoil anyone. Reluctantly, I folded up the soft blanket and switched off the table lamp next to my seat.

"Mademoiselle, your coat?"

The attendant helped me into my jacket and handed me my carry-on bag. I'd certainly never felt this refreshed after an overnight flight. It had been a pleasure, that's for sure. Dad and I left the plane and went to collect our luggage and grab a taxi to the hotel.

Although we'd arrived just after 9 a.m. Paris time, the staff at the lovely Hotel du Palais Royal were happy to greet and show us to our rooms, which were ready for the early arrival. After a quick freshen-up, we met in the hotel's lounge for a pot of tea.

I stirred a lump of white sugar into my Earl Grey while Dad opened his folder, shuffled through it until he came to a particular sheaf of notes. "So, Madame Moreau said that we should report first to the Office of the Prefecture of Police. They will have the initial research records there waiting for us."

His focused approach came as an enormous relief to me. Not for the first time—nor, I was pretty sure, would it be the last—I was so very glad I'd taken him into my confidence. The extraordinary circumstances of this discovery and the search had become over-whelming. I had known I wouldn't be able to continue without support—emotional, and frankly, also financial. And whom else could I trust, if not my father?

"Dad, thank you. Thank you so much." I reached out and put my hand on his arm. Instantly, he reciprocated, covering it with his other hand while his grasp was warm and encouraging. My eyes threatened to fill, but I blinked hard. "I still can't believe you were able to locate the information we needed so quickly through your connections. I'm lucky you have such great ones. Evidently, it makes all the difference."

"It helps, that's for certain. Dominique Moreau is an old friend of mine. I met her at an international scientific summit some years ago, when she was at the Center of Cinematography, before she became the minister of culture for France. I'd been in touch with her just before the holidays, anyway, to congratulate her on her coming ele-vation to director-general of UNESCO. She's a powerhouse, and at her request, the research team at the préfecture hopped to it and found the leads we need."

"Well, I'm incredibly grateful. And also glad we didn't need to reveal all of our reasoning for wanting the background information. It helps not to have to release the details. At least not yet."

"I agree, Zar. There'll be plenty of time to figure out how to pro-vide the right people with the news. That is, if there will be anything to divulge at all. So... are you ready to go treasure-hunting?"

I dropped my napkin on the table, shrugged into my coat, threw my bag over one shoulder, and off we went to the Préfecture de Police, Place Louis Lépine, on the Île de la Cité.

We entered the imposing building ensconced in the shadow of the Cathedral of Notre-Dame's gorgeous spire and gave our names to the receptionist to be quickly and efficiently ushered into the office of Monsieur Durand, the prefect. In perfect English, and exceedingly politely, he greeted us and welcomed us to Paris. The entrée we had gained via the recommendation from Dad's friend, Madame Moreau, was sure as hell impressive.

On Durand's immaculately ordered desk lay a single, thin file, sealed within an official Préfecture de Police de Paris envelope. He told us that he'd included all the information which had been readily accessible by the police, but he felt certain we would be able to discover more at the Bibliothèque de l'Arsenal, where the library archives staff already awaited our arrival. In turn, he shook our hands, wished us "bonne chance" on our search, and guided us to the door.

My anticipation couldn't be contained, so the second we were settled in a cab headed for the Library of the Arsenal, rue de Sully, I ripped open the envelope. My heart started to beat fast, for there, on the title page, in beautiful Copperplate Gothic script, was inscribed:

1752

Dossier de Police sur

M. Adolphe Toussaint

Involuntarily, I grabbed Dad's arm and we stared at each other for a very long moment. In that instant I could tell—just as I had been when I slipped my finger between the pages of that little note in the Papal Library months before—that he was hooked. Rod, line, and sinker!

In a small private reading room in the Library's archives, we sat and chatted quietly with Sylvie Piton, a young university professor of languages who'd been recommended to Dad to help with translation and interpretation. We'd been assured that she was both talented and very discreet. The police dossier we'd been offered, although minimal, was more than enough with which to make a start. In brief it recorded that Monsieur Toussaint had become a notable, and very affluent, personage in Paris. It was known that his fortune came from ownership of several immense plantations in the Caribbean islands, primarily Saint Domingue, now known as Haiti. Apparently, M. Toussaint, like most of the wealthy, noble and socially elite male populace of eighteenth century Paris, was steeped in what was termed the *demimonde*: the sexual subculture which was an accepted element of Parisian life at that time.

The report went on to say that there were volumes of records about kept women and their patrons, all having been carefully and thoroughly documented by two inspectors of the Gendarmerie at that time. The first, Inspector Jean-Baptiste Meusnier, ran the unit which followed such women and their male—and female—clientele from the late 1740s until just prior to the French Revolution. Another, Inspector Louis Marais, who'd succeeded Meusnier, had also kept dossiers on hundreds of women. And buried in those files were references to one Adolphe Toussaint. They should be available to view at the Bibliothèque.

With Sylvie's help, we combed the catalogues. Almost immediately, we had a hit on Toussaint in the Bulletins rédigés par l'inspecteur de police Meusnier sur la vie des filles galantes de Paris les plus remarquées. In fact, there were frequent entries which included his name. The document's English title was: "Newsletters written by Police Inspector Meusnier on the life of the most famous Paris girls galantes".

"Dad, what on earth are 'girls galantes'? Do you have any idea? It sounds glamorous!"

"I could not tell you, Zar. Look it up."

So I popped up a new tab on the library's computer and typed in the words. "Here's what I found: 'Girls galantes' were the most elite prostitutes serving the upper social echelon of 18th c Paris.' And wait till you hear this!" I read aloud, "'...they were courtesans, or *courtesans du bon ton*, or *femmes galantes*: in essence, the prominent, yet notorious, mistresses of eighteenth century Parisian society—and their numbers included the famous Madame de Pompadour, Madame duBarry and Madame de Montespan—the latter mistress of Louis XIV.' Well now, isn't that interesting," I mused.

"It most definitely is," Dad said. "I do know that the time in France before the revolution was full of decadence—for the rich, at least. Hence, the revolt of the peasants."

"So, this entry goes on to say that 'the women who were coveted courtesans commanded big money and wielded great power: especially those few very exclusive madams who ran their businesses selling sex to privileged men of incomparable wealth.' Dad! It seems as if our pirate, Toussaint, must have been a very wealthy, and very frequent, customer."

Dad looked at me, and let out a low whistle.

Chapter Twenty-nine

SPRING AND SUMMER 1752

FAUBOURG SAINT-HONORÉ
PARIS

Assisting LouLou to negotiate the narrow doorway of the Paris Opéra was proving quite an ordeal for Monsieur Adolphe Toussaint—she being attired in a gown which, representing the pinnacle of fashion, featured enormous hooped *panniers*. As Madame Lou-Lou's voluminous skirts bobbed and billowed with the effort, a great puff of sweet orange blossom and French iris wafted heavenward. The scent was so overpowering it almost caused Adolphe to gag. Why in the name of Erzulie Fréda did Parisian women insist on saturating themselves with scent? To be sure, there was no *vodou* goddess more beautiful or sensual than Fréda, and *she* didn't find it necessary to bathe in perfume! He'd never understood it. Even now, despite having lived on the European Continent for nearly forty years, it was undeniably refreshing to return home to his islands and enjoy the womanly scents of the ladies there. Natural... earthy.

Even though every woman on Saint-Domingue wanted to emulate the Spirit of beauty and passion, Maîtresse Mambo Erzulie Fréda, they didn't feel it necessary to stifle their personal aromas with contrived fragrances.

LouLou tucked her arm intimately through Adolphe's as they passed beneath the ornate arch of the Palais-Royal and out into the street, where they commenced their stroll. It was such a splendid, late spring evening in Paris. Streetlamps flickered under a deepening violet sky; lilacs, clustered on every corner, added lush sweetness to the temperate air; the horse chestnuts, which bordered the entire length of the boulevard, fluttered their fresh green leaves in the light breeze. He did enjoy walking with her, and it was only a short way to her townhouse on rue Faubourg Saint-Honoré.

The boulevard was alive that evening with couples and families sauntering along, greeting each other and sometimes stopping under the chestnut trees to visit. LouLou was a well-recognized figure and many men who passed by bowed and tipped their tricorne hats to her. Their women would roll their eyes, then size up LouLou's gown, annoyed to find it more stylish and expensive than their own.

Lou's lilting voice trilled continuously. "Did you enjoy the opera, mon cheri? I know I did! I have seen *Castor et Pollux* several times, but wasn't it especially lovely this evening? And how about our little songbird? Wasn't she simply merveilleux as Telaire? Oh, I thought she did a superb job with the aria, yet I know she was so very nervous! All day, every day, I would hear her practicing 'Tristes Apprêts'. In fact, I feel as if I could perform it myself, I have heard it so many times! It is not an easy piece to sing. But she sounded wonderful, don't you think, Adolphe?"

"Indeed, I do. You really have worked wonders with her, Lou. How fortunate she is to have found you. Of course, you were able to recognize that she possessed all of the basic requirements for success. Beauty, talent, and enough intelligence to converse at least passably well. So, it was mutually beneficial, to be certain, that you discovered her."

Louise Périer, known in and about Paris as Madame LouLou, smiled with satisfaction. As they continued their promenade, she nodded and waved to almost every passer-by. Yes, Madame Lou was indeed a luminous figure in the upper echelon of Parisian society. At forty years of age, she was one of the wealthiest and most successful businesswomen in the city. A reputable and extremely discerning madam, the clients of her desirable femmes galantes consisted of only the most affluent, the most noble, and even the most royal men in Paris. In fact, Lou was even well known to, and greatly admired by, the handsome and beloved King Louis XV himself.

Lou had been born into an impoverished family, so by necessity she discovered at an early age what men liked and wanted, and with her golden curls, curvy figure, and almond-shaped blue eyes, she'd become a highly sought-after mistress in her youth. When her patrons boasted of their business ventures, she'd always listened carefully, and asked intelligent questions. They thought it so very charming, but Lou nurtured a plan greater than to remain a courtesan to rich men. She intended to acquire her own wealth. Thus it was, by employing the tutelage supplied by her lovers, and seeded by the small fortune provided by rich financiers during her years as a working girl, the tiny and delicate LouLou had ultimately become a woman of power and status. She ran the most profitable and desirable brothel in the demimonde—an integral part of the elite culture of the day. To be certain, any girl whom Madame LouLou decided to take under her wing knew she was lucky and ultimately would be very prosperous.

Lou's own long-time patron, who, these days, was both her lover and business partner, was the prominent, respected tycoon, Monsieur Adolphe Toussaint. They had met in December of 1730 at a petits souper—one of the elegant supper parties organized by madams for the purpose of introducing men to young ladies for hire. Toussaint had been 35 years old at that time, fabulously rich and exotically handsome, possessed of a rhythmic accent to his cultured French, and stylishly sporting a unique mode of dress no other man in the city could match. Lou, who at 18 desired a permanent patron of ample means, if not good looks, had glanced his way and in a single instant set her sights on winning him over. She intended to be his mistress—his only mistress, if she could manage it. Although a number of the men in attendance that night vied for her attention, she had eyes only for Toussaint. Midway through the soirée, he approached Madame Broussard, Lou's employer, and with a grand gesture intended to attract the full attention of the room, spilled an astonishing mound of golden louis' on the table.

As everyone watched with inquisitive fascination, he announced, "My offer for one night in the company of the exquisite Mademoiselle LouLou."

Lou's heart, and avaricious soul, was won, and that night she strove to please him with every technique she had learned. He was different from the men she'd previously associated with. His skin radiated a golden cast, not like the milky paleness of most others, and his voice had a melodic quality to it that she found unsettlingly attractive. She was well pleased, even though there was something about him, something rather primitive, that she both feared and relished. He was quick to disrobe completely, and his lean, muscular frame was something else she found unusual. Many pampered clients she served were soft and paunchy. He also displayed several scars, strangely exciting ones, and when she inquired about them, he merely said they were acquired during the vagaries of his youth. He stood naked before her, except for one item he didn't remove. She reached up to touch it—a soft suede bag on a golden cord about his neck. He caught her wrist, and although not exactly harsh, his manner stopped her in mid-sentence.

"You are lovely, indeed, Miss LouLou, and may be able to connive much from me… but never take my gris-gris. Do you understand?"

"Oui, Monsieur. Bien sûr. Of course. I promise."

His grip slid from encircling her arm to delicately lifting her palm to his lips.

"Monsieur Adolphe… what is it? Can you at least tell me that?"

The odd turquoise blue of his eyes had deepened while he stared at her. "It is my talisman. It never leaves me, and its magic protects me. But it can have quite the opposite effect if taken by anyone else. So, if we are to continue the arrangement we have begun tonight, you must know: it will remain private to me."

"I am only too happy to comply, sir. But if I may presume, where did you come by this most intriguing item? I am curious."

"Well, aren't you the bold one, Mademoiselle? Only because your beauty is extraordinary, and your appeal quite bewitching, do I feel any inclination to tell you. I do not inform others, you know. It is a part of my culture, a part of my heritage. I am a follower of vodou, the religion of West Africa, and that of many peoples in the islands where I was born. And that is all I will say about it tonight."

"I see, Monsieur. I find it interesting. In my eyes, it but adds to your power and your allure. And I do hope that our arrangement will be a long one. I will make sure you won't have a need to look elsewhere."

On the following day a package had been delivered, addressed to Mademoiselle LouLou, at the town house of her madam. Inside was 20,000 livres, and a necklace laden with diamonds, and thus was their long- term relationship born.

AS NIGHT FELL, LOU and Adolphe walked briskly. Their destination was in sight, so they stopped for a few moments, and Adolphe helped her be seated on a bench—no easy matter, since the *pannier* hoops women wore to create incredible volume in the skirts of their gowns all but prevented them from sitting, or even from moving, very easily. From her jewelled bag, Lou withdrew a tiny, golden compact. She opened it and peered into the mirrored side, patted a few stray hairs in her elaborately curled coiffure, and, after critically surveying the effect, from the compact selected two tiny silk face patches: one shaped like a crescent moon, and the other a star. Carefully, she applied the star just under her left eye. The moon was affixed to her right cheek. "How does that look, 'Dolphe?" Her black eyelashes fluttered in that special way she had perfected. Lou was ever the *coquette*.

Adolphe took a healthy pinch of snuff from a small box, the enamelled surface of which bore a primitive African design. He tucked it between his cheek and gum, then grinned at her. "You are ravishing, as always, ma beauté." He raised her gloved fingers and lightly brushed them with his lips.

They rose, and as Lou adjusted her gown, Adolphe inquired, "Do you know if Cèlie will be joining us for supper? You'll recall that I invited several gentlemen who wish to make her acquaintance?"

"Yes, chérie, of course I remember," Lou rejoined. "How do you think I have built my fortune? Through a habit of forgetting? I think not. The house staff will have the dining room set for 18 guests as planned. You and I will arrive well in time to have a sherry, and supper will be served promptly by 11 p.m. All the details have been arranged, just as I have always handled them."

She offered him her special, sweet smile. Although she truly did love Adolphe, that smile was a practiced technique to disguise her impatience with the general insensibility of men. Weren't they just impossible at times?! When it came to Adolphe, though, she really had no complaints. He'd kept her as his mistress for many a year—and had paid her handsomely. Now, she and Adolphe were a couple—not a married couple, but a pair none the less. It was just that their personal arrangement was rather unusual; however, it suited them both perfectly well. They were committed to each other, but that did not preclude either one from having an affair or a dalliance elsewhere. Lou was not a jealous woman, and she was attractive enough at forty that she had more than her share of admirers. Adolphe was typically quiet about his occasional diversions, and never flaunted them in Lou's presence. Anyway, although they shared the beautiful, elaborately appointed townhouse on rue Saint Honoré, Toussaint regularly rented other properties in the city: his pied-à-terre, to which he could retreat when he chose. A happy arrangement, even more so as Adolphe had always been enormously helpful by guiding certain men of impeccable financial qualifications to services offered by Lou's girls. And he shared in the profits of Lou's business, but no one other than the two of them knew the nature of their partnership.

Her chatter lingered as they crossed the threshold of the grand three-story stone house. The sounds of a refined party, the clink of glassware and light laughter of women accompanied by men's voices, were heard wafting from the second floor as servants quickly relieved Lou of her silk wrap, and Adolphe his walking stick. They ascended the graceful, curved staircase together, and were greeted with delight upon entering the dining room.

Lou swept the room with her perfectionist's gaze. How beautiful it was, and how proud it made her to know she owned it! A perfect rendering of le style du jour, designed and decorated by the foremost architects and interior designers in Paris. That evening, the glow from a sea of candles was reflected in Venetian mirrors which lined the walls, equally from the abundant silver bedecking the room—candelabra, tureens, salvers and wash basins filled with rosewater… The golden light suffused the room in such a way as to offer everyone their very best advantage. Women looked dazzling—jewels and glimmering embroidery on their attire lighting their complexions to a milky sheen. The men's pale-colored waistcoats and satin breeches set off lace jabots at their throats, powdered hair brilliantly white in the soft light. Elegant crystal coupes of champagne were held in hands gloved in finest kidskin, to be sipped delicately and never quaffed indiscriminately. Lou's girls knew proper comportment. They had all been well-schooled by their astute madam on how to entertain men of high breeding for the night, or to accompany them on any outing desired.

The evening's soirée was well underway. Supper would be served shortly, and men were absorbed by the prospect of choosing with whom they wished to dine. Adolphe sought Lou out from a corner of the room near the hearth, where she was deep in conversation with an older gentleman. "Excusez-moi, Monsieur. I will only borrow Madame LouLou for a mere minute." Taking her aside, in a low but insistent voice he pressed, "Where is she, Lou? You said she would be here. It's getting late, and there are a few men who are quite impatient. Is she coming?"

"As I told you, I believe so, 'Dolphe. But you know how she is. She's not the quickest girl. It will take time for her to change from her costume, and there is no doubt she will be visited in her dressing room by a myriad of admirers. I made sure there would be a carriage waiting for her at the stage entrance of the building. The driver was instructed to bring Célie and her friend, Justine, directly to the townhouse. I do hope they make it in time for supper, but I can't be certain."

"Who is this Justine? I've not heard of her. Is she good-looking?"

"That I do not know, my love. She is a close friend of Célie's—one of the actresses at the Comédie-Française. I am told she is enchanting, so I'll be interested in observing her. Célie likes her very much and has said she might be a worthwhile addition to my group of girls." Lou laughed, and others glanced momentarily up from their tête-á-têtes. "Of course, Mademoiselle Justine will have much to prove before I consider drawing up a contract to engage her services for the long-term. But we shall see. This little supper party will be a good test."

"Well, I hope she has something to offer because Célie can only be in one place at a time, and the financier général has been breathing down my neck."

"Yes, I know darling, I do see him huffing and puffing about the room. And then we also have the irritable Comte de La Marche. He will insist upon competing with the financier général. It seems that whomever Général Gautier beds, le comte must have her too. Poor La Marche... he must feel so emasculated. I've been told he's desperately searching for a new mistress since his former, Demoiselle Coraline, apparently continued to empty his pockets, all the while sleeping with that young and handsome Signore Casanova." She chuckled. "Hmmm... the much older man abandoned for a young gigolo. That never seems to go well, does it?" And with a final giggle and flutter of her fan, she moved off to attend to her social duties.

THE *HORS D'ŒUVRE* SERVICE had been completed, and footmen were again moving from guest to guest, offering selections from platters laden with slices of *boef madrilène* decorated with gold leaf spangles, or, from a deep silver basin, scallops bathed in oyster liquor. The men were very obviously enjoying the meal; the young women ate next to nothing, occasionally nibbling on the tiniest bite, but mostly leaning into their dining partners and whispering in their ears, or giggling behind their fans, always posing at angles which allowed the gentlemen to have an advantageous view of their bosoms.

In mid-service a peal of laughter was heard in the stairwell and making a grand entrance worthy of a duchess, into the dining room floated Mademoiselle Célie. Such was her captivating presence that all stopped eating or drinking or flirting to stare at her. Justine, who had followed Célie, was a strikingly pretty girl, tall and willowy, but it was as if she simply faded into the background, as Célie assumed center stage. It certainly was no wonder she'd been delayed—the completion of her supper toilette must have taken forever. Her *robe à la française* was a vision in shimmering pink silk laden with lace, ruffles, and bows. Corseted to achieve a waistline that could easily be encircled by a man's hands, the gown was so scandalously low cut at the bodice that even the girls galante thought it brazen. Her blonde hair had been arranged in a high, soft pouf, wound throughout with jewels, flowers, and feathers. And her makeup was flawless—a pale, perfect complexion with just a hint of flush at the cheek, dark pink lips, and a single black silk star just to the left of her mouth.

"Oh, bonne soirée à tous!" she sang. "I do apologize for being detained. It was just that I had so many visitors to my dressing room after the performance. I hope we haven't disrupted what is clearly a wonderful party. Please, take no notice of me. Continue enjoying your supper!" And with a wave, she and Justine found the places which had been laid for them. It was not ten seconds before Célie was surrounded by men who had leaped from their dinners to greet her. She and Justine were quickly paired with gentlemen who monopolized their attention.

Madame LouLou kept a keen watch over all from her position at the head of the table. She observed which girls were most desired by the men, and she was prepared to offer the gentlemen the opportunity to spend the night with the girl of their choice in a house she owned for just such a purpose. It stood nearby and was quite beautiful. Accommodations were available for a number of couples should they choose to stay. Her own home she employed only occasionally, but just for select entertainments; no trysts were ever conducted within. Lou glanced along the table, and noticed that Général Gautier, who had won the place next to Célie, was enthralled by one of her cunning techniques: as she leaned in to converse and laugh, she allowed the bodice of her gown to slip just enough so her breasts, with meticulously rouged nipples, were on full view. Naturally, her partner's stare would be riveted, and blithely she would continue her conversation, feigning any notice. It was a very effective flirtation, and Célie had perfected it.

Lou then studied the young Justine, who had quickly acquired several men's interest. Just as the madam determined all was well and thought to take a bite or two of her supper, out of the corner of her eye she became aware that Adolphe's gaze was riveted, and that he'd assumed a certain expression she'd come to know quite well in their years together. It was cat-like, almost feral, in a way, and his intensity at times gave her chills. She knew, when that look appeared, he would not be denied. So, she'd learned to acquiesce. Discreetly she watched him, and her intake of breath was sharp. The object of his fixation was Célie.

At first, Lou felt a pang that was almost visceral. But then she thought, Why should it affect me so? 'Dolphe has had a myriad of women in the time we've been together. He always returns to me. Be that as it may, the situation continued to bother her greatly. All the while, Célie seemed completely unaware, still performing her craft masterfully with the financier général, who looked for all the world like the cat that just stole the cream. The evening wore on; brandy was served. Several couples slipped away, including Justine accompanied by the comte, who looked much less crestfallen than he had earlier, when the général had bested him to the place next to Célie.

Célie and two other girls excused themselves for a few moments and disappeared into the ladies' salon to freshen their toilettes after supper. Lou engaged the général in discussion to distract him while he waited. He informed her that his intention was to spend an evening or two with Lou's lovely protégée and, should all go well, perhaps consider taking her on as his maîtresse-en-titre. Restlessly he paced and awaited her to reemerge, frequently glancing toward the doorway where she and the others had disappeared. One by one, the other girls returned and joined their patrons, gathered their wraps, and departed for the evening. Still, there was no sign of Célie, and

Général Gautier was now very agitated. Lou did her best to soothe him, and offered, "Monsieur Général, allow me to have a look. I will find her. You will see: she is quite charming, but never prompt! I will be right back."

Lou ducked into the salon near the dining room. No one was there. Brushes and combs, feather fans and perfume bottles littered the area, but not a girl in sight. She peeked into and down the long gallery to see if she might catch a glimpse of her stray demoiselle. The hall was echoingly empty. After several minutes Lou knew she had no choice but to confront the général and tell him—but perhaps Célie had returned while Lou was looking? Hopefully, she re-entered the dining room. The only person remaining was Général Gaultier— and he was not a happy man. Lou squared her shoulders and approached him. She would have to make some reasonable excuse. Perhaps say that Célie had suddenly been taken ill, had sent word, and promised to meet with the général soon. Lou worked her magic, and shortly the stout, bewhiskered officer had calmed a bit, his spirits somewhat revived by the assurance of a rescheduled rendezvous with the actress—for a reduced fee, of course.

At that, the graying gentleman was quickly ushered into his eve- ning cloak, handed his stick, and placed in a waiting carriage. With a heavy sigh, Lou returned to the dining room and looked around. She knew exactly what had happened to Célie.

Because, unsurprisingly, Adolphe, also, was nowhere to be found.

LOU WAS SLEEPLESS ALL that night. Amidst her tossing and turning, she occasionally thought she heard him return to the house and slip quietly into his bedchamber, which was just across the hall. Once, she even got up, threw her satin robe about her shoulders, and tiptoed across, lightly pushing his door ajar to see if he slumbered in his bed. But of course, the room was empty, the bed still pristine.

She returned to her own room, and aided by her stepstool, clambered back into bed, and lay wide awake with the coverlet pulled under her chin. She'd not succumbed to jealousy in the past... so why now? It was because she'd seen it—that look of desire on his face as he watched Célie. It was the same expression which, in the past, had been reserved for her—and her alone. Her heart was heavy; there was no denying it. She loved him. Loved him as if he'd been her husband all these years. He'd cared for her, supported her, lavished her with money and gifts, and praise, for her beauty, her ability to attract men, and as they grew older together, her innate ability to run a successful enterprise. In fact, Adolphe's opinion meant everything to her. And now, at 52, he was still a covetable catch for a young woman seeking to become someone's mistress. While Lou knew she had plenty of money to care for herself through the end of her days, it wasn't the money she wanted—it was his devotion. Perhaps he was even preparing to leave her? She had nothing, really, to tie him to her. Nothing except their business dealings and a private, personal commitment. They weren't married; there was no contract.

And what about Célie? In the dark of night, Lou simmered with anger. She was betrayed by someone whom she had nurtured and mentored, and whose livelihood she still directed. How dare she?! But then, she knew. She knew how Adolphe was when he wanted something. Audacious. Almost diabolical. And relentless. Adolphe got exactly what he wanted. Always. So, after all, how could she blame Célie? She'd had no choice. Of this Lou was certain.

Finally, her thoughts settled, the sleep which had evaded her came in the early morning hours. She drifted, dreamless.

At mid-morning she was awakened by her maid, who threw the curtains open and then carried a heavy silver tray into the room bearing an aromatic pot of coffee, sugar and cream, along with delicately thin bone china cups. While Lou was assisted in donning her day attire and having her hair dressed, she determined to release her resentment from the previous night. It was, with any likelihood at all, a short-lived, obsessive fascination he'd harbored, and he would be well satisfied by a single night spent in Célie's company. Lou concluded she would not dwell overmuch on what had taken place. She emerged from her rooms confident and restored, ready to carry out her business matters of the day. Once those were completed, she knew precisely how she intended to put closure to the prior evening's matter.

By late afternoon, Lou had finished a good deal of work. She'd written necessary correspondence, sent payment vouchers to service people to whom she owed money, had overseen the week's menus for the household, discussed the supply orders with her house steward, and conducted meetings with three of her girls to finalise contracts she'd arranged for them with patrons. She decided to take a refreshing walk in the garden and had just slipped through the door when she heard the crunch of gravel behind her. Turning, she was greeted by Adolphe, who placed his hands gently on her shoulders and kissed her cheek.

"Good afternoon to you, Madame Lou. I've not seen you the entire day. How are you?" He offered her his broad grin.

In a moment's decision, she suppressed her pique, and instead smiled charmingly in return. "I've had quite a lovely day, thank you. I accomplished much. I assume my productivity must have come from the unusually restful and deep sleep I had last night. And you? Comment vas-tu, mon cher? Did you sleep well?"

"I did, merci. By the way, had you told me we were expected to dine at Dame Chevalier's house tonight?"

"Yes. We're to arrive at nine. You'll be ready?"

Lou followed Adolphe's gaze as he glanced away. "I will be ready. Have the carriage waiting. However, I cannot stay late. I have an appointment at eleven. I'm sure the main course will have been served by then, correct? I'm sorry I will need to leave, but this is an important engagement with someone interested in buying a good deal of this year's sugarcane. I can't afford to miss it."

She noticed with a pang that he avoided her gaze as he spoke.

"Is that so? Well, darling, we wouldn't want you to neglect your business just for a silly dinner party. Of course, you must go when you need to. I'll remain until dessert has been served, then make my excuses and have the carriage drive me home."

"Perfect." He was visibly relieved. Together, they walked back into the house, and she continued on to her sitting room, while Adolphe bid her leave and went up the stairs to his shrine room for prayer.

Lou, as soon as she'd stepped into her personal suite, summoned her maid and told her to dispatch an urgent message to Célie. She was to be advised that Madame LouLou would shortly pick her up for a drive along the boulevard. And to be ready. There would be no other options.

She knew Adolphe wouldn't descend from his shrine for some while. When he spent time there, it was usually for a rather long duration; it clearly provided an escape for him. When Lou had purchased the townhouse with financial help from Adolphe, he insisted he would have a special place which would be solely his—a room which would not be open to visitors, even to Lou. In this room, he established a sanctuary where he could conduct his worship of Bondye, the Creator, and the Loa spirits, according to his beliefs. Over their years together, 'Dolphe had educated Lou, at least to some extent, about his religion. Lou found it fascinating and very complex. And while she had always expressed interest, he'd never invited her to worship with him, or even to see much of what he did while ensconced in the shrine he created. She thought it was a little frightening, actually. Sometimes rhythmic drumming could be heard from behind the door, often accompanied by chanting. He would also burn incense—the acrid smell permeated the house. And, more than once, she had seen him take brightly colored birds into the room. What he did with them, she didn't know. But none of them ever emerged.

Lou gathered her small, beaded purse and a parasol and was helped into the coach. She settled herself and looked forward to the ride. She'd just acquired a new, light and agile landau coach and was proud that she owned one of the early few which had been spotted on the rues des Paris. It was drawn by a pair of beautifully matched, dappled grey geldings, and her coachman's livery was impeccable. She'd changed into a new afternoon dress of peacock blue watered silk, and she wore the diamond necklace Adolphe had given her after their first, unforgettable rendezvous. Her display of wealth and power was intended to remind Célie that although she might bear the bloom of youth's beauty and with it attract the attention of men, it was her madam, Louise Périer, who remained firmly in command.

"Bonjour, Madame," Célie offered respectfully as she was assisted into the seat facing Lou in the open-air carriage.

"Bonjour, Mademoiselle. And how do you fare today? Well, I hope?" Lou responded with a raise of one eyebrow—a particular expression that her femmes galantes knew quite well and paid close attention to.

"Merci beaucoup, Madame. I am well, if but a little tired. I had rather an exhausting night."

"Ah, yes. I am quite certain you did." The madam's voice oozed sympathy. "Your performance at the opéra was scintillating. It must have taken a tremendous amount of endurance, no? Afterward, I'd assumed you probably felt unwell since you departed so suddenly from the supper party. I must tell you, Général Gaultier was sorely disappointed. I had to scramble to make excuses for you, about which, as you might imagine, I was not at all happy. I had to promise him time with you in the next day or two at most. So, did you retire early? Go directly home?"

The landau skimmed along the streets of Paris and headed out onto the tree-lined Boulevard de la Madeleine, where many other carriages transported passengers for a sunny afternoon's drive.

As she awaited the girl's reply, Lou nodded and acknowledged others when they passed by.

"Well, I... ahh... Oh, Madame! I cannot lie to you! I am so very sorry. Truly I am! I spent the night with Monsieur Toussaint. But Madame—please believe me—I had no choice. You simply must believe me. He is... how should I say it... persistent?" She looked at Lou with pleading eyes. "For that matter, he wants to meet me again tonight, and I would very much prefer not to. Can you help me? Please?"

Madame Lou did not quickly reply. She gathered herself, because she had no wish to display even a shred of jealousy to her young protégée. Eventually, she said, "I am well aware of how coercive Monsieur Toussaint can be, Célie. He's an unusual man. This I have known for many a year. He is very attractive but he's also a man with many quirks. And secrets. He carries secrets that he holds close to him."

"Yes! Isn't it odd?" the younger woman rushed to agree, sensing she might not be cast out by her madam, and her transgression would not be held against her after all.

Lou was silent, surveying white puffy clouds as they undulated with the air currents overhead. Then, "Alright. I will take care of the arrangements for this evening. You will not be troubled by Adolphe tonight."

"Thank you, thank you so very much, Madame. You are much too kind."

Lou swept right over Célie's last comment. "Instead, though, this very morning I received a request for the pleasure of your company, from someone who saw you perform last evening at the opéra. It arrived in a beautifully written letter, on a magnificent letterhead, stamped with the seal of the Sovereign Order of Malta. The gentleman's name is Monsieur François Marraud—actually, he signed the note 'Commandeur Marraud'—and is a Knight Commander in the Order. In fact, I inquired about him, and he is related to the Grand Master Pinto da Fonseca. Fonseca resides in Malta, but he heads the Order around the world. Hence, he is a very, very wealthy and important man."

The coach bumped along a rutted road, and the ladies gripped their seats to avoid being tossed about. "What is this 'Order', Madame? I know nothing of it."

"A large and hugely influential religious group. The Order is ancient—and its Knight members, especially the officers, come from noble and wealthy families. They do charitable work and care for the sick and needy. But I am told their leverage is significant in many other areas. They are mysterious and are closely tied to the Catholic Church and the pope, in Rome. Let us just say that when one of their Knights makes a request, it is not wise to deny it. And religious they may be, but after all… they are men. And this man, apparently, wishes for discretion above all else. Therefore, I will arrange a meeting for you with the Commandeur. I believe this evening would be expedient. You will have time to get ready, yes?"

"Oui, of course I will, Madame. Just provide me with our meeting time and location, and I assure you I will not disappoint."

"I know you won't, Célie. You are, after all, a good girl, and I do care for you very much. I hold no ill will over last night but, in return, you must be firm with Toussaint. I will speak with him, but as you have already learned, he is a man of his own mind. And that mind is unlike others'."

Feeling both relieved and vindicated, in a moment of convivial spirit, Célie suddenly had an additional thought. "Oh! And Madame! It was the strangest thing. The monsieur showed me his shrine room late last night. It is extraordinary, n'est-ce pas?"

Lou was utterly taken aback. Apparently, the sounds she thought she had heard the night before were no figment of her imagination—Adolphe had returned to the house! And worse, he had not been alone. Yet he knew their rules. They had long ago promised that neither would ever bring a paramour into the home they shared. And even more disturbing: why had he taken Célie to see his vodou shrine, a sanctum into which even she, his long-term partner, was seldom invited? It made no sense.

"And to me, the strangest of all, Madame, was this: among all those icons, and statues of his Spirits? I think he calls them the 'Loa'? What about that magnificent double portrait? Have you ever seen anything else like it? I certainly have not! Although you, of course, own many beautiful paintings, I must be truthful and say I haven't seen any to compare to this, not even among the art which I am told is displayed at the Palace of Versailles! I found myself speechless when confronted by it, really."

LouLou didn't respond. She felt like she had been punched. Adolphe rarely invited her into his shrine room. Yet he had allowed Célie to spend time in there and ask questions.

The girl was still chattering. Lou caught the last few words. "… there were deep scratches across the queen's face. So, to repair the canvas, he painted over it himself."

Célie offered an apologetic smile, hoping the story wasn't further exploiting her madam's displeasure. "I suppose he fancies himself an artist, but I don't think he did a very expert job, to be honest. But of course, I would never dare say so... would you?" Lou's expression was one of studied indifference, so Célie forged on. "Anyway, he showed it to me, and then he told me about the Loa, Erzulie Balianne. At least, I think that is her name. He warned that she is the spirit called the 'Gagged', and that she protects all secrets and I would have this Erzulie watching over me, and I shouldn't tell anyone about the painting. It's rather frightening! But I know I can trust you and am certain you will have seen it many times."

Lou remained silent for the rest of the journey, flabbergasted that Adolphe, on their very first assignation, had taken Célie into that bizarre shrine which Lou, herself, had only been privileged to enter on occasion. Yes, of course she had seen the painting and knew that Adolphe had somehow come by it while seeking his fortune in the Caribbean, where it had previously been in the possession of some pirate. He adored it and kept it on private display as the most coveted trophy in his collection of riches. She knew it had been rent down the middle during the sea crossing, and he'd worked on the repairs himself, not wanting anyone else to see or touch it. He had told her that, among all he owned, he knew this artwork held the most value. He believed it had an extraordinary, hypnotic significance. That idea seemed mind-boggling but did explain why he kept it so carefully—obsessively, one might argue—under lock and key.

Minutes later, they pulled up in front of Célie's residence, and before she stepped out, she promised Lou that she would be ready and waiting for her assignation with Commandeur Marraud of the Knights of Malta; and that she would report back to Madame Lou in the morning.

"But, in the meantime, Madame, please, I count on you to hold Général Gaultier at bay, while dissuading Monsieur Adolphe from seeking any more dalliances with me."

Célie kissed Lou's gloved hand and stepped down to the street. Before pirouetting to enter her doorway, her madam called to her. "Oh, Célie! One moment, please?"

Her young protégée returned expectantly. "Madame?"

Most elegantly, LouLou removed one snow-white kidskin glove, and a resounding crack was heard as she used it to slap the actress across one delicately rouged cheek. Sharp enough to sting, but not quite hard enough to leave a mark, thereby damaging her investment.

"You appear a little confused, ma petite chérie." She smiled, while beckoning her stunned coachman to drive on. "It will be entirely up to you to deter further dalliances with Monsieur Toussaint. Comprends-tu?"

THE SILK OF HER gown swished rhythmically against marble treads as Lou descended the grand staircase. She'd taken extra care with her dress and makeup for the evening out. Her heavy satin frock of pearl grey featured a rhapsody of pink ribbons, flounces and ruffles, and nestled neatly in her bosom was her favorite piece of jewellery—Adolphe's diamond necklace. On her face, she wore several silk patches. All the fashionable women of Paris wore at least that many, or even more, designed either to accent their finest features, or in the worst case, to cover imperfections. Her hair had been coiffed carefully, close to her head, featuring finger waves adorned with diamonds, crescents, and aigrettes. That night in particular, she'd felt the need to look her very best, and when she knew she did, it gave her confidence. Awaiting Adolphe, Lou informed her coachman that she wished him to drive around the Saint-Germain before delivering them to the townhouse of Dame Chevalier on rue du Dauphin. She would indicate when he was permitted to proceed to their destination by a sharp tap on the outside of the four-in-hand.

Lou and Toussaint settled themselves in their carriage. Lou reached across Adolphe to pull the curtains closed. She rapped on the ceiling and the driver snapped the reins, signaling the horses to trot off. As soon as they were in motion, Lou turned to Adolphe. "My darling. How long have you known me?"

He seemed surprised at her opening, but calmly answered, "Many a year, Lou. And, may I add, they have been the best years of my life."

"I would agree. Wonderful years they have been. But during all that time, have you known me to be a fool?"

"Why would you ask that of me, Lou?" Adolphe replied patiently. But he was now wary.

"I don't wish to make an issue of this, but I am well aware of what transpired last evening between you and Célie. I was surprised to hear of your conduct. It violates the promises we made to each other: never to bring anyone into the home we share. And, why would you take her into your shrine? When you have rarely allowed me access in there? I don't understand."

Adolphe turned his face away, parted the curtain and peered out into the darkening evening as the carriage bounced along the cobbled street. He was a man whose intensity intimidated many of his acquaintances, but not Lou. She was not fearful. No, they had shared too much over the years; she would not be cowed by his passionate nature. So, coolly and with little fanfare, she told him precisely what she thought about his night with Célie. She made clear her displeasure that a valued client had been embarrassed and kept waiting—a situation which had necessitated her wheedling him back into her good graces, and to provide him a second opportunity with a girl for whom he had already paid handsomely. "And what's more, Adolphe... you hurt me." She paused. "And that is all I have to say."

At this, Toussaint silently turned back to her, and took her gloved hand in his. While he hadn't intended to hurt LouLou deliberately, he'd remained unmarried for a reason. And it was simply this: ultimately, he wanted no one or nothing to tie him. He wished above all to be free to live his life as he chose—and that he fully intended to do. So, when Lou demanded he never have another tryst with Célie, he replied, "I have a trip planned. In a matter of days, I am going back to Saint-Domingue to inspect my plantations and complete some pending transactions. It's a good time to sail; the weather is cooperative."

At this sudden news, Lou was disheartened. "How long do you intend to be gone, 'Dolphe? I understand your need to oversee your business interests, as you've done in the past. But on those occasions, I miss you desperately and, oh, how I do worry about you making such a formidable sea crossing."

"Don't fear, my Lou. I'm an old salt. Should the crew fail in their duty, I shall be there to instruct them. And instruct them I will, as I've absolutely no intention of succumbing to Neptune's embrace. I will return by autumn, before the fiercest storms again begin to build in the open waters of the Atlantic." He smiled a little ruefully then. "And as a bonus, dear one, the trip will far remove me from Célie's presence. You, then, can be at ease."

"I will never be completely at ease, 'Dolphe. I love you and will long for you through every minute, every second, of our separation." She laid her hand on his forearm. "You know you are and will always be the only man in my life, the one I have counted on to be there for me when needed, the one I am partners with, the man I trust. We are a pair, Adolphe Toussaint."

"Take fortitude, mon amour. I hope you know I feel quite the same. We follow the same star. And I won't be far from you; numerous vessels will be making the same crossing over the coming months, so we can write to each other. I will keep you apprised of my progress, and when I'm scheduled to return. The time will go by in a flash, you will see. And in the meanwhile, have no fear about me with Mademoiselle Célie. Let us say, the evening was a mistake on my part. To be quite truthful, I found her rather boring. Like a beautiful cake piled high with glorious icing. You see it, you crave it, but then you take one ill-advised bite only to find it dry as chalk, perhaps even stale." He shook his head, perhaps a little too adamantly. "Not at all to my liking, although I'm sure those of your clients with whom she is currently engaged do find her altogether exciting." Toussaint grinned then, but his expression was derisory. "Those portly Parisian lovers may fancy themselves expert at le langage de l'amour, yet in truth, they are nothing but deluded amateurs. It requires Caribbean blood to quicken the breath and bring the flush of pleasure to a paramour's cheek. And that I well know."

BAGGAGE WAS PILED HIGH in the foyer. All that remained prior to his departure was their final goodbye, conducted in Lou's private office. He held her closely, kissed her mouth and nuzzled her neck. "I shall miss you, my love, but I promise to return by mid-September at the latest. And you can write to me, as I will to you. Cargo galleons depart almost every other week for the Spice Route, and they will all harbour in Nassau, where I can pick up your mail. I know you can take care of the house, and yourself. You may only be a woman, but you're mighty in your own right."

After a final kiss, he abruptly recalled that he might not have locked the door to his shrine, so he ran up three flights of stairs to have a final look around, and ensure the entrance was tightly secured. Although his statues, icons, and other vodou art remained in the room, he'd removed the painting, as he had done on other occasions when he'd travelled. He never, ever left it unattended for any lengthy period of time. It was far too precious to him. The container he'd stolen from La Buse, instead of holding treasure maps as he'd expected, revealed a painting at once gorgeous in its mastery and execution, and mystical in its aura. He immediately had known that it was worth a very considerable amount of money, had he wished to sell it. But it spoke to him. The imagery, the icons... he knew it conveyed a powerful message. So he'd placed it, himself, in a golden frame he bought, hung it in his room, and quickly decided he would keep it. He knew he would hide it, just as the pirate LeVasseur had attempted to do, because he wanted no one to know this enigmatic painting was his.

He constructed a special compartment in the attic in which to store it. Meticulously enshrouded in multiple layers of cloth and leather to protect it from nesting rodents, it was placed inside a box and nailed shut, then hidden behind a wall with attic boards covering it. Once concealed, it was virtually impossible to tell that secret void existed. Only he and Lou knew where it was. It seemed a great deal of trouble to hide it so painstakingly each time he travelled abroad, but he dared not take the chance to leave it exposed to any casual house-breaker. It was too precious a relic—and had been too hard-won to take the chance.

LouLou Periér watched until Toussaint's carriage disappeared from sight. She waved goodbye until he turned the corner, then slowly went back into the house, alone. Their relationship was a complicated one, for certain. But he was everything to her, and she knew she'd never find a man his equal.

IT WAS A STICKY, hot July afternoon, but under the shade of the trees it felt almost bearable. Célie fanned herself continuously, wriggling irritably as she felt rivulets of sweat trickle slowly down the small of her back and between her breasts. Her head was aching, and the large hat she wore didn't help. Nonetheless, she had to smile prettily and allow her patron to think she couldn't have been more delighted to be standing in the middle of the Bois de Vincennes watching horses race around in a great circle. Oh, how she longed to strip off her gown, hoops, corset and chemise and lie, naked and alone, in the breeze from some cooling window. But as a working girl, that was not to happen. She was on the arm of Knight Commandeur Marraud while he, for his part, was preening and enjoying showing her off, just as he puffed with pride at the horses he owned, which were dominating the races. He was winning piles of money.

In fact, he felt so good about his augmented fortune that he decided to depart as soon as the last race was complete and he and Célie would drive back into town where he would stop at a jeweller's he favored in the Marais. There, he would allow her to choose a necklace, or perhaps a brooch. He wanted to reward her, because she'd been a surprise and a great pleasure to him. His successful conquest of Célie, the most beautiful and desired courtesan in all of Paris, had become all the more delicious because he believed his acqui-sition vaulted him to the top of Parisian social standing, hopefully even above the prominence of the outrageously wealthy and suave Adolphe Toussaint—whom he despised out of jealousy. And equally satisfying was the fact that the pompous Financier Général Gaultier had been lusting after her for quite some time.

A grin of satisfaction broadened his cruelly aristocratic features. He'd finally decided to make the young woman his official mistress. It would be fortuitous for her, and exceedingly convenient for him. He would purchase an apartment for her, fill it with exquisite furnishings, take care of all her expenses, buy her many gifts, and most signifi-cantly, would pay her a substantial stipend in livres, every month.

It was an extravagant commitment, this the commandeur rec-ognised, but he felt sure it would be worthwhile. She was delectable, and he would have ready access to her whenever he chose. Essen-tially, she would be his: another feather in the cap which represented Marraud's success and power. Naturally, though, his family would remain in the expansive home he owned, where his wife and three children were well attended. He could certainly afford them along with a full-time mistress. He glanced over at his Célie with desire. The heat had given rise to a bloom and glow on her complexion, and as she perspired, her hair had become damp, as if she'd just emerged from a bath. It felt very intimate. Oh yes, she was a catch. And after all, he, Knight Commandeur Marraud of the Order of Saint John, deserved only the best.

"OH, COMMANDEUR, WHAT A fabulous jewel! Do you really intend it for me? I am not sure I can accept such extravagance!" Célie sat at a table in the jeweller's shop where, before her on a swath of black velvet, was spread a truly stunning array of gorgeous gems: necklaces, brooches, rings. After much deliberation, she had chosen a string of sapphires and diamonds. It really was an incredible piece, spitting fire in the sunlight which flooded the exclusive shop, and certainly unlike anything she owned. Being given such a lavish gift allowed her to temporarily forget the cool bath and nap she'd been envisioning.

"On the contrary, my precious. It was made for you. You will have it, and I wish to see you wear it this evening when we meet for supper. D'accord? Oh, and wear that apricot silk gown - the one with the exceptionally low neckline. I wish to see the jewel clearly displayed on your lovely bodice."

"Oui, oui, Monsieur. I will be only too happy to comply with your wishes. You will drop me at my townhouse now, if you please, so I can bathe and be ready to see you later?"

The carriage clattered toward her residence, and at the door, he kissed her and promised that he had other surprises in store. With a sense of relief, she slipped through her entryway, desperately looking forward to her bath and a short rest before she would be called upon to perform again that evening.

PALE LIQUID GOLD IN crystal flutes, the champagne fizzed and bubbled. They were alone in a beautiful salon in the house that LouLou maintained to facilitate the romantic encounters of her select clientele. The staff knew precisely how to prepare the room for the evening—candles and lanterns positioned just so, and bottomless champagne cooling in silver buckets. On this very special evening, Marraud had even requested a violinist to play softly as they dined.

While nibbling on pheasant and oysters, Marraud admired the stunning necklace which lay perfectly around Célie's neck. She regularly stroked it with her hand and expressed her gratitude and glee at his very generous gift. The footman appeared briefly to refresh their glasses. How she loved good champagne! The bubbles tickled her tongue, and the flavor was heavenly. And it was so refreshing to drink a beverage carefully cooled in Madame's cellars. In the end, she had no idea how many glasses she'd consumed.

The commandeur wasted no time. Within minutes he had told Célie that he cared for her very much and wanted her to be his maîtresse. Her thoughts swam a bit, but then he described the terms of the arrangement whereupon—oh my!—there was nothing to do but agree. With what might have been construed as unseemly haste, they retired to the bedchamber reserved for them so Célie could properly express her gratitude.

The next morning, she and the commandeur lay abed, and a light repast was delivered to them. She sipped coffee, hoping it would cure the throbbing head and upset stomach which had awakened her. Marraud was jubilant. He'd not spent a night like that in many a year, if ever. And as they breakfasted, they conversed. He knew that the girls employed by top madames were always a source of the most delectable gossip about his competitors, even enemies: desirable ammunition to hold should he ever need it for extortion. Specifically, he wanted information about a man he considered his nemesis: Adolphe Toussaint. He'd hated him since they first had met some years before. Actually, it was a hatred born of envy, but Marraud wouldn't admit that to himself. Instead, he wished the scoundrel nothing but ill-fortune and yearned to put an end to his seeming ease at living well, with his money, looks and charisma.

"Now that you are mine alone, darling girl, you simply must tell me: what do you know of the inscrutable Monsieur Toussaint? I do find him so unusual. While it's said that he is an intelligent and skilled businessman, he's also, shall we say, peculiar? I've even heard, in the salons of the city, that he is vodouissant. And that his maternal family is from Sierra Leone in West Africa which, of course creates speculation that his mother was a slave. Can you imagine that? I know his father was a Parisian citizen—in fact, my grandfather knew him quite well before the entire family moved to the Caribe. A daring ploy, I say, but I guess it paid off, certainly for Toussaint. I'm told he inherited sugarcane and tobacco plantations. Profitable ventures to be sure, but apparently not at all due to his own acumen... acquired instead by nothing more than his family's good fortune."

"Well, as I understand it, Monsieur François, it is true that he owns property and businesses in the Caribbean. But I know less about him than one might think. My madam, LouLou, is exceedingly close-lipped when it comes to Toussaint. But I know they have been partners for many years. She cares for him greatly."

Idly, he reached over and stroked her, moving aside her robe so her breasts were exposed. "Nevertheless, my darling, what do you know? I've heard that he used to sail in the Caribbean Sea. And I've also heard gossip that he was a close acquaintance of some notorious marauders during his early years. In fact, it is often claimed that he was a buccaneer himself. Have you seen or heard any evidence of that in your visits to their home? And isn't it odd that they live together and share that house when they are not married? Of course, LouLou herself is a very unconventional woman."

He waited expectantly. Célie realized she was being pressed to offer more. "As I mentioned, Monsieur, I do not know much. I have been a guest in their home only a very few times. But you are correct. Toussaint does follow the vodou religion: so much so that he has a special room dedicated to that purpose, complete with many statues of the Spirits they worship. There's an altar... and incense, drums, books..."

"Really? You don't say? How freakish it must be! Did you witness his rituals? What else is in there?"

"No, I didn't observe his worship..." She knew he would not be satisfied with simply that comment, so, against her better judgement, she continued. "He also has a most unusual painting hanging in the room's center. It's not part of the vodou collection, you see, but he told me it is actually an English work of art—a valuable portrait of the King Henry VIII and his second wife, standing together by an open window."

Marraud knew he was striking gold with this chat. Toussaint an idol-worshipper? He knew the man to be an eccentric. And he owns a painting of King Henry VIII and one of his queens? Marraud wondered how much a work of art like that might be worth—if he knew Toussaint, he'd bet it was almost priceless. So he pressed on. "Fascinating," he murmured as he caressed her neck and shoulders. "Do tell me more, ma petite cher. What of this painting?"

"Ummm, I believe it to be very important in historical terms, since the king and queen look as if they want to convey a special message to whoever views it. Monsieur Toussaint told me there are many religious overtones incorporated within it." She stopped then, feeling guilty. "But I am not supposed to say anything about it, so I've already broken that promise. François… you would not tell anyone, would you? You will protect me?" And she looked up at him with her most beguiling expression.

"Certainly, I won't speak of it to anyone, ma poupette. Now, come here…"

LIFE COULD NOT HAVE been better for the Knight Commander. He'd found a lovely, spacious apartment for Célie on rue de Moulins; close to the theatre in the Palais-Royal where she rehearsed and performed for the Paris Opéra. He visited her at least five nights out of the week, and occasionally in the afternoon as well, rendezvous which he especially enjoyed. Squiring her about the city, he ensured she wore the most alluring and seductive gowns money could buy from the leading Parisian couturiers. The truth was that Marraud revelled in other men's covetous glances each time they appeared in public together. His home was splendid and his family life peaceful, since his wife was fully accepting of his barely concealed dalliances as long as her status and social standing remained firmly in place.

And now, to top such triumphs, it seemed as if he'd stumbled upon an intriguing piece of information which, at the very least, demanded further exploration.

When Célie had revealed her description of Toussaint's shrine, something she'd mentioned perplexed him. The unusual but specific account of the portrait Toussaint owned seemed to jog a distant memory. But the recollection evaded him, so, as he was unable to stop thinking about it, he decided to investigate.

And thus it was, on that very same evening, Marraud casually wondered aloud during a gentlemen's dinner he attended which included several of his fellow officers of the Order of St. John of Jerusalem, the Knights of Malta, whether anyone had ever heard tell of a portrait of the English King Henry VIII posed side by side with his second wife Anne Boleyn, the queen he'd subsequently had executed, a painting which was rumored to have had significant religious implications.

At this query, Commandeur Marraud was met with blank-faced responses from his dining companions. The senior member of the group, though, Knight Commandeur Gilles Marillac, had no sooner heard the question posed by Marraud than he abruptly replaced his wine glass on the table and leaned forward.

"Gentlemen! Do you not know of the legend? I thought all Knights were well versed in the ancient tale. It caused a quiet furor among the ranks of the Order in the mid 1600s. It is reputed that the King of England, Henry Tudor, had planned to violently overthrow the pope, and with it, the Church of Rome. In fact, at that time it was believed he'd already begun raising an army to march on the Vatican, destroy the papacy and everything associated with it. It was whispered that he'd represented his intention in a painting—sacrilegious—which had been created by the royal court painter of the time, Hans Holbein."

And with that, the memory came flooding back to Marraud. Of course he'd heard this legend, back in the early days of his membership in the Order. How could he have forgotten?

Commandeur Marillac continued in a conspiratorial tone only those at the table could hear. "Then the mystery of the painting deepened. Quite inexplicably, it was said, the great work of art vanished, but not before word of the impending crisis, and of the painting itself, had somehow been reported to our magnificent Grand Master at the time: Phillippe Villiers de l'Isle-Adam. L'Isle-Adam received the dreadful news, and had no choice but to tell Pope Clement VII. Suddenly, after sending his message, the Grand Master became sick—very sick. They suppose it must have been poison. And knowing he wasn't long for the world, he also shared the distressing tidings with a young Knight whom he trusted—one whom he felt showed great integrity, fortitude and promise. That Knight was none other than Jean Parisot de Vallette."

At the name 'Vallette', the revered former leader of the Order, all the men said, "Ah, yes!" nodding knowingly.

He enjoyed the rapt attention of every man at the table, so Marillac continued, relishing his opportunity to provide the remainder of the legend as he knew it. "The story goes that L'Isle-Adam implored Vallette to make it his priority to repress the uprising, find the painting, and send it immediately to the pope, whoever he might be at the time. Some years later, when Vallette became Grand Master, he issued a proclamation to every Knight, in every corner of the world, to seek the portrait, and should they find it, return it to him.

"Well, whatever became of this alleged uprising, headed by Henry Tudor?" Marraud asked breathlessly, intoxicated as he was over the enigma.

The most elderly member of the dinner guests piped up. "Well, we know, don't we? Of course we do! With the benefit of hindsight, we realize that, thanks be to God, it never did occur. It would be my guess that the Tudor realized the error of his ways and modified his heinous plans."

"Yes, I'm certain that was it." Marillac at last sat back in his chair and rewarded himself with a hearty swill of wine. "But the Order has never lost sight of the threat posed by the English king. After his death, his successors waged bloody internal wars between the staunch Catholics and the rebellious Protestant reformers. But through that conflict, the threat remained that the English monarchy might use the portrait as an emblem of insurrection and threaten the lifeblood of our Church. This is why the painting was so desperately sought, and even is today. No one knows where it went, for that matter, if it even remains in existence. It may well have been destroyed many, many years ago."

"What would happen if someone were to stumble upon it now? As far-fetched as that seems, one never does know, after all," interjected Marraud.

"Well," offered Marillac, "I feel sure that the reward which was promised in the 1600s would remain in place. The recovery and return of the painting is to be accompanied by the greatest spiritual indulgence the Church offers: complete absolution of any and all lifetime sins, and a guaranteed place in heaven to sit among the holy and mighty."

As they each pondered such a magnificent benediction, Marillac was satisfied that he'd provided his dining companions with the most exciting narrative they'd heard in quite a while.

Commandeur Marraud, though, sat dumbfounded. He did recall being told the story, but had simply forgotten about it. After all, it had been over two hundred years since Grand Master Vallette had died, while Henry VIII the Blasphemer had long been consumed by hell's inferno. But the account he just heard had him questioning whether it might be at all possible—against every odd—that the painting Célie had described to him was the very one sought for all those years. His head was nigh to bursting with the chance it might be so. He sat quietly, keeping speculation to himself. He shivered with the thrill of imagining that he, François Marraud, could wrest it from the pagan Toussaint and possess it. He could then decide what he chose to do with it: retain it for his own advantage or avail himself of Grand Master Vallette's promise of eternal absolution for every sin he had ever committed.

The choice would be difficult. But exquisite. Either way, he could not lose.

THE NEXT EVENING OVER a late supper, Marraud questioned Célie again. She immediately grew withdrawn, and he could tell she wished not to speak of it. But he would have none of that. She was his now and would do as he asked.

"Tell me everything you can recall about this painting, Célie. I am most interested."

"But François, you promised me you would keep it secret!"

"Fret not, my dear. I have no intentions of telling anyone about it. I am curious, though, and I want my curiosity satisfied. So do tell me all you can remember."

It wasn't for the first time that Célie regretted her quick decision to become Marraud's mistress. Madame LouLou had been in agreement of the contract, though she did say there was something about the man she disliked. But the decision had been made, so now Célie was paying the price: she was being interrogated, and desperately needed to provide some answers.

"Well, let me think. I only saw it for a very few minutes, you understand. It was certainly large—almost, but not quite life-size. It was without a frame, instead it was stretched on a big board. And the likenesses of the king and queen were quite incredible. In fact, it was hard not to stare at the queen, Anne. She looked captivating.

Her arm rested on his, and the king had his hand extended, as if he was giving a blessing. And I think there were many symbols painted all around: a bowl, some keys, a walking stick… things like that. The colors were vivid, but of course there were some areas he'd painted over."

"Who—Toussaint? He painted over it?"

"Yes, he told me it had been damaged in an ocean crossing, so he'd tried to restore it. Not too well, I might add. But it's still breath-taking."

"Célie, do you know if he left it hanging while he went abroad? Is it still in his room?"

"Truly, Monsieur, I do not know. I have no idea."

"Would Madame Lou know? She surely must. After all, it is her own house!"

"That I do not know, either. I do not think the painting is of much concern to her."

Célie desperately hoped this would put a lid on the subject. She didn't like talking about it, and even less did she like Marraud's greedy expression. "And I'm afraid that is all I can tell you. I know nothing else about it."

"Well, thank you for what you have offered, ma chérie. You've been helpful. Most helpful."

He picked up his fork to resume eating but was uncharacteristically quiet for the remainder of the night. As if lost in thought.

Célie moved food around her plate. But her stomach felt sick with guilt. Although Marraud paid her little attention that night, she recognized his distant gaze. It was marked by the same covetous, obsessive look he'd had when he sought to make her his mistress.

AS DAYS PASSED, MARRAUD could not stop brooding over the painting. What if the long sought-after icon *was* there in Toussaint's shrine, virtually within arm's reach? If he could be the one to recover it, and hand it to his cousin, the present Grand Master—or better yet, to Pope Benedict XIV in person—not only would he be absolved of every sin he'd ever committed (and for just a brief moment his thoughts lingered on Célie, and the other women before her who'd lain, naked and subservient, on his bed) but his name would live forever in the history of the Sovereign Order of the Knights of Malta. It was far too tempting a prize. He determined he would find it and claim it for his own.

Slowly his course of action was formed. First, he would pay a friendly visit to Madame LouLou. He'd do it under the pretext of wanting to consolidate his arrangement with Célie and settle the fee that was due to the madam. While there, he would inform Lou that he knew about the painting, and ask—no, positively demand!—to view it. Should she refuse, he would find something with which to blackmail her, although he doubted such a tactic would be necessary. After all, he was a powerful and very important man. She would not deny him.

He arranged his visit for 6 p.m. It was unlikely that there would be many people about at that hour, since it was before supper and evening social events. Nor would she be meeting with her girls then, either.

With the head of his walking stick, he rapped on the door, and it was quickly opened by a maid. She saw him to a side parlor, and he'd just been seated when Lou appeared, polite and practiced as ever.

"Monsieur Commandeur, how lovely to see you!"

"And you, Madame. I hope all is well? I understand Monsieur Toussaint is traveling abroad, seeing to his business. I trust that you fare comfortably while he is gone? If you require help of any kind, please, you have only to ask for my assistance."

"How very kind of you. I seem to be surviving just fine. And he will be back in Paris at summer's end, so that isn't long to wait."

"No, it's not. I'm here, actually, to tell you that I am very pleased with my arrangement with Célie. She is a delight and suits my needs.

And my contract with you, a thousand livres per month, is that satis-factory? While, of course, I will fund any incidental expenditure that Célie may accrue, as well."

"That is very generous, Commandeur. More than satisfactory. And I hope the arrangement continues to please you. Célie is a very engaging girl, and will strive to make you happy, this I know."

"I'm sure she will." He tipped his hat and stepped toward the door to take his leave. Before crossing the threshold, though, he turned toward her again. "Oh! And Madame—one more question in pass-ing, before I depart..." He shrugged airily, as if the matter was of little importance. "Célie did happen to mention a certain painting—a most unusual work, owned by Monsieur Toussaint. I have a deep interest in historical portraiture, and I would be inordinately grateful if I might be permitted to view it."

Immediately, Marraud could see that he'd hit a nerve. Lou grew very uncomfortable and avoided his gaze. "I know not to what she refers, Monsieur. As you can see, I own many paintings displayed here in the house. But none of them are the property of Adolphe."

"No, I do not think I am mistaken, Madame LouLou. Célie dis-tinctly told me of a portrait, owned by Toussaint, which hangs in his shrine room—a painting depicting a certain English king and his queen. If what Célie told me is correct, then I respectfully ask you to show it to me. And if she lied, well, then... I will have to address that with her. It could well turn out to be a most unpleasant interview."

His face became a sneering mask. Suddenly, Lou felt a chill; his arrogance nauseated her. She should have known better than to con-tract her Célie to this odious man. Her lips tightened.

"Monsieur Toussaint does indeed own some artwork which is his alone, Commandeur, but I do not, and will not, encroach on his pri-vate apartment. Beside which, it would be quite improper for me to show you that which belongs to him while he is away. You must take it up with him upon his return."

"That is very, very unfortunate, Madame. And I thought you were a reasonable and astute woman. If there is such a painting in this house, I demand to view it, now. And believe me, you would do well to agree, since you are but the madam of a stable full of prostitutes, while I hold high office in the most respected religious order in the world."

Lou's nostrils flared and she straightened her back. How dare this contemptible wretch threaten her! She'd stood up to men who were far more terrifying than the appalling Commandeur Marraud could hope to be at his worst. She rose and took a deep breath, trying to contain her anger, while opening the street door wide.

"Be that as it may, it will not be available to you, and that is all I have to say—other than that I shall require your payments to be made promptly by the 15th of every month, while assuring me of nothing but the best treatment for Célie—a beautiful young lady who deserves no less. Now, I have other business to attend to, so bonsoir, Monsieur Commandeur Marraud."

She opened the door, and saw him out, closing it firmly behind him, but not before registering Marraud's expression as he left her. Irate, murderous!

After he'd gone, she sat for some time, thinking about what had just occurred. Disappointingly, Célie had opened her mouth, and done exactly what she'd been instructed not to do. However, Adolphe had no one to blame but himself. Why, presumably in a foolish moment of weakness, he'd allowed the actress into his most private quarters to see his very personal belongings, she could not imagine. But the damage was done, and now word of the portrait, which he'd guarded and sheltered all the years since she'd known him, was out. Lou didn't like the poisonous look Marraud had given her, not one bit, and doubted she'd heard the last of him. Why he insisted upon seeing it, she knew not, but it certainly wasn't out of scholarly interest. Somehow the fool must be aware of the value it held.

As the distasteful meeting continued to weigh on her, she decided to write to Adolphe and tell him. He would have to advise her of how to handle the situation. Perhaps he would even return home early, and confront Marraud himself? So, as the light waned, LouLou sat at her desk, took up quill and paper, and prepared to warn Adolphe that his treasured painting was at risk.

Dearest Adolphe,

I do miss you so terribly, just as I knew that I would. It is now mid-August, and I trust that your business transactions have gone well while hoping that you are almost ready to depart for your return to Paris, and my welcoming arms.

I must tell you, though, that a disturbing event has taken place. I was visited today by one Knight Commandeur François Marraud, who is now the primary—and only—patron of Célie. She has become his maîtresse-en-titre, his official mistress, and he is paying us a fortune, not only for her contract but to support her every whim. Regrettably it appears that she, in her youthful naiveté, has already made a grave mistake. She told him about your painting—the one you allowed her to see while it hung in your shrine room? I know not why you even took her in there, but that is not the topic of my letter. It's done, and now Marraud knows of it and, I suspect, knows enough about its provenance that he perceives it to be a work of great value. He came to my house this evening demanding to see it.

Of course, I refused—and refused even to discuss it with him. But 'Dolphe... I did not like the look on his face, or how ugly he became over it. I fear he will abuse Célie as retribution if he doesn't get his way. And I also know, with certainty, that he will be back— I've not heard the last of him. I fear, however, I cannot withstand his pressure. So, I ask you, mon amour, are you able to return home sooner than you'd planned?

I desperately need you here.
Please come back!
Your devoted Louise

On an early morning in Nassau Town, Adolphe Toussaint read Lou's letter. His rage at the man who dared threaten her, and Célie, whom he didn't blame for his own neglectful mistake, was explosive. Had he been in Paris at that moment, Marraud would be kneeling, hands clasped in supplication, pathetically begging for his life. Quickly he decided he would wrap up his business, bid adieu to the islands he loved, and catch the first cargoman putting to sea homeward bound.

Chapter Thirty

JANUARY 2017

1ST ARONDISSEMENT, PARIS

It was just after 11 p.m. and the din had become so raucous that I could barely hear my dad, even though he was elbow-to-elbow with me at our tiny bistro table. We'd taken to dining very late, as did the native Parisians, which suited me perfectly because I was a confirmed night owl. Dad seemed to enjoy it too. And anyway, there was no big rush to get up and out early in the morning. So, there we were, hanging out with the post-theatre, post-opera, and general partying crowd of jovial locals.

Dad dug into his roasted marrow bone, nestled alongside a thick, perfectly grilled steak and a mess of frites. He never ate like that at home, but after all, when in Paris…? And we were enjoying what had become our 'regular' dinner haunt—the small but wonderful Chez Denise on rue des Prouvaires, only a brisk walk from the hotel. It was the quintessential Parisian bistro: red-checked tablecloths, framed sketches and portraits lining the walls, and waiters quick to refill everyone's glass with sturdy wine. Even though it was super-crowded at most hours of the day, the maître d' had come to know us, and with a quick call ahead, usually saved us a coveted table, for which we were grateful. My salmon with mustard sauce looked lovely, but I only picked at it. I had no appetite, which perhaps was a good thing since I'd been over-indulging, and the food in Paris was much richer than that which I was used to in Rome. But my lack of interest in dinner wasn't so much from a desire to refrain as that my stomach had been fermenting with anxiety.

Every day for the past week, Dad and I had followed the same routine. We'd meet in the hotel café for breakfast. Over tea, toast and soft-boiled eggs, we would discuss the day's strategy. I'd suggested, "Dad how about if we work toward the middle? You look at the more recent documentation and I'll hunt through anything which might give us a lead starting in the late 1600s. Eventually we will connect."

He had agreed right away. "That makes sense, hon. There's less chance we might miss something. I know anything, even the littlest signal, could be important. If you are finished your tea, let's go."

We walked through the halls of the ornately decorated and gilded Bibliothèque de l'Arsenal and found the special nook we'd claimed in the cozy reading room. Settled in our corner, we spread our papers, notebooks and reference material. We worked clear through to one o' clock, went to the lunchroom to grab a quick bite, and returned directly to resume our dig. It was disheartening to learn that there were over 75 hundred folio pages of dossiers, and other assorted documents generated by those 18th century policemen who'd followed the madams, their girls, and patrons. And it wasn't as if there was a neat index anywhere in the mound of files to quickly source names or places. Page after page we turned, hoping to see Toussaint's name appear. With every folio, I scanned while obsessively twirling a lock of hair. By mid-afternoon, my shoulders were stiff and my head pounded.

In the meantime, I'd received an email from the department head of paleography at Sapienza. Professore Ruggieri politely reminded me that I was due, upon resuming the term, to submit an abstract of my thesis for review. And honestly, I had no idea what I intended to offer. After that email, my dad watched me mope about. Finally, he said "Zar! What's up? I know this effort is really tiring, and we're finding out less than we'd hoped. But you seem troubled. Can I help?"

"Nice of you to ask, Dad. But I don't think so. It's my embarrassment, and it's mine to fix. The truth is, I've yet to submit a proposal for my thesis to the department head. Just that fact alone is humiliating. But I'm also struggling with the idea that perhaps I should just write up this very search, bite the bullet, and go for it."

"Well, there's no question it would provide an incredible, unique platform for your research and dissertation. But you have to feel convinced it's the thing to do. Are you?"

I didn't answer right away. But then, "No. No, I'm not at all convinced. In fact, my gut vehemently tells me not to do that—not to release any information about this discovery. The risk is too great that my paper would be used against me. To beat me to the conclusion. To steal my work and give me no credit. I can't do it."

Dad looked me straight in the eye. "Then, don't. It's as simple as that. Come up with something else to work on. You're smart enough to do both. So... just get on with it, Zara."

TO ADD TO MY angst, Lina had called me. Oh sure, I was glad to hear her voice as always, but in no time, she'd needled me in that forthright way she had. "Zara! Where in the name of hell are you? I haven't heard a word from you in weeks! Are you planning to move to Paris? Because if you do, you will regret it, Tesoro! The Parisians think they are so *stupendi*, but we all know Paris can't compare to Roma! *Roma è fantastica!* So... *quando?!* When are you coming home?"

I had decided to confide in Lina—about the portrait, and also about my dilemma with Antonio, but I wouldn't do it over the phone. So, I said, "I miss you too, Lina! I'll be back soon enough. I probably have no choice but to be there for the start of the term, but to tell you the truth, I've thought about asking Ruggieri if I can take leave of absence. I guess it's not a good idea, since I'm already out of his graces because he's waiting on my proposal, and I don't have one ready. Hell, I don't even know what I want to work on. Or even if I want to submit anything at all."

"Well, whatever you and your papa are up to there, digging around for some crazy secret information, can't that help you come up with an idea? What are you doing there, anyway?"

"I promise to tell you all when we get together. I just don't want to do it over the phone."

"Mamma mia! Sì, sì, sì, of course. But what about Antonio? Why can't he know, too? I ran into him the other day and he asked when you would be back. I guess you aren't speaking with him?"

"No, I'm not. That's another subject I can't get into right now, but I do want your advice. Once I'm back, we'll talk."

"Okay, amica mia, if you say so… let's solve the riddle of why you aren't more appreciative of the attention of a man like Antonio—oh and by the way, there's a party one week after start of term. It's a big one, and tutti saranno lì. I mean everyone will be there. So, I will take no excuses from you. You must come!"

The thought of a big party quickly reactivated the discomfort in my stomach. I dreaded the prospect. But if Lina was with me, I resolved to at least make an appearance.

"I think you should invite that cute Luca you were seeing in December, Zara. What do you say? I might invite Giancarlo. I'm thinking about it."

"Well, you keep thinking, Lina. As will I. I hope to be back by then. If for some reason I'm not, I will let you know beforehand. Sound good?"

"Okay. Suona bene. Sounds good to me. I miss you! Come back! Ciao ciao!"

"Ciao, Lina."

I ended the call, and sat there, morose.

Chapter Thirty-one

SUMMER 1752

PARIS

Justine was worried about her friend. They shared a dressing room backstage at the Théâtre du Palais-Royal because on that evening, Justine was to make her first appearance in a performance with the Comédie-Française. She was all too aware of how important this trial was for her. She'd been a regular, onstage with the Paris Opéra, but to attain a position with the Troupe de Comédie-Française would be a significant step up in her pay and prestige. Already in costume, they sat on a bench in front of the mirror, while splayed out before them were brushes and pots of all sizes: thick white foundation to cover their complexions and make them appear smooth and pale, deep scarlet rouge to effect blushing cheeks and red lips, and cork charcoal, which they'd already applied to draw the perfect brow. Tonight, they would appear in Les Femmes Savantes, the comedy by Molière.

While Justine had a minor part, Célie was to portray Henriette, the premiere female role. And Henriette's costumes were all cut low to expose her décolletage. The problem was that Célie bore angry purple bruises on the top of one shoulder, and on the left side of her neck, which Justine was doing her best to camouflage with thick layers of stage makeup and powder.

"Célie, this is terrible. You understand, don't you? How can I simply sit by and watch this happen to you? You are so desired—my God, all the men in the audience tonight will want to be with you—yet that disgusting troll dares to treat you in this way?"

Justine had to blink back tears. Her much loved friend—she of the quick giggle and sweetest of faces—was not the same. The light was gone from her formerly sparkling temperament. She seemed hunched, shrunken somehow, while Justine noticed that she flinched whenever someone near her moved quickly. She knew she had to do something but wasn't sure what.

Reflected in the mirror, Célie's eyes were wet. "Justine, I cannot talk about it right now. If I do, I will break down and won't be able to perform tonight. And of course, of all performances, this is the one when King Louis and the Marquise de Pompadour are in attendance. Somehow, I have to calm myself or I'll have no hope of remembering my lines. Ohhh…" Her groan came from deep within. "Oh, how I wish I were anywhere else right now. No! Not anywhere—anywhere but here, with Marraud awaiting me in the foyer."

Justine stood back and squinted into the mirror, studying the result of her efforts. They looked passable as long as Célie didn't sweat too much. It could get impossibly hot in the theatre, especially on stage. And if she did, the makeup would melt and slide right off. She pulled up a stool, and when Célie turned around, they were face to face.

"I tell you now, dear one: this is the last time I am going to help you disguise the damage that pig does to you when he beats you. Either you will go to Madame Lou and tell her, and demand she extract you from that contract, or I will. And the next time I see him, I will hawk the biggest gobbet of spittle you ever saw, and it will hit him right between the eyes. I'm known for my great aim, you know."

At that, Célie let out a nervous laugh, but Justine wasn't to be deflected. "Well?" she challenged, staring Célie down.

"Alright, I'll do it. I will slip over to see LouLou tomorrow evening while Marraud attends an engagement with his wife. But Justine... will you come with me? Will you? It's not that I am afraid of Lou. Of course I'm not; she is almost like a mother to me. It's just that I'm so emotional I may not be able to tell her without sobbing. It would be a great support if you were there."

"Oh, I will! I am so relieved you are going to do this. You need to be away from him—as far as you can be, while Madame needs to know what kind of monster he is, so she will never contract him to any other girl. Lord knows there are many kind and generous patrons in the city, men like mine, the compte, for example, to put girls' lives at risk with that brute."

"Thank you, my dearest friend," Célie sniffed. "You give me strength. We will both go to Lou tomorrow evening and end this nightmare, which I foolishly stepped into with willingness."

She smiled bravely, and hugged Justine. "Now, let's go out there and offer our royal audience the show they expect to see!"

KNIGHT COMMANDEUR FRANÇOIS MARRAUD had fumed for days after his abortive visit to Périer's house. He didn't know what aggrieved him more: the fact that he hadn't been permitted even a glance at the painting which Célie had clearly told him was displayed in Toussaint's private rooms, and he now coveted; or the insolence of that arrogant bitch, LouLou Périer. Who did she think she was, damn her? Refusing him?! He was a high-ranking officer in one of the most benevolent, sacred institutions the world had ever known. And just by virtue of his position, his word should be respected—*obeyed*! After all, she was nothing but *La Pute*—a great whore who had made her money by prostituting others. It made no matter that he, himself, had taken advantage of her business. Every time he thought about how the woman had summarily ushered him from her house, after he'd agreed to pay her a fortune for his harlot, his fury festered until he was barely able to control himself. And woe to Célie, if she just happened to be nearby. Another slut! Well, too bad for her that she bore the brunt of his anger, but that was part of the arrangement he'd made for her. It felt good to slap her, even better when he put his hands about her neck and squeezed until she gasped for air and begged him to stop. Best yet? When his rage culminated in forcing her down beneath him and he caused her to cry out. Why shouldn't he show her who was master? After all, he intended to take full advantage of that for which he was paying so dearly.

Ultimately, Marraud decided to make a return visit to the home of Madame LouLou Périer. This time, though, she would not refuse him—oh, no! He could be certain, from what he'd been told by Célie, and especially from the look on Périer's face when he'd touched on the subject of the painting, that it certainly did exist, and that the heathen, Toussaint, did indeed own it. Well, not for long. Soon, it would be his! Whereupon he would magnanimously offer it to the men of the True Faith: the pope, and the Grand Master of the Sovereign Order, to do with as they chose. And by virtue of that single act, he would become famous while all his sins would be expiated, the slate of Knight Commandeur François Marraud wiped clean in the eyes of God.

It would be best if he surprised the madame when she would be returning home from an outing—wait and confront her as she entered the house. It was easy, then, for him to place a coin or two in the pocket of one of Périer's scullery servants to send him word confirming she'd gone out and what time she was expected back. The very next afternoon, the eagerly awaited signal arrived, and Marraud promptly set off, instructing his coachman to discreetly park around the corner from the house, and remain there until his master's business had been completed.

It was dusk when the madame's carriage driver helped her down at her door, then departed on a clatter of hooves. As she fumbled in her bag for her key, from the shadows emerged Marraud. "Bon soir, Madame. I thought I would visit you since, as you probably recall, our last meeting was cut short. Rather rudely, I might add."

Lou was startled, whirling about. "What are you doing here, Marraud? I told you to merely send me your payments by the middle of the month. Otherwise, I have no need to see you in person."

"You are most impolite, Madame. I would hope you might invite me in. There is a matter I wish to discuss with you."

"Thank you, but I'd prefer not. Send me a letter, if you must. Otherwise—" She finally unlocked the door and held it only barely ajar. "—otherwise, good evening to you." She prepared to step inside, but Marraud placed his foot on the threshold, preventing her from entering.

"Move aside, Marraud. Now!"

"That I will not do. You will allow me to enter, or we will stand here all night."

Lou looked around; there was no one in sight. Most of her service staff were off duty, and she knew there would be but a single night maid on the premises. "Oh, alright. Come in if you must. But I tell you, make it quick, because I have little time to spare you."

At this insult, his anger spiked. They got inside the foyer, and he said, "Let us talk civilly, in your office." So, Lou led him across the foyer, to the end of the long hallway, and into her spacious office. Once inside, she purposely left the door wide open.

"I trust you do not expect refreshment, Marraud, as there won't be any. Just tell me your reason for arriving unannounced. What 'matter' is it that you wish to discuss?"

"It's simple, Madame. I spoke of it when I was here before. I know that in this house you harbor a painting I wish to inspect. My reason for wanting to view it is significant enough to warrant this late call. It would serve you well to agree and allow me access to it. I am giving you another chance to do so."

Lou was incensed. The man was a detestable lout, and she had absolutely no intention of giving in, or even to allow him to witness her unease. She clenched her fists and spoke very clearly.

"You are mistaken, Monsieur. Sadly mistaken. There is no painting here such as the one you've described. While even if there was, you would be the last person on earth to whom I would show it. This is my house, you arrogant boor! You will NOT make demands of me in my own hallway—I will make them of you! And they are that you immediately gather your hat and coat and leave. Meanwhile, we will consider the contract for the services of Célie null and void as of this very minute. I will happily return every last centime of your fee to you, but you will not go near her again. Do you understand?"

Marraud heard only half of her spirited protest. His head throbbed and felt about to explode, and in his ears he heard nothing but the roaring of blood. His breath came ragged; a vein pulsed on his forehead. Maniacally, he scanned the room until he spied a silken cord holding back the draperies. In one swift movement, he ripped it from the window, lunging at Lou while her back was turned. He wrapped the makeshift garrotte tightly about her snow-white neck and yanked until her back was pressed against him.

His stinking breath came hot against her pearl-studded ear. Through her fear and revulsion, she heard him snarl, "I afford you one last chance, slut! Reveal the painting's whereabouts, or I end you right here!"

Lou, caught completely unaware, and with the noose already about her neck, flailed wildly, hoping to strike her assassin as he stood behind her. As her sight dimmed, she remembered that on her desk was a lethally sharp letter opener, which she struggled to reach. Summoning every scrap of strength, she rammed her elbow sharply into his groin and heard him cry out like an enraged bull.

In that second, his grip loosened just enough… free of his vise-like clench, she lurched forward, knocking over a large plant stand, sending the porcelain pot flying to the floor in an explosion of shards and compost. One outstretched hand scrabbled for the knife. Her fingers enclosed its razor-pointed surface and she grasped it tightly, cutting herself but not caring that her blood flowed. If she could but clasp its handle, she might drive it deep into his throat. Her bloodied fingers wrapped around the shank and as she turned to strike, he leaped on top of her and flung the cord again about her neck, this time jerking and twisting it like a tourniquet. Lou's grip on the knife began to loosen as Marraud wrenched the snare tighter… and tighter….

She valiantly fought waves of blackness washing over her, desperately gasping for air but unable to draw even the shallowest breath. Maybe it was a mere instant, or maybe long minutes passed as she struggled to remain conscious. But ultimately, she knew she was about to succumb. Her thoughts became a jumble of darting images; her past replayed before her. Lou's agonized grappling slowed, and her final vision was of Adolphe. In the flash of an instant, she saw him standing before her, welcoming, smiling.

And then LouLou Périer slumped to the floor.

Marraud stood over her, panting. Had he killed her? He hoped so. With the toe of his boot, he shoved at her head. He saw no throb of a pulse in her exposed neck, just an angry purple welt. She had surely invited death, or even worse—he might have raped and tortured her before allowing her the escape of her demise. His mind raced. Should he ransack the house now, and look for the portrait? What if he was discovered, along with her dead body? He couldn't risk it, so he quickly moved to flee. He'd create some way to gain access to her house once her death had been discovered and attributed to a burglary attempt.

He opened the front door a crack, peering nervously up and down the street. It was empty: no carriages, no witnesses. He threw his cloak over his head and silently went out, pulling at the door behind him. He slithered around the corner and heaved himself into the carriage, commanding his driver to take him home.

THE MADAME HAD BEEN very welcoming when she'd received a note from Célie asking for some time to talk, with urgency. She'd responded by inviting the girls both to dine with her that very evening. So, arms linked, Justine and Célie walked briskly in the deepening twilight along rue de Rivoli. They were headed to the madame's house.

"I am so glad you are coming with me, Justine," Célie whispered. "I'm anxious to tell Madame Lou, and even more anxious to get released from the horrid clutches of Marraud. I just hope he doesn't stalk me once the contract's broken."

"I don't think he will. And anyway, we can always find you a protector. There are plenty of men who would be happy to jump to your defense. So, he'd better not harass you or he'll find himself taking a swim in the Seine wearing bricks tied to his hands and feet!"

Célie gave a nervous laugh. "We're almost there. Just around the next bend. Madame said that I could just let myself in, since her servants are off for the evening."

They were nearing the corner of Passage Delorme, where it intersects with rue Saint Honoré. Parked beneath the trees on the opposite side of the street was a carriage. As they passed it, Célie glanced over her shoulder. "That's strange. I swear that's Marraud's coach and driver. What would it be doing waiting here? Maybe I'm mistaken; it's dark. Anyway, it makes me jumpy. Let's get to the house as quickly as we can."

Still arm in arm they hurried a little faster along toward the turn onto Madame's street. As they rounded the corner and her house came into view, the girls hesitated as its front door opened, only

slightly at first, then wider. The light from within the house silhou-
etted the figure of a man seemingly peering cautiously up, then down
the street.

Quickly Justine grabbed Célie's arm and pulled her behind the
broad trunk of a tree, hiding them both from his sight. They watched
as the man threw his cloak over his head and moved quickly, stealthily.
In a few strides he'd reached the carriage they'd passed and climbed
aboard, closing the door with a slam. Aided by a streetlamp which
had just been lighted, they were able to see detail clearly. Therefore,
it was without any doubt that they both witnessed François Marraud
lean out of the window to tell his driver to take him home. "Avec
rapidité"—with all speed!

"What was that about? What was Marraud doing at Madame's?"
Célie whispered, thinking it could not possibly be anything good. His
gait and his posture were even more sinister than usual. And the
cloak thrown over his head? Her heart hammered in her chest. "Justine, let's hurry. We have to get to Madame's—something isn't right."

Holding their skirts high, they ran to Madame Lou's. The
door had been left ajar after Marraud's hasty exit. With great trep-
idation they pushed it open, then, carefully closing and locking it
behind them, crossed the empty foyer. "Madame?" she called, her
voice echoing in the empty hallway. "Are you here? It's Célie. With
Justine... Madame?"

The sound lingered, then trailed away. No response. It felt terribly
ominous. Célie wrapped her arms across her chest against a sudden
chill as they travelled the length of the hall, peering tentatively into
each salon. There seemed to be not a single soul about.

The girls' footfalls came slower, ever more cautiously against
the wooden parquet floor as they traversed the space. The last
chamber on the left was Madame's office. Célie had been in there
but once, when she signed her agreement to be employed by Lou-
Lou, so she knew its location. They hesitated again before reaching

the doorway; light from the room spilled out into the hall. Célie noticed that she was holding her breath. Silly girl, everything will be alright, she thought uncertainly. Madame was probably upstairs in her boudoir. Perhaps she'd even forgotten their meeting and gone to bed early. That must be it. Célie took a deep breath, pushed open the half-closed door, and peeked around the corner into the room...

...and screamed! The kind of unearthly shriek that emanates from the worst of all nightmares—a keening wail that threatened to raise the dead slumbering in their catacombs beneath the streets of Paris.

BY EARLIEST DAWN, THE two working girls, eyes raw and red-rimmed, still dressed in the finery they had worn for dinner at Madame's the night before, sat in the office of Paris police Inspector Jean-Baptiste Meusnier. Meusnier was well known to Célie since he, too, had been acquainted, even friends with, the poor, deceased Louise Périer. He held a senior position within the *gendarmerie* and was known to be a kindly man disposed to helping the less fortunate in society. It was his job to report on the girls and madams well known in the demimonde. He also tracked those often dangerously powerful men who were their patrons. Most importantly, Meusnier was the only person whom Célie felt she could trust.

Sitting on hard wooden chairs, both girls had managed to recount their woeful tale of the evening prior, although often they broke down while they sobbed into lace handkerchiefs. The inspector quickly dismissed any suspicion he might have harbored regarding the two young women's involvement in the killing. Instead, he felt aghast, saddened, as he had admired Madame LouLou very much despite her dubious profession. He knew her death would come as a sorrowful blow to a wide community. He wondered, too, what would become of the girls she'd nurtured and cared for. Mostly he felt for Célie, whom he'd secretly held in high regard, and who was now utterly distraught.

"Inspector—please—you simply must do something! That beast Marraud murdered her! I know it. We saw him slinking away from the scene of the crime! I know he believes himself to be all-powerful and invincible, but he did it, Inspector, and I beg of you to have him arrested. He's a killer… just look!" And she showed him the bruises he inflicted when he'd practiced his lethal stranglehold on her. "I have confidence in you, Inspector Meusnier. I know you will avenge Madame Lou. Please…please… you must!"

"I shall do my best, but you need to be aware that he is a man with money and connections. Bringing such predators to justice is not always a simple matter, while Lou was, after all, a madam of the dames entretenues. a precarious path of her own choosing. On the other hand, she was also a respected businesswoman; she gave generously to important causes, and her women are being kept by some of the most influential men in France. They will demand a quick resolution of this case in order to mitigate the scandal about to explode, so we have that on our side. While what of Monsieur Toussaint? He must be informed of Madame Lou's untimely end with the utmost expedition."

This elicited a fresh round of weeping from Célie. "I believe he is attending to his business in the Caribbean. Oh, his heart will be simply shattered. I can't imagine what he will do without LouLou. I will see if I can obtain an address so that you can send him a communiqué to return home with the greatest urgency."

"And what will he do to the culprit when he arrives?" The inspector reflected grimly. "I am not at all sure what will be worse for the murderer… restitution inflicted by Toussaint, or a life in prison."

AND SO IT WAS that, less than a fortnight later, the Marraud family was roughly awakened in the hour before dawn by a relentless pounding on their door. Moments later, four gendarmes stormed in and arrested Knight Commandeur François Marraud by force, binding him in shackles.

"Monsieur Marraud! By royal command of King Louis XV of France, you are under arrest for the murder most foul of Madame Louise Périer!"

"Arrest? ARREST? I am guilty of no crime!" the Knight bellowed as he was dragged through his house before the terrified eyes of his wife and children. "The king has commanded this? I am not guilty and will be proven so! And where am I being taken, anyway? I demand immediate release!"

As they yanked him across his threshold, out into the street and a waiting police tumbril, they replied, "Why sir, that would be impossible. The prefecture has received direct orders from His Highness the King. As for where you are going, well, Monsieur, you need hardly ask. We hope you enjoy your stay, for even if you retain your head, it will undoubtedly be a long visit. Probably lifelong."

Whereupon the shrieking sham of an officer of The Order of Saint John was thrown roughly into the cart, to be summarily incarcerated in that water-filled, rat-infested stone fortress, Le Bastille, awaiting a trial which would not be arranged until—and only if—the king so mandated it.

BIBLIOTHÈQUE DE L'ARSENAL
PARIS

Seven straight days scouring a mountain of information with no positive result had taken its toll on me. I was exhausted, and frustration added to my sour mood. The entire effort had been an intense test of our collective brainpower, not to mention stamina. We'd flipped through page after page of documents, each one a challenge due to our limited abilities in French. Every time I turned another pointless leaf, I swore under my breath. Finally, Dad flashed me a look that meant 'Can you not restrain yourself, please?' So I made an effort. When we became desperate for help, we asked one of the curators, who had generously offered to assist if we got stuck. I was beyond discouraged and at that point, toyed with the thought of just giving up. After the initial tantalising reference to Adolphe Toussaint, we still hadn't found mention of his name anywhere else.

"I think we should pack up, Dad. It's useless."

"I'm drained, too, Zar. But look, we have two more books here. The archivist said they were some sort of addendum the police created after completing their record-keeping. Why don't we at least flip through them before we go?"

My sense of defeat was self-directed. I was disappointed for making the decision to spend so much time on something futile. We'd spent days here. Was I going to waste them, though, without seeing the search through? I could pack up right now, go back to Rome and be busy doing what I was in Rome to accomplish. Get my degree. I sat for a few minutes letting the thoughts churn. Give up? Was I going to confirm my worst fears—that, although I might be smart, I was also a loser? The ugly word reverberated, bouncing around in my head. It created a visceral reaction, my stomach clenching in objection.

"Dad. You're right. We're here for a reason. You go to the café and rest. Give me those two damn books. If there's nothing in them, I'll be the one to call the search off."

He gave me an admiring smile and a pat. "I'll wait for you." And off he went.

I opened *Tome Un*. Book One of the miscellaneous materials the prefecture had collected over the years. This time, the volume had a sort of an index at the end. So I flipped to it and ran my finger down the neat columns of blue-inked handwriting. And, lo and behold, within minutes, there he was. The target of our scrutiny. And, holy hell: it was his address! The entry listed under 'Toussaint' read: 'M. A. Toussaint était l'amoureux de Madame Louise Périer. Monsieur A. Toussaint was the lover of Madame Louise Périer. They lived in rue St. Honoré, in the fourth house near rue de L'Echelle...' in the old, feathery Gallic hand it added, 'the house was large and magnificent, being the physical manifestation of Toussaint's and Périer's great wealth.'

Pulse fast, adrenaline rushing, I scanned the lines again and again. So, he lived with a woman! In fact, with one of the very prosperous Parisian madams. He was known as her lover, and together they owned an impressive townhouse. I found it fascinating that, unmarried, she had a relationship favorable enough that they owned a house together—this in a time when probably very few women owned property. I could almost picture her... Madame Louise Périer... She must have been very beautiful. And fierce—in an 18th century sort of way. Rich, powerful in her own right, a homeowner. And the partner of an influential man. Somehow, I just knew they had loved each other, and found the notion to be inspiring.

I couldn't wait to tell Dad what I'd found. I grabbed my bag and ran to the café, knocking into an older gentleman on the way. "Pardon!" I threw the apology over my shoulder, saw Dad and skidded into the booth next to him. Barely able to catch my breath, I grabbed his arm. "Guess where we are going tomorrow? To Chez Toussaint! On rue St. Honoré!"

Chapter Thirty-three

AUGUST 1752

NORTH ATLANTIC OCEAN
OFF THE AZORES ARCHIPELAGO
THE BRIG *TWO SISTERS*
Latitude 37° 47' 40" North: Longitude 29° 32' 16" West

Toussaint lounged on his cramped cabin bunk nursing a glass of rum and a fine Cuban cigar, while thinking back to a previous evening on his Saint- Domingue retreat; already, it seemed a very long time ago.

On that peaceful occasion he'd been on his veranda, reading yet again all of the letters he'd received from LouLou since his departure from Paris. The summer had proved delightful on the island, mostly spent sitting on the porch of his plantation house, lulled by the whisper of palm fronds in the warm tropical air and the lap of foam-edged turquoise surf against the white sand beach.

As the summer had worn on, he'd been giving serious thought to moving back to the Caribbean permanently. His plantation afforded such respite from the vacuous, frenetic social whirl of Paris—not to underestimate the luxury of year-round warm weather set against the cold rain and soot-contaminated French snow in winter. But his current isolation had also made him acutely aware that he would miss Lou desperately, and he was compelled to consider inviting her to move to the islands with him. He had, in fact, made a decision while in Nassau, on the fateful day that her final letter had arrived.

He thought he would return to France, help her sell the house and dispense of the business she had diligently run for many years, consolidate her cash, and have her sail with him to live for the rest of their days in one of his homes in the islands. How she would love it! They had more money than they could ever spend, and it was time for them both to live life more tranquilly. He'd lost that restless fervor of his early years, and no one made him happier than did his LouLou. Yes, it was the right thing to do—finish up his local business dealings then return to Paris before the winter Atlantic storms season set in. Over the festive period they would arrange to move—lock, stock and barrel—including, above all, his beloved portrait, to Saint-Domingue by the spring, as soon as the ocean crossing again became feasible.

But then, Adolphe Toussaint had opened Lou's envelope, and begun to read. His jaw clenched tight and immediately his rage had grown, billowing out of control, a wrath unlike any he'd experienced since his youth. That the self-important Marraud would dare to threaten his woman, and demand to see his belongings in his absence! But of course the swine had waited until there was no man in the house to protect Lou: a coward to his bootstraps!

Oh, he was well acquainted with that so-called Knight Commandeur François Marraud—had detested him since their very first meeting, in fact. Adolphe found the overbearing man to be envious and sullen, prone to spitting offensive remarks when he felt his superiority to be in question, while furtively trying to outdo others at every turn. But the stupid lout had now taken a misstep too far, for which he would pay. Oh, make no mistake, he was going to pay dearly.

Clutching the letter in his fist, Toussaint went immediately to the dock to book passage on the first ship outward bound for Europe.

No sooner would he arrive in Paris than he'd surprise Marraud with a very special meeting. How that cur would regret his decision to harass Lou, and Célie, and beg for his pitiful life and release from the punishment which Toussaint would slowly mete out!

Adolphe tied up business dealings on his island, then sailed to Cuba where he'd boarded a tramping merchantman, the brig Two Sisters of Bristol, scheduled to depart from Havana, call briefly at the port of Philadelphia to take on more cargo, then sail for Dover, England. Once there, he would have to cross the Channel to Calais and finally undertake the last leg of his journey by coach to Paris, a wearying and convoluted trip to be sure but the best he could manage on short notice.

Two Sisters turned out to be a small brig, and reasonably fast although nothing could get him to his destination as quickly as he would have wished, not unless he could fly like a bird. But at least, he reflected wryly, her captain and crew seemed competent, and kept to their business. Their cargo consisted largely of tobacco and cigars, indigo dye, oranges, hides, and sugar, some of it from his own plantations, destined, eventually, to be sold both in England and on the European Continent. Hard lying or not, he'd been lucky to be able to book passage on the ship the very day of its departure from Havana.

A soft whimper interrupted Adolphe's daydream, and he reached down to stroke the silky ears of his companion, who lay tightly curled at his feet in the cramped cabin space. An island dog, she had taken to him, cunningly wheedling herself into his affections at the beginning of the summer. Thereafter she'd followed him constantly, and finally he'd started calling her 'Odette'. Before long, she'd been permitted on the veranda where he would feed her scraps from dinner until, eventually, brazenly following him into the house itself where Odette's adoring gaze was always firmly fixed on him, her warm brown eyes and eager expression invariably melting his heart. So rather than leave her behind, he'd loaded her on board with him where she'd proved a seaworthy mate, and had no problem adjusting to the pitch and yaw of the vessel. The one thing he'd discovered that she did fear, though, were coming storms. She seemed to be able to sense the heaviness in the air and would find someplace to hide until it had passed.

Toussaint stubbed out his cigar, drained his glass, and decided to have a pleasant stroll on deck before turning in for the night. With Odette at his heel, they emerged on the deck, where a stiff westerly wind filled the sails and drove the two-masted ship along at a fast clip, skirting the Azores islands.

He stopped to have a congenial word with the captain, then, with a final glance at the star-strewn sky, went below to retire for the night.

It must have been just before dawn that Toussaint rose to relieve himself in the piss pot. As he climbed back into his bunk, he noticed Odette, and frowned. Curled as tightly as she could manage, pressed into the corner, she trembled piteously. She looked up at him and started panting, eyes filled with terror. He patted the dog and told her to hush, but she only became ever more agitated. Realizing he could hear the wind, which had clearly risen since he'd fallen asleep some hours ago, he pulled on his breeches and went above to check on conditions.

His seaman's sense immediately told him a full gale was brewing, and the deckhands were rapidly raising the storm sails. Already the helmsman was struggling to steer the ship's head into the weather, but the seas were getting bigger by the minute. Dawn was breaking, and when Adolphe looked forward, he saw wave tops already cresting high above the main deck. As the swell increased, and the wind grew to a piercing wail, he returned briefly to his cabin where he tucked a blanket around his trembling Odette, patted her reassuringly and told her to stay where she was, that she'd be alright because he'd make sure she stayed safe.

He crawled to the foredeck where, battling against the lashing rain and now screaming wind, the crew struggled to keep the ship from broaching, as the storm increased with alarming intensity. Adolphe joined the seamen on deck, hauling frantically to bring the sails in. By now the ship was staggering to climb waves increasingly immense while, as it plummeted downward from each crest, the motion sucked the air from his lungs with its dreadful speed. The sailors swore mightily, laboring as best they could to reef even the single storm jib while lashing the helm to run downwind, hoping it would stabilize the careening craft. But the tempest which had developed, seemingly from nowhere, pulled them, with merciless power, into its center. Rain lashed sideways, unseasonal hail pelted the men with the force of leaden shot. Adolphe had little time to be fearful, or even to think, as he reacted instinctively from his years at sea, but just as it seemed they might be able to run ahead of the storm, a colossal wall of water exploded against the starboard side of *Two Sisters*, capsizing her like a child's toy while hurling every last despairing soul of her crew into the roiling North Atlantic.

Adolphe was stunned at the raw, bone-numbing cold of the water as he hit its surface. His head was sucked under, but he was able to thrust himself upward to grab a heaving breath. The sea dragged at him mercilessly, and he quickly realised it would be impossible to survive such conditions for long. As he rode each huge wave, he fought to keep track of the capsized ship, hoping he might swim to it and pull himself onto its bilge keel to take refuge above the maelstrom. But within seconds his only potential salvation had been swept far from his reach, with the current carrying it further and further away. Close by he could hear other men crying out but sighted never a one. Toussaint did his best to tread water while praying he might come upon a barrel, a wooden grating, some wooden spar, any scrap of flotsam that would sustain him above the surface.

He caught sight of the seal a moment later. Atop two wave crests away it was swimming steadily towards him. How curious that there should be a seal here, adrift in this violent storm, Adolphe reflected gravely.

It was only then he realised it wasn't a seal, but a dog! A shiny-wet dog with big floppy ears sleeked back against the sides of its head and paddling determinedly towards him. He recognised it now—Odette, his devoted island companion of the wide, brown, implicitly trusting eyes.

Hopelessly he called out, "I am so sorry, my faithful friend! Sorry I have broken my promise to keep you safe."

But then Odette had passed him by, whimpering, swept helpless by the current. And, the next time Adolphe looked, the sea—that ally, upon which he had sailed, fought, and thrived—had swallowed one of the very few true friends he had ever possessed in his unusual, impassioned life.

As he watched, helpless, the subsequent breaking roller submerged the already lost man and caused him to inhale a great draught of sea water. Toussaint choked; his arms and legs felt leaden, frozen. He fumbled for his gris-gris, which miraculously had remained about his neck whereupon, gripping it tightly, prayed to his Vodou spirits until the force of the next wave ripped even that false comfort from his hand. The cord snapped—and his final hope for salvation was lost to the sea's savagery.

Adolphe Toussaint: fearless buccaneer, man of brilliance and spirited tenacity, accepted his life had come to its end. So… he simply let go. As he sank, he was surprised by how peaceful it was beneath the sea's surface—found, in fact, that the adventure of dying was not at all unpleasant.

While Adolphe spiraled bottomward, eyes open and long hair splayed like tentacles about him, he was surprised to see his beloved LouLou drifting nearby.

He tried to call out to her, but it wasn't really necessary. She knew he was there, and, smiling, reached out to him and lovingly, reassuringly, clasped his hand.

And, together, they slipped into the soothing, dark depths.

Chapter Thirty-four

LATE JANUARY 2017

PARIS

Morning offered a miserable, slate grey sky and raw, biting temperatures. Icy pellets of sleet bounced off umbrellas, our feet dancing
and sliding in the fast-accumulating slush. Once Dad and I arrived
at the corner of rue St. Honoré and rue de L'Echelle, we identified
four houses on the side of the street which seemed most likely. We
couldn't figure out whether the corner building was included—and
for that matter, if the number of buildings would have been the same
as they were in 1755 when the report had been issued. But I carefully
counted to include the corner building, the fourth structure was a
narrow but stately townhouse rising three full stories above street
level. It was now the Parisian store of the British couturier, Vivienne
Westwood. Number 175.

We stepped inside, careful to leave our sopping umbrellas by
the threshold. I couldn't do much about my wet parka, much less
my boots. Immediately, I became terribly self-conscious because the
store, along with the other businesses in that block, was an emporium
of high fashion. My glance swept the shop to take in a wild array of
garments, clothing of the most avant-garde colors, prints and shapes
hanging neatly on racks. The store itself was sleek and minimalist, but

the old wide-plank wood floors were highly polished, adding needed warmth to the spare look. A friendly young woman with pink, spiked hair and a print mini-skirt stepped over to us and asked if she might help. Dad immediately piped up, as he knew I would probably be a bit overwhelmed. "Bonjour, Mademoiselle... parlez-vous anglais?"

Thankfully she replied that she did, indeed, speak English, so Dad told her we had an unusual request: we needed information about the building. She held up her hand and hurried off to beckon the manager. When he arrived—a young man equally whimsically attired, and quite friendly—we explained to him our purpose for the visit. His English was passable, but with the help of another salesgirl who translated, we were able to convey that we were doing research and wondered what information might be available about the building from its early days in the mid-18th century. "Truthfully, I do not know the answer, but I can give you the name, address, and phone number for the landlord who should have records of all of the buildings' owners and tenants. With any luck," he offered, "you may find what you seek. In fact, I will be happy to call for you to see if you can meet with her, perhaps even today?"

Once we started talking about the building and its age, I relaxed a little. "Merci beaucoups, Monsieur. We would be very appreciative if you might do that for us," I said. I hoped he could make the connection. I was anxious to get any info possible about this edifice and the secrets it might hide.

True to his word, the young man disappeared, returned and handed us a sheet of paper with the contact for the property manager. Paper in hand, we went back out into the bleak afternoon, directed toward the management company's office.

In reception, a middle-aged, and very elegant woman greeted us and led the way into her office.

"Good day, sir and mademoiselle." She was brisk and efficient. "What is it you seek today? How may I help?" Her English was precise, but I'd say her initial manner was certainly not overly friendly. So I allowed Dad to lead the conversation, and watched in both amusement and admiration as he turned on the charm. I guess I tended to forget that he was still a very handsome, and distinguished, man. It was hard to think of him in that way—as an attractive and quite wealthy widower. And clearly, his appeal wasn't lost on Madame Armel.

"Madame," Dad said, "we are researching this particular section of the city, especially the houses which involved early residents who may have achieved some notoriety. Any information you might offer would be so gratefully received."

As she listened, I noticed she wore no wedding ring. She asked a few questions, then thrummed the fingers of her left hand on her desk as she considered our—or should I say Dad's—request. With barely a glance at me, she told Dad, "Excuse me. I'll be right back."

I thought it better not to comment, once she had left us alone, but did raise my eyebrows a bit.

"Oh, stop, Zar. I know what you're thinking. You catch more flies with honey, you know."

"Yes, indeed. I do know that… and apparently your brand of honey's pretty enticing to the single Madame Armel!"

"Whatever works…" He fell quiet as she returned.

"I've made a quick call for you, Docteur Rossi. I do not have the information in this office, but there is a historian I happen to know who will be able to help you—a specialist in the arondissements of the earliest parts of Paris. He is willing to assist. Here is his number. You may call him to arrange a meeting. And, by the way, his English is not too good. Would you need a translator? If so, I would be more than happy to help…?"

Oh boy, I wondered how Dad was going to manage this?

With little hesitation he reached for her hand and covered it with his other hand in a gesture of warmth. "Merci beaucoup, Madame.

You are so very kind. However, I think we will be fine. I appreciate your generous offer, though, and the help you have given my daughter and me today. I wish you well and have a lovely afternoon. Au revoir, et merci."

It had been, I thought, a successful visit. All due to Dad's warmth, his ability to make people feel comfortable, and his obvious charm. It occurred to me that I could learn a lot by watching him interact with people. And I got to thinking about his connection with Madame Armel. As we walked down the street, heads down against the still-spitting pellets of sleet, I tugged on his sleeve till we both stopped. "You know, Dad, I don't want you to feel like you couldn't have someone else in your life. It would be okay with me. I know you miss Mom, like I do. And you might never find anyone her equal. But it doesn't mean you shouldn't have someone to share things with."

He linked his arm through mine and gave me a squeeze. "Thank you, my sweet girl. That means a lot to me. I don't know, really, if I will ever find anyone again, but I am grateful for your approval should I do so. And, by the way, I'm well aware your mother hounded you about this, but it would please me very much if you, too, found someone to be your partner—your companion, confidante—someone your equal intellectually and, above all, someone you could trust. It would be okay for you as well, you know. It doesn't mean that a partnership distills who you are into a shadow of your former self. On the contrary, Zara, the right person would do the opposite. Enhance all you are: all you could be. In fact, the right partnership can make life glorious."

He hesitated then and looked into my eyes. "Promise me you won't resist the possibility. Promise me you'll keep your heart open. Will you?"

"Yes, Dad. I promise. I'm not sure it will ever happen, but I'll try to be open."

"Thank you, Zara. Love you. Now let's go call our historian and see what we can find out."

As soon as we'd returned to the blessedly dry warmth of our hotel, Dad dialed the number we'd been given. He said, "Bonjour, Monsieur Castile", introduced himself, and stated that Castile's name and contact info had been provided to us by Madame Armel. Dad clicked on the speaker, and I could tell right away that Monsieur Castile was more adept at English than we'd been led to believe. His fluency was helpful, because in short order, we conveyed what we hoped to learn about the fourth house on rue St. Honore. I was amazed when Castile immediately knew of the building. He told us it was most certainly original to the late 1600s and had been a grand townhome in its day.

I piped up, "Oh, Monsieur, you have no idea how grateful we'd be if you could provide us with anything—really, any scrap of information you might have on the house."

"Oui, Mademoiselle Rossi, let me look for something I recall reading, and if I find it, I will fax a copy to your hotel: if my memory is correct, it was a reference to the property's history from a very early newspaper. But I shall search, and will let you know as soon as I can. Au revoir."

It wasn't even an hour later when we received a return call from Castile. He told us he couldn't access a copy for us, but the reference he remembered was in an old periodical called the Anecdotes Galantes, a deliberately titillating publication containing the sexual gossip of the day, largely produced for the entertainment of the king and his court. It was first launched in 1764 and the article was in one of the earliest issues.

I was dying to know what the piece had reported. "Merci, Monsieur Castile. What story did it cover? Was it about the house we are researching?"

"Well, yes, it appears so. The story described the death of a Knight Commander François Marraud, imprisoned for 14 years, dying in his cell in the Bastille. He'd been incarcerated for the brutal murder of the illustrious Madame Louise Périer, a great favorite of the king's. The murder took place in the home Périer shared with her financier partner, Monsieur Adolphe Toussaint, native to the isles of the Caribe."

I was beyond exhilarated. "Wow! That's incredible! To think there was a mention of him in a newspaper that's lasted until today…"

Castile went on: "The account tells of the prisoner: the murderer—a formerly respected Knight in the Order of St. John—ranting and raving night and day in his cell about his wrongful punishment, which he claimed should instead have been the fate of Toussaint, who'd flagrantly stolen a valuable painting from him. The reporter added that the artwork was in Toussaint's and Périer's house, and when Marraud's attempted to rob them of what he falsely claimed to be his property, he strangled Périer when she was home alone. So the King had him arrested and thrown into the Bastille. He was never released; he didn't merit a trial since he was deemed a raving lunatic."

I shook my head in disbelief. This tale was information I had never hoped to find! "Monsieur Castile, my father and I thank you so very much. You truly have no idea how helpful you've been."

"It was my pleasure, Mademoiselle and Docteur Rossi. Good luck with the rest of your research. Good afternoon."

No sooner had we hung up than I twirled in my chair to face Dad. "What the hell? Can you even believe this? Dad—do you think it could be our painting?"

"I think it has to be, Zar. The murderer's connection to the Order? That doesn't strike me as coincidence. It might have been some other painting, sure, but this Marraud must have felt entitled, and driven to seize it. It's just too uncanny. Particularly as the Knights of Malta had been required to seek it out? I think this is a lead—a good one."

"I believe you're right. And how incredibly sad for that poor woman, murdered in a robbery of something which was never his to belong with. The king must have really cared for her to intervene in such a dramatic way." I was thrilled, and in a moment of self-reproach, realized that I'd almost given up the entire search. "Well…if you ask me, I think we need to go back to Madame Armel to ask if she can gather anything else on the house's history after the murder. Whatever happened to Toussaint, for instance?"

"One has to think there might be additional information about Toussaint… After all, he didn't just cease to exist. Maybe he continued to live there with the painting? Or just left the city following the death of his beloved Louise?"

I couldn't resist the impulse to tease him gently. "Speaking of love… I think it's best left to you to call your lady friend in the property management office to see if, now that we have a piece of the puzzle in place, she might be able to dig up anything else for us about that house. I have complete confidence you will handle it ever so smoothly."

DAD AND NICOLE ARMEL went out that evening for drinks and dinner. I was pleased for him, and he gravely promised he wouldn't return without some additional info to help in our convoluted search. When he'd called her, he said he wondered if she might be able to assist with any records of previous owners or renters in the building, and she'd been delighted to accept his invitation, offering to do a thorough property search prior to their meeting.

"Sounds more like a date," I responded mischievously.

"It's not a date," he defended in earnest.

"Of course not," I said, grinning. Then told him that, either way, I wouldn't wait up for him.

The next morning when we met for breakfast, I could tell he was pleased. He had a lightness about him that I realized I hadn't seen for a long, long time. I had to admit that I envied his good cheer. In any case, I decided to go easy on him, so, as I added a splash of cream to my coffee I remarked offhandedly, "Hope you had a nice time last evening, Dad."

"Indeed, I did, honey. She's a lovely lady, and really quite interesting. And she'd been true to her word and unearthed a further bunch of records for us. In fact, she said she'd meet us for tea and bring along the documents so you can see them. Okay?"

"That sounds great, my charming father. You do a pretty good job as an assistant sleuth, you know?" I was glad, for so many reasons, that Dad had come to Paris with me.

Later that afternoon, the three of us sat in a booth in the back of a local patisserie. Over cups of tea, we examined the records Nicole had pulled for us. It sure appeared that, following Périer's killing, the house remained vacant for many decades. There was no account of Toussaint having continued to live there, in fact, no indication of where he'd gone. We conjectured that perhaps no one wanted to reside in the house after such a notorious murder. The rental records showed there'd been random families in and out, but none for any length of time. Certain reports revealed that the building had, by then, fallen into in a complete state of disrepair, so again, it was abandoned.

While Dad and Nicole chatted, I read every line on each page of the documents she'd pulled from her chic leather bag. Hoping to see Toussaint's name, I didn't, and fought my sense of letdown. But then, my interest peaked. Having nothing to do with Louise Périer or Adolphe Toussaint, still, there was something quite curious about a certain set of entries: records of the building's sale in 1911 by a woman who purchased it as her place of business. It was to be a fashion salon. She was British, a female fashion designer in Paris in the early 1900s. How compelling! Not that I was any sort of maven of fashion—the thought made me laugh out loud—but a British woman as a fashion designer of the Victorian era? In Paris of all places?

I felt a shiver. The thought of an incredibly cool and obviously talented woman living in the house that had been Toussaint's? It was more than exciting. Who was this renegade?

According to the records, her name was Lucile Duff Gordon.

Chapter Thirty-five

LATE MARCH 1912

RUE ST. HONORÉ
PARIS

M umbling around a mouthful of dressmaker's pins, Lucile realized Gamela had no idea what she was trying to say, so instead, she grabbed her mannequin's ankles and shifted her position a bit to the left. Lucile was kneeling on a floor cushion at the model's feet, pinning a hem intended to flow like water rippling from the train of an ethereal gown. Her focus was so intent that she was unaware of two extremely striking ladies who'd just sailed into the room—until they squealed in delight.

"Lucy, darling! We've simply got to tell you how thrilled we are to visit you in your brand new salon! I hope we're among the very first… do tell us. Are we? At least among the New Yorkers?"

Lucile spat the pins into her hand and scrambled to her feet. "My two absolutely favorite ladies! How glorious to see you both. And here in Paris. I'm so sorry… I didn't know you were coming, or I would have been much better prepared. At the very least I shall order tea." And to her mannequin, who'd remained standing perfectly still on the fitting platform, she said "Gamela, let's take the dress off and we'll finish the hem a little later."

Cathleen (Mrs. Reginald Vanderbilt) and her sister-in-law Gertrude (Mrs. Harry Payne Whitney) arranged themselves on a settee beautifully upholstered in rose pink damask, while Lucile's housemaid hurried in with tea service, and laid it on a side console. The ladies, prominent members of the top echelon of New York and Newport society, had become regular clients after attending the first 'mannequin parade' Lucile staged in New York. On that momentous afternoon, as the stage curtain fell behind the last model wearing one of Lucile's gossamer, figure-flattering evening gowns, they'd swooped like fluttering birds, politely but persistently pecking at their fellow finely-feathered canaries in order to be the first to gain Lucile's attention. It seemed that everyone clamored for an immediate appointment—with the objective of commissioning dozens of the unique dresses the mannequins had modelled that afternoon. Never before had a designer staged a fashion show like that, in which lithe and willowy young women floated on a runway, showing the couturière's newest collection off to perfection. The carefully curated audience found the event irresistibly alluring, and the 'parades', as Lucile termed them, were an instant sensation.

Gertrude, a renowned sculptress and painter in her own right, sipped her tea and gazed in wonder at the six-foot, raven-tressed Gamela, who slid gracefully from the fitting platform.

"Will you look at that girl? What a beauty! How I'd like to have legs like that. But seeing as it's impossible, instead I would love to use her as a sculpture model. What do you think, Lucy? Might I be able to borrow her at some point, even though I do realise she's one of your top mannequins?"

"Well, of course you can, Mrs. Whitney. It would be my great pleasure to allow Gamela time to attend your studio. I understand you have a big workspace in Passy, in the XVIth, correct? You just tell me when it would be convenient, and I'll see that she's there."

"Marvelous, Lucy darling! Cathleen and I just arrived this week, and plan to stay in Paris for a few months, so we thought we would stop by to see your new atelier. I'd heard it's stunning. Do show us around, will you?"

"It will be my pleasure, ladies. Let's take the grand tour."

And Lucile proudly led them from floor to floor, salon to salon, allowing them to peek into the many suites where she stored her fabrics: yards of tissue, thin silks, and organzas of the softest colors of the rainbow, closets in which accoutrements were arranged (ribbons, buttons, lace), cutting rooms where patterns were laid out and material readied for assembly, even the sewing rooms in which several Parisian seamstresses were working, stitching together gorgeous confections for the fashionable young Frenchwomen who'd elected to have a special gown, often their entire trousseau, designed and created by the British phenomenon, Lucile. The American women ooh'ed and ahh'ed at each discovery until finally Lucile directed them to the piéce de resistance: the main salon she used as her receiving room, carpeted in thick soft grey, and with floor-to-ceiling windows hung with lilac brocade. Off to one side was a discreet fitting area, veiled by swathes of periwinkle blue chiffon, behind which her clients took to raised platforms to be impeccably custom-fitted.

Lucile refreshed teacups and they nibbled on tiny sandwiches while blithely chatting about the upcoming dress parade. The show would be her first in Paris, and it was of vital importance. Special invitations, hand-engraved on dainty cards, had been sent to the wealthiest women driving the Parisian social scene, each card slyly personalized to create the illusion that it bore a request to attend an elegant afternoon party, rather than a function of business.

"Aren't you at all nervous, Lucy?" Cathleen inquired. She was a lovely woman with arresting green eyes. She already wore a perfectly tailored afternoon dress by Lucile Ltd.

"A bit. I would be lying if I didn't admit it. But I have confidence in the looks I'm designing, and also in my girls. They know how to dazzle; I've not seen them fail yet. And I have a fantastic concept in mind for the event. I'll gladly share it with you, if you like—but you must keep it a secret."

The elegant sisters-in-law, doyennes of American society, giggled like naughty children at the prospect of being privy to Lucy's creative plans. "We will. We promise! Oh, do tell us!"

"Well, I've imagined it to simulate the 1903 Imperial Ball in the Winter Palace of St. Petersburg. The gowns I intend to show will be celestial, bejewelled, and reminiscent of the opulence of the Russian Empire at its pinnacle—a time which, sadly, now seems gone forever."

"Fantastic! Won't that be just brilliant? And will your creations have names?" Cathleen's eyes glittered, and Lucile was again reminded that almost every woman she'd ever met could be transported simply by imagining herself in a gown fit for a princess.

"Indeed, they will. Gamela will, for instance, wear 'Give Me Your Heart': an ice-blue chiffon strewn with silver paillettes which will set off her raven-wing hair. Dolores, she of the lovely curves, will model 'The Meaning of Life Is Clear', a diaphanous white robe edged with black satin ribbon, while our ravishing, golden-blonde Hebe will close the parade in 'Forever Yours', a bridal gown of cream satin covered in sparkling crystals. So, what do you think?"

"We simply must be there! Of course, you can offer us invitations, can't you, Lucy?" Cathleen leaned forward on the edge of her chair in anticipation.

"Certainly! I can and will. I'd be delighted for you both to attend."

Lucile was pleased. A sighting of the two influential American socialites wouldn't be missed by the local social climbers, and it could only help her own acceptance into the closed world of Parisian fashion design, which had been, until her arrival on the scene, the strict purview of French men.

Gertrude gushed, "And it goes without saying, dear heart, that we will both wear our favorite tea dresses, by Lucile Ltd., of course.

One can't get too early a start on planning one's wardrobe for the upcoming season, you know. And we want to be the only women in New York with pieces from your new Parisian collection. Good-bye, Lucy darling. And good luck."

The Vanderbilt sisters waved a fond farewell as they departed Atelier de Lucile Ltd, rue St. Honoré.

THE FADING AFTERNOON LIGHT slid slowly from the ceiling down along the cream-colored walls of the salon when Lucile let her girls go home with their promise to return the next morning by 7:30 a.m. sharp. The show was in three weeks' time and there was an enormous amount to accomplish in the interim. When the last seamstress had stepped out to the street to head homeward, Lucile wandered alone through her studio, admiring the results of exceedingly hard work that had taken place over the last eight months in readying it for her tenancy. Once she had determined—with affirmation from some of her closest friends, and dire predictions of certain disaster from others—to set up business in Paris and challenge the French at their dominance in the world of fashion design, she'd begun to look for a suitable location in which to establish her atelier. She had to acquire something which would command respect from her competitors. So, she seized every possible opportunity to sneak away from her business in London and, with the help of estate agents, hunted for vacant properties along the avenues of the fashion district, until one day, she'd stumbled upon an empty four-story townhouse. It was narrow, its windows looked like eyes staring vacantly into the past, yet it possessed an unmistakeable aura of former grandeur, and seemed to beckon her.

It sat directly on rue St. Honoré, just near the corner of rue de L'Echelle. And, oh my! Wasn't it a right mess! Stepping inside, Lucile blanched. Peeling paint, woodwork cracked and broken, water damage creasing walls and ceilings—but there was something about it. Something mysterious, something enticing. It reminded her of her girls—the future mannequins she had tirelessly sought and plucked from among the working-class young women of London. At first glance, they appeared plain; surely, they wouldn't have been considered beauties by any standard of the day. But if one knew what to look for, there it was: great bone structure. Elegance, style, and grace merely waiting to be polished and coaxed to emerge in glorious brilliance. Somehow, that's precisely how she felt about the house. So, against the vociferous protest of her second husband and business manager, the Scotsman Sir Cosmo Duff Gordon, and her estate agent, she went ahead and placed an offer.

It was promptly accepted. The building was hers.

LUCILE DUFF GORDON WAS an intrepid woman of great imagination and creativity. An early divorce and a resulting lack of finances with which to raise her little daughter had inspired her to call upon the hobby which she'd nurtured as a girl: creating beautiful outfits for herself and for her sister Elinor, mostly cobbled together from bits and bobs of fabric and lace, those few trimmings she could then afford on her meagre allowance.

Until, one day as she sewed a dress for her little Esmé while racking her brain for an idea which would rescue them from their desperate straits, it occurred to her: why not try her hand at dressmaking? There were naysayers of course, including her mother, but Lucile was excited by the prospect and decided to forge ahead. A single order for a bespoke tea-gown, worn by a lady of London society to a notable afternoon party, was all it took to launch her business. The dress was openly admired and commented upon and, from that point, gossip helped spread the word. Suddenly, every stylish woman in London heard about, then desired, a Lucile dress of her own. Her creations flowed over the female body in the most attractive way. Lucile's intuition as to how women wanted to look and feel, coupled with her sense of innovation, propelled her business such that within six months she had many more orders than she could fulfill alone. Quickly, she hired four seamstresses to help, and thus was the design house of Lucile Ltd. born. Everyone who was anyone wanted Lucile to dress her.

As her clientele continued to expand, she acquired a second big property in Hanover Square, London, as her salon. Elegant women came and went daily, and Lucile had the pleasure and privilege of dressing some of the most beautiful, the most influential, and richest women of the day. The British prime minister's wife, Dame Margot Asquith, proved a regular and dear supportive friend as did the Duchess of Connaught with her daughters Princesses Margaret and Patricia; Victoria Eugenie, the Queen of Spain; the Duchess of York; actresses including Lily Langtry; and wives of innumerable ridiculously wealthy businessmen all counted on Lucile to make them look ravishing. When she dared to design lacy and sheer underclothes, a great departure from the Victorian foundations of the past (and a pleasant surprise for husbands who were unfortunately accustomed to seeing their wives in dowdy, stiff, corseted undergarments), certain eyebrows were raised, but in no time, she had completely transformed the way women thought of their wardrobes.

Indeed, Lucile set the fashion world on its ear, and that world couldn't get enough. But for Lucile, all roads led to Paris. More than anything, she wanted to conquer fashion's highest pinnacle. And she wouldn't stop until she did just that. So once the purchase of the house in rue St. Honoré was completed, it was then that the hard work began.

There was no time to spare. She needed a workspace perfectly befitting her design concepts. She decided, then, to travel from London to Paris, remaining there to oversee progress. So it happened that she was present on the last day of demolition: the fourth-floor attic, a spacious area which, it seemed, had rarely been used, was to become a storage space.

Lucile and the construction foreman, Monsieur Ducasse, were deep in conversation on the first floor when a workman, covered in sawdust, stood impatiently waiting for an opportunity to speak. His toe-tapping finally prompted Ducasse to say, "Oui, oui… qu'est-ce que c'est?"

At the same moment, Lucile also asked, "What is it, Monsieur? How can we help?"

The carpenter jerked his head toward the staircase. "Tu dois voir ça. Dans le grenier." And with that he started toward the stair, not looking back.

Ducasse motioned to Lucile, saying, "He wants us to see something in the attic. Says we must inspect it. He's not a man who becomes rattled by much, so we'd best catch up with him."

They climbed the stairs level by level, finally ducking under some boards at the very top and into the attic which was almost cleared with the exception of one wall: the space under the eave of the gambrel roof. The foreman pointed to an area which, so far, had been left intact. "Voyez? Allez chercher vous-mêmes."

"'See? We should look for ourselves'," Ducasse translated. They picked their way across the floorboards until faced with a most curious sight.

A cabinet had been built right into the wall under the slanted roof. When pried open by the carpenters, it revealed a fairly large void—obviously a closet, but one which had previously been sealed tightly so no one would guess at its existence. Holding a lantern in front of them, they peered inside and saw a large flat object wrapped in leather, the skins cracked and dried with age.

"What in God's name could this be?" Lucile was mystified, and it was hard not to be excited as the workmen lifted it from its resting place. Who knew how long it had been in there? It was layered with dust and cobwebs.

Monsieur Ducasse directed the workmen to remove it to a lower floor into one of the finished rooms so Lady Duff Gordon could inspect it in a safer setting. Carefully, the men carried the object to her reception area and leaned it against a table. Lucile's heart was pounding, and she longed to pull the covering apart. But this was an experience to be shared so, instead, she looked at Ducasse and said, "Merci, Monsieur. I believe I will leave it for today and only uncover it when my husband arrives in town. We will investigate its content together, but thank you so much for your help."

COSMO HAD THOROUGHLY POKED into every corner and crevice of the studio as it was under construction, to be reassured that the level of workmanship was up to snuff.

"Well, Lucy, it looks pretty sound to me. Just as well, mind you, we're paying an absolute king's ransom for this work, and that on top of the price of the building."

"Oh, I know, darling. I'm glad I have you to review matters like building plans and construction sites, so I don't have to worry about it. It's your forte, and just one of the reasons why I married you." With a wink, Lucile added, "Other than your enduring good looks. So now, Cosmo, please can we finally examine the mysterious object found in the attic yesterday? I've been waiting for what seems like forever, but I wanted you here."

Lucile tucked her hand through her husband's arm and firmly propelled him towards the reception salon where the object remained, propped against the table, patiently awaiting its moment of revelation.

"What a strange thing... especially since it was packed away in that niche, which certainly does seem as if it was built for the specific purpose." Cosmo untied the crumbling leather bindings and released them only to find further wrappings of material and paper. Before removing the final layer, he wiped the dust from his hands. Then, while Lucy stood back holding her breath, unravelled the remaining wrapping.

It was a painting.

And not just any painting, but one that looked undoubtedly as if it was a portrait of the resplendent King Henry VIII. Lucy and Cosmo blinked in disbelief. They looked at each other while Duff Gordon muttered uncertainly, "What the devil?"

Momentarily speechless, Lucy finally approached the painting, affixed within an ornate gilt frame and began to examine it more closely. "Cos! No question—it's the Tudor king! And I might be wrong, but I feel like he's portrayed with his second wife, Anne Boleyn. Her face has been painted over—it's a bad repair—but you can still see how she resembles the portrait we saw at that reception at Windsor Castle, do you recall? The one by Holbein? In fact, look at her necklace—you can see the 'AB' pendant attached to it. I must say...I'm flabbergasted! How did this thing end up in our attic?"

"Lord only knows. I certainly have no idea. Look closely, though. See the areas which haven't been repaired? They are really magnificent—as if they'd been done by one of the great masters. Yet the table and some of the objects on it have been overpainted by someone who had no skill at all. What a pity!"

Lucy was so caught up in studying the astonishing find, which now, presumably, belonged to her and Cosmo, that she didn't hear him.

"It looks... it's so baffling, Cos. To me, it looks as if Henry VIII is some sort of religious icon. You know how those Renaissance and medieval masters placed saints into landscape backgrounds redolent with hidden meaning? That's what this reminds me of. And then there's Queen Anne with him." She shuddered. Suddenly, the reception salon seemed colder. Unsettlingly so. "Poor woman, I guess this reflected a time when things were going well between them. Before he believed those lies about her infidelities and had her beheaded."

Cosmo pulled a monocle from his breast pocket to examine it more closely. "In the areas where there's no terrible overlay of paint, it does indeed look like someone with the most incredibly fine eye for detail, and even more skilful hand, executed it. I'm no art expert, but it appears to have been painted many years ago—but then, one never knows with forgers. They are rampant."

"Yes, but why would a forger create such an unconventional subject? It's unlike any depiction I've ever seen of a portrait of a king. Especially this king. From what I can see, his face—his expression, rather—it's so benevolent. Wise, knowing, even kind. That's not the Henry I learned about, nor recognised in any of his other portraits. He preferred strong. Arrogant. And there's another aspect to it. One can tell, even though she's been heavily overpainted, that Queen Anne played a very important role in this portrayal—look how he holds her hand in a way that seems as if they, jointly, offer some kind of blessing, or benediction. And even more heartbreaking: to me, she looks as if she's pregnant. In truth, this thing gives me chills."

"Do you think we should look back at the ownership records for the house?" Cosmo mused. "See if they offer some clue as to who owned it originally? For instance, I wonder if there might have been any members of the British royal family who lived here."

"I already have the title deeds. All of them. And I can tell you, never was there a member of our royal family who resided in this house. The records go back to the late 1600s, when the house was built by a wealthy merchant who imported and sold silks and other textiles. He and his family lived here for about fifty years, until it was purchased by a couple with the last names of Périer and Toussaint. Legend has it she was a very famous and wealthy madam, although this was her home, not her brothel. After that it was rented, but then left vacant for a long time until the mid-1800s when another businessman bought it. I think he bought and sold other properties in the Foubourg. And when he died, there were a few tenants, but no owners until we purchased it. So, who knows when the artwork was originally placed in its vault upstairs? Certainly suggests whoever placed it there didn't want it to be found, wouldn't you agree?"

Cosmo sat in a chair facing the painting and lit a cigarette. Through the smoke curling around his head, he mused, "I do. And it may well be worth a great deal of money. I think we should look into it."

Lucile felt the pressure rise in her chest. "Cosmo, my darling, it may well indeed have some value, but I'm under enormous strain right now; I can't possibly begin to investigate this peculiar piece of art which has somehow adopted us. Really, to commence a search for who may have painted it, to whom it belonged, how it got here. And what on earth would we do with it if, and when, we find those answers?" Her lips set stubbornly. "Sorry, but there's no way, Cos. I have an enormous fashion parade to stage in mere weeks—the whole justification for our purchasing this premium property. It simply has to be a success! And then there's New York. Business there is massive, and I'm doing my best to stay ahead of their wretched American tax laws—not to mention London, and the busy autumn season upcoming where I have hundreds of orders to fulfil. And... have you thought of the notoriety we'd attract? If this painting turns out to be an original, it's unprecedented. The press will be all over us! Please, Cos. Let's leave it be for now."

He stubbed out his cigarette. "Alright, love. I understand. But it's not something we can just let languish for years, you understand? At some point in the not-too-distant future we must investigate it. You know, I don't think I have ever heard of a double portrait of both Henry and Anne. I was always told that the scourge on her name, at least in Henry's mind, was so great that he had every painting of her destroyed after her death. The drawing in Windsor, which some people believe is a portrait of her, others discount as not. So, actually, nothing authenticated remains. Wouldn't it be uncanny if we were to have accidentally stumbled upon the only portrait still in existence? Of course, it seems so sad that her face has been repainted by someone who didn't know what he was doing. Makes a chap wonder what lies beneath, right?" Duff Gordon stood and stretched his long legs. "Decision made. Let's get some fabric to rewrap it in. Do you have any muslin, my pet?"

Lucile threw him a withering glance as if to say, 'Do I breathe air?' and went off to gather yards of muslin, which she used to make all her patterns. Together they wrapped the painting, but not without a last lingering gaze on the unimaginable, mystifying treasure which had firmly implanted itself into their chaotic lives.

Finally, for lack of a better solution, and until they could decide what to do with the strange portrayal of the Tudor King, Cosmo Duff Gordon replaced it within its secret attic alcove and nailed the original boards across it, sealing it off from the world once again.

Chapter Thirty-six

END OF JANUARY 2017

PARIS AND ROME

A fter having made our euphoric discovery of Toussaint's former home in the Foubourg, and finding a juicy tip about its early twentieth century owner, the famous female *couturière*, Dad and I raced against the calendar, hoping to uncover anything and everything we could about a possibility that King Henry VIII's painting was resident in the building at one time.

We made calls of inquiry, haunted libraries, read unending microfiched newspaper articles. With Madame Armel's help, we unearthed and scoured building records and title deeds. But luck stubbornly evaded us. Not a shred of evidence presented itself, nor did a single additional source refer to the painting which may have provoked a brutal murder and the demented ramblings of an imprisoned noble. As day followed unproductive day, my despondence grew.

In the meantime, I was now receiving regular emails from Professore Ruggieri urging me to respond regarding my plans to return and submit my Ph.D. proposal. I avoided his communications as long as I could, until one evening, as January drew to a close, my dad leveled his direct gaze across our bistro table, and said, "Zara. It's time."

"Time for what?"

"Time for us both to resume our previous lives, honey. You've put far too much into your studies to let them drift into oblivion now. And, as for me, it's time I went back to work. The hospital needs me, and I've made commitments for a number of consultations—work I've been putting off."

I remained silent, jaw clenched, but couldn't stem the single tear which escaped and ran down my cheek.

"Zara, it's okay! We've made so much progress against a search which we've always suspected could, in the end, prove futile. Hey, I've been engaged almost as much as you have. It's provided the most fascinating journey I've encountered in a long, long while—kind of like unravelling a medical forensic mystery. I know how fantastic it is when you make that final discovery—and you still might! This doesn't mean it's over. But you have to know when to step back and allow the universe to settle into its own cadence. Things can't always be forced into place. Sometimes, when you permit nature to flow, that's when a solution comes."

He looked at me tenderly, and I felt true understanding and empathy. "Allowing things to flow naturally hasn't really been your greatest strength, love." And at that statement—understatement, really—he chuckled a bit, and even coaxed a little smile from me. "Are you hearing what I'm telling you?"

I remained silent for a few more minutes, reluctant to let go of my gloom. Finally, though, as I saw no alternative, I heaved a sigh of acceptance. "You're right, as almost always... almost!" Despite my inclination to wallow a bit longer, I tried to laugh. "Okay. Let's order dinner, then I guess we'll pack up and head out tomorrow." At a sudden optimistic thought, I added, "Dad! Would you want to stop over in Rome with me for just a day or two? I wish you could. You'd meet Lina and Antonio. Maybe even Luca. Lina told me there's a gathering happening this weekend, I think. Maybe you'd come?"

"Sure, sweetie, I'll do that. I'd love to meet your friends. Let's finish up here and go back to the hotel to make our travel arrangements."

I tried hard to release my viselike grip on the obsession over a painting which probably didn't even exist anymore. With conviction, I firmly put it aside, and found that I felt a little bit better about returning to school, and Rome, with the support of my dad, even if he was there for a short stay.

To say Lina was overjoyed to see me—and to meet Dad—would not do her elation justice. It was simply impossible to be around her without sharing at least some of her zest for life, and laugh at her quirky but insightful view of the world.

"Tesoro! Zara! My God, I thought I'd never see you again! For a while I thought you'd met a Frenchman and decided to get married. Elope, even! Oh, *che tragedia*! How I could have borne that news I don't even know! But now here you are, finalmente, and you have brought tuo padre, your wonderful father, with you!"

Dad couldn't stop beaming when Lina was with us. And I could tell he felt relieved in the knowledge that I had such a loyal, fun-loving, and savvy friend. We all shared a happy dinner together in one of the local trattorias, and Lina chattered on about what I'd missed while I was away, "doing my mystery hunting". Although she never asked overtly what was going on, I knew she was curious, and promised her I would tell her, very soon. We made plans to see a few sights in Rome the next day, and then, reluctantly, I agreed to go to the party on campus with her—Dad joining us—the following evening.

"Oh, and Zara…" Lina began, and her sheepish expression told me something was coming that I might not be thrilled about. "I, uhhh, I sent Luca a text and sort of invited him on your behalf. I hope you don't mind, mia cara."

"Well, why should I mind, Lina? After all, I haven't seen or even heard from him in over six weeks!" I was annoyed, but then realized if she hadn't done it, I never would have. So I let it go.

"And also," Lina continued, all of this providing Dad with an unending source of amusement, "Just to let you know, Antonio will be there. And he's very much looking forward to seeing you. I'm certain he will be delighted to meet Dottore Rossi, too!"

"Great!" I pursed my lips. "Sounds like a ton of fun. I simply can't wait."

She either didn't get, or probably chose to ignore, the sarcasm. "Doesn't it? Me too! We are going to have *un'esplosione*!"

"Lina. You mean a blast? That doesn't really translate as 'an explosion', you know."

Dad doubled over, snorting with laughter.

FULL GLASS OF CHIANTI firmly in hand, I moved slowly through the crowded hall in the Museum of Anthropology at La Sapienza. With Dad close behind, we followed Lina, who said she knew where she planned to meet her new friend Giancarlo. It was just like Sapienza to hold a welcome-back party in the most unconventional of spaces: the Anthropology Museum. As we moved along the crowded halls, we passed mummies, preserved skulls, ancient skeletons, and finally ended up in a larger space. Dad loved it. It was a large gallery dedicated to the history of medicine. I loved it too because we didn't have to squeeze body to body, and at least I could comfortably raise my glass to my lips. Which I did. Quite often.

Dad became thoroughly engrossed in the exhibit, making his way around the perimeter of the gallery, while I found a comfortable corner from which to observe. A server walked by with a tray of little bruschetta toasts laden with tomato, and I grabbed two, being hungry. As I wolfed them down, I hoped that they weren't too garlicky, nor would any land on my white shirt—something Lina had insisted I wear, saying it made my dark eyes and hair look great. I was just about to hunt for more when I saw Antonio enter through the far doorway. All of a sudden, I wasn't hungry anymore, so I dumped my napkin on a nearby tray while I watched him glance around the room. I had to admit I was sort of glad to see him. Somehow, encountering him always instilled a nervous energy in me. My gaze must have prompted him to look up, because we made eye contact and a wide grin spread across his face. He made his way over, took my hand and said in his soft and melodious voice, "Zara. It's truly wonderful to see you. It's actually been a while— although to me it feels, perhaps, longer. How are you?"

"I'm well, Antonio, as I hope you are. It's been a busy holiday season. I had a long visit home."

"Yes, I'd heard as much. I trust it was enjoyable."

"It really was. Thanks for asking. In fact, my father's here with me tonight. We took a trip to Paris and he decided to stop over in Rome before flying home. Would you like to meet him? He's over there studying the early surgical instruments."

"Sì, sì, of course I would! Andiamo."

We wound our way toward the exhibit where we found him, immersed. "Dad—sorry to interrupt your study, but I'd like you to meet Antonio. Antonio Moretti, this is my father, Doctor Daniel Rossi."

"Dottore. What a true pleasure to meet you!" Antonio extended a hand, which dad clasped firmly.

"Professore, it's my pleasure as well. I have heard many wonderful things about you."

Dad, are you kidding? I thought, rolling my eyes. To escape the aftermath, I waved my glass vaguely and muttered, "Going to get a refill. May I get you gentlemen anything?"

Wending my way slowly back, fresh wine in hand, I saw Lina with the charming and incredibly handsome Giancarlo. "We were just coming to look for you, Tesoro. Did you find a spot which might be less crowded?"

"Follow me, we can go into the Medical History gallery. There's a bit more space there: probably because it's a little gruesome for many visitors... I left my dad and Antonio chatting there."

Lina shot me a wide-eyed look as she and Giancarlo trailed behind. I'd just turned the final corner into the gallery when I literally bumped into someone, who said, "Zara! Oh hi! It's so great to see you! I've been searching for you in this mob. Wow, to think I bumped right into you!"

It was Luca, sporting an ear-to-ear smile.

"Ciao Luca. It's nice to see you too. Want to join us? We're headed to one of the galleries around the corner where there's a bit more room," at which invitation he happily followed, puppy-like. I, in the meantime, had developed a pronounced knot in the pit of my stomach. This was shaping up to require more socializing than I'd anticipated.

On entering the gallery, I spotted Dad and Antonio still deeply engaged in conversation, so I steered us to the opposite corner, where Lina, Luca, Giancarlo and I clustered, chatting away amiably. My back was to the corner, so it was only moments before I noticed Antonio glancing over to see me and Luca, who paid me very close attention. My dad seemed unaware, and they continued their discussion—who knows what it entailed—but I was aware of Antonio flashing several looks my way. I could tell he wasn't thrilled that Luca monopolized my time.

Eventually, Dad and Antonio finished their exchange. I saw them shake hands and they ambled over, so I introduced Luca and Giancarlo. I felt, rather than actually saw, Antonio assess Luca, who stood close to me as if we were on a date. It made me uncomfortable, so I stepped away, but Antonio announced he was leaving. Goodbyes were said and before he turned to go, he held my gaze long enough that I became flustered. I knew my face had gone red, so I looked down to hide it. I grabbed my dad's sleeve and gave it a tug.

"Dad, I've had enough of crowds. You ready to go back to the apartment? Anyway, you have an early flight out tomorrow."

Before we left, Luca leaned in to say, "I hope I can call you, Zara. I'd like to get together. And I could really use your help on a few documents I'm struggling with. Would you do that?"

I was irritated. It struck precisely the wrong tone with me, and I wondered if he liked me for simply being me or for what I could do for him. I shrugged. "Sure, Luca. You can give me a call. But I'm going to be super busy in the coming weeks. Anyway, good to see you."

With a wink to Lina, Dad and I headed home.

Once back in the flat, we busied ourselves in packing and organizing Dad for his early flight back to the States. All went quiet for a while, but finally he came over to where I was reading on the sofa and sat next to me.

"Honey, I've had the most marvellous time with you. I'm so glad we were able to pursue this adventure together. And I don't want you to be melancholy—I think there's more you'll be able figure out on your search for the painting, but for now, concentrate on your studies. It's what you've wanted."

"It is, Dad. I know that. I'll try not to be distracted and keep my eye on what's important: pursuing my degree." I said it, but I knew I didn't feel it.

"Antonio told me he's never seen a talent like the one you possess. It's his opinion that you're going to accomplish great things by discovering ancient secrets, unlocking lost knowledge. That's really something, you know? There are very few people in the world who have such potential. And Zara—" He hesitated, searching for eye contact. "—by the way, I think you're wrong about Antonio. I believe he is a good man. An honest man. A man who will advocate for you. And... someone who, I think, is in love with you."

Dad tried to assess my reaction, but I kept my head firmly down because I didn't want him to see the spin of emotion I experienced.

Finally, I raised my eyes, blinking hard to keep the tears at bay. "I hear you. And I thank you. Thank you so much—so very much—for coming with me and just for being my rock. I love you. Have a safe trip home, and really, I can't wait to see you again." I gave him a squeeze, then Dad went to bed. I, on the other hand, pretended to read. But I was awake for some time.

Thinking.

Chapter Thirty-seven

EARLY APRIL 1912

PARIS AND THE NORTH ATLANTIC OCEAN

"Cosmo! Look—just *look* at this telegram! God, this is the last thing I need to deal with right now."

Lucy swept into the morning room of the Duff Gordon's Paris apartment on the elegant Avenue Bois de Boulogne, flourishing a paper with "Western Union" emblazoned across the top. She read aloud:

> "*Shipment of gowns being held by U.S. Customs. Cannot get a release. Property for new studio requires your signature to retain. Must come to NYC soonest. Wire your plans. Abraham Merrit.*"

She dropped into a chair opposite Cosmo, who meticulously placed his cigar in the ashtray and neatly refolded the newspaper he'd been reading. "Well," he said thoughtfully, "it sounds as if you have little choice. I thought we'd resolved the customs issues, but evidently there's still something they aren't happy with, and you can't let an expensive order of dresses lie around in a warehouse when your clients are waiting for them. Plus, you've been searching for a bigger space for months now. You've finally found something that suits, so you either forfeit that property and start over, or we travel to New York now, and lock it down. It's never quite convenient, is it, my dear? Happily, though, your fashion parade has been completed and proved a raving success so at least that's behind you."

"Yes, and I now have hundreds of orders to fill as a result. Oh, sometimes the price of victory feels much too costly." Lucy heaved a petulant sigh, and went to the sideboard, pouring herself a cup of coffee from the silver service. Stirring idly, she gazed out the window overlooking the boulevard.

"I'm tired, Cos. I wish we could go away someplace for a restful stay. But that's utterly impossible." She sipped her coffee and studied the carriages and motorcars travelling the length of the sunny, tree-lined avenue below. Finally, she grumbled, "Well, I guess you best go see what you can book for us to sail to New York. Reserve passage for you and me, and also Franks. I'll want her with us to help with all kinds of things while we're there. Oh, and can you send Merrit a wire? Maybe see what you can book first, so he knows when we'll actually arrive. Meanwhile, I'll make the necessary arrangements here to have as many orders as possible completed while we're gone. If I really think about it, I should also stop off in London on our way home to assess the status of business there... so let's return through Southampton, eh? See if you can organize that, Cosmo. Thank you, love. You are, as always, my wise counsel and rock of support. See you at supper?"

She placed her empty cup on the side table, gave Cosmo a quick kiss on the cheek, and bustled off to her atelier for a full day's work ahead.

At 6:00 pm sharp, as every evening, they met in the lounge for a sherry before dinner whereupon Cosmo reported that he'd sent a telegram to their New York business manager, Abraham Merrit, informing him they would arrive in the city in just over one week's time. He was especially excited to tell her about the travel plans he'd been able to make. They would be departing for Cherbourg, the port from which they would board their transatlantic liner, in two days. It would be a six-hour train journey to Cherbourg, so all packing and final arrangements to leave Paris would need to be completed with haste.

"Lucy, as I was making the travel bookings, a thought occurred to me: what if we were to take our strange painting to New York? The art historians and appraisers there are second to none. We could get some answers, and do it in a way that is a little more private than unleashing a hidden portrait, possibly of Henry VIII, on a gossip-hungry London. What do you say? Good idea?"

Lucy shot a look over her shoulder to him, as she went to the drinks table to pour herself a glass. With a roll of her eye, she said, "Look, Cos. I have so much damn work ahead of me I cannot possibly spare a second to think about taking that portrait to New York to deal with. But, love, if you want to do it, you should. Just make your decision, and go ahead with it. Don't add anything else to my overloaded mind to ponder, all right? Anyway, I am dreading this trip. The anxiousness I feel when I have to leave the country is oppressive."

"My darling, I will not bother you again about the portrait. I'll do my own enquiry to see if there are the right people to help with it once in New York City. So don't trouble your head with it. I'll take care of the entire process."

"Good, Cos. I'm sure you will do what's best. So I'll focus on preparing everything I need… which will help keep my mind off of the trip itself."

"JUST YOU WAIT TILL you hear how we'll be traveling to New York. In excellent style! In fact, it will be the finest available crossing, and I've booked us two magnificent staterooms. Darling, you're going to just love the experience."

Lucy wasn't convinced, since she just didn't like travel of any kind, especially when it involved water. "Aboard what, Cos? It had better be awfully good—and relaxing! I have to cram everything I need to do for the business, as well as packing for me and you, into a single day."

"We are traveling, first class of course, on the grandest ocean liner ever built. I've seen the White Star agent's photographs of her. She's magnificent, Lucy! Immense, appointed with every possible luxury and reputed to be not only the fastest liner to cross the ocean, but guaranteed absolutely unsinkable. It's her maiden voyage, and her name is the *RMS Titanic*."

As soon as Lucy heard the phrase "maiden voyage", she bit her lip nervously. "You mean the ship you've booked us on has never actually sailed across even a duck pond before?"

"True. But she's been built from a unique design which, as I said, means she can never founder, no matter what. Most ingenious, hey?"

"My dear Cosmo," she broke in impatiently, "I see you are excited about the prospect, but I'm sorry, I just don't share your enthusiasm. For a start, I'd rather not have to go at all, and certainly don't welcome, for one minute, the fact that this ship is untested. Was there no other option?"

"Not unless you want to wait at least three weeks—which you cannot afford to do. Trust me, darling, you will enjoy it and we will be in New York in a flash. Let's have dinner and begin organizing what we need. We board the train for Cherbourg first thing on Wednesday morning. That doesn't give us much time."

Lucy kept herself busy to suppress her apprehension and, as she always did so capably, went about the business of readying for the trip.

THE TRAIN TRANSATLANTIQUE FINALLY arrived after a long and tiring journey from Gare St. Lazare in Paris, pulling into the quayside terminal in Cherbourg mid-afternoon on Wednesday, April 10.

As passengers spilled onto the platform, pandemonium ensued, with porters attempting to unload piles of steamer trunks and suitcases and sort them for transfer to the ship, which, they were informed, would be late from its channel crossing. Lucy had her secretary, Laura Francatelli (whom everyone called Franks) check in with the arrival desk and find out as much as she could about when they could expect to board the tenders once *Titanic* made its appearance.

Settled for their wait in the terminal, Lucy spotted a number of people she knew, many of them clients. Immediately she identified a tall, thin, moustachioed man. Colonel John Jacob Astor IV was with his pregnant wife and followed obediently by their dog, Kitty. Lucy felt pleased to see them—Madeleine Astor was a regular client. In fact, Lucy had designed her entire trousseau when she wed Jack in the autumn of the previous year. Lucy had found that particular assignment interesting, as the marriage itself was a great scandal, Astor being 29 years older than Madeleine, and she but 18. The facts that he was divorced, had a reputation as a womanizer, and—in spite of his enormous wealth—was not widely liked, required their fitting appointments to be held in secrecy so the press would not hound the extremely shy girl as she entered or left the salon.

Late in the afternoon, the waiting passengers were asked to board the White Star tender, Nomadic. Although rumors circulated that *Titanic* had already cleared the Passe de l'Ouest and was about to anchor off the Central Fort, it wasn't until after seven in the evening that it was ready for its many Cherbourg-joining travellers to stream up the gangways and onto the titan ship, described by many as looking like a massive, five-story building, a chandelier ablaze with light, looming above them in the fading night sky as they approached. Cosmo guided Lucy to step nervously from the diminutive ferry into the entrance foyer, and at once she was overawed by the opulent interior. Still, she gripped Cosmo's arm ever tighter, fighting the anxiety she always suffered upon commencing a journey. He patted her hand reassuringly as they proceeded to the reception room, which came to be well known to all first-class passengers as the Palm Room.

It was entering the Palm when she couldn't help but concede grudgingly, "Oh my. Now this is lovely, darling."

"I told you you'd like it, Lucy. I can't wait to explore the rest."

They strolled arm in arm through the exquisite salon furnished with white wicker, potted palms, sparkling white walls and an ornately plastered ceiling, to the strains of the *Titanic*'s Palm Court Orchestra welcoming the guests' arrival. Shortly thereafter, their Irish stewardess guided Cosmo, Lucy, and Franks to their respective staterooms. They each had their own, and Lucy exclaimed as soon as the door to hers was opened, "Look! Isn't it sweet?"

Spacious, but very cozy, Cabin A20 had white wainscoting, deep azure walls, pink curtains, and a lovely white iron bed with a thick and inviting coverlet. A desk, and a good-sized table with a lamp completed the chamber, along with generous closets. Cosmo's and Franks's rooms proved similar but were decorated in shades of brown and taupe. Each cabin had its own electric heater, which they quickly switched on since the air bore a distinct chill. At the sound of a bugle, everyone dressed for dinner that first night aboard. At the bugler's second call, indicating it was time to make their way to the dining saloon, they then paraded, arm-in-arm and somewhat self-consciously, down the elegant, curving stairway into the Palm Room where cocktails were served, and thence into the restaurant, richly appointed in every detail.

At 8:10 p.m. the Royal Mail ship *Titanic*, the greatest and safest ship ever built and the pride of Britain's merchant fleet, set sail for New York, scheduled to make only a brief stop-over at Queenstown in Ireland to embark her final group of passengers.

Lucy's great adventure of sailing to the Americas in an unsinkable palace had begun.

For dinner on that first evening at sea, the Duff Gordons had been placed with John and Marian Thayer; the Philadelphians George and Eleanor Widener and their son, Harry; and an American woman traveling alone, Margaret Brown. Margaret had been one of the party who'd accompanied Jack Astor and his wife as they trekked through Egypt, now all returning to their homes in the U.S. She vigorously shook hands with everyone at the table, introducing herself. Her broad mix of Southern drawl and Midwestern twang added a distinct flair to her rather brash greeting. "Well, hello there. It's awfully nice to meet you! I don't know about y'all, but I am looking forward to this crossing. If we stay with some good weather, it should be interesting aboard this big ole tugboat, don't you reckon?"

Lucy immediately took a liking to Margaret, who right away informed them that her friends called her Maggie. When she spoke, her eye contact was direct and unwavering, something that the British typically found unnerving. Nevertheless, Mrs. Brown's handshake was firm and warm, and Lucy found her to be very amusing.

"Aren't you the famous dress designer, Lucy? If so, I'm feeling a tad uncomfortable as I doubt my attire tonight is the height of fashion. Mind you, honey, I'm not as slim and willowy as I used to be." She laughed, or rather emitted a sort of braying sound, but it was hard not to chuckle, or at least smile along with her.

"It so happens that I am, Margaret—or may I say Maggie? And I think you look perfectly lovely. You can see what I'm wearing: hardly revolutionary. But I admit, after spending all day every day making delicate, floaty gowns, I've come to prefer practical black. It's strange, isn't it, that I love making beautiful clothes for other women—this business has become my passion—but as for dressing myself, well, frankly, I find it quite a bore. I assume that's a disappointment to many who meet me. They probably judge my ensemble before my character. But in truth, I really don't care."

"I like you, Lucy gal! Let's plan to have luncheon together one afternoon, shall we?"

"Indeed, Maggie. I'd like to hear more about your life in Colorado. I can't imagine what it must be like there. Very 'wild west' I presume?"

"Not really. Although I will say that negotiating the social scene in Denver can seem a bit of a shoot-'em-up at times."

Again, followed the throaty laugh, and with that Lucy felt she'd made a new friend aboard *Titanic*.

After a superb dinner consisting of seemingly endless and exquisitely prepared courses, the couple wasted no time returning to their staterooms which were but a short walk from the first-class lounge. With assistance from her maid, Lucy changed from her evening wear into a sleeping chemise. As she snuggled deep into the warmed and comfortable bed and began to drift, she had the notion that perhaps she'd been wrong to judge the *Titanic* so quickly.

Next morning at breakfast, she couldn't help but remark, "Cosmo, can you imagine this? Strawberries! Fresh strawberries in my compote—and it's only April. And we are out on the open sea, although I never even sensed the ship moving. I must say, we British know how to do things the right way."

Cosmo, busy reading the news digest which was made available to first class passengers each morning, barely glanced up. Lucy, well used to his morning silences, enjoyed her coffee while idly studying the guests as they came and went from the breakfast room. Just then, Madeleine and Jack Astor passed near her table, so Lucy called out, "Madeleine dear!"

When the young woman approached, Lucy stood and grasped her hand. "How are you faring—or should I say 'sea-faring'? And, would you like to have tea this afternoon?"

Madeleine glanced inquiringly at her somewhat distant husband who acceded diffidently. "Actually, I'd love to, Lucy. Shall we meet at, say, four o' clock? In the Parisian Lounge?"

"Perfect: I'll look forward to seeing you then. In the meantime, have a lovely morning." And off they went, the dog, Kitty, following close behind.

After breakfast, the Duff Gordons decided to take a bracing stroll on the first-class promenade deck, and found that the day looked fair, with a mild wind, the sea smooth as glass. They had fun discovering the fascinating aspects of the ship, most of which they'd never experienced on any ocean liner before. Everywhere the décor and attention to detail was astonishing. Eventually they ended up in the panelled, relaxing Reading Room—also used for writing, and sending wires and communiqués ship-to-shore via the incredible, still seemingly magical, Marconi wireless telegraph.

At lunch, most of the talk centered on the smoothness of the passage and especially how fast the ship was going, how many nautical miles had been covered—this information being updated regularly on the information boards.

By later afternoon, Lucy and Madeleine were seated in the elegant Café Parisien, a silver teapot merrily brewing Darjeeling, and a variety of delicate cucumber, egg, and chicken sandwiches, along with scones, Devonshire clotted cream and raspberry jam all beautifully arrayed before them on fine White Star Line-crested china, every morsel just begging to be sampled. Madeleine nibbled on a sandwich while Lucy liberally spread the dark yellow cream on a piece of scone. "Oh my, I'd better beware on this crossing or I'll have to make myself an entirely new wardrobe once we dock in New York. Do you find you have much appetite, Madeleine? You may have been sick, you poor dear, but I do say you look well. When are you due?"

"The doctor said mid-August. I do dread the summer heat in New York when I will be so far along. Perhaps I will have Jack leave me at our Newport cottage until just before I'm to give birth. It's so much more refreshing there by the sea. May I ask you something, Lucy?"

"Certainly!"

Madeleine looked a little bashful and lowered her voice to just above a whisper, so Lucy had to lean in to hear her.

"How did you feel about taking this ship's maiden voyage? I've never done such a thing before. Have you?" Then she added, "Well, actually, I've not had too many transatlantic crossings anyway. I spent most of my time before marrying Jack in school at Miss Spence's. But… were you at all anxious about the prospect of sailing on an untried vessel?"

Lucy hesitated briefly before answering. She didn't want to upset Madeleine in any way, so she tried to sound reassuring. "You know, I never like traveling. I find it dreary, from the packing to the unpacking, different beds every night… just the whole unfamiliarity of it all. I guess I'm just an old fussbudget. So, no, I wasn't thrilled about this ship. But now, I must say, my mind has changed. For instance, here we are, thoroughly enjoying ourselves, over a quite civilized, if I do say so, cream tea while coasting over a sea of glass."

Madeleine relaxed into her chair, visibly relieved. "Oh, I'm glad to hear you say that, Lucy. I admit I wasn't very keen when Jack told me how we'd be returning home. But then, we came over on this one's sister ship, Olympic, and that went fine. So, all in all, I'm sure everything will go well. And may I visit your salon in New York in September? Will you be there, do you suppose?" With a giggle, she added, "I think I will be ready for a brand new wardrobe by then, don't you?"

The ladies chatted, shared tea and confidences for almost an hour, and then decided to meet in the Á La Carte Restaurant for dinner later, joined by their husbands.

BY FRIDAY EVENING, THE third night aboard, firm friendships had formed while the atmosphere at dinner had become convivial rather than stiffly polite. Over a delectable meal, the Duff Gordon's group, including the Astors, Maggie Brown, the Washington D.C. socialite, Helen Churchill Candee, and her companion and admirer, Hugh Woolner, enjoyed lively conversation accompanied by flowing champagne. Maggie entertained them with hilarious stories of life at her ranch in Colorado, and the many bison which seemingly roamed freely across her property. Helen, clearly enchanted by her traveling companion, also proved an articulate and vivid conversationalist. Lucy was fascinated to learn Helen was, like herself, a woman who'd had to provide finances for her two children after having been abandoned by her husband. As a result, she'd become a highly successful writer, and then an interior designer for wealthy Washington patrons.

Throughout, Madeleine remained quiet, particularly during the discussion Jack initiated about the stunning estate in England which his older cousin, William Astor, had purchased some ten years prior, and had spent a fortune on renovating. Once he'd heard Maggie talk about her expansive lands near Bear Creek in Colorado, Jack could barely contain himself until he was able to recapture the attention of the guests at the table.

In his clipped, affected delivery, he stated, "Well, of course, we own many, many properties in the city, as well as in upstate New York, but as a result of familial discord over them, Willy and I did not get along for some time. Not, in fact, until my dear mother passed a few years ago. Due to the friction between them, Willy felt compelled to move out of the country because, it went without saying, if you weren't accepted by the Mrs. Astor, you were erased from the social scale. Although dear old Willy had, in truth, made some terrible decisions which certainly didn't endear him to my inflexibly obdurate matriarch. But that's another story, perhaps for another evening."

At Jack's mention of yet another story, Maggie remained focused on her minted lamb chops, but Lucy caught her wry half-smile and raised eyebrow. Jack, of course, failed to register the guests' disinclination to listen to yet another long-winded tale and doggedly continued his monologue, while the other diners politely offered him as much attention as they could muster.

"...After living in London for a number of years, making various land purchases and initiating different building projects, Willy—by that time we had repaired our relationship and were in communication once again—was informed that a most historic, somewhat ramshackle, property was for sale in Kent. He decided to look into it, being the history buff he is..." Astor paused for a breath and glanced around while everyone graciously stopped eating, forks in mid-air, to nod feigned interest. Satisfied that he still held the floor, the billionaire resumed. "It seemed that the estate was established in the 13th century, and parts of the manor house were begun in 1270. Can you imagine? It had fallen into great disrepair, but the most intriguing aspect of its long history is the period of time in the early 1500s when it was owned by the Bullen family. Meaning it was the home of the young Anne Boleyn and her parents and siblings."

He waited for an appropriate reaction from his listeners. Several had no idea to whom he was referring, especially Maggie, Marian Thayer, and Hugh Woolner. However, at the mention of that name, Lucy felt a start of surprise.

"Really, Jack? How fascinating! Tell us more. How do they know it belonged to the Boleyns?"

Pleased to have some encouragement, Jack surged ahead. "Well, there are a number of land records which show the ownership of the manor house throughout the centuries. And Thomas Boleyn, Knight of the Garter, Earl of Wiltshire, was one of them. In fact, it's documented that King Henry VIII actually courted Anne there, at Hever Manor."

Now it began to dawn on other dining companions to whom Astor referred. Helen Candee jumped in. "You're saying this estate was the home of that wife of Henry VIII's? The one he had executed?"

"Precisely so," came the answer from Colonel Astor.

Upon the revelation that Henry VIII and Anne Boleyn had been together at the estate which was now owned by the Astor family, Lucy nudged Cosmo's knee under the table, and shot him an inquiring glance. Would it be worth adding the story of their incredible find to the conversation? Cosmo responded by the slightest shake of his head, so Lucy let the moment pass.

Helen continued, "Oh my, now that is incredible. Isn't it wonderful to think of buildings which have lasted so long? We, of course, have nothing nearly so old in the United States."

"Well," Jack added importantly, "that is why it was such a noble purchase of Willy's. Not only the acquisition, but the fact that he then spent millions on its restoration including its magnificent gardens. From total marshland, he recreated the most spectacular landscape I've seen anywhere in the world. And his art! I must admit," he boasted, "that it is one of the most impressive private collections in the world! His assembly of portraits of kings and queens of England is unmatched."

At this, Madeleine quietly voiced her assent. "Jack is right. If only you all could see it. To wander the manor house and those gardens is to escape the madness of the world; they are so tranquil. I love it there."

Jack was pleased because he now had the undivided attention of the entire party. "Not only did Willy restore the manor house, but he added an entire village to which people can come, stay, and enjoy the gardens and the history. You should all visit! Next time you find yourself in England, take a trip to Kent and stay awhile at Hever. I'll make sure Willy and the staff know to welcome you appropriately."

With a pensive look, Helen piped up. "So, Jack, tell us. What is the story of this Anne Boleyn who was a wife of Henry VIII? Unfortunately, we Americans know only the bare rudiments of that part of English history. But it's very intriguing—at least, to me."

At last Jack allowed others a chance to add to the conversation. "Lucy, Cosmo—you're both Brits. Perhaps you'd like to provide the rest of us with some historical perspective."

Lucy allowed Cosmo to respond, wondering if he'd add anything about the painting. But briefly, he recounted the story of Henry Tudor: that he'd been married to Katherine of Aragon, the Spanish princess, for many years, but as she aged yet still failed to provide him with a male heir to the throne, his attention had turned to the young, witty, and more attractive Anne Boleyn, a woman who'd been educated in France. Cosmo described how Henry, desperate for a divorce from Katherine, had petitioned the pope to grant him one, and upon being refused, went ahead and married Anne anyway, thus marking the rift with the Catholic Church which ended up establishing what is now known as the Anglican Church.

"So, what went wrong between Anne and Henry, then? Wasn't he happy with her after all that effort?" Helen asked, almost afraid of the answer, having been through a terrible divorce with her own husband some years before.

Cosmo thoughtfully dabbed his lips, the starched white napkin neatly embroidered with the logo of the White Star line. "No… no, Henry ended up being dissatisfied with Anne, despite her having once been the love of his life. She, too, was unable to give him male issue, although their daughter, Elizabeth, ended up being our illustrious Queen—Gloriana. But the last straw came when Henry was told that Anne had betrayed him with his best friends. In a rage, he imprisoned her in the Tower of London before ordering her beheading. Most prisoners at that time died by the swing of an axe. For Anne, though, he commissioned a master swordsman. A French executioner, intending it to be a more merciful end."

The ladies at the table shivered. Helen said, "That poor girl! What a horrible, horrible demise. To know you were about to lose your head—to await that final blow. And to know you were wrongfully accused, but all the while had loved your husband, which I assume she did. My heaven, I can hardly imagine a worse death."

And to that dire pronouncement, they all murmured their assent. Shortly thereafter the sociable party left the table to pursue other pleasures: men to the smoking room, women to the first-class lounge for coffee and after-dinner drinks.

LIFE ON BOARD *TITANIC* continued in a most gratifying way for most of her upper-class guests. Games of cards, walks on the promenade, reading in deck chairs, exquisite meals all became part of the day-to-day routine for the privileged passengers. The Saturday evening dining parade was a spectacle of rich and generally beautiful women in gorgeous attire. All enjoyed a marvellous time. But the most elegant evening, the Grand Gala, was to be held on Sunday. It was known that the ladies would put on a display of their finest gowns and most breath-taking jewellery for the formal dinner that evening, which would be followed by dancing to the Palm Court Orchestra. The first-class maids were put to the test as they scurried to assist women of wealth and status don gowns and jewels which were intended, hopefully, to impress above all others. Many women who made a dramatic entrance were clad in the most recent, the most fashion-forward attire designed by Lucile Limited, much to Lucy's gratification. Couples of great prestige hosted private dinner parties in the Ritz Restaurant. Seated at flower-laden round tables were the who's who of high society, including the Thayers, the Wideners, the Carters from Philadelphia, the Astors, along with J. Bruce Ismay, the chairman of the White Star Line, and even Captain Edward Smith himself. The discreet popping of champagne corks provided a backdrop to fine wines being liberally poured and all agreed that the experience was unmatched—as fine as dining in Manhattan, London, Paris, or Rome. On the upper decks, it was an evening to remember, with the soft clinking of crystal, click of fine silverware against bone china, and the light shimmering on women's jewels providing a magical aura.

Many women now included fur wraps to crown their ensembles, as over the past several days, the temperatures had steadily dropped. On Sunday evening it felt particularly frigid, and any brave soul who ventured onto the outer decks for a constitutional hurriedly returned to the warmth and light of the accommodation to ward off the chill. Dinner conversations included rumors that there were icebergs in the seas ahead, yet passengers also became aware that the engines were now producing a higher pitched sound. The ship was being coaxed to maximum speed in the hope that the crossing record might be broken. Everyone wondered whether they might arrive in New York earlier than had been scheduled. Some speculated that it could be inconvenient, as arrangements for their pick-up would have to be altered, but nothing dimmed the brilliance of the spectacular event.

Lucy and Cosmo enjoyed dining with several fellow travellers they had befriended en voyage, and everyone commented on the number of women wearing designs by Lucile. Shades of rose and lilac, pale gold and sky blue wafted by with the soft rustle of expensive silks. The couturière herself wore a fitted dress of black velvet, her pearl earrings, and a fox fur stole draped across her shoulders. After dinner, many retired to the lounge to enjoy coffee where Lucy and Cosmo sat with Edgar and Leila Meyer—Leila being the daughter of the owner of Saks Fifth Avenue.

Just before ten o'clock, the Duff Gordons, along with several other guests, decided to return to their staterooms for the night, since it was far too cold for a stroll. In the passageway Cosmo said goodnight and went into his cabin. Lucy and Franks huddled awhile in Lucy's, with the heater on full blast. Finally, Franks went to her cabin, and each climbed into her own bed, eventually feeling warm. They dozed.

Only an hour later, Lucy was startled by a strange, seemingly distant rumbling noise followed by an even odder silence. Fully awake, the ominous quiet, absent the low hum of the engines, told her the ship had stopped. Wondering what had happened, she crept across the passage and woke Cosmo. Over his snoring, she had to whisper loudly, "Cosmo. Cosmo! Do you hear that? No engine sound? Why did the ship stop?"

He turned over in bed, mumbling, "What? The ship hasn't stopped. You are dreaming, Lucy. Go back to bed and let me sleep."

She lay awake for some time, hearing noises on deck, but no sounds of alarm. However, she couldn't shake her anxiety, so got up and threw on a robe to cross to Cosmo's suite. "Cos, please. Please will you go up top and see what's going on? The ship isn't moving and I'm becoming rather concerned!"

Reluctantly, he clambered out of bed, pulled on his clothing, and went out. As she waited, her apprehension grew, until at last, Cosmo returned, his concern now evident. "Lucy, get dressed. Wear the warmest clothes you have and wrap yourself in a thick coat. There's word the ship has hit an iceberg. I'm not sure how extensive the damage is, but we must be prepared."

Awkwardly, her heart pumping, she fumbled into clothes pulled from her dresser. Franks arrived white-faced to announce she'd been on deck, the lifeboats were being readied, and that she had water in her cabin. At that moment, a steward knocked on the door, telling them that Captain's orders were to dress warmly, put on their life-belts, and to get out onto the open deck.

By the time Lucy, Cosmo, and Franks arrived on the upper deck they were met, to their horror, by a scene of utter chaos. People running madly everywhere, women and children crying in panic. On the port side, people were being herded into lifeboats, and Lucy heard cries of "Women and children first! Stand back!" Unbelievably, shots were fired.

Cosmo, feeling his wife's legs beginning to buckle, supported her and shouted, "Let's go to the starboard side to see if it's any better." He steered her across the deck while she clung to him with all her strength.

"Cosmo! How could this have happened? And my God, what are those women doing, leaving their husbands? I will never leave you, no matter what. Do you hear me?" Cosmo saw the terror and determination on her face, and knew she meant what she said, so they waited starboard while lifeboats were being filled one by one.

Suddenly, it seemed that they were almost alone on that portion of the deck: just Lucy, Cosmo, and Franks. There remained only one small emergency boat being prepared to launch, and Cosmo asked a passing officer if his little group could get in. The officer agreed, and they scrambled into the boat, along with a few of the ship's stokers, one seaman, and two American men who followed.

As they were being lowered into the inky blackness, upon reaching the glassy, icy water with a splash, they heard the officer call out from above: "Pull away from the ship as fast as possible and row as far off as you can. You hear me?" At that moment, screaming rockets pierced the night sky, obliterating for just a moment the carpet of stars which illuminated the heavens. The men began heaving on the oars; the small boat swayed and corkscrewed; and the remaining lights of the doomed ship provided no solace at all in that most horrifying of moments.

Lucy, almost immediately, was hit with a wave of nausea. The rocking of the small vessel didn't cease, and after she had vomited over and over the gunwale, she lay down on the ice in the bottom of the boat and curled into a fetal position with a scarf wrapped around her head. Only when she heard the anguished cry, "My God, she's going!" did she raise up to watch as the remaining rows of lights, which had once cast their glow on scenes of cheer and revelry, winked out one by one. The final porthole light was doused by the unforgiving sea, and a booming explosion followed. The 12 passengers aboard emergency lifeboat number 1 couldn't stop from staring at the ghastly image. Another enormous detonation threw the Titanic's stern heavenward; its towering bulk raised up and fully out of the water, a sight never intended to have been witnessed. And then, with a massive rush, the unsinkable liner was sucked into the depths, leaving the surface of the deadly sea eerily smooth.

There was silence aboard their little vessel. Lucy's retching had stopped. The stars glittered brightly, reflected by the ghostly berg lying still and serene just a short distance away. One might have thought the world was at peace.

But the night wasn't without sound.

From across the God-forsaken expanse came the pitiful wails and shrieks of the dying: the poor souls who were freezing to death in the ice-strewn waters of the North Atlantic during the earliest hours of Monday, April 15, 1912.

EVENTUALLY, LUCY AND COSMO returned to their London home after having been rescued along with other survivors by the brave crew of the *Carpathia*. It immediately became clear that life would never be the same for them. Although grateful for having been spared, the sorrow the Duff Gordons experienced left a permanent imprint upon their spirits. While, to add to their misery, an intended act of kindness by Cosmo while aboard lifeboat number 1—to provide each of the now-unemployed stokers with a small contribution of cash—had been misconstrued as a bribe to keep them from rowing back and recovering other passengers desperately treading for their lives. Indeed, the boat could have held 40 persons, and it carried only 12; but Cosmo claimed his intention was never, ever, to save himself, his wife and her secretary by sacrificing the lives of others.

Both Lucy and Cosmo were called to appear at a court of inquiry in Buckingham Gate. On Monday, 20th of May, 1912, Sir Cosmo Duff Gordon was questioned for over two hours before a packed hall, and while they had many supporters in the audience there to hear not only Cosmo's testimony but that of the other *Titanic* survivors, it did little to relieve him of his misery. Ultimately, the Duff Gordons were vindicated, but Cosmo never fully recovered his former joie de vivre after that experience. For him, a pillar of British society, there was simply nothing worse than to be accused of cowardice. Lucy's heart broke for him, but there was little she could do.

Equally sad was news of the many friends they had lost on that terrible night: Colonel John Jacob Astor IV, Major Archie Butt, Edgar Meyer, John Thayer, father and son George and Harry Widener... the list went on and on.

But Lucy ached, above all, for Madeleine Astor and wondered how the traumatized widow had fared after returning home to New York, realizing that her baby was to be born but would never know its father. In August, Lucy learned that Madeleine had given birth to a boy, whom she named John Jacob Astor VI, but whom the family called 'Jakey'. Lucy sent a telegram of congratulation to Madeleine, who responded with her thanks.

IN THE SPRING OF 1913, the Duff Gordons went back to Paris to resume their business dealings there, since the demand for Lucy's creations had barely diminished despite the adverse publicity received following the tragedy. It was only then that they recalled, with some astonishment, the intriguing portrait they'd uncovered the previous spring. At the very last moment before they'd traveled to board *Titanic*, Cosmo had decided against packing the deteriorating canvas and sailing with it to New York. He thought he'd deal with it once they were back in Paris, figure out the best approach. So he'd never taken it from the special cabinet which had been built by someone as its hiding place. And now that they were back home, his life—their lives—had significantly changed. He found that he had no appetite for assessing the validity or value of the portrait. Lucy, also, was less inclined than ever to deal with it, especially since she and Cosmo desired no further notoriety.

Until one day, that was, when, as Lucy sketched a series of new gowns, her mind had idly wandered to their discovery and a thought occurred to her—what if she were to gift it to Madeleine? Lucy recalled how much her friend loved William Astor's English estate which had, after all, been the former home of Anne Boleyn, the painting's presumed subject.

That very afternoon, acting on impulse, she sent a wire to the Astor residence in New York and was informed that, indeed, Madeleine had taken Jakey, his nannies and nurses, and had travelled to Hever to retreat into relative anonymity while she mourned. A knowing smile spread across Lucy's face on hearing the news. She'd always suspected that Madeleine's beloved gardens were exactly what the young widow needed to help restore her wellbeing.

So, Cosmo carefully prepared the painting for shipment while Lucy wrote Madeleine a long letter, describing their find, and telling her that perhaps it belonged in a place which might seem like a proper home for it. She also invited her to visit any Lucile Ltd. salon once she felt up to facing the world again, for a fresh new wardrobe.

Adding their love and best wishes, the Duff Gordons despatched the painting to Hever Castle, Edenbridge, Kent.

As they watched the peculiar painting, well wrapped and packaged for its journey, pull away in the Royal Mail van, Lucy stood at the door with Cosmo. She rested her hand comfortingly on his arm. She wanted to do all she could for him in hopes he might recover from the trauma and heartbreak they had endured. He'd been there

Sandra Vasoli

for her when she'd needed him, and she would now do her best to be his pillar of strength.

The van turned the corner and disappeared. Wasn't it curious, though? The second it was out of sight, they clung to each other, and both breathed great sighs of relief.

Chapter Thirty-eight

FEBRUARY 2017

ROME

O nce Dad had returned home to the USA and our exhilarating trip to Paris was over, I intended to fulfill my promise and attempted to concentrate on my studies. I'd made an appointment with Professore Ruggieri, first diffidently apologizing for having been delayed on my return to classes and my neglect at not having submitted a proposal for dissertation study on time. He was kind but direct in admonishing me, and gave me a two-week extension in which to develop my presentation and offer it to him for review. With relief, I thanked him and left his office with the committed intent of rallying and suggesting an exceptional concept. So, I parked myself in the library by day and aimlessly searched. When back in my apartment at night, I pecked at my computer and thought. But I just couldn't come up with any ideas which gave me that thrill of anticipation or discovery. After all, what could possibly compare to the enigma of the painting that absorbed all my attention and thought? It just wasn't feasible, though, to disclose my efforts in order to provide the centerpiece for doctoral study. Finally, in desperation, I pulled a concept together which involved the study of medieval medical literature. It would please Dad, and hopefully satisfy the department heads while being something I could accomplish with just a modicum of effort.

But despite some initial optimism, as I worked on the paper, I struggled to make progress. When my thoughts wandered, which they did frequently, I yanked them back to the subject at hand, but try as I might, I couldn't stop dwelling on the impasse my dad and I had met in our search for the portrait. It bubbled away in my brain incessantly. How could we have come so very far and no further? I couldn't escape the crazy notion that the painting was calling to me... that it wanted me to keep digging, keep searching, and if I did, somehow it would triumphantly emerge from its elusive shadowy past.

One night, tossing and turning as I did so often, I fell into that weird half-sleep. That time of night when everything in life seems more dramatic, when the mind won't stop churning, even though it knows we should be sleeping. My thoughts drifted and bobbed, like I was on a ship. As I wandered, in my imagining, throughout the ship's interior, I thought it was unusual. Some of the rooms were entirely wooden—rustic, like a whaling ship perhaps—other rooms that I entered were beautiful, luxurious. At last, I drifted down a long corridor. At the end, in dim lighting, hung a framed painting on the wall. With interest, I approached the painting. But when I finally stood in front of it, it was maddeningly out of focus. I blinked and squinted, to no avail. I couldn't make out the subject. The effort woke me. And I found that I was left tired, and with a deep sense of gloom.

THE ALLOTTED TWO WEEKS ticked by, day after useless day. I knew my paper wasn't up to the standards which were expected of me. Lina phoned regularly; of course, she was doing fabulously well in her studies. And in the meantime, I grew more and more withdrawn, spending a few hours every day pecking away on my proposal, but for the rest of the time, I just languished in my flat. I had no interest in going out, even to classes on campus, much less to see people I knew.

Late one afternoon, I agreed when Lina asked if she could come by for a visit. She arrived with ingredients to make panini sandwiches. As we sat at my kitchen table, she said, "Zara. I worry about you. Why are you so distraught? Tesoro, you're not yourself at all. Although I know—oh, how I know!—you can get in those moods. But this time seems different."

I shrugged. "I feel lost, Lina. Here I am, in Rome, studying what I thought interested me most, and lately I'm not sure I even care anymore. In fact, I wonder if I should continue with my degree. I think to myself, 'what the hell am I going to do once I have my doctorate? Teach?' Ha! That doesn't sound much like me, now does it? I think maybe my mother was right. Maybe I'm headed down a path which will never make me happy. I do know this—I'm not happy right now. The problem is, I don't have any idea what real happiness is. Do you? You seem to. You are always sure of yourself. Just like Mom. She always was so confident. So... comfortable. What am I doing wrong? Like, what actually allows someone—a woman, I mean—to feel content?"

Lina exhaled a long, slow whistle. "Oh boy, cara mia. You are really in what they say is a pickled dilemma—aren't you? Ascolta, Zara—listen to me. I can't pretend I know all the secrets of life, but I do know this: you have everything you need to be happy—to be truly, magically happy. It's not something that happens to you, you know. You gotta make it happen. Happiness and contentment are about being glad of what you have—right in front of you. And as far as I can tell, you have it all! You're so smart, you're clever and funny, you have amazing talent, and you're so, so pretty... except maybe..." She hesitated.

"What? Except what?"

"Except the willingness to allow people to get close to you. Whether it's friends or maybe a boyfriend, those relationships help us to be happy, don't you see that? Maybe this is what your mom was trying to tell you all along."

I got up from the table and went to the sofa. I sat with my legs pulled up, arms circling my knees. I remained still for a while, as Lina gave me time to think. It hurt, what she'd said, this friend who was maybe the closest I'd ever had. After all, it was so easy for Lina to embrace people—to be warm and friendly, laugh quickly, develop close relationships… have fun. For me—it was always a struggle. And why did it hurt? Because she was right. I knew she was. I knew that the things we are most afraid of are the ones we will do anything to avoid facing. And I'd done anything and everything to avoid dealing with my anxiety around people. I looked up from the little cocoon I'd wrapped myself in, there on the sofa, and our eyes met. "You're right, Lina. I know this. I just have to figure out how to change."

"You will, Zara. I know you will."

Her belief in me touched deeply. Normally, I would change the subject, or make a wisecrack, or even just ignore what had been said. Instead, though, I went over to hug her, and said simply, "Thank you."

Lina got up to go. I stopped her. "Do you have just a few more minutes? Because I guess there's another thing bothering me. Actually, it's keeping me up at night."

"So… what is that?"

"Can you promise to keep it between us?"

"You can trust me, Zara. You should know that by now." She dropped her coat and bag, went to the counter to pour herself a mug of coffee, then sat at the table with me.

"I do trust you. Of course I do. Okay. Well, remember when I told you about the discovery I made in the Vatican Library, way back in the autumn?" She nodded her recall, and I proceeded to tell her about the note I'd found—it seemed so long ago—and how I'd searched and hunted for the painting described by the little document, an art-work lost to history which had been considered a dire harbinger of threat to the 16th century pope. I talked about the strange ways in which its existence had been revealed to me, including my visit to the Magistral Library where Luca helped me find the cryptic letters tracing it to Paris. Then I told her that I believed it called to me in some indescribable way, even though I'd come up against what seemed like an insurmountable impediment.

"Whoa, that is crazy! I've never heard of a search like this, Zar. Well… what are you going to do about it? What if your search, as studious as it's been, is at an end? What will you do? You can't just stop your life, you know? Life has to go on."

I released a bleak sigh and pushed aside my untouched sandwich. "Does it? I'm finding it very hard. Between my failure to find a way forward with this search, and my wondering if I've chosen an entirely wrong direction in life, I do feel hopeless. Maybe I should drop out of school and devote all my time to finding the painting. I feel like it's got some sort of a grip on me… and I've got to say, that grip isn't a pleasant one."

My ever-bubbly friend scooted over and draped her arm over my shoulders. She made me look at her directly, and her tone was tough. "Don't even think about doing that, Tesoro. Hopeless is a terrible word; you worry me! Hopeless means things can never turn around. It means you are desperate, and that your goals are pointless. That's not true! Tell me you can see how wrong that is!" Her dark brows knitted together, beautiful face a mask of concern, she said, "You must stay here! Stay in Rome, with your studies. It's a hump you have to overcome. You are strong. I know you can do it. I can help! I will help you in whatever way I can. Promise me you won't quit. Promesso!"

"Ok, Lina. I'll think it over. I won't quit yet. But if I can't get some relief from these bleak thoughts, I truly don't know where I'll be six months from now."

OVER THE FOLLOWING DAYS I put forth my best effort to pull together a paper which was worthy of submission to the department. Several times each day my phone buzzed, and each time, it was a text from Luca. He wanted to meet me for pizza. He wanted to chat with me about his thesis. He missed me. Could I help him with a document he'd had trouble with? Why hadn't I come to the Magistral Library to see him? And with every message I grew more and more irked by his behavior. No doubt it was exacerbated by my own dilemma, but that was just the point. He took no time to ask how I was, had no idea I was struggling. And it seemed plain to me, he didn't care. I might have been more disappointed had I not been in my own quandary, but not only did I feel apathetic about pursuing the friendship with him, I actually told myself I was relieved to discover that he was far too immature before we'd become further involved. Eventually I texted him in return saying I was too busy to meet with him, so please stop messaging, and good luck with his degree. I guess he got the point because that was the last I heard from him.

In the final push to complete my proposal, I didn't leave my apartment at all, for several days. And that was fine, because there was no one I wanted to see. I rummaged in my little pantry for food, ate what I could assemble, worked, and slept. I knew I looked a fright, but then who cared? I'd no intention of being seen by anybody anyway.

I was laboring over the final edit—none too pleased with how it was progressing—when my phone rang and startled me late one afternoon. Mindlessly, I grabbed it and answered the call. It was Antonio.

"Zara? Zara, where have you been? I haven't seen you around campus at all, and now I understand you are having a tough time. I mean, with your paper." I realized he must have spoken with Lina, and before I could object, he forged ahead. "I'm coming over to see you. I'll be there in 45 minutes. And I won't take no for an answer. A presto. Ciao." And he hung up.

I sat there for a moment, thoroughly indignant. I picked my phone back up and started to dial his number to tell him flat out to stay away. But then… I felt a nudge of anticipation. I raked my fingers through my dirty hair and suddenly thought, Shit! I look like a troll! And I might even smell bad! So I leaped to my feet, ran for the bathroom and took the hottest shower I could stand. I didn't have time to do much else, but at least I was clean as I swept through my apartment clearing away the detritus of the previous days, shoving things into closets where necessary. By the time I heard the sound of his Vespa pulling up outside, it looked somewhat passable. At least I hoped so.

My heart beating faster than it should, I opened the door and there stood Antonio, two bottles of wine in one hand, and in the other, a sack filled to the brim, crusty loaf of bread peeking out the top. For just a moment, I froze, taken aback by how glad I was to see him.

"May I come in? These bottles are rather heavy…" He grinned eventually.

I took the package from him and held the door so he could step inside. "Oh! Of course. Let me help."

We unpacked the satchel. In addition to the bread, he'd brought a wedge of sharp provolone, sliced prosciutto, two different kinds of salami, and a tomato and olive tapenade. I hadn't realized how hungry I was until I unwrapped the packages. We assembled everything on platters, poured two glasses of Montepulciano rosso, and pulled up chairs to eat. Antonio didn't jump right into a conversation about my absence from school, and I was appreciative. Instead, we chatted about my dad's medical career, my hometown, the chilly weather, how delicious the prosciutto was from the specialty shop he loved… and I began to relax, even felt a little happy for the first time in weeks.

We finished the first bottle of wine, and then moved to the sofa, where he opened the second, an Amarone he'd been saving. "…So, I said to myself: Antonio, what are you waiting for? Let's drink it, enjoy it. And I thought you could probably benefit from it, Zara. Right?"

I curled up, tucked my legs under me, saying, "How could any girl ever refuse a good Amarone? Thank you for sharing it with me."

"My pleasure. So now, what have you been up to? Tell me, what's going on? Are you progressing with your proposal?"

Antonio's voice was soft and kind. When I looked at him, sitting next to me on the sofa, despite my hesitancy, I liked what I saw. He was handsome, no doubt. The wine encouraged a loosening of the tightness I'd had in my head for weeks, so I told him how I was unengaged by the process of coming up with a suitable dissertation theme. He waited, knowing that if he gave me enough space, I would continue. I added, "And… there's something else I've been grappling with. Actually, for quite some time now."

"Well, I hope it's not causing you distress, Zara. I'd never want that for you. You know—or I hope you know—I would always be happy to help you. In fact, there is nothing which would give me more happiness than to support you."

His expression was so very earnest, soft, and deep—and for the first time, I saw something else. When our eyes met, I felt… understood, somehow. Was that right? Did he in fact really see me? Maybe I'd been mistaken about him and his motives all along. I wondered how I'd missed this quality. Then I remembered what Dad had told me, and I felt a deep blush creep up my neck.

Antonio's gaze never wavered, and his face drew close. The moment was overwhelming, and I felt the grip on my emotions give way. A single tear escaped. Roughly, I brushed it away. But I'd lost the internal battle, and before I could regain control, I began to cry.

Gently, Antonio took the wine glass from my hand while my sobs grew until they were heartbreaking. Quickly, he moved close to me and took me in his arms, and I'd never felt such comfort and strength. It only provoked more tears; my shoulders shook, releasing all the stress and anxiety I'd harbored for months. Slowly my pain dissipated, but he never let go. I knew I embraced him too, and eventually he tilted my head back so he could look into my eyes and kissed me.

I'd not imagined a kiss like that and was surprised at how much I wanted it to happen and the pleasure it held for me. It just felt right, and for a time we sat there, entwined, kissing with a tenderness that soon turned to passion.

Slowly he stood, turned out the lights in the kitchen, and led me into the bedroom.

AS EARLY MORNING LIGHT seeped through my bedroom window I awoke with a start, realizing that Antonio lay next to me. My heart beating with the unfamiliarity of it all, I lay there quietly for a while, turning over in my mind what had happened. Slowly, I realized that my life had profoundly changed. For maybe the very first time since I'd been a child, I felt unguarded. Vulnerable. Hesitating, my fingers found Antonio's and my hand closed around his. He stirred, and the old, familiar tendrils of fear and anxiety probed, trying to gain hold. What if he just got up, grabbed his clothes, and left? I felt I would surely die, right then and there. He reached across to stroke my hair tenderly. No words were exchanged, but when we finally looked into each other's eyes, I knew. My relief was profound. It was no one-night stand. It was real! For the first time in my life, I experienced true romantic love; and it filled me with a deep sense of wonder and exhilaration.

Once we were up, he ran out to go to the corner pasticceria to get us breakfast since I had not a scrap left in the flat and returned with a bag full of sfogliatelle—my favorite, flaky, heavenly pastries. As we sat at the table—where just the night before we'd merely been friends—I welcomed the day with a fresh, new and marvelous perspective. Over coffee, he held my hand, never took his eyes from my face, made sure my cup was refilled. And we chatted—easily, effort-lessly. It wasn't long before I said, "Remember last night when I told you I'd been struggling with something? I think that was when I had my meltdown?"

"I do, and I'm ever so grateful for that, as you call it, 'meltdown', Zara."

There it was—that crinkle at the outer corner of his eyes when he smiled—somehow now that expression seemed oddly familiar, and beloved! How could it be that things had changed so drastically for me, for the better, in just one night??

"Well, I'd like to tell you all about what prompted it. That is, if you have time. Can I share it with you?"

"My love, you can share anything with me. I want you to know that."

Only for a second did I recall the times when I'd felt suspi-cious of his motives. In a flash of insight, I guessed that perhaps my attraction for him was what caused my wariness… the conversation in which I told my dad I was afraid Antonio would steal my work, the moment when he'd moved my notebook in his office and I'd felt sure he'd snooped, his insistence we work together… I'd bundled all those things and layered them on top of my conviction that everyone talked about me behind my back. The negative stories I'd always told myself became real. In that beautiful moment of realization, though, I understood that at the slightest hint of suspicion, I'd slammed the door on anyone and everything that had the power to hurt me. Turned away and never looked back. My God, how wrong I'd been!

Cynicism held at bay, I decided to trust him. So, event by event, discovery by discovery, I told Antonio about what I'd found that day in the Vatican Archives, the note I'd stumbled upon in the last min-utes, and how the strange tale had unfurled since then.

"You know…" he said shaking his head, "…I was certain you'd come across something unusual that day. You were flushed and there was something about your demeanor which told me you had a secret. But I felt guilty questioning you. After all, anything you'd uncovered was the product of your efforts, not mine. I didn't want to demand anything of you, so I let it go. Although I will admit, I never stopped wondering."

"I'm sorry, Antonio. I was unreasonable. But I was so overwhelmed, truly I didn't know quite how to handle it. You should have seen it. Such a tiny scrap, but the power in its message! It leaped off the little page."

"And so, this reputedly 'sacrilegious' portrait of Henry VIII and his queen—you're saying you've tracked its history through the years until you've reached a dead end in Paris in the 18th century? And its power caused the Grand Master of the Knights of St. John to quake with fear? People have died because of it? It's an incredible account, Zara. What's really perplexing is that there's no official record in the annals of art history. Meaning that, as far as you know, historians are unaware that it ever existed?"

"That's right. At least that's what my research—and let me tell you, it's been endless—has determined." I paused while Antonio processed what I'd told him. "So, do you see, now, why I can't let it go? I just can't."

"I get it, amore mio. It's a trail that should be followed, at least until it exhausts itself. You do realize, though, assuming it did exist at one time, it may no longer. There is a serious possibility that it's lost somewhere never to be found, or even that, at some point in its violent history it was destroyed."

"My logical mind tells me that might well be the case, Antonio. But my heart, and my soul, pleads with me to keep looking. I have to!" I took his hand in both of mine and pulled him close. "I never thought I would ask this, but—will you help me? Will you work with me to find it?"

He hesitated for only a fraction of a second. "I will. If you wish it, I will do it." He added, with a rueful grin, "Do you recall, once, I told you that if we worked together on a project, it could be big—really big? Well, I have to say I never envisioned anything like this. But if that damned portrait is out there, let's combine forces and uncover it. And let the whole world gawk!"

I hugged him then, and kissed him with warmth I never knew I possessed. Suddenly, I realized how pleased my dad would be. And my mom; but I wasn't ready to think about her just yet.

As Antonio gathered the few items he'd brought with him, he said, "I have to get back to teach a class. But maybe later we can make plans? How about if we do some research here, and then go portrait hunting over spring break? It's only a few weeks away. In the meantime, finish your proposal. It's a good one and Ruggieri will like it. You must finish your doctorate. Just think, it will give you that much more credibility when we make our big discovery and reveal it to the world. 'Explosive discovery rocks the art world, made by Dr. Zara Rossi and Dr. Antonio Moretti.' Sounds good, doesn't it?"

And with a lingering kiss and a promise to spend time together very soon, he ran down the stairs of my apartment building. Standing in my doorway, I watched until he stepped out into the street and pulled away, his Vespa trailing a little plume of exhaust in the early morning air.

Chapter Thirty-nine

OCTOBER 1935

THE MANOR OF HEVER
EDENBRIDGE, KENT, ENGLAND

On a mild autumn afternoon, golden sunshine beckoned guests to wander in the legendary gardens of Hever. Colonel John Jacob Astor V, Hever's owner, had been called out to business in London, but had nevertheless insisted the cocktail party proceed without him. It wasn't unusual: he positively encouraged the magnificent estate to be utilized for parties and events—always, of course, with people he knew—whether he and the family were present or not. After having inherited the Manor in 1919 from his father, William Waldorf Astor, he seized every opportunity to showcase the spectacular renovations his father had spent so much time and money completing, invariably to people of great importance and rank. And inevitably, those so privileged to behold the property were duly impressed.

On that particular day, the invited guests who gathered for cocktails and hors d'oeuvres included a number of the more conservative British aristocracy. It was intended they meet with several prominent, visiting German officials. Viscount Rothermere was the host, the owner of Associated Newspapers and a great admirer of the principles of Nazi Germany and its führer, Adolf Hitler.

Rothermere was especially keen to encourage as many influential British nobles as possible to meet Joachim von Ribbentrop, whom, it was rumored, would soon be appointed as German Ambassador to the Court of St. James.

Ribbentrop was accompanied by Major General Otto Abetz, an ambassador to France. Trailing behind them, Colonel Max Hansen, a rising star in the SS Verfügungstruppe—Germany's Dispositional Troops—and Ernst Himmler, Director of the Reich Broadcasting Organization, but more importantly, brother of Heinrich Himmler, Hitler's indispensable right hand. Each had been specifically selected by Ribbentrop so as not to overshadow or outrank him, but to impress the British nevertheless. Hardly surprising, Ribbentrop was widely known as an imperious and arrogant man, whose modus operandi was to bootlick Hitler whenever and however he could.

The stunning expanse of green lawn centering the Italian garden was the perfect location for the comfortable chairs and tables spread with starched white linen bearing an array of fruits, cheeses, delicate finger sandwiches, and the most gorgeous cakes. White-gloved butlers milled about offering champagne, wine, or more robust spirits.

In the middle of the cluster of very important people, Ribbentrop and Rothermere held court.

Ribbentrop swirled the pale vintage in his glass and peered at it down the length of his pinched nose. "What is this swill? Astor serves wine such as this to his guests?" He spat a mouthful on the lawn and motioned for the server to come to him. "Junge! Boy, bring me some of what you have in a Spätburgunder, or—" And he smirked. "—since Lord Astor likely has none of that, at the very least a decent Riesling. And I shall taste it before you fill my glass—*verstehst*?"

"Yes sir, I understand perfectly. I will look for whatever the house cellar holds which might please you." Whereupon the butler withdrew to see what he could produce.

Huffing impatiently, Ribbentrop tapped the toe of his highly polished boot and scanned the area, bored and indifferent to the conversation underway between Rothermere and several of the wealthy local landowners.

Baroness Braye and her daughter Eleanor wandered back from visiting the serverie, each bearing a selection of delicate petits-fours on delicate porcelain plates. They sat near Lady Dering, who was accompanied by her niece, since the young lady was to make her debut in a month; her aunt felt this might provide an opportunity for the girl to meet an eligible bachelor. The ladies sat together, chatting quietly. Guests were still arriving, fashionably late. An elegant couple, hands linked, walked slowly along the gravel path leading to the lawn setting, admiring the late blooming dahlias and the strategically placed statuary. When the young woman raised her head, the Baroness and Lady Dering took note and exchanged knowing looks. Her beauty was exceptional, and instantly recognizable. Diana Guinness, born Diana Mitford, strolled with her paramour, Sir Oswald Mosely, the leader of the British Union of Fascists. Not only was this relationship a scandal of London, but it was said that Diana had met with and been entertained by Hitler while in Germany with her sister, Unity Mitford.

Lady Dering leaned in toward the Baroness. "Well, well," she murmured, "suddenly this has become a much more intriguing party, don't you think? Heaven knows, it needed a shot in the arm."

She glanced archly at Ribbentrop, who was spouting instructions based upon his professed knowledge of wine and art.

"I couldn't agree more. I wonder if anyone else will surprise us with a bit of titillation? I do hope so." The Baroness chuckled at her own droll humor.

Ribbentrop continued to hold sway over the guests unfortunate enough to be within his earshot.

"Ja, mein Führer has asked of me, due to my expansive knowledge of art—especially the great German and Netherlandish masters—to seek pieces which the Third Reich will acquire. Our leader is a consummate collector, as he is a masterful artist in his own right. In fact, he intends to build a magnificent center for German culture and art near Linz to display his collection. Which reminds me…" And he snapped his fingers to summon one of the servers. "Junge! Find the house steward. I will view the artwork Astor has in the castle. Do it now!" Turning to the others, he asked, "Who will come with me?" Reluctantly or otherwise, his compatriots, Lord Rothermere, and a few others levered themselves aloft to follow him.

While they prepared to walk back to the Castle, an electric thrill ran through the crowd. From their seats, the women craned their necks as whispers were shared behind hands for, casually joining the assemblage, was the most notorious couple in all of Britain—Edward, Prince of Wales, and his paramour, Wallis Simpson. The Prince was, as ever, impeccably attired in a Savile Row suit, but all eyes were on Simpson. Thin as a whip, she wore a brilliant teal dress, cinched tightly with a print silk scarf. On her left shoulder was an impossibly extravagant brooch—a floral spray made from gold and precious gemstones which fired in the sunlight. Her lips were done in her signature red.

Rothermere and Ribbentrop both about-turned abruptly, literally colliding with each other while scrambling to greet the twosome. Ribbentrop stumbled, thus enabling Rothermere to reach the Prince first, bowing obsequiously.

"Your Royal Highness, this is indeed a most unexpected honor! I had no idea you would grace us with your presence today." Almost as an afterthought, he acknowledged Wallis. "And Mrs. Simpson! How lovely to see you! Please, may I offer you a drink?"

Ribbentrop was red-faced when he regained his balance and bowed to the Prince. Upon greeting Simpson, he hesitated for a moment, uncertain how to handle the situation. Those who watched closely saw the two exchange penetrating looks. The German took her hand, clicked his heels and nodded curtly, saying nothing.

The Baroness and Lady Dering, along with every other woman present, enjoyed a charge of excitement at this utterly riveting social interaction. The buzz at every recent dinner party, every high society gathering in London, was that Simpson and Ribbentrop were, in fact, passionate lovers. To actually observe that threesome—the Prince of Wales, the shockingly bold divorcée, and the high Nazi official—in the flesh was a treat no one had anticipated. For many, it instantly transformed what had been a somewhat tedious garden party into one of the most intriguing social events of the early season.

Obviously still nonplussed, Ribbentrop turned to see Hever's chief steward, Mr. William Snowsill, waiting patiently, having been summoned by the server.

"Sir, I will be happy to show you and any other interested person some highlights of Lord Astor's art collection. If you will follow me, please?" And he set off at a good pace, headed for the manor house.

Once inside the ancient walls of the stunning Hever Castle, the guests moved from room to room, admiring the many paintings and objets d'art amassed by Astor and his father on their travels. Some spaces appeared almost as if they'd been untouched since Tudor times; others were updated to meet the demands of modern residents: the Drawing Room, Library, and Morning Room particularly. In every nook and cranny hung paintings both contemporary and venerable.

Ribbentrop, it was clear, was having a hard time overcoming his earlier resentment. At last, when the tour appeared to be over, and finally having regained his bluster, he faced young Snowsill. "Is this all? This is the totality of Astor's collection? I must say I am disappointed. I see nothing here of value."

The steward, flustered, replied, "Er, no sir. Of course, this is not the full extent of the Astor holdings. We curate the exhibits every so often—rotate them with other pieces so nothing is overexposed."

At that moment, the Prince and Wallis joined the group in the Drawing Room, where the interaction was taking place. When Ribbentrop was satisfied that they, too, were listening, he barked at Snowsill, "I demand to see the rest of the collection! Where are they stored? Show me, immediately."

Snowsill protested, indicating they were kept in a locked area of the castle.

"I don't care where they are kept. You will show me the additional works of art owned by Astor, or I will complain to him that you are a disrespectful, lackluster steward!"

Snowsill decided it would be more prudent to allow Ribbentrop to have a look than to continue a public argument he knew he wouldn't win, so he led Rothermere, Ribbentrop, and Himmler to a large space on an upper floor. He unlocked the door and they entered. Stacked against walls, filed in special shelves, even hanging from the rafters, were paintings of all kinds. Ribentropp scanned the room, grunting in disgust at several impressionist works, muttering "Degenerate graffiti! It cannot be called art… Have you nothing by German masters, man? Nothing which represents the greatest works ever executed?"

"Sir, what we have in this vault is all that I am familiar with. Perhaps Lord Astor has other pieces, but I know not where he keeps them."

It was then that Ribbentrop spied a canvas lying in a remote corner of the room. He stalked over, and moved it in order to look more closely.

Propped carelessly against the wall, it was old and showed every bit of its age. Its surface was crackled, dusty and had been obviously retouched heavily by someone who was in no way an artist, yet it intrigued him. It was bewildering. Across great proportions of it were awkward swaths of paint; faded over time. Other sections, though, seemed as if they'd been done by someone who had infinite skill, definitely in the style of the great Flemish masters. And the subject was interesting. It appeared as if it was an English king, joined by a queen. He turned to walk away, but then the faded artwork seemed to call to him, and he twisted round to look again. This time, he studied the canvas intently. Then he barked, "What is this, Steward? Who executed this painting, and where did it come from?"

"Sir, that I do not know. All I can tell you is that it was given to Mrs. Madeleine Astor, but on arrival, it reminded her of the terrible time she endured on the Titanic, losing her husband, so she had it stored so she wouldn't have to look at it. It's been here ever since."

"I want it, Steward. Have it wrapped. I will take it with me today."

Snowsill grew tense. There was no way he could let this abominable man take one of Lord Astor's paintings without express approval and he was not about to be cowed into submission. "I am truly sorry, sir. I cannot permit you to do so. I must have Lord Astor's consent."

Ribbentrop's face grew florid. "What on earth do you mean, junge? Do you have any idea to whom you speak? If you know what is good for you, you will obey!"

But William Snowsill—as British as roast beef and possessing valor worthy of a knight at King Arthur's Round Table—knew he had not the slightest intention of obeying the loathsome German. So he simply replied, "Yes, sir," and stood silently watching the small band of Ribbentrop devotees file from the room to return to the party downstairs.

The second their footfalls had ceased, he cast a glance around to be sure no one was lurking nearby. Muttering to himself, "You disgraceful son of a bitch, do you think I would allow you to loot Lord Astor's treasures? You won't get your hands on anything as long as I am here." He grasped the painting, carrying it gently due to its age and condition, and secreted it to a small room on the top level of the house.

Grunting with the effort, he pushed a large and heavy armoire in front of the door. He sat in the single chair in the room, telling himself he'd wait there all night if need be. "You won't outsmart me, Nazi swine." He examined the strange painting as he sat there, wondering at its baffling subject, hard as it was to discern, covered by dust. He made a commitment that he'd wait until all of the partygoers had departed, hoping Ribbentrop might have forgotten his order.

And as Snowsill's luck would have it, once the German delegates returned to the Drawing Room, they were greeted by a cluster of interested aristocrats, including Wallis and Edward. The conversation turned to the state of affairs of the burgeoning Nazi party, and Ribbentrop quickly became engaged bragging about his important role in its growing success. It wasn't until later that evening, back in his London hotel, the odious diplomat remembered the puzzling but provocative painting, having been too busy with carnal thoughts of Wallis.

"Oh well," he mused. He determined to send Astor a note in the next day or so, telling him in no uncertain terms that he would claim it to add to Hitler's collection. He'd bring it home, have it cleaned and restored, and just perhaps der führer would award him a coveted accolade, which was, after all, what he lived for.

Chapter Forty

MARCH 2017

ROME

How life had changed for me in just one sweet, short month! True, there were moments during which I felt like a silly, sentimental teenager, but I couldn't help myself. It was as if a filter—that grey wash through which I'd previously viewed the world—had been lifted. I awakened each morning feeling a sense of joy.

I was in love.

And the best part? I was certain Antonio felt the same. Despite our busy schedules, we spent as much time together as we could manage. And although I was skittish that our initial ardor would wane, it hadn't. His devotion to me was evident; he displayed it in so many ways—not only physically, but in sweet thoughtfulness. A relationship of such intensity was entirely new to me, but I was shocked at how easily I slipped into it. It felt right, straightforward. And that was the best part: there were no games of cat and mouse.

Of course, we were discreet on campus. News like ours would have traveled fast, and neither of us wanted that scrutiny. So, by day he taught while I studied, working on my dissertation—my proposal had been readily accepted by Professore Ruggieri and the committee. And in the evenings, we either stayed at his flat or mine, searching, digging, excavating any and all sources we could think of to find that next critical clue, if one was to be had, in our pursuit of the painting which seemed to have vanished without a trace.

Late one afternoon, as we sat in a local trattoria waiting for our dinner, Antonio said, "Hey. You know how I had planned to get you another appointment at the Papal Library? Well, why don't we go together?" And then, with a wry smile, added, "I did, you may recall, ask you this question before. But you were just a bit skittish and shut me down right away. Didn't you?"

"Ummm, yep. I do remember. I had my reasons... I wasn't sure your motives were above board. But now, well, things are different. So... sure. Why don't we go? That is if you can get approval for my admission again. Hope that woman archivist doesn't remember me. Maybe I'll wear a disguise!"

He laughed, reached over to squeeze my hand, and then added, "How about I see if we can get approval to look at the note under x-ray fluorescence? Think it will offer any more clues? The part which was unreadable?"

"It's a great idea, Antonio. I'd love to see what else might show up. Let's do it."

So, with Antonio's connections, we went to the library. My excitement at passing through the impressive doors had not waned one bit. I was nervous... maybe even more so since I was with Antonio. I certainly didn't want him to regret accompanying me.

In much shorter order than at my previous visit, we had the same volume, Cap. 239, placed before us on the table. Sitting close together on the bench, holding my breath, I opened it to the very back, and there—precisely where I'd replaced it months ago—was the notoriously small square of parchment. Antonio's eyes grew wide as we opened it and looked through our magnifiers. I turned to the page in my notebook where I'd transcribed all that was visible and we tracked those words against the original. Then he looked up and motioned to the scriptore, one of the archivists, who quickly responded. In Italian, Antonio told him we'd been approved to study this document under x-ray fluorescence, so we were led to a small study chamber near the Reading Room. There, the archivist helped us set up the equipment, and soon we had the note situated under a special camera. On a screen, the results of the investigative process were displayed.

"I'm so anxious," I whispered to Antonio, as the images on the screen came into view. "Gosh, do you think we might find anything else—anything that might be an indication of where it is?"

"Well, we will soon find out." Antonio and I both squinted and stared at the letters swimming into view. And indeed, there were additional words which were now readable! I carefully copied each word as Antonio and I both read aloud. The first lines, which I'd not been able to discern before, were now clear.

'My esteemed Holy Father…
…must inform you of an ominous message I received from a respected Knight.'

Then an unreadable section, followed by the words:

' this portrait…with symbols…as the blessed St. Peter'.

A smeared and blurred group of words preceded:

'and our spies signaled great danger.'

The rest was text I had already transcribed. Nothing more revealed itself to us. My disappointment was all too apparent.

Still, I rallied enough to spend the rest of the day hunting and pecking in the vast library collections to see if we just might, possibly, find any other reference to this damnably obscure relic. But not a line, not a word, presented itself.

As we left the Vatican grounds and went to a bar for a drink and a bite, Antonio put his arm around me. "Cheer up, Zar. This doesn't mean we'll never find anything. I know it feels like looking for—what is that English expression—a needle in straw? But we will persist. If it exists, we will discover it! I have confidence in you. And me! Together we will get there. We make a great team, you know?"

"I know, Antonio. I'm glad you're with me. I really am." His words buoyed my spirits.

A little.

Regardless of the intensity of our collective research, though, not another hint was uncovered. Our continuing failure to unearth any leads at all was leaving me bitterly disillusioned. I was fearful that, one day soon, Antonio would tell me we had no choice but to give up. Then what would I do? Abandon the entire quest? Proceed once again on my own? The thought caused a knot to twist in my stomach.

AT THE STUDENT CAFÉ one afternoon with Lina, she asked me whether or not I'd told my father about Antonio.

"No, I haven't. Not yet."

"What are you waiting for, Zara? This is the most fantastic news, the most *incredibile*—la cosa più bella: the most beautiful merging of soulmates I've seen, maybe ever! I kept waiting for you two to get together. I knew it! I just couldn't figure out why you refused to see it. Oh, it makes me so, so felice! Happy, happy! Your dear dad deserves to feel the same way."

"Yeah, yeah, I know you're right, Lina, but I guess I've been sort of waiting to see if it's real. I just never expected to be in a relationship like this… maybe ever! And now I look back and think about how I mistrusted Antonio. I kind of knew all along that he felt something for me, but I confused it with thinking he just wanted to use my talents and didn't care for me as a person; as a woman."

Lina cocked an eyebrow and burst into laughter. "That is hilarious! Not so often do you hear about a girl being afraid her boyfriend only wants her for her brain, and not her body! But with you, cara mia, I am not so surprised!"

I laughed too, but then reflected, "You know, sometimes I feel like I'm living a dream."

"Yes! Yes, that's what love is like, Tesoro! It is a dream, and very wonderful. You are a different person, you know… just look at you! You're not the same adorable mess you were a few months ago."

I smiled at her—a smile which originated deep within, infused with the gratitude of having such a friend. How lucky I was, and I hadn't fully realized it until now. "You're right… I will call my dad. I need to find the best way to tell him. But then, maybe he won't be too surprised, either. I guess the only one who was caught off guard by this is me. I know he'll be happy, though, and heaven knows he does deserve it. I've certainly put him through enough angst." I hesitated for a moment. "As I did my mom."

Lina wisely chose to not comment on my last statement. Instead, she reminded me, "Don't forget, we said we'd have dinner together this evening—you, Antonio, and me. Then Giancarlo will meet us later for a drink, after he's finished work. We are going to Sapori di Casa, right? See you at 8! Gotta run to class."

And she gathered her books, and was gone.

WE WERE SEATED AT a corner table, in the back and away from other diners that evening. Our orders had been taken, and we poured wine, munched on bread with olive oil, and quietly talked about the search we had underway. Lina asked many questions, and I had no reluctance in answering them, or encouraging Antonio to do so. She listened as we spilled all that I'd been through, described the investigation my dad and I had undertaken in Paris, essentially ending at 175 rue St. Honoré, the salon of the former designer Lucile Duff Gordon, and now of another British designer, Vivienne Westwood.

"Woo, you were in the Vivienne Westwood store, Zara? I am impressed!"

"Yeah, well, you should have seen me that day. It was sleeting and I had a wet parka, wet snowboots, and bedraggled hair. Stepping inside wasn't my most comfortable moment."

"Well, I'm sure it was worth the trip... or was it?" Lina glanced from me to Antonio.

"In a way it was. We found out a bit of the property's history. And for all we were able to discover, it seems as if the painting was certainly in that house at one time. But then the trail runs cold. And try as we might, we can't get a hit on anything else."

Our food was delivered, and we fell silent while we started to eat. Lina seemed lost in thought.

Abruptly she stopped, mid-bite. "I have it! The solution! It's molto semplice! Easy as a piece of bun—"

"Cake," I corrected, smiling.

"Cake! You do a connectivity chart. Something like a Venn analysis, but you draw a chart with every fact you know, and you see where the connections lie along the pathways. And when you find the ones that are connected, you pursue those. See?"

Antonio laughed out loud. "Lina, I think you're on to something! It's may not be quite as simple as it sounds, but it just might be completely brilliant. You are a wonder."

She waved away his complement offhandedly. "Sì, sì, this I know already. A wonder in a glamorous package, that's me."

We had a great time for the rest of the evening, and I enjoyed watching Lina and Giancarlo, who seemed really happy together, joke and laugh. But mostly, I couldn't wait to get home and start on the diagram. I hoped Lina's inspiration would work. It felt like our last resort.

IT WAS CLOSE TO 11 p.m. when we unlocked the door to my flat. Antonio had an early class the next morning, and I was scheduled to meet with one of my professors at nine. But the instant the door had closed behind us I whirled to face him. "Please? Please Antonio, I can't wait till tomorrow or the next day to do the chart. I know we have a busy day ahead, but we've both pulled all-nighters before. Isn't this worth it? I have to do it, even if you go to bed and I stay up alone."

"Well, that's not going to happen. I can't sleep with you working away by yourself. Flash up a pot of coffee—strong enough to stand a spoon in—and let's get started."

I gave him a quick, forceful hug, thinking how lucky I was to have his love and encouragement. Hurriedly, I set up a strong pot to brew, then scrounged in my closet and withdrew a big pad of chart paper with self-stick top, and some Sharpie markers.

We spread our notes on the table, pasted some of the chart paper to a blank wall, and looked at each other. "How do we start this?" I queried dubiously. "I'm pretty good at figuring out writing from the 12th century, but not so great at analytics."

"Let's begin by listing every name you've become familiar with in your research thus far. We'll leave enough space around each name so we can then go back and add any event, fact, or connection we learn about each person. Let's see what pops up for us, if anything. Once that's done, we'll draw connections. Maybe something will emerge that'll drop a hint in our laps."

So that's what we proceeded to do. As the hours passed, the charts became filled with names: Henry VIII and Anne Boleyn, Pope Clement VII, Philippe Villiers de l'Isle-Adam, William Weston, the Knights of Malta, the royal painter Hans Holbein, the pirate Olivier LeVasseur, his brother Louis, buccaneer and landowner Adolphe Toussaint, his lady Louise Périer, the imprisoned Knight François Marraud, Lucile Duff Gordon and her husband Cosmo. And around each name, we wrote—stopping to research if necessary—any and all recorded events or unique circumstances attributable to each. Often our research prompted us to add new names to the array, and several times we needed to expand the paper by attaching one to another and rewrite our burgeoning chart. By 4 a.m., I could see that Antonio was flagging. I refused to stop there, so I went to the kitchen and made him pancakes with syrup. He gobbled them and was renewed with a fresh energy.

Next, we started the tedious process of making connections. At times we were stuck, so we moved to another section of the chart and worked there.

"Look at this, will you?! It's like spaghetti." I stood back and squinted at the tangle.

"That's why we used different color markers." Antonio rubbed his eyes. "I'm pretty exhausted and my brain isn't working very well. I don't know, Zara, maybe we are just wasting our time. It doesn't seem that we are getting anywhere."

He took one look at my expression of dejection, drew a deep breath, and offered, "Okay. Let's really study the Duff Gordon period. Although the painting was in their house at one time, it's at least possible they may have passed it on. So, who and what are they connected with? What events did we record for them?"

"Well, by definition Lucile knew many famous names, so any one of them might provide a clue. But…what about this? She and her husband both survived the *Titanic* sinking! My God! How many people did? Not many. Maybe we should study everyone they seemed to be acquainted with on board the ship."

So, we went to the computer and began reviewing a list of first-class passengers: the survivors and the deceased. We were able to determine those whom the Duff Gordons definitely knew and were friendly with, so we starred their names. I thought it might be helpful to verify who among the women might have been her clients, and a few names emerged. We thoroughly researched the survivors who were also her customers, listing their unique attributes. Antonio probed backgrounds of the New York and London clients, and I focused on Madeleine Astor. The Astor family was fascinating, and as I read on, one piece of almost-trivia caught my attention. Her husband's cousin, William Waldorf Astor, had moved to England and owned numerous properties. In July of 1903, he purchased Hever Castle.

I added that factor to the chart and stood back, staring at it for long minutes. Hever Castle… Hever Castle… where had I heard that before? My tired brain couldn't summon the details, so I grabbed my phone and looked it up.

Hair on the back of my neck stood up, as carefully, very slowly, I drew a thick line from Lucy Duff Gordon to Madeleine Astor… to Hever Castle: the childhood home of Anne Boleyn. "Antonio!" I almost screamed and he jumped. "Look! Look what I found!" I described the connection to him and then retraced the line. "What do you think? Could it possibly mean something? Could the Astors have had a link to the painting? I know it may be far-fetched, but it's the only connection that makes any sense at all. What's your opinion?"

He didn't answer for a long minute and I began to despair. But then…

"I think, over spring break, we go to England. To Hever Castle. We have nothing to lose."

I shrieked, threw my arms around him almost knocking him to the floor. "I'm so excited! I wish we were going tomorrow!"

"As for me," muttered poor tired Antonio, "I just hope I make it through tomorrow! Let's get an hour or so of sleep."

Chapter Forty-one

MID-MARCH 2017

HEVER CASTLE AND
ST. PETER'S AND ST. PAUL'S CHURCH
EDENBRIDGE, KENT, ENGLAND

M r. Nigel Lewis, warden of St. Peter's and St. Paul's Church—the church which had been associated with Hever Castle for centuries—was anxious to conclude his long conversation with the three elderly ladies, some of the most dedicated members of the congregation, and lock up for the day. It was now late on a chilly and damp Sunday afternoon, and in his role, he'd spent the entire day greeting parishioners, handling church business, conferring with the vicar, and after services, answering questions from the many visitors who stopped in to see the lovely old building—many of them expressly there to view the brass plate which marked the gravesite of Sir Thomas Boleyn, grandfather of Queen Elizabeth I, and father of Queen Anne Boleyn.

He braced his back with his hand to try and relieve the ache and did his best to straighten up, although it was impossible. He suffered from an acute case of scoliosis—a curvature of the spine. As he'd aged, the curve had become more pronounced, and very painful. Now into his seventies, it caused him trouble mostly all the time. That, and a vexing heart condition, told him it was time to retire. But he couldn't quite bring himself to do so. Not yet. Just a few more years…

Selecting a large iron key from the ring he carried, he lovingly, deliberately, secured the lock on the ancient wooden church door, waiting until he heard the click, then turned to go to his car, and home. Nigel lived nearby, in the village of Marsh Green, so it was never much of a drive to or from the church. Once he'd arrived and stepped inside the little whitewashed cottage, he moved about switching on lamps, lighting the rooms against the encroaching dusk. Finally, he put on the kettle for a bracing cup of tea, placed his worn leather carryall on the table, and picked up the most recent edition of the Art Newspaper, thankfully lowering himself into his chair—the soft padded, well-worn chair he favored—to relax and read.

Nigel, a lifelong bachelor, was a man of habit. He'd lived in the same cottage for close to fifty years and served the church he loved for just about as many. He was a pleasant little chap, but in truth, even though he was familiar to St. Peter's and also to the staff at Hever Castle, which lay just adjacent to the church, no one really knew him well, or much about his personal life. Once his job was done, and he did it conscientiously, he retreated to his house, and kept to himself whenever possible. He was a deeply contented man; there were three things Nigel Lewis loved above all else: his church, the appreciation of fine art, and the Most Venerable Order of the Hospital of St. John, the highly respected and restored version of the Order which Henry VIII had abolished in 1540. The new English Order was a charitable, religious group, and Nigel was proud of his role in such a long-standing royal order of chivalry. He was a member; his father had been appointed before him, and by virtue of Nigel's many years of dedication to St. Peter's and the good outreach work the parish did to care for the poor and infirm, he, too had been embraced by the Order. His was total commitment. The only piece of frippery Nigel ever wore was a gold ring bearing the insignia of an eight-pointed Maltese cross, the ancient symbol of that which had once been known as the Sovereign Order of St. John of Jerusalem, or the Order of Malta. The ring had been given to his father; it was now his, and he treasured it.

After he'd eaten the sparse supper his housekeeper had left on the stove for him, he read a while longer then decided he'd best go to bed. The next day would be challenging. A specialty carpentry company would be at the church early to assess the condition of the belfry, and make any repairs or restorations deemed necessary. The bell tower at St. Peter's had been in place since the 15th century, and in addition to its impressive age, was unique in design. Its structure had been made of English oak, much of it, including the narrow, leaning stairway which led up to the landing from the vestry below, petrified to near stone-like hardness. Every Saturday and Sunday, a specially trained team of bell ringers climbed the tilting staircase to a tiny space, stood in a circle and rhythmically pulled on the ropes which allowed the bells to cast their music out and across the countryside, calling its congregation to worship.

Nigel would meet the carpenters and lead them to the stair, and of course, he would have to accompany them into the tower—a task made ever more difficult due to his impairment. He had another reason, though, for wanting to be at the church early, much before the carpenters arrived. There was something in the bell tower he needed to ensure would remain out of sight. An object he revered above all else—his personal secret.

IN NIGEL'S EARLY TWENTIES he'd come to work at Hever Castle as a junior caretaker. When he had breaks from his regular duties, he would often remain in the big, medieval house closely studying the artwork displayed there. One day, he was approached by the Chief Steward, Mr. William Snowsill. Everyone in the employ of Hever knew Snowsill—a highly respected, knowledgeable gentleman who'd run the Castle with dedication and attentiveness for just short of half a century. At seventy years of age, Snowsill had been ready to retire, but his love of the Castle and everything in it remained apparent to all.

"Good afternoon, young Mr. Lewis. Haven't I seen you on numerous occasions studying the paintings while you should be on break? Is there something in particular you are looking for?"

'No, sir. It's just that I have a great love of fine art, and it's a privilege to be able to study paintings such as the ones displayed here, on a daily basis, and up so close."

"I understand, Lewis. Actually, I feel much the same way. This is a special place, and we are lucky to have access to the incredible works of art Lord Astor has acquired. And apparently, young man, you agree."

"Oh, I do, sir. I wouldn't wish to work anywhere else. This place— Hever—has an entrancing quality. That's about the best I can do to describe it."

Mr. Snowsill chuckled his approval at the caretaker's perceptiveness. "You've been working here for quite some time, isn't that right? And I've heard good things about you and your dedication to your work. How would you like it if someday I show you some additional art owned by the family which is stored upstairs?"

"Sir—Mr. Snowsill—really? I would be honored, and so very grateful. Please let me know when it would be convenient, and even if it's before I start work, or after, I would make myself available. Thank you very much. I will look forward to it."

Shortly thereafter, true to his word, Snowsill and Lewis climbed to the storeroom early one morning. The sun was just rising over the horizon, and it cast a brilliant beam of light into the space, which, to Nigel's amazement, was filled with paintings and other artwork: sculptures, bronze statues, and furniture.

Observing Nigel's awe at the accumulation of masterpieces assembled in the storeroom, Snowsill led him up and down the rows, stopping to comment on pieces he was particularly fond of.

Nigel had never seen such a collection of riches, and ooh'ed and aah'ed at many of the works. Pausing in front of some, unable to tear himself away, he heard Mr. Snowsill say, "You know, Nigel, over the years, I've discovered something extraordinary. When you observe certain paintings day after day, they begin to speak to you. Not all of them, you know. But some do appear to move and change and, on special days, actually whisper to you. It's like they want to tell you how they were born, and why, whom they've known and seen. I find it to be quite magical, really."

Nigel's eyes lit up. This was precisely how he'd always felt about certain paintings but had been too shy to reveal to anyone. "Oh, sir. Thank you for saying that! I've thought that same thing for years— well, at least as long as I've been exposed to art—but I've never known anyone else who recognized it. It's strange, but wonderful, don't you think?"

He felt that his heart was about to burst as he wandered through the room, studying masterpieces by early artists, and contemporary ones. It was a magnificent collection. Reluctant to have his precious allotted time come to a close, he walked ever so slowly, willing it not to end.

Rounding the final corner, he saw, tucked way back and almost out of view, a most curious canvas. It was plain, merely attached to a wooden frame, with no ornate gilding to encompass its aged appearance. He carefully moved it away from the wall to have a closer look and saw that it betrayed evidence of a pentimento—a hasty overpainting by the artist—either that, or it had been ineptly repaired by someone else. With surprise, he noted that the subjects of the painting appeared to be Henry VIII and, presumably, one of his queens, though he knew not which one. The work was in a sorry state, but to him that mattered little. Instantly, he was drawn to it. He leaned closer and was able to detect sections, though dirty, which were rendered with a fine hand. It was hypnotic; he had a hard time sliding it back into its corner. But reluctantly, he replaced it and turned to follow Mr. Snowsill down the winding stone staircase, back to work.

But all through that day, and every day thereafter, he thought of the painting, the portrait. It haunted him, until early one morning when he was alone, sweeping the courtyard of the Castle, and Snowsill happened to pass through to go into his office.

On an impulse he called out. "Mr. Snowsill, sir. May I ask you something?"

"Certainly, Lewis. How can I help?"

"Well, sir, I so appreciated you taking me into the storeroom to see the artwork. It was a special morning for me. But I have a question: do you know of the old, very dirty painting tucked away in the back corner? The one that's damaged? I wonder... if you're aware of the item I'm referencing, can you tell me anything about it?"

Snowsill knitted his brow trying to recall, but then said. "Aye, Lewis, I know which one you mean. Strange looking canvas, isn't it? I believe I do remember just a bit about it. Yes, yes. I was just a lad, and had only begun working at the Castle in the previous year—meaning we're going back to, let me see, about 1934. I'd heard the story from other castle staff. At one time, the painting had been sent here as a gift to Mrs. Madeleine Astor—of course, she's long dead now—by a close friend who, like her, had survived the sinking of the *Titanic*. Apparently, this friend thought it might be appropriate, since it's said the queen in the portrait is Anne Boleyn and this was her home. Anyway, Mrs. Astor wanted nothing to remind her of the tragedy in which her husband drowned, so she ordered it put away, never to be placed on view." He was silent for a moment, reliving shadows from his past. "Oh, and yes! How could I possibly forget? There was an event held in the gardens, attended by some of Hitler's henchmen, in the mid-thirties I believe. One of them—Von Ribbentrop, a thoroughly horrible man, I have to say—saw it and wanted it." He stopped, thinking back to that day, and chuckled heartily. "Wasn't I just the young whippersnapper then? He pulled rank and demanded to take it with him, but I stood firm, looked him right in the eye and refused. He was red as a tomato, he was, but I wouldn't budge. All those damned Nazis. Who the hell did they think they were?"

Nigel listened, transfixed. The stories surrounding his painting (for he had begun to think of it as his painting) made it even more intriguing. Before he had time to reconsider, he blurted, "Mr. Snowsill, I have a bold request. Do you think it would be possible for me to rescue that canvas, and perhaps place it somewhere… maybe the church? It wouldn't have to be on full display, but what if there was a discreet place, like the vestry, which would allow it to be seen in the light of day? I know the warden and could ask him."

Snowsill had no reason to refuse. It was immaterial to him, and certainly not one of the treasured Astor pieces which were carefully kept under lock and key. "I don't see why not, young Lewis. You talk to the vicar, and the warden and, if they are agreeable, you can have it moved to the church. Maybe if it's dusted off it will look a bit better, but I'm not sure."

Joyfully, Lewis had expressed his deep thanks, and within a week, after convincing the warden it would be positioned unobtrusively, the painting was rescued from its imprisonment, and transplanted to St. Peter's Church, propped in a corner of the vestry. There, almost no one but Nigel Lewis paid it any attention as the Edenbridge parishioners busily came and went.

Nigel had cleaned the dust from it as best he could. The more closely he inspected it, the more convinced he became that it had lived an important life and had a compelling tale to tell. He grew ever more protective of it as the years passed. And then, one day when he'd been in London for a meeting of the Order, he'd visited the library upstairs at the Priory of St. John in Clerkenwell.

Nigel settled himself into a chair at a table with a stack of books piled before him. He sighed with pleasure. He loved reading about art almost as much as viewing it, and he had the entire afternoon ahead. So he began poring over books and records of a collection which were the exclusive property of the Order until, quite by chance, he stumbled upon a personal journal written by a Knight in the Victorian era. Included was a curious section about art which carried legends, and within was the tale of a painting of Henry VIII and his second Queen, Anne Boleyn. The author reported a possibility that the extremely rare double portrait had been created by the Tudor royal court painter, Hans Holbein the Younger. This particular painting's legend revealed that the work was intended to position the King as the new leader of the Christian Church, following his conquest of corrupt papal forces.

The Knight's somewhat fanciful tale alleged that the painting had gone missing shortly after its conception: seemingly vanished into thin air never to be found again despite every Knight in the 16th century having been put on notice to seek and find it, whereupon they were under order by the Grand Master to deliver the elusive work to the pope in exchange for great indulgences. Riveted, Nigel flipped the page, hoping for just a bit more information, but there, the scribe's reportage ended.

At that very moment, with an old, forgotten, musty volume open in front of him, Nigel knew there was no flight of fancy in the Victorian author's claim. Indeed! Folding his hands before him, he bowed his head in thanksgiving to his God above for the revelation. He, Nigel Lewis, knew precisely where the lost painting was.

At long last, he also knew the reason he'd been irrevocably drawn to the piece of canvas he'd seen in the castle storeroom years ago. Just as Mr. Snowsill had said, the painting had been speaking to him all that time, trying to tell him its story.

Hard as it was to believe, it was now his painting. He would keep it. He knew he would protect it with his life.

And never would he let it go.

Chapter Forty-two

MAY 2017

HEVER CASTLE
KENT

A ntonio and I arrived at Hever on a chilly and drizzly afternoon. The mist shrouded early blooms in the gardens and seemed to enhance the dreamlike aura surrounding the exquisite castle and its moat. I made a great effort to contain my nervous anticipation as we bought admission tickets and entered the stately building. Its beauty and quiet grandeur was unexpected, and slowly we toured, spending time in every corner, absorbing the profound sense of the past. In each room, I inspected the paintings, every piece of art which was displayed on the ancient walls, and when standing before the Hever Portrait of Anne Boleyn hanging in pride of place at the right of the Great Hall's magnificent hearth, I remained for a long while, intently studying her features.

Beckoning Antonio to stand with me, eye level with the lovely painting, I sighed. "What a pity none of the portraits actually created during her lifetime have survived, isn't it, though? I just wonder if she truly was this beautiful? If she actually looked like this in the portrait of her and Henry? Oh, how I'm dying to track the remainder of its journey, to be able to see it… to touch it!"

Once we'd completed our tour, we asked to see the castle supervisor. After a short wait in the office, he appeared: a warm and helpful man. Earnestly, I told him we were interested in any information which might be traceable to a painting of both Anne and Henry. He shook his head, saying he had no knowledge of any such artwork, but, after a moment's thought he said, "You know what? It comes to mind that perhaps you two should speak with the warden of St. Peter's Church, just up the road: a Mr. Nigel Lewis. He's an older gentleman and has been an art aficionado his whole life. There's very little he doesn't know, and I'm certain if there was ever anything similar to what you've described at Hever, he'd have been aware of it. Good luck!"

We thanked him and headed for the church.

As soon as we stepped inside, we were suffused with the peacefulness and grace of the small, historic church. Apparent was a perception of the myriad souls who'd prayed within its structure over the centuries; unquestionably, those ghosts had left an indelible spiritual mark. In a whisper, we inquired about seeing Mr. Lewis, and were told he was out but, if we chose to wait, he should be back shortly. We sat in a pew while I nervously fidgeted, until Antonio placed his hand over both of mine to quiet them. At last, a stooped and bespectacled man approached, motioning for us to join him in the vestry. There he offered chairs in that small but tidy space filled with vestments and other clerical items. Once seated, he asked how he might be of assistance.

"Well, we have a somewhat unusual request, Mr. Lewis, and we've been told you are the expert with whom we should be speaking," I began. "I am Zara Rossi, and this is Professor Antonio Moretti. As part of the research supporting my doctoral dissertation, we're seeking information on an artwork which may, at one time, have been known to someone affiliated with Hever." I was dying to forge ahead, but tried to be careful not to disclose too much, handling my approach lightly, almost casually. "It would have been an unusual painting, with religious overtones: a portrait of Henry VIII and his queen, Anne Boleyn, posing together. We think it may have been produced during her reign, and not posthumously. Might that description ring even the faintest bell for you?"

Lewis glanced down, and when he raised his head, he'd paled visibly. As he prepared to reply, I noticed his left eyelid begin to twitch. There was no doubt in my mind that his demeanor had changed at the mention of the painting. I sat on the edge of my chair, holding my breath, until he finally spoke.

"Let me think… it's possible there may have been such a painting here, but I believe it would have been many years ago. Well before my tenure. In fact, I do recall a report which had circulated in the mid 1930s. It implied that a delegation of Nazi officers who visited the Castle may have stolen a number of works from the Astor collection. As you know, the Nazis looted and amassed art which appealed to Hitler. Maybe the canvas you seek was one of them. At any rate, I can confidently assure you nothing like it exists anywhere within the Castle collection today."

He dropped his hands to his lap, wringing them restlessly.

Unable to ignore the movement, I looked at Mr. Lewis's arthritic knuckles, and something glinted. He held them still just long enough for me to gain a clear view of his left hand—and on its third finger was an insignia ring. He shifted that hand again, and the emblem came into focus. It was imprinted with the Maltese Cross… the symbol of the Sovereign Order of Malta.

Forcing myself to remain casual, I asked, "Are you quite certain, Mr. Lewis? That you've never actually seen any work of art resembling the one which we describe? What if it was damaged? Or perhaps overpainted in parts? Would you have any recall?"

"None at all, I'm afraid. I am sorry I can't be of more help. Is there anything else I can do for you? If not, I apologize but it's getting late and I really must lock up."

"No, of course. We understand. And thank you for your time." When Antonio reached across to shake his hand, the left curled up, almost as if to conceal his ring. We stood, said goodbye, and stepped out of the church into the deepening twilight.

As we began to walk to our car in the parking lot behind the castle, I whispered, "Antonio! He knows. Did you watch him? Did you see his eye twitch? And how pale he got as soon as you mentioned it? And especially, did you see that ring? He's a Knight! I bet he knows. And you know what else? I think he's got the painting. I think he's hiding it. I feel it…"

"I'm not sure, Zar, though I did see him tense as soon as we mentioned it. It's weird! But anything is possible, I guess. I wonder why he might have it—and furthermore, be hiding it?"

"Okay. This may sound crazy, but do you want to walk back and wait until he gets in his car? Should we follow him?"

Antonio at first looked at me as if I'd lost my mind. But then, reconsidering, he said, "That's outrageous! But oh… what the hell. This whole quest is extraordinary. So… yeah. Let's go. What else do we have to do tonight but maybe go to a nice pub and get a beer and some good food, sitting by a warm wood fire? After all, what fun is that? No, let's follow our strange little suspect."

We hid from the headlights of oncoming cars by pressing ourselves along the hedgerows as we retraced our steps. The church lights were not yet extinguished, so we tucked ourselves into a shadowed spot with a good view of the door, near the parking area, and waited. Within twenty minutes, the lights winked out, and the door slowly opened. In the pale moonlight, we could clearly make out his bent form, limping across the lawn to the carpark.

And under his arm, carried with some difficulty, was a large rectangular object.

I jabbed Antonio in the ribs with my elbow. "Look!" I hissed. "That's it! Oh my God. He's got our painting. I knew it. I knew it!"

Antonio grabbed my hand and we set off running to reach our car in order to follow Nigel Lewis. We eased out onto the road when we saw his little VauxHall pass by, slowly. And, keeping our distance, but never losing him, we tracked him until he pulled into the gravel drive in front of a cottage in a neighboring village. We parked down the street, sunk low in the front seat, and watched. Surely, unbelievably, he emerged from the car, walked around to the passenger seat, and withdrew the object. Now we could see it was wrapped loosely in cloth. He unlocked his door, looked around, and went inside. Slowly, lights came on in several of the downstairs rooms.

I gripped Antonio's arm. "Now what? What do we do? We obviously can't knock on his front door. But—I'm not sure I can even believe it—could this obscure man actually have the painting we've been looking for for so long? Antonio, is it possible?"

"You know what, cara mia? In this world, truth can be stranger than fiction. So, sure, it's possible. But at the moment that's all we know. That he hastily transferred an object which looks suspiciously like a painting to his own house immediately after we questioned him. But we need to think carefully about our next move, and frankly, I'm affamato—or as the Brits would say—bloody starving. Let's go get some food while we figure out how we should proceed."

So, in the local pub, over a couple pints and dinner, we talked about it. I was so agitated I could barely eat. It had been such a long road. Was it imaginable that it could end here, in the placid countryside of Kent?

I sat in the booth, stewing, while Antonio demolished his dinner. Burrowing my forehead in my hands, fingers pressed into my temples, I was absolutely desperate to continue questioning Lewis. The more I thought, the greater my conviction that he had the painting we'd been pursuing. But, what if he did have it, and what if he owned it? Then I'd have no right to do anything. No legal right to even see it!

I was in turmoil. Antonio finally put down his fork, reached across and lifted my chin, and said, "Zar! You realize there may be nothing else we can do, right? We can't break into the man's house and ransack it."

"Can't we? Because I'm just about ready to do that. I'm sorry; I'm not taking that flimsy answer he offered us as closure. No way. We are going to see him again. Tomorrow."

Antonio was beginning to read my expressions and moods quite well, so he knew better than to push back. So, maybe reluctantly, he agreed that we'd go to Lewis's house the next day, and politely ask if we might pose just a few more questions, seeking anything at all he might remember about the paintings which were stolen. Maybe, just maybe, we could make some headway. And if great luck was with us, perhaps he would show us what he'd so clandestinely brought home with him this evening. Determining this to promise our best course, we went back to the inn and fell into an exhausted sleep.

On the following morning, we were up and out, driving the short distance to Nigel Lewis's house. What if the painting was there, now concealed within his cottage? Or worse, what if we were entirely wrong and simply caused a gentle old man unbearable embarrassment? I wasn't sure what unnerved me more—if we were to finally see it, or if he were to abjectly refuse, even chase us away. My hands were shaking when we turned the corner into Lewis's street. As we did, we were startled to see police cars and an ambulance in his drive, while a small crowd of curious onlookers were contained behind hastily strung police tape. We parked and walked toward the cottage, until a policeman stopped us. "Sorry, but you can't come any closer."

"What happened? We've come to visit Mr Lewis. We just saw him last evening."

"Are you family?"

"Friends," retorted Antonio. "Why?"

"I dislike having to tell you this, but Nigel Lewis is dead. Found this morning by his housekeeper. Lying at the bottom of his stairs, he was. We think he was robbed. Still trying to determine if he was a burglary victim or not. So, no one can cross the tape. There's a full investigation underway, you understand."

As I strained to grasp the implications of what the officer had just reported, I felt my knees begin to wobble and give way, and in slow motion, I crumpled to the ground. Antonio grabbed me under the arms, but waves of blackness washed over me.

Before losing consciousness, a vision swam before my eyes.

It was that of a faceless portrait fading slowly away...

Chapter Forty-three

JUNE 2017

ROME AND FLORENCE

M y stomach churned walking into the office of the Kent police chief. I was exceedingly anxious, knowing that this appeal might be our only chance to gain access to Lewis's household belongings. Before we had to return to Rome.

Once seated, I delivered a well-rehearsed fabrication about being old friends with the poor, deceased Mr. Lewis, and that my family had loaned him a painting, thus Antonio and I simply must see his belongings to regain the artwork.

We were immediately and definitively refused. The police chief detected my intensity, and he didn't like it one bit. He was suspicious, glared at me over his half-spectacles, and told us firmly that if we challenged the privacy of the estate, we would be liable for legal prosecution. He added that he'd be on watch for the two of us.

As I stepped over his threshold on our hasty way out, I muttered, hoping he'd hear me, "Thanks a lot, you dumb copper." Antonio jabbed me, but I didn't care. I was furious.

And so, without other options, we traveled back to Rome, empty-handed.

I was disconsolate. Although I felt emotionally drained by the search, I couldn't stop thinking of Lewis's furtive departure from the church that night, carrying the large parcel and loading it into his car with difficulty, then ushering it stealthily into his house. Had Nigel Lewis been the key? In my heart I believed so. But we weren't his family, so the door remained firmly closed to us.

That roadblock gnawed at me incessantly, and I was miserable. I wasn't in the mood to see or talk to anyone. Antonio wanted to stay with me at my apartment, but I made excuses. Instead, I huddled inside, by myself, going out only when I absolutely had to. My days and evenings were spent in internal conflict. Was it finally the end of the road? How the hell was I going to come to terms with that?

I tried so very hard to convince myself that the riddle was going to obstinately remain unsolved. It was a bitter pill to swallow. I'd marshaled every resource I could think of to decipher the enigma of a lost portrait which had caused dire alarm and had signaled such an ominous conflict in the religious world of the 16th century. And what did I have to show for it? Failure. But damn it, I knew I was close. It was enough to drive me crazy. How could I possibly let go without ever examining it to know what it was that enraptured its owners? Or should I say caretakers, because indeed, it had moved from hand to hand over the course of its history. I brutally berated myself that even my greatest effort had not been good enough—and it was this very demon which had preyed upon me my entire life. Something I'd wanted so very much—to solve a unique historical riddle, to achieve an accomplishment no one else had, an achievement which would, at last, have allowed me to feel I was worthy of respect, of self-esteem, even worth being well and truly loved—had eluded me, regardless of my monumental efforts. That realization plunged me into a deep dejection. In that state, I wanted to see nobody, wanted even less to talk to anyone. Especially not Antonio, or even Lina.

Sandra Vasoli

One afternoon, as I slipped out of a class I absolutely had no choice but to attend, I furtively made my way across campus to catch the bus home. Creeping around the corner, hoping to be invisible, I ran smack into Antonio. I couldn't meet his probing look, so I moved to one side, trying to sidle around him to continue to the bus stop.

"Wait, Zara! Where are you going? I thought you might be coming this way. What's up with you? What's going on? We haven't seen each other for almost two weeks. And you won't even answer my calls, much less tell me why. So, just spit it out, will you? Are you finished with this relationship—with us?"

I glanced up. One look at his face, lined with concern, caused my defensiveness to crumble. As my lip trembled and I struggled not to lose control, he led me to a sheltered spot behind the building and took me in his arms. I stayed there, secure, until I could talk without blubbering.

"I'm so sorry, Antonio. Look at me! I'm a mess, and I know it. I'm not sure how you can tolerate me. You have to see, by now, how flawed I am, how weak and unstable I can be. Why would you want to saddle yourself with someone like me?"

"Oh, my Zara. You are anything but weak, mi amore. And flawed? Aren't we all? Why would you think that everyone else is confident, secure and perfect all the time? No one is like that! And, my God, what hurts me is that you suspect I might just turn away and leave you behind. I'm not shallow, you know."

"I never, ever have thought of you as shallow! I'm incredibly grateful you see in me some qualities that are worthy of love. Because… because… I do love you, Antonio." I stopped and couldn't say more. That pronouncement took every ounce of courage I had, or ever thought I would have. I held my breath until he reacted to my blurted announcement.

"Yes, Zara. Sí. And I love you. Very, very much. So… here we are. And what shall we do about it?"

"I can't say that I know. I've never felt this way before. What does one do about it, especially when it gets real messy? Because, as you can see, 'Messy' is my middle name."

I brushed away my tears and wiped my nose, and looked at him with guilt, mixed with hope.

"Well," he said slowly, "I think we pick right back up where we left off. And we move forward, not looking back. How does that sound?"

At his response, my heart swelled. What was he telling me? With an exhilaration I'd never known, I suddenly realized what it was: commitment. Commitment. A word previously foreign to me, but one that now sounded glorious.

Was he truly mine? With all my heart, I hoped so.

However, I knew one thing for sure and for certain: I was his.

AFTER SUPPER ONE EVENING, I sat cross-legged on my bed, laptop at hand while Antonio graded student papers on the kitchen table.

I was in the process of making arrangements to visit home and my dad for several weeks over the summer and I hoped Antonio would accompany me, at least for part of the time. I was busy comparing prices between a nonstop from Rome into Boston or a layover in London, when I quit searching mid-click. I dropped my head into my hands, staring blindly at the keyboard.

"Antonio? Antonio!" He didn't answer, and I assumed he hadn't heard me. I was about to shout even louder when he came into the room and sat on the edge of the bed. "Che cosa? What's up, cara? Why are you yelling?"

"I have to go back."

He looked at me blankly, shaking his head in confusion. "Go back where? Home? What are you talking about?"

"No, not home. To England—to Kent—to Lewis's house. Antonio, I have to go! I have no choice. I will be tortured for the rest of my life if I don't. Somehow, I have to get into his house. I've got to see if the object he carried in there the night before his death was my painting—our painting."

Antonio hesitated, clearly trying to grasp my intent. His dark eyes searched my face, then he quietly asked, "Well, Zara, how do you plan to do that? His house is closed, you know. Locked up. Even before we saw the police chief, I called Lewis's solicitor—the policeman at the house that day gave me the man's card—expressly to inquire whether we might learn about a certain artwork we believed Mr. Lewis owned. And the solicitor informed me there would be no access until the entire estate is disposed of. Which is, of course, what we were told in no uncertain terms by the chief. Apparently, Mr. Lewis had a very brief will and testament, and a few items were to be given away. The rest will be sold at an auction sometime in the future, the money donated to his church. So, I can't fathom how you would be able to examine his belongings."

I felt my jaw tighten. "I will find a way. I swear to God, if I have to break in at night, that's what I'll do. If I'm caught and arrested, so be it. I don't care. It means that much to me. I have to get in there and see if he was hiding that painting." After a moment, I softened when I saw Antonio's dismay. "Look, I don't expect you to be a part of this, anyway. Last thing you need is to be fired for breaking and entering, especially in another country. I will go myself. I'll be fine. Don't worry about me."

"Mio Dio... my God, Zara. Loving you can present a challenge, girl." He sighed. "But love you I do. And come with you... I will. We better get there soon, before the house is stripped bare."

I exhaled slowly. "What makes you such a wonderful, stupendous man? And why on earth did you choose me? I have no idea. But I'm awfully glad you did. Let's leave tomorrow, can we? Let's just get there and get inside. Better to ask forgiveness than permission. At least, that's what I've heard." And I wriggled across the bed to hug him tightly, feeling a small sliver of hope parting the cloud of gloom which had settled on me since our return from England. With purpose, I went back to making travel plans—this time, Rome to London to Edenbridge, Kent.

IT WAS LATE AFTERNOON before our rental car pulled into Nigel Lewis's road in the village of Marsh Green. I was nervous, but even more so, I was determined. I hoped there would be a way Antonio and I might be able to gain access without breaking the law, but I was ready to break and climb through a window if that was my only choice. As we rounded the final turn, we saw a good-sized lorry parked in Lewis's drive. The back doors to the truck were open, and there were two men carrying furniture from the cottage and loading pieces into the truck. The lights were on in the cottage and as we drew near we could see that the little rooms appeared empty. The house was being cleared.

My breath came quickly as we pulled up alongside the truck, which was labelled Kent Auction Galleries / Valuers & Auctioneers. The car had barely rolled to a stop before I jumped out and called to the two truck drivers. "Helloo! Excuse me… is there any chance I could see what you've loaded onto the truck? I'm a friend of the man who owned the house and I'm looking for something which holds sentimental value. Please?"

"The workers looked at each other, and the foreman began shaking his head. "I don't think so, miss. Don't think my boss would like that."

I turned to Antonio and whispered, "Help! Can you help?" Even as I was asking, I saw that Antonio had pulled a wad of cash from his pocket. He jumped out of the car and talked to the men, handing one of them some bills. The man hesitated only another minute, then jerked his head toward the open back end, saying to me, "Go ahead. But make it quick. We're due back at the shop real soon. Give you ten minutes."

I didn't waste a second. Climbing into the back of the packed truck, I squeezed past a pile of chairs, a table, a disassembled bed, some lamps, and a small dresser. I tripped on a carpet roll, cursing under my breath, but maneuvered to the front, where, wedged between a side table and boxes of books, I saw what I was hoping to find. A large wooden crate containing a tight stack of framed art. I slithered into the very small space and shifted the box just enough that I could move the frames one by one. There was so little room in the crate that it was impossible to determine the subject of any single painting. My fingers shook as I maneuvered each one, futilely straining to see as much as I could. The fit was so tight that my knuckles scraped against the rough wood, and they bled as I gripped each frame to move it enough to inspect the next piece. The second to last painting was frameless: just a simple canvas pulled over wooden stretchers. I reached in to wiggle it free, and as I brushed its edge, a jolt coursed through me—as if I'd touched a live battery. I yanked back, stunned. Waiting at the back of the truck, Antonio saw me flinch, and the instant our eyes met, he squeezed past me to help, pushing and shifting the paintings, somehow making enough space to wrest the canvas free. Pulling carefully, he lifted it from the rest. It was large, clearly old. The outside light, though, had faded to the point where we couldn't examine its subject.

But I didn't need to see. I knew.

Shaking, I went to the men and told them I wished to buy the item we found. They looked dubious, and the foreman crossed his arms over his chest. I was close to being frantic, so Antonio handed them his card, saying he would call the auction house that evening to be sure he paid a fair price. The men were hungry, tired, and more than ready to go home to dinner and a pint or two, so they agreed. We lifted the canvas from the truck, they closed up the back, and drove off.

And there we stood. The village was quiet. Not a sound marred the deep silence. The blue twilight was dimming into velvety black night. There were no lights to illuminate what we'd just recovered from the auctioner's truck. Imagining this moment as I had so many times, I would have thought I'd do anything—even strike a match against the pavement—to glimpse what I felt sure was what I'd sought so achingly.

But somehow, I was at peace. It was there, with us. I could wait to see it.

Finally, finally, it was in my possession.

BACK IN OUR ROOM at the inn, with every light on at highest wattage, the painting stood. It leaned against the bed, and we could not stop staring. To say it was a mess was an understatement. It wasn't dirty, exactly—it seems that Lewis had dusted it regularly—but it was cracked, yellowed, painted over by a crude hand, and parts of the canvas had begun unraveling. The subject was almost unrecognizable.

Almost.

But when studied, the image was definitive. A king and his partner, standing together, the king's hand extended in a gesture of blessing while the queen's rested lightly on his arm. The significance of their gesture of unity was unmistakeable, despite the dirt and yellowing of the pigments. But sadly, the glory of what had once surrounded the figures was lost to the ravages of time.

I stood before the canvas and emotion overpowered me. Tears ran freely as I witnessed the probability that this tattered piece, covered with faded paint, was the object of my own passionate search, and the potent target of so much unbounded ambition over centuries.

Blowing my nose, and wiping my eyes with a tissue, I looked at Antonio. "What on earth will we do with it? Look at it! I never expected—if found—it would be so ravaged. How do we even know for certain that it's what we hope? I just didn't think this far ahead... I guess I never actually figured we'd come close to finding the real thing."

Antonio, who was equally mesmerized by the strange, compelling image, thought for a moment, then went to his iPad and typed for a bit. He looked up at me and said, "I have an idea. There's a very famous school of art restoration in Florence. I have colleagues who are well connected there. Tomorrow morning, I could contact them, and see if they will accept this painting, work on it, and be able to tell us something about it. If they accept it, we can have it shipped to them first thing tomorrow. I'll request they restore it right away, as they may be busy. I know we don't want to wait too long for the results. What do you think?"

My thoughts were so scattered, and the next steps were to me, a quandary, so I went to Antonio. We held each other for a long time, both unable to tear our eyes from the painting. It cast a spell which was palpable. In the protective circle of Antonio's arms, standing in the pool of energy flowing from that ancient artifact, I stared at the connection between king and queen. Her hand on his arm: a gesture of assurance, of solidarity, of promise to her king. The sight filled me with a deep sense of contentment. I held Antonio tighter, and realized with a shock that I was happy! Happy to trust him, happy that with his help, and Lina's, and my dad's, we had made this indescribable discovery. And most amazing of all, I was happy to be his woman. Then I thought of my mom. This time, I didn't chase her ghost away. I realized she must have experienced these very same feelings once she'd found my dad! At last, I got it. The moment seemed to erase all the years of mistrust and misgiving. I wanted to hold on to it forever.

Eventually, we released our embrace. And I was left feeling light, tranquil.

"Your suggestion is perfect, Antonio. And can I tell you something really strange? With every fiber of my being, I hope this painting is the one we have searched for. But, if it isn't, I'm pretty sure I won't collapse into a state of desolation. I think I've actually found what I've been searching for."

OPIFICIO DELLE PIETRE DURE
GABINETTO DI RESTAURO

THE YOUNG APPRENTICE REPORTED to his supervisor early that morning, eager to begin his next restoration task. He was excited, since this project would be his exclusively. The school was busy with an overload of work, but someone well known to the director had requested a fast turnaround, so Giovanni had been instructed to repair a stately but badly damaged double portrait.

Soon Giovanni's area was set up: the painting propped on a stout easel, swabs, brushes and cloths at hand. Before him was an array of solvents he would test to liquify old varnishes and some which he would carefully apply to uncover areas which had been overpainted. And so, the restoration student began his task, deploying cotton swabs to fastidiously lift layers of centuries-old grime from sections which seemed to show the artist's original work.

As he commenced softening and wiping away the yellowed varnish and detritus of years, Giovanni drew a sharp breath. Although termed a "master's apprentice" at the Gabinetto, he was in fact a doctoral candidate, and no novice to the history of art. Uncertainly, he ceased cleaning to inspect the canvas using a magnifier—then shook his head, dismissing such initial speculation as preposterous, resuming his tedious labor of love: dissolving, carefully wiping, thus ultimately revealing the strokes of the original painter's brush.

As Giovanni inched further along and more widely across the canvas, the questions persisted. Why, for instance, was this work painted on a very early form of canvas which he well knew was infrequently used? And these highly unusual pigments? They were unmistakeably colors of a most extraordinary quality and brilliance, rarely found in late medieval work, and certainly only afforded by the most wealthy, the most influential of patrons. What about the objects depicted on the table? They may have, at first glance, seemed randomly selected, but he knew iconography was of critical significance in early modern portraiture. What might the items mean?

Arduously, Giovanni brought back each image's original lustre: a ring of golden keys, a rustic wooden bowl, an exquisite storm-tossed jewel of a ship rendered in fine gold leaf, a white taper, and, at the epicentre of the painting, an ornate golden cross so finely wrought it appeared real, touchable. Cleaning further, he uncovered cryptic notations which were depicted in various places on the image: possibly scriptural references... while the male subject's foot rested on some artefact particularly obscured by grime. He had to work hard to delicately reveal it. And once exposed, it appeared to be a mangled tiara, its gems still sparkling bright. Perhaps most enigmatic, at the bottom of the canvas, his efforts disclosed the following caption: 'Obedientiam'. Giovanni was awestruck, having never touched, nor really even seen, a work like this.

He labored gingerly on the face of the woman, exposing the superlative craftsmanship of the original artist. Standing back to regard this astounding painting, apprentice Giovanni finally concluded he must call to his supervisors.

"Dottori! See what is being revealed! I am astonished. But perhaps I am wrong? Your eminent opinions are requested."

The team of master restorers peered at the composition, first with expert eyes, then more closely with magnification. They dissolved and wiped, just as Giovanni had done, then solemnly conferred.

Over the following days the Gabinetto di Restauro's investigative scientists interrogated the increasingly puzzling work by means of high-resolution computers, infrared spectroscopic dating and reflectography, duroflexometry—every known technique available in their forensic armory. Learned men conversed using terms such as "craquelure" and "pentimenti", "crystallinity" and "fluorescence", while simultaneously taking minute samples of the underlying pigments for microchemical analysis.

Finally came their determination.

Gathering his entire staff, since such was the import of the moment, Direttore Renaldi pronounced, "Look on with veneration, each and every one of you, for we conclude that this institute has been entrusted with a masterpiece of immense historic magnitude. The only composition of its nature in the world, we believe this acquisition to have been executed by the magnificent 16th century portraitist, Hans Holbein the Younger. Even more extraordinary is the uniqueness of the painting's configuration: a remarkable dual portrait of the English King Henry VIII and his second queen, Anne Boleyn, in a religious, rather than secular, representation—the like of which is not known to exist in any international collection. Of course, we will engage the world's top experts to provide their own assessments of its true provenance, to say nothing of the Holy See's study of the masterpiece's theological connotations, but..." Typically an undemonstrative academic, Renaldi could hardly contain his exhilaration. "...but by all accounts, revered colleagues, this work may well prove the discovery of a lifetime."

ANTONIO HAD BEEN CONTACTED by Director Renaldi, who had breathlessly informed him that we should make a journey to meet with him, as soon as humanly possible. He concluded the call by saying he had some monumental news to share. So, we arrived in Florence after a short train journey from Rome and went directly to the hotel to leave our bags and freshen up. I was beyond anxious to get to the institute.

My excitement was uncontainable. We would take a cab from our hotel to Viale Filippo Strozzi, where the laboratories of restoration were housed, in the Fortezza di Basso. We were told to ask for Direttore Renaldi, who would guide us.

In the hotel room, I quickly unpacked the few things I'd brought with me. No jeans this time; instead, a linen skirt, crisp white shirt, and tailored jacket. At my request, Lina had come shopping with me—and single-handedly transformed my entire wardrobe. She kept shaking her head, marvelling at what she called the "Nuova te'—'Cara mia! It's a brand new you!'" But I was new. And it felt very good.

Digging around in my suitcase, I unloaded all the remaining items, placing them either in the closet or drawers. With a thud the bag's lid closed and I shoved it under the bed. As it slid away, I heard something rattle inside. Annoyed, I stooped to retrieve it; I was certain it'd been fully emptied. Still kneeling on the floor, I unzipped the case and felt around inside, and sure enough, there had been an object left behind. I pulled it out and was confronted with a small grey velvet box. For a moment or two, I was completely perplexed.

And then the realization hit me. My throat constricted, tears filled my eyes and ran unbidden down my cheeks.

How, though, did the box end up in my suitcase? Certainly, I'd never put it there. In fact, I hadn't laid eyes on it since deciding I couldn't open it when Dad and I had our Christmas party. That day, I'd carefully and decisively replaced it in my drawer at home…

Moments later, Antonio and I climbed from the cab, paid and tipped the driver. Above us loomed the imposing Fortezza di Basso in which the Gabinetto laboratories were housed. I took a deep breath, sensing every individual beat of my heart.

"Well, we're here," said Antonio. "Let's take a few moments to collect ourselves, shall we? After all, look at that place. It's been standing there since the 14th century: I don't believe it's going anywhere in the next ten minutes."

I tried to smile but was far too anxious. I placed my hand on his strong arm to steady myself. My mind flashed to the sight of the queen's hand on her king's arm, which symbolized so much about their liaison. Fleetingly, I wondered about this simple but universal gesture, how it signaled so much intimacy between two people, as it did now, between Antonio and me.

The sun, glancing off a circlet of gold studded with ten sparkling diamonds on my wrist, caught Antonio's eye.

"Tesoro, what is this? It's beautiful! I've never seen you wear it before."

I blinked hard, squeezing his hand in an effort not to cry.

"Antonio… it's my mother. She is here with us this morning. She's going to witness what will be my triumph—and the fact that you are here with me, well, it's our triumph and I know that will bring her, and my dad, great joy."

He drew me to him in a tender, reassuring embrace. And I knew I didn't need to explain further.

We both looked toward the fortress, inside which awaited an inscrutable piece of canvas that so many had pursued, and at such great cost.

Antonio turned to face me, placing his hands on my shoulders. He gazed at me with unmistakeable admiration. "Against all odds, you unearthed the first clue," he said, "and followed Henry's ill-fated symbol through the fog of centuries. You established its provenance through consummate skill and dogged perseverance, and now... now, you will reap the rewards of your efforts: the acclaim and great respect you so well deserve." His eyes were shining with pride. "I'm honored to accompany you today. So... it's time, Zara Rossi. Andiamo. Let's go, shall we?"

And together, we walked through the doors.

THE END

AUTHOR'S NOTE

T here's no doubting it: historical fiction is a passion of mine. In fact, I've loved it from as far back as I can remember: my earliest days as a kid, hiding to read endlessly in the local library. Stories of the past, filled with vivid characters following their dreams, struggling with obstacles, and living their dramatic lives... well... to me, that's the pinnacle of storytelling.

Pursuing A Masterpiece is a product of that passion. A work in progress for almost six years, it is my hope that readers will be transported through place and time, following Zara's journey and that of the mysterious and beseiged portrait, as they both seek their capstones.

How thoroughly I enjoyed placing real-life icons of times past into the midst of my created story! Henry VIII, the larger-than-life Tudor king; his courtiers Cromwell, Cranmer, Kratzer and the Westons; the master painter Holbein, who most surely created at least one contemporary portrait of Queen Anne Boleyn—paintings which are lost to us today: these people were more than capable of providing the foundation of an imagined narrative, yet one which seemed to me to be altogether plausible. The fascinating Order of the Knights of Malta—their noble and brave Grand Masters L'Isle-Adam and Parisot de Vallette—whose biographies ring with valor ; the notorious and colorful pirate LaBuse, Olivier LeVasseur; the trailblazing couturiére Lucile Duff-Gordon, her husband and fellow travelers aboard *Titanic;* and the dastardly Nazi Joachim von Ribbentrop— art thief: they all interacted with people of my imagining. Together, they attempted to elude the heroine, Zara, with whom—although a completely fictional character—I believe many of us can relate.

In order to conduct research necessary to convincingly portray the time periods which were settings for the portrait's journey, I sought and received an enormous amount of extremely generous help. To these friends and supportive colleagues I am hugely indebted.

For assistance with concept creation, expert crafting, word wizardry, and for all around dear friendship, I thank Brian Callison, master storyteller of thrilling exploits on the high seas. Offering advice, shoulders to lean on, and never-ending encouragement, my gratefulness extends to the wonderful novelist Adrienne Dillard; administrative guru Catherine Brooks; friend, historian and social media influencer without equal, James Peacock; podcaster and author extraordinaire Natalie Grueninger; social and cultural historian and gentleman for the ages Dr Owen Emmerson; historian and witty author David Lee.

For willingly offered information and guidance about the golden age of piracy, I truly thank Cindy Vallar and John Boyd. And to Deb Weinstein for providing me with a gris-gris to guide parts of the story, I am indebted.

Inspiration and editorial prowess provided by my editor Katie Zdybel was an integral part of bringing the novel to its culmination, and Zara to the fullness of her character, and I am very thankful.

Thank you to the wonderful, patient beta readers for working through numerous iterations of the tale as it developed: the readers from History Quill, and my personal group of very generous critiquers: Dr. Robert Ketterlinus, Maria Maneos, Camille Sullivan, Donna Bolno, and Luisa DiCapua-Rasiej.

Some years ago, I had the good fortune of seeing the incredible photography of Yelena Strokin. I immediately knew I would wish for her to do a special photo for my cover, and when it came to fruition, I was enthralled with the result: thank you for your creative vision.

To match her artistry, cover and interior designer Domini Dragoone has brought the book to life, and I could not be more delighted with the result.

KLEIO Global, partnering with me in a venture about which I am so excited: the unique opportunity of creating a multi-sensory experience reading by a candle which will evoke ancient texts in the Vatican Library is something new and completely different and I am very appreciative.

Finally, in no small measure, to my dear family, who have listened, steered, suggested, nudged, and in every way been all I could ask for in this pursuit of my own masterpiece, I thank you and love you: Christopher Vasoli and Caitlin Sullivan, Stacey Miller, and my husband without peer, Tom.

And to you, dear readers—if you've reached this far, you've read the book through. Thank you from the bottom of my heart!

—Sandra Vasoli
GreyLondon Press

ABOUT THE AUTHOR

S andra Vasoli grew up in a suburb of Philadelphia, Pennsylvania, USA. As a child, she developed an abiding interest in objects and stories from a long-ago era: historic houses, antiques, period clothes, and tales from the past. A passionate reader and enthusiastic writer, she also spent her formative years caring for dogs and riding horses; the love of animals factors large in her writing.

She earned degrees in biology and English from Villanova University, and then pursued graduate work in organizational development during her long career in human resources. As a human resources officer for several global companies, she honed her ability to observe and read the behaviors of people, which contributes to her poignant character development.

After leaving the corporate world, Vasoli wrote and published her debut novel, *Struck With the Dart of Love: Je Anne Boleyn*. Uniquely positioned as Anne Boleyn's memoir, it is the story of the tumultuous relationship between Boleyn and Henry VIII of England. With a deep appreciation for meticulous research, Vasoli was permitted rare access to the Papal Library at the Vatican on two occasions, to read and study the original love letters penned in the 16th century by Henry VIII to his second wife, Anne Boleyn. She has also done extensive research in the British Library, viewing the beautiful *Book of Hours* in which Henry and Anne both inscribed lovers' messages to each other, and documents attributed to a mysterious letter purportedly written by Boleyn while she was imprisoned in the Tower before her execution. The result of that research has been published in *Anne Boleyn's Letter from the Tower: A New Assessment*, widely recognized as the definitive study on the letter.

Vasoli is now at work on a narrative non-fiction story behind the Love Letters from Henry to Anne, proposed publication early 2024.

You can follow Sandra on Instagram (@sandravasolibooks), Facebook (Sandra Vasoli Author); Twitter (@queenannefan) Goodreads (Sandra Vasoli) and LinkedIn (Sandra Vasoli). Comments, communication, and reviews are always happily received!

Lightning Source UK Ltd.
Milton Keynes UK
UKHW030653221022
410889UK00001B/7